LOVE NEVER DIES

LOVE NEVER DIES

The Porn Star Brothers Series

L.J. DIVA

★ ROYAL STAR PUBLISHING ★

Chances is an imprint of Royal Star Publishing
www.royalstarpublishing.com.au

First edition paperback published in 2018
All Rights Reserved, Copyright ©L.J. Diva 2018

Trade Paperback ISBN: 978-1-925683-55-4
Dust Jacket Hardcover ISBN: 978-1-922307-33-0
E-book ISBN: 978-1-925683-54-7
A catalogue record for this book is available from the National Library of Australia.

Cover design: Royal Star Publishing and Odyssey Books
Cover photos: Sunset: PrazisImages/Shutterstock.com
Boys: Istock.com/Squaredpixels
Typesetting in Minion Pro by Royal Star Publishing

Dedications

In 2014 a vague idea to write a book about a porn star came to me. In 2015 the idea brewed and grew and when my idol, Jackie Collins, passed away, the idea flourished with a vengeance.

Jackie Collins is the only inspiration in my life when it comes to writing. She had the passion, the brains, the ballsy rollicking attitude, and the kind of life that made me want to *be* her.

Without her, these books would not exist, for I would not have had the inspiration to follow in the same 'write whatever you want' league. Without her, I will continue trying to write the kind of books she wrote. Real, ballsy, and bonkbustingly good.

Jackie,

the Porn Star Brothers book series is dedicated to you as so many of my other books are. I thank you for the inspiration you have given me and hope you continue giving me, to go on and write more. I hope that you are well and having a good laugh wherever you are. I miss you and will continue doing so. Sometimes I think I feel you egging me on with my writing. Maybe that's true, and maybe it's just my rampant imagination; the same imagination that has given me the books I have written so far in my life. And sometimes, I really wished I could be you. You will forever be my idol and inspiration and I thank you.

RIP, Miss Jackie C.

And to the three Stefanovic brothers, Carlos, Pedro, and Tomas, without whom I would not have had names for my porn stars.

February 1980

"Oh, my, God, I can't believe we're back in New York," Carlos Stephanopoulos, the world-famous ex-porn-star-turned-writer-producer said to his supermodel wife, Vivian Villiers, as they danced up a storm at *Studio 69* on Valentine's Day.

New York's hottest club was the place to be, regardless of what time of year you were in NYC, and it was all because of his little brother Pedro, who was not only an ex-porn star like himself, but the resident DJ. He swung Viv around and bumped and ground to the sounds of *Relight My Fire* by Dan Hartman as he cast glances around the room.

His brother Tomas was with his husband, Roger Dencott. Both were ex-porn stars like him. There were his parents, Jenny and Spiros Stephanopoulos, and Pedro's wife, Angelina. Their daughter, Alena, and his and Viv's daughter, Diana, were being babysat by his grandparents, Sarah and Matthew Marsh, on the sidelines wearing noise-cancelling headphones to block out the noise so they didn't go deaf.

Having spent their last birthdays and Valentines at 69 because Pedro had been working, the family had then spent most of the year travelling. They had taken off to Europe for summer the day Angie started her break from Juilliard, and had travelled first class through Great Britain, France, Germany, Switzerland, Italy, and many more countries, getting back just in time for Angie to start her third year at school. Then they had flown to Australia for December and January to spend Christmas and New Year's with their family back in Armidale, N.S.W., visiting Sydney for the NYE celebrations, spending time in Melbourne, and on the Gold Coast in Queensland. It was summer in Australia, and they had chased the warm weather around the globe.

But now, Angie had to get back to school, and that was important to Jenny. No matter what, Angie must finish her four years at Juilliard before doing anything else work-related. Never mind the fact they had nearly two-year-old Alena to contend with while they worked and studied. But Jenny had been a big help in that department, having moved from Mykonos to NY just to help out with setting them up, and had then decided to stay in NY so she could help raise her grandbabies and be closer to her sons.

That's why she'd bought an entire apartment building for all of them to live in, made him and Viv move from Hollywood to New York, made Tomas and Roger move from Miami, and made them all get out of the porn industry. They had been the Porn Star Brothers in '77 through '78, with the biggest selling movies of all time. Especially, *The Greek Gods,* which had broken all the records and still held them today.

Back in '77, he had left home with the help of Viv and her friend, Connie DeLuca. She was one of his conquests on a nightly basis and the mother of his co-bartender, Antonio DeLuca. Porn was an easy step when they suggested it. He'd been fucking women since he was eighteen and had been paid well for it. So, why not star in movies? He found out months later, after a harrowing kidnapping attempt, that his brothers Pedro and Tomas were in the business too, and had also been kidnapped.

A group of FBI agents, detectives and cops had filled them in on who was responsible, and Carlos recognised the name. Stefano Papadopoulos. Going home to Mykonos to talk to their father, they found Stefano. He was also responsible for the death of Carlos's lover, Rosalee Brentworth, the kidnapping of world-famous photographer, Aneeka Ne Masta, and was his dead grandfather's ex-brother-in-law.

His great-grandfather, Giorgio Stephanopoulos, took care of Stefano and the whole ordeal was over, ending in three weddings and them moving to New York. That was two and a half years ago and so much had happened since. Now, they were celebrating their birthdays. He was twenty-seven, Tomas twenty-five, and Pedro twenty-three, thanks to Mama having them all on the same day two years apart and it being Valentine's Day. He stared adoringly at his amazing wife.

"It has been a whirlwind year," Viv said above the din of *Stomp*, the latest hit by The Brothers Johnson, as it burst through the speakers. "And all thanks to your mother." She grinned at his sappy expression and flicked her long golden-brown locks over her shoulder. Pinned back by colourful combs, it rained down her back in a riot of soft curls to brush against her pert ass in its pert satin pants. The matching top brought out the blue hints in her green cat-like eyes. She was back in fine form after giving birth, not that she hadn't been during, exercising throughout her pregnancy, but it had taken some time to get back the shape she had before. And while she was in demand as a model still, it wasn't like before when she did shoot after shoot.

No, younger, skinnier models were now in demand and pushing her and the likes of Bashiel, the forty-five-year-old African American beauty, Dante, the Brazilian model who was hitting forty, and Marica, the French-Swiss stunner, out of the way. With the older ones not as much in demand, the question was being asked, were they too old to model?

In Viv's case, the fact she'd had a baby at forty-one, just two years ago, definitely seemed to put a dent in her career. But, being a new year and a new decade, she was considering other avenues of income, such as a beauty line, perfumes, and as suggested by Cabot Conroy, one of NY's youngest, hottest photographers, an exercise program such as how to keep in shape in your forties. Viv had been seriously considering it, going so far as to write up a business plan, make contacts, talk to people, and find companies that would be interested. They'd all said yes, and she was ready to get it all going in June that year. The holiday to Europe had afforded her the chance to see what was coming, what was in the process of being made, and what companies would be a good fit.

"Yep, Mama knows how to take care of her babies." With a double spin, Carlos dipped Viv, pulling her up against him to grind around in circles.

Jenny had asked for Stefano's estate as he had no blood relative for it to go to, and they were the closest to legal relatives he had. She planned to blow it all on her children after what he'd done, and that's what she was still doing.

"She certainly does. She's even going to put some money up for my new business venture, *Villiers Inc.*," Viv told him.

"So, you're going ahead with the exercise tapes and cosmetics?" Carlos asked.

"Absolutely." She nodded enthusiastically. "I don't know how much longer I'll model for. My bookings are already down from two years ago, so I have to find other options for income."

"Well, I'm behind you a hundred percent," Carlos said, holding her close. "Whatever you want, I'll back you up."

"Will you? How did I get so lucky?" She grinned and planted a kiss on him.

"How did *I* get so lucky, you mean?" He twirled her around the floor.

Tomas grinned at his brother and sister-in-law as they flew past him, then slid his arms around his husband's neck. "How did I get so lucky as to meet you?" he asked, gazing adoringly into Roger's big brown eyes.

Roger smiled lovingly down at his husband. At six feet three, he had four inches on Tomas, or T as he affectionately called him. But they matched each other where it counted. In bed. At a long, strong twelve inches, they suited each other perfectly, and he loved to hold Tomas and rest his cheek upon his head.

They'd met over two years ago in Miami, Florida where he'd been at *The Joy Stick,* a popular free and open dance club for all kinds to hang out, dance, and be free. He'd been on his own when he'd spied the beautifully tanned God on the dance floor with an older woman. The way he moved, the way he looked at him with his black eyes had made his heart race. He'd gone over to the bar and chatted him up, introduced himself, and given him a friend's business card instead of his own. And how stupid had that been? If it weren't for the ladies Tomas knew, he'd probably never have gone to *Seralift Productions*, a porn movie studio, and he would never have found Tomas again. But he had, and they'd gotten to know each other, very quickly falling in love *and* into bed. Even though Tomas was seven years younger than him at twenty-two and very inexperienced when it came to love and gay sex, and he was twenty-nine and quite experienced, they'd known what to do from the start. Coming together, it was like they had known one another their whole lives. And even through past lives as well.

There was a deep connection between them, something they couldn't really explain. But it was there, and they loved each other, cherished and adored each other, and knew it was for eternity.

And thank God for Mrs S, Roger thought.

Seeing that love, she had organized a wedding ceremony for her gay son, so he didn't miss out when his brothers were married. Rings had been secretly bought, and the whole family had gotten involved, plus she'd stolen a marriage certificate, so they could sign it and hang it on the wall. It took pride of place in their apartment along with a wall of wedding, holiday, and anniversary snaps.

"It was meant to be," Roger finally murmured in his lover's ear. "We were meant to find each other and be together."

A love song came on and they slowed down.

"Yes." Tomas kissed his husband. "Definitely meant to be." Not that he ever meant to be gay, or straight for that matter. It just hadn't happened for him until he was twenty-two. He'd never had feelings for girls or boys, women or men, and felt nothing at all, unlike his brothers, especially Carlos, who couldn't keep his cock in his pants. Carlos had bedded half of the world and loved it, whereas he'd never been interested until he'd met a man that changed all of that. Luiz Manning had been his first lover, not his first love. He hadn't fallen in love with Luiz, that's not what it was. It was lust and passion and exciting; a new experience he'd never thought would happen, never believed existed. But Luiz had made him want men.

And it had come with a price.

Guilt.

A very heavy dose of it.

Luiz was engaged to one of his clients, Bertha St John. As a personal trainer, Tomas had trained her every day at the resort's gym, hearing all about Luiz, her twenty-five-year-old fiancé, and his prowess in bed. And then he'd experienced it firsthand and loved it, until finding out who he was, and that's when the situation had gotten really sticky. After a guilt-ridden weekend away of non-stop hot passionate sex, Tomas had confessed all to Bertha, and she'd forgiven him, knowing all about Luiz's exploits and his being bisexual. They decided to both dump him and go to Miami. Tomas stayed, and there, he met Roger. But unbeknownst to them, Luiz was causing all manner of trouble behind the scenes, killing four gay porn stars from *Seralift Productions* where they worked, all in the vain hope of framing Roger and getting him away from Tomas. But he'd also poisoned Tomas then kidnapped him from the hospital. Tomas didn't have recollections of that time and only remembered the airport when he was found in the trunk of the car he'd been kidnapped in, by Papadopoulos's man that is. He'd killed Luiz and taken an unconscious Tomas from the hotel room.

Since then, he'd come out to his family, married the love of his life, left the porn business, become an uncle twice over, and travelled the world, all while not feeling a hundred percent well after the poisoning. He'd probably never fully recover, but wouldn't let that stop him from enjoying life. And after two years of travelling the world with Roger and his family, he was back at 69 celebrating another birthday. The big 2-5, a quarter of a century. And if his great-grandfather lasting until he was a hundred and one was anything to go by, he had a long wonderful life with Roger still ahead of him.

Jenny Stephanopoulos lifted her granddaughter Alena into her arms. "Are you having fun?" she asked even though Alena couldn't hear her with the headphones on.

With jet-black hair like both of her parents, and big blue eyes like Pedro, Alena was the spitting image of her father, with cherubic cheeks, a cheeky grin, and a personality to match. At twenty months of age, she was dynamite to be around, loved music like her parents, and adored her grandparents, especially her grandma who spoiled her rotten. She waved at her daddy on stage.

"Yes, wave to Daddy, wave to Dada," Jenny said, holding her on her hip and waving Alena's hand.

Pedro caught a glimpse and waved back, flashing his big toothy Stephanopoulos grin before going back to spinning the records.

"Dada," Alena said, waving both of her hands.

"Yes, Dada," Jenny replied and started moving around, dancing with her granddaughter.

Spiros came back from the bathroom and saw them. "How are they doing?"

"Dada." Alena double fist pumped in her own way with her chubby little hands.

Spiros laughed. "She's definitely taking after her father."

"Yes, she is." Jenny bounced her on her hip, getting a giggle in return. She'd done it since she was born, doting on her as if Alena was hers, and to a degree she was. She had finally revealed to her sons upon the birth of their daughters that they had a baby sister who didn't survive. Jenny had named her Alena, putting her name on a Christmas bauble and stocking. The boys never knew the whole story, had never been told until Angie had given birth nearly two years ago. It brought back all of the memories for Jenny. Bad memories. Memories of giving birth to a dead baby girl. A child she had wanted so desperately. A child she'd had cremated just days later. Her ashes were in a small pink and blue urn on Jenny's bedside table, and it travelled with her everywhere, even to Europe last year.

Pedro and Angelina had proudly christened their daughter Alena Jennifer Stephanopoulos in honour of his sister and mother, and Jenny had all but raised her granddaughter herself while Pedro worked nights and Angie went to school during the day. But she didn't mind. With Angie and Pedro being nineteen and twenty-one when Alena was born, Jenny had taken over, getting a second chance at raising the daughter she'd never had.

Angie herself had filled a big chunk of that hole. Being five-foot-five with long black hair and big brown eyes, she was exactly how Jenny had pictured her Alena would have looked. And now she believed that her Alena had come back for another go at life with Pedro and Angie and that's why she'd been so hands on. They both had another chance; Alena at a life, and Jenny at raising a daughter.

Of course, Diana, Carlos and Viv's daughter, didn't go without. With golden-brown hair like her parents, and her daddy's big blue eyes, she was a gorgeous child. She was bright and full of life, and whoever looked at her knew she'd be a world-famous model just like her mother when she grew up.

Jenny spied Diana in Sarah's arms on the couch and indicated that she would take her.

Sarah lifted Diana and Jenny wrapped her left arm around her, fixing her on her hip.

"Is Diana enjoying Uncle Pedro's show? Mmm? Did Diana and Alena enjoy their Daddies' birthday cake?"

"Ah, ah, da," Diana cried, trying to remove the headphones from her head.

"No, leave it on, sweetie, we don't want you going deaf," Jenny said as Spiros came behind her and gently put them back on Diana's head.

He pointed to Carlos and Viv on the dance floor. "Dada, Mama."

Diana zeroed in and gurgled. "Dada, Mama."

Jenny bounced up and down to the music. "Yeah." She pulled faces at the girls, making them laugh. "Wanna dance?" She bounced them a little higher, a little faster, and the girls waved their hands. Jenny sighed in delirious happiness. "I luv you two sho mush." Nuzzling Alena then Diana, she looked over her shoulder at her husband. "And I luv you sho mush too," she told him, making him laugh before he kissed her.

The last couple of years had been a learning curve for the two of them. In fact, their whole relationship had been one. Spiros immigrated to Australia in 1950, met Jenny on the dock as he descended, and found his relatives lived next door to her in Armidale. She taught him English, and fell in love with him. They married in 1952, and had Carlos nine months later, with the other boys following. In 1967 they moved to Mykonos upon the death of his father for him to take over the meat shop and be the head of the family as the eldest. His mother got to spend time with her grandsons before passing two years later, and they had inherited the house. Ten years later, in 1977, her own babies started leaving home under suspicious circumstances, but fortunately, that was all cleared up and over with. With weddings and babies on the way, Jenny had decided to go where her babies were to help out, and that happened to be New York, where her youngest, Pedro and Angelina, were working and going to school. They were going to need more help than Carlos and Viv, and her decision had almost ruined her marriage to Spiros. When she decided to stay for the boys' birthdays two years ago, he had stormed out and gotten drunk at some bar, only to wake up the next morning in a strange woman's bed. Believing he had cheated on Jenny, he'd left her and gone back to Mykonos, leaving the boys to pick up the pieces. Finally, Jenny found out he hadn't cheated on her and called him, demanding he come home because home was now New York. Realizing Mykonos was cold and empty without her and the boys, he'd packed up and arrived in New York in time for Viv to give birth to Diana. A day later, Angie gave birth to Alena.

Putting the dramas behind them, they helped raise their granddaughters and explored the city, renewing their vows on their twenty-seventh anniversary last year before setting off for their European vacation. Everyone had loved it, especially the girls, getting to celebrate their birthdays in Paris with lots of photos and videos. She'd made sure that everything was documented for prosperity. Every moment, every smile, every outfit, every little thing, and not just of her grandchildren, but her sons. She had done that forever.

Especially with Tomas after the whole Luiz ordeal. The fact she'd nearly lost her son to poison and a ruthless ex-lover appalled her, and she'd vowed to give Tomas and Roger whatever they wanted, send them wherever they wanted to go. She had a bad feeling about the repercussions of Luiz's actions and had decided to do whatever she could for her son. And that meant getting as many photos and as much film as possible. Something told her she needed to document her son's life for future use. And *that* she planned on doing.

Gazing over the club, she saw Tomas in Roger's arms. A bright smile on his face, he radiated happiness from every pore, and Roger radiated it back. Jenny knew Roger was it for Tomas, and vice versa. She'd never seen her son happier than with the man he'd found. When she'd met Roger, it was after the kidnapping and poison, and when he'd reunited with Tomas, she saw the love that flowed between them and knew Tomas had found the person he wanted to spend to rest of his life with.

Smiling, her gaze wandered to Carlos and Viv. Their sixteen-year age gap made no difference to them. Yet, she worried for her son, as Viv would always be older and would more than likely die long before him. And future children? Tomas and Roger certainly weren't having any, but what about Viv? At forty-two, Viv had all but sworn off having another child, but had never said the word no. So, who knew what was going to happen. The love they had for each other rivalled Tomas and Roger's. It was forever.

She moved her attention to Angelina, who was joined by Pedro on the dance floor. They made the most incredible-looking couple. While Viv and Carlos were the golden couple, Pedro and Angie were the exotic couple. Dark hair and fair skinned, he towered over her at six feet to her five-five frame, but they made the cutest pair too. They were both still so young and raising a baby.

Pedro picked Angie up and swung her around, her long black silky hair trailing behind her as her head flew back with her laughter. Sliding down his sweat soaked body, she pushed him away, laughing when he leaned in to kiss her cheek. They danced next to his brothers. A fine family of fine-looking men and women, all hard workers, all wealthy in their own right.

The girls strained to get out of Jenny's arms, leaning toward their parents. Laughing, Jenny carried them over.

"Hey, Alena." Pedro's face lit up when he saw his daughter, and he took her and swung her up into the air.

"Ah, ah, Dada," she cried, clapping her acceptance.

"Diana." Carlos pulled his daughter into his arms and sat her on his hip. "Are you having fun?"

Viv took Diana's hand and waved it. "Having fun, my baby girl?"

Diana threw her arms up in the air and bounced along to the music, making her parents laugh.

Alena, not to be left out, did exactly the same thing, trying to outdo her cousin and get the attention back on herself.

Jenny laughed, glad to be surrounded by her family. "This is what you have to look forward to. The girls trying to get your attention every second of the day. I have a feeling they'll always be in competition with each other no matter what they do."

The boys grinned their big Stephanopoulos goofy grins.

"Why would it be any different for the girls, Mama?" Pedro asked. "I was always competing with Carlos for the girl's attention."

"Glad you said *you*, little brother," Tomas called. "'Cause I certainly wasn't competing with *either* of you for girls."

Carlos threw him a cheeky grin. "Just as well *we* weren't competing for boys."

Tomas blushed, but couldn't stop himself from laughing.

"Now you'll have the girls competing for everything. Clothes, shoes, jewels, bags, boys, grades, jobs, you name it, they'll make it a competition," Jenny said as Spiros slid an arm around her. "They're going to be just like their parents."

Amidst the music, glitter bombs, and roller-skating waiters, Jenny watched her family live. Her parents joined them on the floor, and they laughed and danced. Seeing her boys over her husband's shoulder, she rejoiced in the happiness she had coming out of her in spades. The love she had for her sons was abundantly overwhelming and would never die. Neither would her love for her husband, or daughters- and son-in-law, regardless of what happened. Regardless of who got in the way, her family would always come first, always be in her heart, always be the one thing she fought for and won for. No one and nothing would ever come between her and her sons. Not even her husband. After the last few years, she knew he was on her side and they were a united front. No one would ever come between them, or the family, and the love they had for each other.

*****

"I can't believe how adorable that kid of yours is," Mike Gatos said as he and Pedro dressed at the end of the night. He was the bartender and had started the same time as Pedro, the two of them becoming fast friends. He also dated Angie's best friend, Maggie.

Both men wore tiny gold shorts and lace-up boots for work and couldn't wait to get back into normal clothes at the end of their shift at six every morning.

"I know, can you believe it, she's nearly two." Pedro pulled his t-shirt over his head. "So damn adorable."

"Adorable? Who, me?" Leon, their roller-skating waiter, came in. "Of course I am, I always have been," he continued, but ended with a hacking cough.

"Whoa, germs." Pedro covered his face. "Winter flu?"

Leon pulled his coat from his locker and slammed the door shut. "I seem to have caught something from one of my many lovers," he quipped. "But then you know I'm a lover, not a fighter, and I couldn't *bear it* if they gave it to me on purpose. What would I say to them? I'd probably get my cock sucked to shut me up. Ah…" He sighed. "I love *too* much." It may have been 1980, but black men, especially flamboyantly gay ones, were still seen as scum on the streets regardless of how many gay men there were in New York. They just never got a fair go. He coughed again, a dry hacking cough.

"Jesus, Leon, go and see a doctor. You don't look so good," Pedro said. "Have you lost weight?"

"Ugh, it's this off again, on again case of diarrhea I have. Nothing I eat stays in me; it just keeps coming out, and I'm dropping weight like crazy." He flung his coat around his shoulders. He was still wearing his tiny gold shorts, but had paired them with a tight gold top. "I even had to get smaller shorts from Eddie because I couldn't keep my old ones up."

"You're not going home dressed like that are you?" Mike asked, pulling on his coat. He couldn't wait to change out of his shorts every morning.

"It's the day after Valentine's," Leon said, topping off his outfit with a huge fake fur hat that matched the coat. "I'm going to see if I can still get lucky, toodles." With a wave of his hand, he flounced out the door.

Pedro traded a glance with Mike. "Did you see how unhealthy he looked? The weight loss, the muscle tone, there's definitely something wrong. And how long has he had that cough?"

"A couple of weeks, I think," Mike said as they walked out the back door into the alley. "But it doesn't seem to be getting better, just worse."

"He should see a doctor then," Pedro said and unlocked his car.

"Have you ever known Leon to see a doctor?" Mike took off down the alley with a wave.

Pedro climbed in and sat thinking a moment. If Leon had something contagious, would he be carting it home to his family? Remembering how ill Tomas and Roger had been at Christmas in '77 when Angie was pregnant, he'd been worried about her health. With a shake of his head, he started the car. "I'll ask him about it tomorrow."

But Leon wasn't in the next night, having called in sick for the fourth time in a month.

Eddie threatened him with the sack if he didn't get a doctor's certificate, and Leon promised to have one to him as soon as he saw a doctor.

*****

"Cabot, darling, how are you? Do you have a minute?" Viv asked New York's hottest photographer, Cabot Conroy, as she paraded into his Greenwich Village office. She'd modelled for Cabot off and on for five years, and they'd become good friends. He'd even taken some

Christmas and birthday photos of them for Jenny and Spiros.

"Of course, darling," the thirty-something schoolboy prep photographer managed before coughing. "Come in." Quickly wiping his hands on his checkered handkerchief, he sat behind his desk.

"Oh, dear, you don't have the flu too, do you?" Viv covered her mouth with her paisley scarf. "I don't want to take anything back to my daughter."

"Oh…" He groaned and waved a dismissive hand. "Probably. It's knocked me out for weeks. I'm having night sweats, and I'm short on breath. I've barely been working." He sat back in his chair and studied the delectable Vivian, disappointed that she hadn't brought the tasty morsel that was her husband, Carlo Stefan. Although Carlos was retired from porn, that hadn't stopped Cabot from reliving the videos over and over with every lover he had, and he had a new one every week, sometimes every night. While he tried to keep his sex life to himself, dressing like an asexual schoolboy, he loved men and knew how and where to find them in the most secretive of places. He never went back to *their* places, or his; he didn't want to be found out. As much as he desperately wanted the world to know, he was afraid everything he'd worked so hard for would fall apart if the world *did* know. So, he kept it to himself.

"Are you okay, Cabot? You look a little…thin." Viv studied his face. "And you're very pale."

"Oh, darling, I've *always* been this colour." He nervously adjusted his bowtie. "But I think I've dropped a pound or two. I haven't been eating much."

"You don't want to get *too* thin darling, that's *our* job." Although Viv had never been a model to succumb to the pressures of taking drugs to stay thin, preferring diet and exercise, she knew many who did.

"So, what did you want to talk to me about?" He coughed into his hanky.

"Well," Viv started, "I've decided to branch out into other avenues of business and wondered if you'd like to be my official photographer."

"What sort of business avenues?" Cabot tried to hide the pain starting to flare in his stomach.

"I'm going to be doing exercise videos like you suggested, so will need photo shoots for promotion. Plus, I'm getting into cosmetics and perfume and will need photos for those as well. Will you be my official photographer, Cabot?" Noticing the queasy look on his face, she wondered what he was hiding. As much as he'd never revealed his sexuality, everyone who worked for him, or with him, knew he was gay. Hell, even some of *them* were gay and were either hiding it or openly out about it. But Cabot hid it, and she wondered what was going on.

He couldn't hide it any longer, the pain was too much to bear, and he bolted for the bathroom at the back of his office, barely making it to the toilet before soiling himself. He glanced up at the fresh clothes hanging on the rack within reach. He'd kept them there for the last few months since the damn diarrhea started. His weight was falling, he was having difficulty breathing, and he'd started seeing blotches pop up on his face and chest. He pulled his shirt and knitted vest up to see a few more of them on his torso. He knew he had more; he counted them every Monday morning when he showered and knew they changed, and grew, and moved around. Finishing up, he cleaned himself and changed his pants, leaving the soiled ones in the shower stall. He'd take care of them later; burn them if he had to. He could afford a hundred of them, all the same, all of them from the same place in the same size. He bought them, wore them, and then threw them out. A germaphobe from way back, he couldn't wash and wear clothes a second time. He'd tried, but couldn't. He had no idea why he was germ-phobic; he certainly wasn't when it came to men. He loved freely and openly in the moment and had absolutely no trouble with it. But washing clothes and wearing them again, forget it. After spraying man's cologne around the bathroom, he exited and went back to Viv.

"Are you okay, Cabot?" Viv was concerned. She'd come to Cabot for help with a job, but he was sick, and she was having second thoughts as she watched him sit back behind his desk.

He smiled grimly. "It's this bug I've got. It's made me pretty sick, but don't worry about it, darling. Now, about this venture of yours, it sounds fabulous, and I'd love to do all of your photo shoots."

Viv leaned forward in her seat, frowning. "Are you going to be well enough? It may not happen until late spring early summer, and we're only in February."

He waved a hand. "Don't worry about it. I'll be better by then. Will that delectable husband of yours be joining you? I haven't seen him since when…May '78 when I did those photos of you and your sister-in-law with your big bulging bellies."

Viv laughed. "That seems like a lifetime ago, yet it was only two years."

"How come I haven't seen you much?" He popped a breath mint into his mouth.

"Well, we travelled most of the last year, and I was busy getting used to a new baby the year before. I've done some modelling in between, but not much. Older models aren't really wanted anymore as the youngsters are on their way up the ladder. Younger, thinner, no boobs. Not very attractive, but it seems to be what companies want now which is a pity," Viv said. "It's putting us older women out of work. After all the years we've put into our careers, we're being pushed aside by children, which is why I'm thinking of new avenues to make money. Cosmetic, perfumes, helping women in their forties look good, feel good, be good."

"It all sounds fabulous, darling." Cabot leaned on his desk and held his hands in front of his face. "Just let me know when and I'll book you in. You know I'm generally busy all year, but like to have some time off over summer for parties and lavish holidays."

Viv remembered some of the parties she'd attended with Cabot. "You always do throw a spectacular soiree," she said, gathering her things. "I'll give you a call to set it all up. But as I said, it won't be for a few months."

"That's okay. I'll see you then." He rose slowly, escorted her to the door, and held it open.

She watched him a moment. "Do take care of yourself, Cabot."

"Of course, darling," he replied, air kissing her. He waited for her to enter the lift and waved goodbye before closing the door and running back to the bathroom.

*****

Jamal Devron, a police officer with the NYPD, was now thirty-nine years old and still hadn't climbed the ladder. He'd applied for his sergeant's exam five times in the last two years, and failed every time. When questioning why he hadn't passed, he'd been told his attitude was a problem, and until he sorted it out, no promotion for him.

He scowled, looking at himself in the mirror. Six feet of black man with a close-cropped hairdo and newly trimmed moustache looked back at him. He felt something scratchy in his throat and coughed. He'd been trying to kick a bug for weeks. That was the problem with February, it may have been the end of winter, but the bugs just weren't disappearing. *At least it's not like the flu I had last year,* he thought.

It was the weekend after Valentine's Day, and he had only just celebrated with his lover. This year it was an older man. Normally he went for the younger men, hot Latin, Brazilian, Middle Eastern, all twenty-something so he could be the big man in charge with his badge and cuffs. But over Christmas, he had met Stephano DeLuca, a fifty-something Spaniard in incredible shape with a head of jet-black hair and blacker eyes. He had a body to die for and a cock that could perform magic. And it performed magic on him. Jamal had first seen Stephano before Christmas when he'd come into the precinct to file a complaint of theft. They'd spied each other across the room, and sparks had ignited. He'd found a business card waiting for him at his desk with Stephano's name and number on it, but he'd thought nothing of it until seeing Stephano at 69 that night.

Pedro wasn't there, and there were fewer people, but he'd gone anyway as it was one of the best places to pick up. And pick up he did. Stephano had taken him home and hammered away until the sun came up, performing trick after trick with his magic dick, and his magic tongue, and his magic fingers. And God how those fingers had Jamal in the palm of their hand. "Oh, God." He groaned as Stephano's hand moved back and forth on his cock. "I really have to get dressed for work," he breathed, his eyes closing against the rush of blood.

"Not just yet, not until I have my final fill for the morning," Stephano told him, taking him into his mouth and getting what he wanted before forcing Jamal onto his back on the floor and sitting on his face while shoving his own cock into Jamal's mouth. "Suck it," he commanded. His legs pinned Jamal's arms down as he leant forward to kneel and thrust his magic dick back and forth into Jamal. "Suck it, suck it. Oh, God suck it. Yes, yes, yes, oh, God, I'm coming, I'm coming. Yes, oh, God, yes, yes, yes." Sitting back, he moved and mounted Jamal's hard cock, slowly going up and down while he got his breath back. "Oh, yes," he moaned, feeling the width of the man he was on. "Oh, yes."

Jamal let him do all the work and lay back, noticing the marks on his lover's body and the scratches from him. He coughed and tried to sit up, but he kept coughing, and the movement stirred Stephano further.

"Oh, God, yes," he groaned. "But stop coughing, you are ruining the moment."

"Can't help it," Jamal rasped. "Damn bug I picked up at Christmas." He looked down, and that's when he saw the small spots on Stephano's dick. He'd seen them before on other lovers, especially in the last two years. Damn genital ulcers, no wonder he'd gotten them last year. It seemed to be a thing going around, but he'd gone to a doctor and had been treated. But, here they were again. "I gotta go, Stephano," he rasped, his throat worse than usual. "I gotta get to work."

"Just one more," Stephano said, bouncing along like the bullfighter he was. "Just…one…more…ah…" He stiffened, his eyes widened to the size of saucers and his jaw dropped open. "Ah…" The air slowly left his body and he stared at the ceiling.

"Stephano?" Jamal hadn't seen him act like this before and it worried him. "Stephano?" He poked his arm.

"Ah…" Stephano released and settled onto Jamal. "Sometimes you just need to hold it all in and let the release take its toll."

"Its effect, you mean." Jamal eyed his lover's face.

"Whatever." Stephano shrugged and got to his feet. "Now, you must not be late for work, and I must not be late for my flight." He eyed his abs in the bathroom mirror before stepping into the shower.

"Flight?" Jamal looked up sharply from his spot on the floor. "You didn't tell me you were going anywhere." He slowly clambered to his feet.

"I wasn't, but my wife is back in Spain after her long sojourn around the world, and we need to sort some paperwork out."

"Wife!" Jamal exclaimed. "You didn't tell me you had a wife."

"Well, I didn't tell my wife I was gay, and we have lived separate lives for many years. But we occasionally catch up for old times' sake." He turned off the faucets.

"So, am I the only man you've fucked?" Jamal stood in the middle of the bathroom watching as his lover towelled down.

"Of course not." Stephano shrugged. "There have been many men, especially these last years."

A noise came from Jamal as he stared in disbelief and understanding.

"What?" Stephano asked. "You didn't think you were the only one, did you? Just as I am not the only one for you."

Jamal finally got his act together. "No…no…I guess not. I just didn't expect a goddamn wife. At least have the decency to be free, especially from a woman."

"I am." Stephano walked into the bedroom of his small hotel apartment. "We are just bound by law, nothing else."

"That's bad enough," Jamal replied. "But you also got ulcers on your dick and should get them seen to."

Stephano looked down and shrugged once more. "I've had those for ages. Everybody has."

"Yeah, well, I certainly don't have those blotches on my body." Jamal pointed to the reddish-purple spots on Stephano's feet.

Another shrug. "Ah, old man's disease. They can be covered."

"Really?" Jamal pulled on his pants. "Old man disease? So you're old? You're so old that old man disease has spread to your torso?"

Stephano glanced down. "Dry skin, bruises, of no importance."

Jamal shook his head. What the hell had he gotten himself into?

An older man who'd made no mention of a wife, an older man that had the same sexual diseases as every other man he'd been with had. *Jesus fucking Christ, is the whole gay community fuckin' disease ridden?* Fixing his cuffs and doing up his tie, he looked in the mirror. His uniform stared back, *glared* back, yet his eyes were haunted, dull, and the frown lines were deeper, more evident, and so were the spots, small, around his ears, one near his collar. He figured it was an African thing, having seen those on the continent with the same markings in books and on TV. But after seeing similar ones on his lover's body; he was beginning to question what they actually were.

*****

"Hey, boys," Eddie said a week later to Pedro and Mike as they finished up on Saturday morning. "Would you mind going around to Leon's and seeing if he's there? He hasn't been in all week, and I couldn't get that medical certificate he promised. He's not answering my calls, so I need someone to check."

Pedro matched Mike's groan. "Yeah, all right. I'll do it."

"Here's the address. Not far from here, so it shouldn't take long." Eddie handed over the piece of paper. "Call and let me know."

"Sure thing, Eddie," Pedro said and followed Mike out back. "Wanna come?"

Mike shrugged. "Sure. I always wanted to see where he lived."

Taking Pedro's car, they stopped out the front of Leon's worn down apartment building in Harlem fifteen minutes later, getting out to black kids and men watching and waiting, even though it was six-thirty on a cold Saturday morning.

Finding no elevator, they walked the six flights to Leon's and knocked. And waited. And knocked. And waited.

"Leon?" Pedro called. "You home? You in there?"

"He ain't there," a voice from behind them said.

They turned to see a little old black lady in curlers and a purple terry robe and matching slippers.

"Do you know where he is, ma'am?" Pedro asked. "We work with him, and he hasn't shown up all week."

"He in tha hopital," the gnarled old woman said.

The boys exchanged a glance. "Hospital?" Pedro asked. "Which hospital?"

"Tha NYC Health an' Hopital here in Harlem," the old lady said. "Tha ambulance came an' took 'im away."

"Um, okay." Pedro glanced at Mike. "Thank you very much." They made it downstairs and to the hospital to find Leon in intensive care and a doctor coming out of the room.

"Doctor, we're here for our friend, Leon Talley, how is he?" Pedro asked.

"Dying," was all the doctor said, without looking up from his chart.

"What?" Two pairs of stunned brows flew up. "Say that again."

The doctor put his serious face on as he looked at them. "His CD4 count is less than 200 microlitres; he is chronically dehydrated, wasting away, has candidiasis of the oesophagus, trachea and lungs, and is suffering from gonorrhoea, chlamydia, diarrhea, and has genital ulcers. He has swollen lymph nodes, and what we've just found out today is, he has pneumocystis pneumonia and probably has had for some time. It's shutting down his liver and kidneys. He also has a rare cancer that's only found in old men. Kaposi's sarcoma. But from what we know, it can affect Africans. Basically, he's a walking, talking cesspool of diseases. He's gay, isn't he?"

Pedro blinked. All of those words he didn't understand and yet the doctor had rattled them off just like that. As if he was reading a shopping list.

"Yes, he is," Mike barely managed, stunned out of his mind. "What's that got to do with it?"

"Everything," the doctor said. "We've been seeing a lot of gay men with those symptoms, but not all together like this."

"You said he's dying," Pedro said softly, his heart plummeting towards his feet.

"Yes." The doctor sighed. "I'm sorry, since he's your co-worker. Did you know he'd been so sick?"

Pedro slowly shook his head, thinking, his hands in his jacket pocket.

"He's had a bug for a while," Mike said. "Coughing a lot, had four days off this month alone."

"Have you seen any sores on his body, loss of weight, diarrhea, weakness?" the doctor asked.

Mike mentally went through the list. "We saw he'd lost weight since Christmas, didn't seem to eat much, loss of energy."

"He was wearing a shirt the other night," Pedro said. "We normally wear shorts and boots, but he's been wearing t-shirts and tanks."

"Yeah." Mike nodded. "He started covering up."

"When did you first notice the symptoms?" the doctor asked.

"I noticed during December, especially before Christmas." Mike turned to Pedro. "You weren't here, though, so you wouldn't have seen anything."

"No, but I certainly saw the difference," Pedro replied. "Can we see him?"

"You'll need masks and gloves. Don't touch him," the doctor warned and prepared them. "Two minutes only. Say your goodbyes now because you may not get another chance."

They covered up, entered the room, and stood by his side. He was frail, thin, sunken cheeks and hollow eyes. He had a ventilator mask on and tubes sticking out of his arm. "Leon."

Leon opened his eyes. "Hey, porn star," he said softly, his eyes closing from the lack of energy to stay open. "You found me."

"Eddie got worried when you didn't turn up for work," Pedro said. "Sent us around to your place. The old lady across the hall told us the ambulance brought you here. You're really sick, Leon."

A soft smile came to Leon's face. "I know. They told me to write out my will a few days ago and who to give it to. I chose you, porn star."

Pedro frowned. "Leon."

"No, no," Leon breathed. "You only need to see to it that my mama and grandma get the money in my bank account and my fabulous clothes and shoes. Everything else can go."

"But I don't know who your—"

"They're in my black address book by the phone in my apartment.

Under M for Mama and Grandma. See to it that they get everything," he said.

With a glance at Mike, Pedro agreed. "If that's what I can do for you in your time of need, then I'll do it."

"Good boy," Leon rasped, looking at them through hazy yellow eyes. "It's been good knowing you, porn star. Real good. I'm just pissed I never got a chance at your brother."

Pedro grinned. "I bet he's glad you didn't."

The soft smile came back to Leon's lips. "At least I got a chance to know you all. Say goodbye to that wife and baby of yours, and that mama. She's awesome."

"I will, Leon. Anything else?" Pedro asked.

"Mike, say goodbye to Maggie for me. She loves you."

"I know," Mike said. "And I will."

"Porn star. Tell everyone at 69 it's been a ride, and make sure to have a wake for me and unite all of my ex-lovers. They're in my little black book. Use my money to throw the funeral and service. Make it a blast, porn star. Make it a blast."

*****

"He's what!?" Eddie exclaimed ten minutes later. Pedro had called and told him about Leon. "What the fucking hell!"

"Yeah," Pedro said from the hospital telephone. "The doctor said he hasn't long to live, and he has so many problems they can't fix them all. The antibiotics just haven't done the job."

"And the doctor said it's because he's gay?"

"The doctor said they've seen a lot of these symptoms in a lot of gay men, but not all together. He said Leon was a walking, talking cesspool of diseases."

"*Jesus fucking Christ*," Eddie said. "What sort of fucking germs has he spread around my business? God knows what diseases he's passed on."

"From the sound of it, and from what the doctor explained, some of them are sexually transmitted, some are non-contagious, like the cancer and pneumonia. We can't catch them."

"Just as well, but not the point. I'm gonna have to get the place fumigated." Eddie was on the verge of breathing fire.

"Yeah, well. We've said our goodbyes, and he's written his will. He wants a lavish funeral and reception at 69. Wants us to send him out in style."

"Mmm well, I'll see what I can arrange. You'd better get home, kid."

"Yeah." After hanging up, he and Mike silently went their separate ways. Pedro went back to the apartment, finding Angie feeding Alena.

She glanced up from the table. "What took you so long? It's after nine."

He sighed and dumped his bag on the floor next to the coffee table. "You would not believe what I've just been through." Throwing himself onto the couch, he put his feet on the coffee table and wearily gazed at his wife and daughter.

"From the way you look, I'd say someone's died." Angie carried Alena over to him.

"Alena, my baby girl," he said, taking his daughter into his arms and kissing her cheek. She snuggled into his side while sucking her bottle.

Angie sat next to them. "Who died?" she asked.

He sighed. "Dying."

"What!" Her eyes widened. "I was kidding."

"I'm not," Pedro told her. "Leon says goodbye to you and Alena. Mama too."

"Leon, oh, my God," she gasped. "You're kidding? What happened?"

"We don't know," he replied. "Mike said he'd had some bug since Christmas and hadn't shaken it. He's lost weight, I noticed that, and he had a really bad cough. He didn't make it in last Friday, so Valentine's was the last time you'll see him."

"But what does he have?" Angie urged.

"Everything," Pedro said. "Too many diseases to remember, but I remember the sexually transmitted ones. The doctors said they've ravaged his body on the inside. He doesn't have long."

"Oh, my God," she said again. "Leon…oh, my God."

"Apparently, a lot of gay men are showing up with the same diseases, just not all together. He also has pneumonia and cancer."

Her face fell. "Oh, poor Leon."

"Yeah. He looked terrible. Said the hospital staff made him write out a will and he wants me to make sure it's all done."

"You?" She frowned. "Why you?"

He shrugged and looked down at his daughter as she looked up. He saw the worry from his eyes reflected in hers. "He didn't say. He *did* say he was glad to have met us and says goodbye to you and Alena and Mama. Wants me to make sure his mama and grandma get everything, and that we throw him a funeral, and a reception at 69."

"How long does he have?" Angie saw how much it had taken out of her husband.

"Don't know." Gazing at his wife he saw the pain. "Hours, days, *any* day now."

Fifteen minutes later they were in the penthouse telling everyone.

"Oh, that's so sad," Jenny said. "He was always so nice to us, and now he's so sick. That's horrible."

"Yeah." Pedro slowly shook his head. "You should have seen him. So different, even to Valentine's Day. It's like he wasted away in one week."

"What's going to happen to his effects?" Spiros asked.

"He wants me to give his money and clothes to his mother and grandmother. And send him off in a lavish funeral, then a reception at 69. Eddie's already said he'll put something in motion."

"We'll have to do something," Jenny said. "He's been there from the start."

"Yeah." Pedro wearily sat on a couch in front of the fireplace in the lounge room. "We have to do something."

*****

The next day, Pedro received the call. Leon had passed away, and it was time to do what was needed. Back at the hospital, he collected

Leon's effects and the will he'd written out. It was all fairly easy and straightforward, and he enlisted the help of his parents who'd offered the day before. Tomas and Roger tagged along. They made their way to Leon's armed with boxes ready for packing. According to his paperwork, the clothes were to be given to his mother, and everything else to the Goodwill. He wouldn't need it anymore. Not that there was much of that. After folding clothes and personal effects into the boxes and piling them up by the door, they moved on to a few photos on the walls and phone table. There were pictures of Leon with his mother and grandmother, pictures with Pedro, Mike and the 69 crew. The photo that sat front and centre was one with Leon and all three Stephanopoulos brothers and Roger.

Pedro chuckled. "He always went on about Carlos. Would have loved to have made him a conquest." He picked up the photo. "I want to keep these."

"Then keep them." Jenny peered over his shoulder. "Any of him and his family, send on. Any of him with others, especially you or the boys, keep."

After a look around, and boxing up anything extra, they carried the boxes down to pile them into the van they'd hired. The Goodwill people arrived and loaded the truck with everything else, and Jenny gave the place a quick sweep and mop.

"That's it." Pedro saw the last piece of furniture off and looked around. The walls, floor, and rooms were bare.

"That's it," Jenny repeated. "You just have to get his things to his mother. You have her address?"

"Yeah, in his little black book. Said his lovers are all in there and wants them all to celebrate at his funeral."

"And his bank accounts? Did he have the money to pay for the funeral?"

"He had twenty-five thousand, but..."

"But?" Jenny looked at her son. Twenty-five thousand more than paid for a funeral, so she wondered where her son was going with his thought process.

"But I'd like to pay for it, give his mother all of the money, and pay for the funeral and the reception myself. As a parting gift." The tears welled in his eyes. Leon had been a great friend. They'd hung out on occasion and got along well at work. But not once had he been invited to Leon's apartment. But then…he'd never invited Leon to his either.

"Ready to go?" Spiros came back in. "Those stairs are really killing me."

"Don't say that!" Pedro turned sharply. "Don't *ever* say that."

"I didn't…" Spiros, concerned for his son's emotional welfare, went to his side.

Pedro relented and sighed. "I know. It's just…"

"Being here is getting to you," Spiros said, putting his arms around his distraught son.

"Yeah, yeah." Pedro shook himself out of it. "Let's get out of here."

They walked downstairs, and Jenny went with Pedro to Leon's mother's home where they explained about her son's illness and how he wanted a lavish funeral.

Betty Talley patted her tears and nodded, knowing her son lived the life he wanted, *how* he wanted, though she knew it would end up killing him. She accepted the boxes of clothing and accessories, laughing at the fake fur animal print coat and matching hat. "He always had a flair for clothes," she said. "Thank you for bringing them."

"Leon wrote that he wanted to be buried at the Chelmsford cemetery near here, so you could go and see him. He asked me to organise it and get a reception together at 69 where he worked. Would you want to come?" Pedro asked.

She looked up from a photo of Leon and her. "The funeral yes, but I'll have a wake for my son here, with my friends."

Pedro nodded. "Okay. I'll call and let you know about the funeral. It will probably be next weekend."

Betty touched a finger to her son's face in the photo. "Thank you for doing this, young man; if he asked you, he thought a lot of you."

A sad smile touched Pedro's lips and tears welled in his eyes. "I thought a lot of him, too. So did my wife. And he loved her and our baby girl. I'll call during the week. Goodbye."

"Goodbye, young man."

With a sad sigh, Pedro left with Jenny following. The drive back to Fifth Avenue was a quiet one. A sombre one. One full of thought.

*****

On Monday morning, Pedro rang every number in Leon's little black book. After a few failed attempts, and being given numbers to ring, he contacted everyone he could, telling them details of why he was calling and asking if it was possible for them to attend. The news he received was shocking, and he even had two hang-ups.

*****

Jamal slammed the phone down. He was at work in the precinct, and the call had been put through to his desk. Pedro Stephanopoulos calling about Leon Talley and his funeral.

Funeral!

Fuck!

Jesus, he was dead!

Leon was dead?

Having slammed the phone down, he had no more details because one utterance of that name and the fact he was dead was enough to make anyone slam the phone down in shock. He'd kept his sexuality a secret for years and wasn't about to let it out now, especially having another new work partner.

Carmichael Burns had retired the year before, along with Giancarlo Gardo, the detective in charge of the Stephanopoulos case from 1977. Gardo had taken his leave because of his new kid and walked away from it all. They had met Pedro Stephanopoulos and his brothers, plus Roger Dencott, when they'd moved to New York. Dencott had known of him, known a mutual friend, and made it known that he knew he was gay. So, Devron backed off and had nothing to do with them again. But he'd lived life in the very secret fast lane, fucking a lot of men in a very short time, including a quick night with Leon two years ago. But the new cop partner didn't know he swung like that, while Burns had and didn't care. And even though it was 1980, his new partner was a homophobe and had made it very clear. No, Jamal would never tell anyone. He'd keep it to himself and make a note of the papers to see if he could find Leon's death notice. Just in case…

*****

Stephano DeLuca put down the phone, cutting the conversation short, thinking about what he'd just been told. He'd been in Leon Talley's little black book, and Leon was dead, and a young man by the name of Pedro Stephanopoulos had wanted to know if he'd be attending the funeral on Saturday.

"What did he die of?" Stephano had asked.

"Many sexually transmitted diseases, cancer, pneumonia, a whole bunch of horrible icky stuff," Pedro had replied.

"My, that's horrible," Stephano said. "Thank you for telling me, young man. You wouldn't happen to be related to a Carlos Stephanopoulos, would you?"

Pedro had baulked. "Why?"

"My son once worked with a Stephanopoulos."

"Your son?"

"Antonio DeLuca, in Mykonos."

"Oh, right. He worked with my brother at the resort's summer bar. Why?"

"He fucked my wife for money. I won't be attending Leon's funeral, but thank you for calling."

He sat thinking about Leon and sexually transmitted diseases. He knew that he, Stephano DeLuca, had some of his own. What man didn't? But that was normal, right? He glanced down at his bare ankles and saw the blotches creeping up his legs. They appeared here and there on his torso, but disappeared after a week or three. He hadn't seen a doctor for them, and knew that his father and grandfather had had them as well. He knew it was a Mediterranean

29

thing that older men got, so there was no need to worry about it, right?

He dashed off to the toilet where his bowel relieved itself, and saw himself in the mirror. He'd dropped a few pounds from the diarrhea, and his skin was looking a bit grey. Thank God he'd had a quick fling with Connie before the diarrhea started. Otherwise it would have been a mess.

She was always up for a good time. They'd been married long enough. But they'd gone their separate ways with separate lovers over five years ago. She had hers, he had his, but every now and then they came back together for a quickie, and they always enjoyed it.

Clearing up, he stood only to be overcome with cramps and shortness of breath. "Ugh. What is this? I must have caught Jamal's damn bug."

*****

Pedro was still sitting in contemplation when Angie got home from school.

"Are the funeral arrangements made?" She dumped her bag and coat by the door.

"Huh? Yeah. I rang the funeral home and the cemetery. They'll do it on Saturday."

"Ring his mother with the details?" She bent down and kissed his cheek before going to the kitchen.

"Yeah."

"Are all his exes coming?" Getting no reply, she turned from the fridge to see her husband in thought. "Are his exes coming?"

He finally looked up. "You would not believe what I've been told today. My God, Angie…" His head moved side to side. "My God."

"What? Tell me!" Moving over to her husband, she sat beside him at the table. "Tell me."

"I…can't…not yet…when we're all together," he said dazedly. "I want to tell you all together."

An hour and a half later, when the family was seated at the

penthouse table having dinner like old times, he told them what had happened.

"I made lists of the names in his little black book. Besides his mother and grandmother, there were five other names, me and Angie, Mike and Maggie, Eddie for 69, his doctor and a dentist. Of all the other names in the book, there were one hundred and fifty-eight of them. He told me all of his lovers were in that book, but you'd never guess what, and I can't even believe what I was told." His head shook in disbelief.

"What?" Jenny was intrigued and hanging on to every word.

"Out of one hundred and fifty-eight lovers, from what I could tell, just in the last five to ten years at least, oh, my God, I could not believe this. I went into shock at the stories I was told." Running a hand through his hair, he stared wide-eyed at all of them.

"Well, tell us!" Carlos snapped impatiently. "Come on."

"Okay." Pedro wiped his hands on his jeans and pulled the pages from his pocket. "Out of one hundred and fifty-eight lovers, only forty are coming to the funeral."

"Is that all?" Carlos rolled his eyes and put a forkful of food into his mouth.

"I'm not finished," Pedro said. "Forty are coming to the funeral, eighteen are very sick at home, twenty-three are sick in hospital, thirty have a disease, a *sexually transmitted* disease, two won't be coming, and get this…out of one hundred and fifty-eight lovers, *forty-five* are dead, just in the last few years." He watched everyone's faces as it sank in and murmurs went around the table.

"You're kidding?" Jenny said.

"Nope." Pedro shook his head. "I spoke to parents, or partners, or carers. All of them have, or *have* had, a disease, or *are dying* from that disease, or *are dead* from that disease, mostly sexually transmitted. Many also had cancer or pneumonia just like Leon. The forty that will be coming to the funeral are, apparently, according to them, disease free. The rest blame Leon, or someone else who had it. Oh, and get this," he looked at Roger and Tomas, "there were two familiar names in that little black book, and both of them hung up on me. Neither will be coming to the funeral by the way."

"Who's that?" Tomas asked, scraping some sauce onto a piece of his chicken parmigiana.

"Officer Jamal Devron of the New York City police department."

"You're kidding!" Roger exclaimed. "Bloody hell. I knew he was, but I didn't picture him as Leon's type."

"Who was the other one?" Carlos asked, giving Diana a piece of carrot.

"Stephano DeLuca…"

Carlos's head shot up. "What! You're kidding! Antonio's father?"

"*Connie's* husband," Viv said pointedly at her husband.

His head spun to face his wife. "Connie's…fuck…"

"Carlos!" Jenny said sharply.

"Fuck," Diana repeated.

"No, no, no Diana, you do not say that word," several said at once, only for Diana's lip to quiver and her blue eyes to well up with tears at the telling off and raised voices. She promptly burst into sobs.

"Oh, baby, no, no, it's okay. You just don't say that word is all." Viv took her into her arms and soothed her. "You don't say that word, that's all. It's a rude word."

A sly giggle was heard from across the table, and Alena pointed to her cousin, her giggles getting louder as she laughed at her cousin's mistake.

"Alena," Angie chastised. "It's rude to laugh at someone's mistakes."

Alena looked up at her mother. "Wude."

Angie looked down. "No, *rude*."

"Wude." Alena giggled again.

"And who's Connie DeLuca to you?" Jenny asked, taking the attention away from the girls to hush them. "Oh, you mean the Connie Deluca who came to Greece after the kidnappings. *That* Connie Deluca?"

"Yes. The woman who helped get Carlos out of Mykonos that night. One of his conquests actually," Viv said dryly.

"Yes, with *your* help, darling, or did you forget?" Carlos asked.

"Oh, for God's sake Carlos, we don't need to hear about the

women you've bedded. Who's up for dessert?" Jenny asked.

"Yeah, well, Stephano DeLuca certainly knew who *you* were," Pedro said watching his brother's reaction.

"What?" Carlos's head turned from Viv to his brother. "What do you mean, *knew?*"

"He asked if I happened to be related to you, I asked why, he mentioned his son worked with a Stephanopoulos, I asked about the son, he said Antonio DeLuca in Mykonos, I said right, he worked with my brother, and he said he *beeped* my wife." He substituted the word which was just as well.

"Beep, beep," Alena cried. "Beep, beep."

"He said he won't be attending Leon's funeral, so you won't need to worry about running into him," Pedro finished.

"Bloody hell," Carlos muttered. "Bloody hell. Stephano DeLuca and Leon…bloody hell."

"Stephano DeLuca *and* Connie DeLuca. You did it, he knows. Is there something to be worried about?" Viv asked as Diana crawled from her lap back to her seat, her tears all gone.

"God, I don't think so." Carlos ran a hand through his hair. "I was always safe with everyone."

"Well…not everyone." Viv nodded at their daughter.

Carlos grinned. "Yeah, but that was after we got together and there was no one else."

"Just as well," Viv replied.

"Maybe I should call Connie." Carlos's mind changed tack.

"And tell her what?" Viv asked.

"Tell her one of her husband's male lovers is dead from sexually transmitted diseases and to watch out for her husband," he said.

Viv thought about it. "No. As far as I know, they went their separate ways years ago. From what Connie told me, they had their own lovers and never went back."

"Doesn't mean they don't now," Carlos replied. "Some women go back to men. Look at us. We went our separate ways, you worked, I had Rosalee, you came back, and we got back together. That was it."

"Yes," Viv replied with a small smile. "But *we* were different."

"How?" Carlos asked.

"We weren't already married and separated and screwing around," she replied.

"And that makes a difference how?" he went on.

Pedro butted in to end their conversation. "Well, *I* find it very strange that so many of his exes all had similar, or the same diseases as him. And the parents were rude about it. The carers were okay, as were the hospitals. But God, some of the people I spoke to." He leant both elbows on the table.

"Are they coming to the funeral?" Roger asked. "What about other family and friends?"

"His mother will invite her friends over and have her own wake. I'll let everyone at 69 know later tonight. Are you all coming?" Pedro asked.

"Yes, we are." Jenny laid out hot apple pies and ice cream. "We will be a united front. And if he only has a mother and grandmother, then he'll need his other family to be there."

March 1980

A week later, on Saturday the first of March, the public funeral for Leon Willmore Talley was held at the Chelmsford Church not far from his mother's home. The place was full, with at least thirty people from 69, forty ex-lovers, about fifty friends of Leon's mother and grandmother, and lasted for about forty minutes. Leon's favourite music was playing, his casket was gold, and he had his favourite outfit on. He lay peacefully, hands on heart, but incredibly thin and gaunt.

People got up to speak about him, telling wild stories and anecdotes, and they filed by at the end, saying small prayers before they followed the casket to the cemetery for the burial.

Once it was over, Pedro said goodbye to Leon's mother before leading his family, the crew from 69, and Leon's ex-lovers back to the club where they started the party early, playing Leon's favourite songs and drinking his favourite drinks. The ex-lovers told even wilder stories, and co-workers shared good times. After four hours they stopped, turned off the music, stopped the disco ball, and raised their glasses in the air.

"He was our co-worker, a lover, a friend, the life of the party. The glitter in the air, the disco ball that never stopped." Pedro looked up at the massive ball hanging from the ceiling. "To Leon, may you always be our disco ball here at 69. When we look up, we'll know you're looking down on us. To Leon."

"To Leon," staff, family, crew, and lovers all said.

And, as if on cue, the glitter bombs went off, the music started playing, and the ball started spinning, even though no one was at the controls.

*****

"Happy birthday to my darling wife, Viv, another year older, but still just as beautiful," Carlos said, glass in the air. "To Viv."

"To Viv," everyone toasted.

It was her forty-third birthday, and the family was celebrating at *Santiago*, one of New York's hottest restaurant bars.

"Thank you, thank you, thank you all for being here, it means a lot. It does," Viv told everyone at the table.

Spiros and Jenny were beside Pedro and Angie who had Alena between them, with Tomas and Roger on Jenny's other side. Diana was sitting between her parents and squirmed in her chair to roll onto her mother.

"And I thank you for being here, Diana." She kissed her daughter on the head. "Yes, I do. You are the best thing I've ever done."

"Mama." Diana pointed up at her as she leaned backwards across her mother's lap. "Mama."

"Yes, I am, Diana, and I'm so glad I have you. Thank you all for the presents. The locket's beautiful," she said to Carlos and gently touched the gold locket with small inlaid rubies. "I love it." He'd put a picture of himself and Diana in it and the rest of the family on the other side.

"Good. It's getting hard to buy for you Viv; all I keep giving you is jewellery." Carlos casually rested his arm across the back of Diana's chair. "You're gonna have to tell me what else I can give you, otherwise you'll have enough jewellery to open your own store soon."

She laughed lightly. "Hardly, but I have a good start. And thank you so much for the investment in the company," she told Jenny. "I wouldn't have had enough on my own, and I didn't want to give my company and me away just to get financial backing."

"You're welcome. I needed something to do with it besides blowing it on my kids and grandkids. I've set up trust funds for them too. But there's still plenty, so I need things to spend it on." Jenny smiled brightly at her grandbabies.

"Thank you, anyway," Viv said. "Once again I've had a *very* happy birthday."

"So, when do we start this new venture?" Jenny asked, excited at the prospect of owning a large chunk of *Villiers Inc.*

"Well…we have scents for the perfumes; they'll come out sometime in April or May, followed by the cosmetic line which I hope will be done. And we'll film some exercise videos in the park in May in time for summer, all about how to stay fresh and trim during bikini season."

"You look awesome in a bikini, babe," Carlos told her.

Viv smiled brightly at him. "Aw, you say the sweetest things, Carlos."

*****

Cabot Conroy studied the negatives and photos from the last shoot he did. It was two months ago, and he hadn't been well enough to do another since. But here it was, late March and he had a photo shoot to do for Viv. "Gotta pull yourself together, Cabot. The shoot's the second week of April. Gotta pull yourself together." Sighing, he leant back in his chair and stared out at the view of the city skyline.

He loved his job, loved what he did, but he felt like absolute crap. His breathing was worse, he was being treated for candida of the mouth for Christ's sake, but it wasn't getting better. His lungs were giving way, his body was almost bone thin thanks to a disease called Cachexia, his hair had thinned to almost being gone, *and* he had resorted to wearing a wig.

Holy fucking shit balls, he thought. *What the fuck is wrong with me?* He was awaiting more test results from the blotches on his body, and his diarrhea had determined that he had parasites. *Fuck! Fucking parasites. Some dirty little faghead gave me fucking parasites up the ass.* He hadn't had a fuck since the Christmas New Year period, so must have contracted them sometime before that, and here it was, nearly April, and he was just finding out now. Nearly three months he'd been sick, and it definitely wasn't getting better. If anything, it was getting worse, even though the doctor said it was all treatable. Sexually transmitted diseases weren't to be sniffed at or taken lightly, and his diseases needed tough treatment.

Looking around his empty office space, he glanced over all of the photos on the walls. Photos of him and all the top supermodels, actors, actresses, celebrities. He even scored himself pictures with the Porn Star Brothers which took pride of place in the middle of one wall. And it was blown up as big as he could get it. It was taken back in '77 when he'd photographed them for their parents' present. And then there was the photo of Viv and Angie with their bellies painted.

On a table under the photos were awards of all shapes and sizes for photography and art. He was prolific at what he did, had been doing it for nearly two decades, and had more than proved what talent he had. And everyone had flocked to him. Every supermodel wanted him, Cabot Conroy, to take their photos because they knew he took it in the best light from their best side, and no matter what he did, he *never* took a bad photo. Of *anyone* or *anything*.

The office was quiet. He'd sent home his assistants weeks ago when he knew he didn't have the strength to work, but, he still made it to the office. He had to, just for his own peace of mind to feel like he was doing something productive instead of wallowing in his bed in self-pity. He picked up the paperwork from Viv; a detailed plan of what products they were selling, what the names were, and how she wanted the photo shoots to be. She also wanted aerobic shots taken for her exercise videos, and it all needed to be done together. The plan was for one week. To get everything done in one week.

"Jesus fucking Christ I don't know if I'll last that long," he muttered. At a week and a half away, he was going to need all of his strength to do it. *I wonder if I can get it all cut down to two days? If I set up different scenarios in the studio, have someone bring over samples beforehand, and then all she'll have to do is change, and I could keep taking the photos. Once it's done, it's done, and I can go back to my seclusion.*

Calling his assistants, he told them he had a job for them.

April 1980

"Happy birthday, my darling husband." Tomas kissed his lover's cheek as they woke on the first of April. It was Roger's birthday, and he had special plans for his husband, besides the family dinner his mother had planned.

"Mmm," Roger moaned softly at the hand around his cock. "Morning."

Tomas went to work and took charge, taking care of his husbandly duties, and making his husband very happy on his birthday. "So, I have plans," he said as he finished. "A nice breakfast, a walk in the park, maybe the zoo, rudimentary family dinner, and then I will make you very happy all night."

"Guess I'd better save up my energy then." Roger pulled Tomas into his arms.

"Not so fast, Roger Dencott Stephanopoulos," Tomas said, and rose to the occasion.

After a fine spring day followed their every step, they dined at home with the family. Roger received gifts of records, books, and tickets to his favourite basketball team for the entire year from his in-laws.

"Thank you so much." He gaped in surprise. "This is awesome."

"You're welcome," Jenny said, carrying the cake to the table. After a loud rendition of Happy Birthday, he blew out the thirty-two candles, and Jenny cut and served it.

Afterwards, Tomas and Roger retired to bed where Tomas showed him just how much he loved him.

*****

On Monday, Viv arrived at Cabot's studio for her photo shoots. She'd been called the week before about doing all of it in two days and agreed if he had the time. He did, and now she was getting her make-up and hair done for the first shoot for her perfume, *Vivian*. In time for summer, it was a light, fruity scent that smelt perfectly of warm summer days. A new one would come out every three months in time for a new season and new buying frenzy. And she had the perfect names for all of them.

The perfume for fall would be *Diana*, the one for winter was *Angelina*. The following spring was *Alena*, summer was *Jennifer*, next fall was *Sarah*, and the next winter one was *Villiers*. It had to start and end on her name after all. She'd come up with other names down the track if she kept producing more perfumes.

After donning a bright floral summer dress, she wandered over to the perfume set. The background would change for the first three as she already had them prepared, plus the clothes on the racks for her to wear were divine.

The next set was for the cosmetic line, and round pedestals held her beauty creams all ready to go. She had face washes and toners, body moisturizers, and make-up. Those were just the samples. The products were in the final manufacturing stages and on their way for a late April early May sale start. The final set was bright and colourful and full of aerobic gear. Steps, light weights, jump ropes. Cabot had gone all out to get it done in as short a time a possible.

"Where is Cabot?" she asked one of his assistants working on the perfume set.

The assistant checked her watch. "There's a few minutes. Okay everybody, in your places. We need everything ready to go and start straight away the minute Cabot arrives. There is no time to be wasted. Lights." The lights were turned on. "Fan." A fan was turned on to make Viv's hair and dress billow. "Places." Everyone got into place. She turned to Vivian. "Don't be shocked when you see him; it will affect the look of the photos."

"Is he still sick?" Viv asked, worried about her friend.

The assistant blinked. "He looks like death. Don't be shocked, keep your face neutral. Okay?"

Viv nodded, and the assistant walked away, coming back moments later with Cabot sitting in a homemade wheelchair consisting of a peacock chair on a trolley being wheeled by his two assistants.

"Cabot?" Viv put her hand up to shield the light. "Are you still sick, darling?"

"Yes, darling. So, this will be my final shoot." He slid the ventilator mask off and took his camera from the assistant. He was weak and frail, but determined to do this last job. "Model for me, darling." Holding up the camera he clicked away, going through several rolls as Viv modelled the perfume.

"Time for a break and change of clothes for Ms Villiers," the assistant said and wheeled Cabot back into his now empty office. He'd taken down all of the photos, and packed up all of the awards. The furniture was bare, as were the file cabinets. He'd signed release forms, releasing all of his photos back to the model or celebrity in them. He couldn't take them with him, so he sent them on to their new homes. He sucked back on the ventilator, his lungs slowly dying. Just like the rest of him.

Viv quickly changed. "I didn't get to see much of him. Is he *that* ill?" she asked the make-up artist.

"He's gravely ill," Evie, the African woman in the tight turban and colourful earrings said. "On his death bed from the looks of it."

"Jesus," Viv muttered as her hair was twisted up. "Poor thing."

Cabot was wheeled back in for the next shoot and wheeled back out while Viv changed again. He grew weaker by the minute and didn't know if he'd last the day. His schoolboy prep tie and vest hung on his tiny frame; his pants were too big even though they were the smallest he had. He was malnourished, borderline anorexic, all because of some stupid disease he had. He was wheeled back in for the final perfume shoot before stopping for lunch. He hid in his office while everyone else ate, knowing he didn't have long. Knowing the make-up shoot would take too long, he told his assistant to tell the others they'd be doing the aerobic shoot instead, and half an hour later Viv was on set in a bright pink lycra outfit with electric blue leg warmers, sweatbands and belt.

They shot for thirty minutes before she changed into an electric blue outfit and pink accessories and did the exercise scenario once more. With two more quick changes into red and green lycra outfits, and skipping, jumping and lunging her way around the set, they were done for the day.

"That's a wrap, come back tomorrow for the beauty and make-up products." The assistants wheeled Cabot across the hall into his office and set him up on the couch. He'd be staying there instead of going home as he didn't think he'd make it back. He strapped on his ventilator. The private doctor he'd hired came in to watch him for the night as he struggled to breathe.

Viv changed, said goodbye to everyone, and went home, She told the family about Cabot as they all sat around for dinner.

"Oh, that's so sad," Angie said. "I remember him from the photo shoots."

"Yes," Viv murmured. "So sad. He's just wasted away, and the assistant said he's dying and had to wheel him in and out of the studio."

"Is he?" Jenny asked. "Do you know that for sure?"

Viv shrugged. "I didn't get to speak to him, so I don't know. But by God, he looked awful. Thin, weak, bony. I think he even had a wig on. Definitely *not* the Cabot Conroy of a couple of years ago."

"Disease can ruin a body," Spiros said. "Look at my grandfather. A disease of the heart in heartache at the loss of his children. A disease of the brain in hatred and anger. He was eaten away with everything that had happened. Disease is a dangerous thing."

"I think Cabot has a disease of a different kind, though," Jenny told her husband.

Viv sighed. "I plan on having it out with him tomorrow. That's if he's still alive."

*****

He was, barely.

They started with the face washes with Viv washing her face over a basin and splashing water on her. The next shoot was the moisturizer. Photos of Viv lathering her arms and legs and face were taken before breaking.

The next shoot was going to need longer as Viv was releasing four make-up palettes, one for each season, and was going to have the make-up artist completely redo her make-up in each palette, so it was going to take time.

Summer was up first and luckily, Evie, the mak-up artist from yesterday, knew her stuff, getting Viv into shape in just under fifteen minutes. Wearing a summer dress and with her hair pinned up, she settled on stage for her moment.

Cabot was wheeled in, took a couple of rolls and was wheeled back out.

That's how it was for the rest of the day until the end when she finally marched up to him. "Cabot, *please* tell me what's wrong." She stopped short at the sight of him up close. "God, you look awful."

He smiled, or at least tried what could be described as a smile on his thin bony face. "I'm dying. I don't have long. I hung on for you, darling." He waved a hand at his assistant who handed Viv a plastic bag full of film canisters. "Your photos from the last two days. My good friend Vincenzo Vasarelli said he'd process them for you because I can't. I'm too weak and sick, and I think this is it."

"Oh, Jesus, Cabot." Viv looked at her friend, and her insides died right along with him. He looked awful. "What do you have?"

"Besides a couple of sexually transmitted diseases?" He grinned lightly. "I have no idea. My doctors have no idea. I've just wasted away, and I'm dying. Take the rolls of film; they're yours. I've sent all my photos off to their new owners, so they don't have to be dealt with. The sets will go back to where they came from. My office is empty; I am done. My will is done, my funeral arrangements are done. Vivian, you have been a wonderful, amazing woman to work with and I thank you. Now please, go home to that beautiful baby of yours and that tasty morsel porn star husband. Love to you all and your family. Everyone, time to go."

With arrangements for the sets to be dismantled and sent back the next day, everyone left. Cabot was taken back to his luxurious penthouse that overlooked the ocean, and was placed in a comfortable chair to watch the warm April breeze waft over the water. He passed two hours later with his doctor and lawyer by his side. His doctor declared him dead, and his lawyer rang Vivian to tell her.

"Oh, no," she murmured. "That's awful. Did he suffer?"

"No, the doctor had him on morphine and a ventilator. He died peacefully."

"Thank God for small mercies." Viv made a small cross symbol with her fingers. "Was everything as sorted as he said it was?"

"Yes. I'm ringing to let you know of his passing and that the funeral is this Saturday. Got a pen?"

Viv wrote down the time and place and asked what Cabot had been suffering from.

"A few things. Low cell count, his lungs were filled with diseases, and that meant he couldn't breathe. It was eating him alive. He also had parasites and some kind of cancer."

"Oh, no…that's horrible." Viv's hand went to her mouth. "Is there anything I can do?"

"No. He planned his funeral down to the last detail. Just show up."

"Okay, thank you for calling." Hanging up the phone, she turned to Carlos who sat on the couch with Diana, reading a book.

He looked at her dead expression. "Viv?"

Glassily, she looked at him, not quite seeing him, more through him.

"Viv?" He wondered who had called and what they'd said to affect her so much.

"Mmm?" She drifted back. "What? Sorry."

"Who was that?" Curiosity got the better of him.

"Cabot's lawyer. Cabot died a short time ago. His funeral's this weekend."

"Ow, geez, babe, I'm sorry. I know you two were close." His heart went out to her.

"Dada read," Diana demanded, not liking being ignored.

"Wait, Diana," he said to her then turned his attention back to Viv. "What happened?"

"Apparently, he passed away after getting home. Quietly and comfortably. The lawyer said he was suffering from cancer, and his lungs were dying which is why he couldn't breathe. And he had parasites."

"Ew." Carlos screwed his face up. "Yuck."

"Yuck, Dada." Diana screwed her cherubic face up to imitate her daddy.

"Yes." Viv's mind wandered off in thought about the job the lawyer now had. "Yuck."

*****

The lawyer started the long, arduous process of contacting every person Cabot had remembered having sex with, to inform them he was dead. Even though he was paid well, that was a job he didn't want, because either they didn't want to know, or many of them were too sick and blamed him for making them sick, or were already dead themselves. Cabot wanted to be dressed in his famous schoolboy prep outfit, had picked out a coffin, knew where he wanted to be buried, and had listed everyone he wanted certain things to go to. He'd closed up his business, sold off his possessions, and dotted every i and crossed every t right down to his will.

The funeral of Cabot Charles Conroy was a weird affair, and it was held in the St Baptist Church. He'd asked for every model, actor, and celebrity he'd photographed to be there, and most of them had made it. The weird part, he'd asked for all of them to wear a bowtie and tortoiseshell glasses like his own, and asked for his casket bearers to wear the same outfit he used to wear, and was *still* wearing in his dramatically expressive coffin. This was his famous schoolboy prep outfit. Khaki pants, white shirt, knit vest, bowtie and glasses. An outfit that had been his trademark since leaving the horrendous boarding school he'd gone to nearly twenty years ago. He'd become head photographer at a fashion magazine, earning his way to the top within two years, and he hadn't looked back until the last three months when he'd looked back a lot, and made plans from the day the doctors had told him he was dying. And here he was, lying in his white coffin with its white satin lining being passed by all of the people he loved. The one photo that he wanted displayed above all else, next to the coffin, was the one with him and the Porn Star Brothers and Roger Dencott.

"Jesus Christ," Carlos muttered when he saw the photo. "What the fuck has he got that there for?"

The family paused in the aisle of the church to look toward the coffin, seeing the photo, smiling, and shaking their heads, before taking their seats. They had all gone to pay their respects even though Viv was the one who knew him best. Mike and Maggie were watching the girls in the penthouse.

The service went for hours with countless people wanting to get up and tell everyone their own story or anecdote about Cabot. He loved his model and celebrity friends, and they loved him back, and were all showing it with the tie and glasses tribute. Their tears were genuine, their stories funny, their pain real, and they all shared in it until there were no more stories to tell.

Finally, the coffin was closed and rolled out to the car, and they followed it to the St Baptist cemetery where he was laid to rest. While the priest read from the Bible, thirty-five white doves were released, then thirty-five white balloons with his name on them. Thirty-five white roses were laid on the coffin before it was lowered. Thirty-five to mark his age, his years on the planet, his years full of life.

After the service, everyone went to the Four Seasons hotel for the whitest, swankiest party that was *so* Cabot Conroy. Known for his love of white decorations when it came to throwing his soirées, the reception had everything Cabot would have wanted. But then he *did* plan it that way. White balloons and streamers, white champagne and wine, white chocolate and white finger food, white roses. It was all very Cabot and his parting gift to the people he loved.

*****

They celebrated Angelina's 21st birthday at *Maxim's* which had a 360-degree view of the city. Everyone she wanted was there; Mike, Maggie, and a few other friends from Juilliard, as well as all of her family. She was dressed in a slick black and silver bodysuit with matching bolero and studded heels, plus she was wearing all the jewellery Pedro had given her since their marriage. He matched her in a black suit and shirt, and little Alena was dressed in a white party dress with a ribbon in her hair. The birthday cake was a violin coming out of a grand piano with twenty-one sparklers sticking out of it.

"Yay." She clapped her hands excitedly. "I can't believe I made it to twenty-one."

"I can't believe you're in your third year at Juilliard," Maggie replied. "After everything you went through in the first six months, I'm surprised they allowed you to stay."

"Yeah, well, they knew how good I was and who I was related to." Angie grinned.

"Blow out your candles, babe," Pedro urged and quickly caught Alena as she went for the cake. "It's not yours, Alena, it's Mama's."

"Mama no, cay my," Alena cried, reaching her chubby little hands towards it, looking from it to her father and back again. "Cay?"

"Not yours, Mama's," he repeated.

Angie laughed. "Guess I'd better blow it out, so she can have some." After blowing out the sparklers and cutting it up, she handed a piece to her daughter. "Alena want a piece of Mama's cake?"

"My cay." Alena grabbed the piece and smeared it all over her face. "Cay."

Everyone laughed, and several cameras went off to capture the moment.

"Definitely takes after her father," Jenny said, watching her granddaughter on her son's knee. "And look at those big blue eyes. Just like Dada's."

"Mmm, mmm," Alena agreed around another handful of cake.

"Just as well we took photos already; she just smeared it over her dress." Pedro wiped some off with a napkin as Angie finished passing the cake around and sat down to eat her own.

"It doesn't matter, it will wash out," Jenny said. "It's only cake."

"Cay," Alena agreed and reached for her father's piece that was right beside hers. "Cay."

"No, Bubba, that's mine," Daddy told her, moving his plate out of her reach.

"Oooh, my…" she whined, looking up at her father and frowning. "Me more cay?"

"You haven't finished the piece you've got," Pedro told her.

"Doesn't matter, let her have some more." Angie laid another piece on her daughter's plate, capturing her attention.

"Cay," Alena squealed and dug in.

Once the cake was eaten, they filled the restaurant's small dance floor, going until the sun came up when they decided to stay for breakfast.

May 1980

Viv's new fragrance campaign went live on the first of May. Her new scent, *Vivian*, was in all the stores of New York. Department stores were top of the chain, followed by exclusive boutiques and perfumeries, followed by pharmacies and chain stores. Posters dressed the windows, and billboards dressed the buildings. Displays sold out in hours. Alongside the fragrance were the new body and face ranges, and the make-up lines. The gorgeous Vivian Villiers could outsell anyone, and she did, with shelves being restocked twice a day for the first week.

Cabot's last photo shoots proved to be the best he did, of Vivian that is. He made her look incredible. They were his parting gift to her, and she cherished them dearly.

May was also the time to get started on the exercise videos and health and beauty segments for her lifestyle plan, and she got to it quick smart, doing her first video in Central Park close to home.

"And we step." Viv stepped in place. "We march to warm ourselves up. We have to get our blood flowing, our fluids moving, our muscles working, and sidestep. Right and left, and right and left." After taking five minutes to warm up, she launched into a twenty-minute workout that was basic level and ended with a five-minute cool down. "And we come to a slow march, so our breathing regulates, we bring our heartbeat down, and everything settles back into place. And stretch." She threw her arms over her head. "And once more stretch and down." Straightening, she faced the camera as the other girls in the video gathered around her. "Good job everyone, see you next time." She wore the same hot pink lycra outfit and blue accessories as in the photo shoot Cabot did, so the photos went with the video.

"And cut," the director yelled. "Great Viv, let's move on to the next spot."

Because Jenny was supplying the money, they were able to have cameras and lights already set up in each spot so all anyone had to do was run to the next stage.

Viv and the girls towelled down, changed outfits, and had their make-up reapplied before doing it all over again, but at a slightly faster pace and with slightly more complicated moves. There would be several in the series. Basic, intermediate, advanced, super advanced, the five-minute workout, the New York workout, the seated workout for people unable to stand, and the floor workout where you worked on your abs and glutes.

She had come up with so many ideas for exercise videos it excited her, and she'd even recruited Angelina and Maggie into some of them. There was a set of dance videos planned, which she was hoping to film at *Studio 69*, plus she had a set planned for using workout equipment such as jump ropes, the step, the ball, the hoop and weights.

Villiers Inc. was dashing ahead, and Vivian was planning to run, because on top of all that, she had a beauty video planned where she would show everyone her own routine to glowing skin. They were all a part of her five-year plan because that was as far as she'd thought ahead with the videos. She was also considering taking her exercise routine on the road and travelling to foreign countries to show off the landscape. Oh, yes, *Villiers Inc.* was in production.

"And perfect, cut, let's move onto the next one. What is it? Advanced?"

"Yes," Viv called. "Whew, glad I'm doing this now and not in the middle of summer." Another change and they continued filming.

After watching the first two times, Jenny went back to the penthouse across the road and found Carlos holding Diana and standing at the edge of the rooftop terrace. "There you are. Watching

Mama?" Jenny waved Diana's hand around. "Hello, my baby, hello Diana."

"Mama," Diana replied. "Mama da." She pointed to the park where they could just make out Viv in bright red lycra.

"Yes, Mama's there." Jenny kissed her granddaughter's chubby cheek and slid into Spiro's lap as he lazed on an outdoor lounge.

He wrapped his arms around his wife. "How's it going down there?"

"Really good. And if the perfume and cosmetics sales are anything to go by, *Villiers Inc.* is going to be a massive money earner. She looks hot in lycra. I wish I looked that good."

"Have you ever tried lycra on?" Spiros asked, nipping at his wife's neck.

"No."

"Why not?"

"Because it doesn't suit me."

"Have you ever exercised?"

"No, never needed to. Are you saying I'm fat?" She swatted her husband's arm. "Spiros Giorgio Stephanopoulos."

He laughed. "Hey, I'm just saying you should try it on and see how you look. My bet is, you'll give Viv a run for her money."

Jenny scoffed. "I hardly think so." She grabbed Diana as she came racing over and launched her into the air and down onto her grandfather.

"Oomph." He pretended to be winded. "Diana."

"Gampa," she gurgled in delight. "Gampa."

"See what you would have missed out on if you'd stayed in Mykonos all by your lonesome," Jenny teased. "Being called Gampa by your firstborn grandchild."

He laughed once more. "You're never going to let me live it down, are you?"

"Nope." She kissed him on the cheek. "Gampa."

*****

Over the next two weeks, Viv filmed video segment after video segment, laying out, step by step, her beauty routines for body and face, like her make-up routines with different looks for day, evening, working out, and dating. She added her simple diet plan for how to stay fit and healthy, and a cooking segment showing off some of her favourite meals. Everything was ahead of schedule and going to plan.

*****

"To my darling wife, Jenny, you are my everything. I still regret missing out on your fiftieth two years ago, and I've tried making up for it ever since. You are my whole world, my life, my love, and I am so glad you chose this little Greek boy to love, marry, and give your heart and soul to. I love you; happy birthday and happy anniversary."

"Happy birthday, happy anniversary," the kids chimed in.

Jenny smiled. Her boys and their partners and children were all around her, and she was in her element. Every year they celebrated her birthday and their anniversary together as they were only two days apart. This year she was fifty-two, and it was their twenty-eighth anniversary. They were celebrating at *Star Tower*, one of the hottest restaurants to open in years.

"I love you too, my darling," she told her husband, kissing him. "And our babies and *their* babies."

"Ooh, ooh." Alena and Diana banged their fists on the table.

Jenny laughed at their antics. "And their mamas. And I am *beyond* deliriously happy that we are all together in the one room, in the one place."

Two years ago, at the most important birthday of her life, Spiros hadn't been there. The cheating scandal had him back in Mykonos as they were separated. He'd called the day after, but she'd hung up on him, and that was the worst, most horrible time in their relationship and her life, besides losing her own daughter, Alena. But they had made up, she had a second chance with Alena who'd come back as her granddaughter, and she had never been happier, having gotten to see Europe last year, and Australia and her family once more. Her world was complete.

"Open your presents, Mama," Pedro urged, bouncing Alena on his knee.

Laughing, Jenny ripped open the bright coloured box and pulled out a specially framed photo of Alena in a gorgeous blue dress sitting with her hands in her lap and a huge smile on her face.

"Oh, she's beautiful," Jenny said. "Yes, Alena, you are beautiful." She waved her granddaughter's hand. "Yes, you are, look it's you." She showed the picture to her.

"Ma ooh, ooh, A-ena," she replied, pointing to the picture.

"Yes, Alena," Jenny said. "A-lena."

"A-e-na," Alena repeated, banging her hands on the table.

Carlos and Viv gave her a similar photo of Diana in a blue dress, and Roger and Tomas gave her a silver engraved ornament of an open bible with the Corinthians passage she had read out at their wedding on one side. On the opposite side was a picture of the two of them in their tuxes on their wedding day. Under the passage was inscribed *Love Tomas and Roger, May 1980, thank you for being our biggest supporter.*

"Oh, my boys." She teared up. "It's beautiful."

"Oh, Mama, we didn't mean to make you cry." Tomas rushed around the table to hug her. "We were trying to come up with something different."

"You did, and it's beautiful. I'll treasure it always, thank you." She stood to take him into her arms. "I love you so much, Tomas. So, so much. I want you to see the world and enjoy yourselves, you hear me. Enjoy every waking moment that you have because none of us knows when it's over. None of us knows when our time is up. So, enjoy every single moment you and Roger have together." She pulled back and kissed both his cheeks. "Enjoy every single moment, Tomas. Promise me that."

He couldn't read her expression; it was a mix of love, sorrow, worry and something else he couldn't put his finger on. "I will, Mama. I promise."

"Good." She brushed his long black hair aside. He'd grown it out for a different look, but she didn't like it. "Look at you. Long hair, happy, in love." Smiling, she kissed his cheeks again. "Never go to bed angry, and always tell one another *I love you* when you wake."

He grinned. "Yes, Mama."

She turned to Roger who had come up beside her. "Thank you, Roger, it's a beautiful gift."

"You're welcome, Mrs S." He gave her a kiss and a hug.

*****

Jamal rolled out of bed.

His feet hit the floor, and then he did.

"Jesus fucking Christ." His legs had failed him, weakening until they'd folded, and he was on his knees, bent over, and feeling like shit. "Jesus fucking…" He hefted himself back onto the bed and tried again, managing to stand.

He wobbled into the bathroom and saw the gaunt version of himself. He'd lost weight lately, having bad bouts of diarrhea, but that had stopped, and he hoped to gain some weight back. His eyes were sunken; his teeth seemed longer. He checked them, peering closely at his gums. "Fuck! What's that? Damned red blotches, fuck." He checked the rest of himself, finding blotches on his cock and torso. "Fuck this shit, what is it?" Checking his mouth again, he noticed his gums seemed to recede. His face had thinned, making his teeth look bigger. "Ugh. Fuck."

Standing in the middle of the small room, hands on hips, he knew something was seriously wrong. This wasn't just a case of STDs anymore. With Leon dead, he'd contacted his ex-lovers and found most of them had similar experiences, but some had actually passed away…dead. *Fuck, they're dead. Three ex-lovers dead, over twenty infected with something.*

"Jesus fucking Christ what's going on?" he swore, but it took his breath away and he gave a hacking cough. That was the worst, always making him weaker and leaving him in pain.

He turned on the hot water taps in the sink and shower to get the steam going. It seemed to be the only thing that helped every morning. The steam moistened his throat and helped him breathe. He hadn't seen a doctor, was too scared to go, and with everything he'd been reading in the death notices, it freaked him out. People he knew, people he had grown up with, were dying way too young. So, what the hell *was* going on?

The shower helped relieve the aches and pains, and he dressed for work. Maybe he should take time off to rest and take some meds, try and get his strength back. One thing he *had* done was gone without sex. Since Stephano, and learning about Leon, he'd sworn off sex and lovers. Not going out partying, not going out to hook up. He'd sworn off it until this thing died down. But at the rate *he* was going, things were definitely dying faster than expected.

June 1980

"Oh, my God, you're kidding?" Roger said into the phone. "When?"

"Last week. Johnno an' Evan just up an' died. We didn't even know they were sick. They certainly didn't look it, but one minute they're here, the next, they're in the morgue," Freddy said from Miami. Freddy Highmore was the owner of *Love Stick*, the restaurant bar where Roger had taken Tomas on their first day out together.

"Jesus, Freddy. What the fuck's happening? My brother-in-law's co-worker Leon died. My sister-in-law's photographer died. We're reading of friends and acquaintances being sick. Jesus."

"Yeah, I hear you. A lot of guys down here are sick. STDs are goin' 'round; some are comin' down with pneumonia for God's sake."

Roger sighed. "When're the funerals?"

"This weekend. We'll have the wake here at *Love Stick*."

"Okay, ah…" He glanced at Tomas who had a worried look. "Are we free this weekend?" he asked his husband.

"Yeah, absolutely." It was barely June, but the girls' birthdays were next week. "As long as we're back by Monday."

"Yeah, Freddy. We'll leave tomorrow and catch up with you. Can we stay in your spare room, or do we need a hotel?"

"You can stay with me, man, everyone else is bunkin' in with someone."

"Okay. We'll see you tomorrow." Another sigh escaped Roger as he hung up.

"What's going on, Roger?" Tomas moved to his side. "What's happened?"

A deeper sigh. "You remember Johnno and Evan from *Love Stick*? We saw them occasionally." He received a nod in return. "I saw them a fair bit before I met you, but obviously after I didn't see them so much. Well…" He wandered over to the window.

"Roger?" Tomas moved with him.

"They're dead." Roger shook his head in disbelief. "They're dead. Just like that."

"You're kidding?" Tomas covered his mouth in shock. "How? Why? Of what?"

"Don't know," Roger said. "Freddy reckoned they were fine and then they were dead. The funeral's this weekend. The wake's at *Love Stick*. Freddy said we could stay at his place."

"Yeah, absolutely." Tomas nodded. "Yeah. I'll go let Mama know, you go and start packing."

*****

They flew down to Miami the next day, heading straight to *Love Stick* to see Freddy. He showed them to his spare room then sat them down in his small lounge. He lived above the restaurant in a two-bed apartment.

"So, what's going on, Freddy?" Roger asked.

"What's goin' on is that guys are gettin' sick," Freddy said. "They got all sorts of STDs, some have the goddamn flu in summer, an' others look like hell chewed them up an' spat them out. While others," he shrugged, "look like there's nothin' wrong."

"What *is* wrong? Is it just the gays, or girls too?" Roger tried for more information.

"None of the girls are sick, just the gays." Freddy swigged back his beer.

"How many have passed?" Roger leant forward in his seat.

"All together?" Freddy raised a brow.

"Since we left in '78," Roger pushed.

"Hmm." Freddy thought. "Johnno an' Evan make ten in two years."

"Jesus!" Roger exclaimed. "And how many sick?"

"Hmm, about twenty."

"The regulars that I knew?" Roger's heart sank, and so did his head…into his hands.

"Most of them." Freddy nodded. "There's a few new ones that have come along since you two left. Some of them are sick."

"Jesus." Roger sat back in his seat. "So, it's just the gays?"

"Just the gays."

"What time's the funeral?"

"Midday. We'll come back here after."

Roger nodded. "We'll fly back home Sunday." He looked at Tomas who had been quiet the whole time. "We'll make it back for the girls' birthdays."

Tomas smiled softly. "Okay."

*****

On Saturday, they attended the church service of Jonathon Ranks, a.k.a. Johnno, and Evan Stewart. Their caskets were closed, the service only fifteen minutes long, and everyone gathered back at *Love Stick.*

"Jesus." Roger glanced around the restaurant he'd loved spending time in, at all the people he knew and didn't know. It had always been light and airy, and full of life and fun. A safe place for gays to hang out, and he remembered back to the days he'd taken Tomas there. It had been fun and casual. And now, everyone was sick, the décor not up to its usual standards, the atmosphere as sick as the crowd. It was definitely not the place it used to be, and all in two and a half years. What a waste. "Look at them."

Tomas stood by his side, almost hiding from them behind Roger. He didn't feel comfortable in Miami anymore, and definitely didn't know these people.

"They look ill," Roger said, taking in the gaunt, sickly, yellow complexions, the blotches, the coughing.

"Roger, I don't think we should be here. I don't want to get sick too." Tomas's nerves clenched his stomach. He wasn't sure why he was so nervously sick, but everything in him was telling him to get out. Get out and go home and don't come back. Never come back.

"Hey there, oh, my God. Judd and Ethan. Oh, my God, you guys look awful." Roger hadn't seen them since New York in '77 when they'd come to watch Pedro play at 69. "Jesus boys, what the hell happened to you two?"

"Sex." Judd shrugged. "Lots of it means rampant diseases. They're taking a toll on my body." The former bodybuilding champ was a wasted version of his old self. His blond hair was long and straggly and thin, his features gaunt.

"You on something, Judd?" Roger noticed the redness around his nose and the ulcers on his lips. He had blotches over both arms. "Speed, crack, heroin?"

"Hey man, what I do is my business." Judd didn't even have the strength to get angry.

"You're doing heroin?" Roger asked, dumbfounded. "Fucking hell, Judd. What's wrong with you? You used to be so clean and healthy."

Judd scowled. "Yeah well, you try making a living on weightlifting Mr Big Shot Porn Star. I'm not living in New York on Mommy's money." He sneered at Tomas who shrank back. "Shit happens." He walked away leaving a very scared and ill Ethan standing there.

"Ethan?" Roger said.

"It's…" the skinny brunet rasped through ulcerated lips. "He's just a…" He weakly shrugged a shoulder. Ethan was a former surfing pro; now he looked like regurgitated shit.

"On drugs like you? You should be ashamed of yourselves." Watching Ethan saunter after Judd, Roger sighed. Where were all the healthy-looking guys he knew, he'd *known*? He'd been going there for two years before meeting Tomas, and everyone had always been so healthy and alive. Everyone looked after themselves, *and* each other. Looking out for friends and keeping them safe. But Jesus, who the hell *were* these people? He knew their names, but they were all shadows of their former selves, and it was scaring him.

He was scared for what it meant for them and him and Tomas.

Scared for the parts of life that no longer existed. The good old carefree days. Scared for the present and all he saw, and scared for their future because he seriously didn't believe any of them had one.

If they had gone downhill in two and a half years, then he doubted they'd survive *another* two and a half. He doubted if any of them would even survive the year.

"You're right, T. We shouldn't be here. It's not for us, anymore. Come on. Let's go home."

*****

"Happy birthday, dear Diana, happy birthday to you. Hip, hip hooray, hip, hip hooray, hip, hip hooray."

They were celebrating Diana Villiers Stephanopoulos's second birthday in the penthouse. The whole room had been decorated with pink and blue streamers and balloons, and presents were piled on the sofas in the sitting area. They were gathered around the dining table, set up with cake and finger food for the babies, and finger food for the adults. But it was all about Diana, even though Alena was disapproving.

"My berfday," Alena wailed. "My cay." She reached for the birthday cake Diana was digging into. It was a castle with Princess Diana written on it in icing.

"No, Bubba." Pedro lifted his daughter into his arms. "*Diana's* cake. Yours is tomorrow."

"No," she cried. "*My* cay." Her bottom lip quivered, and her big blue eyes welled with tears. This was her birthday, was it not? Why was her cousin eating her cake?

"No, Bubba." Pedro wandered into the lounge room to get his daughter away from the table. "Alena's birthday is tomorrow." No matter which way he stood so she didn't see the table, she would quickly turn her head to watch. "Alena," he said sharply to get her attention. "It's not yours. *Your* birthday is tomorrow. You can have *your own* cake tomorrow."

"Cay." The tears flowed down her cherubic cheeks.

Jenny wandered over to her son with a small piece of cake on a plate. "Alena, would you like some of *Diana's* birthday cake?" She held it up for her granddaughter to see. At six feet, Pedro was four inches above Jenny, and with him holding Alena in his arms it made her higher still, so Jenny had to hold the plate up.

"Cay?" Alena whimpered, looking from the piece to her Dada and Gamma. "Cay?"

"Yes, Alena, you may have a piece of *Diana's* birthday cake," Pedro told his whimpering daughter.

She looked once more from the cake to him and back before grabbing a handful and putting it in her mouth.

"Good?" Jenny smiled.

"Cay," Alena said and went back for more.

Pedro took the plate and sat down on one of the couches to finish feeding her.

Jenny went back to the table. "She really doesn't like sharing, does she?"

Angie shook her head. "We're going to have to teach her that not everything is hers." She nibbled on her own piece of cake.

"It's to be expected the first few years." Jenny sat next to Spiros at the table with her own piece of cake and watched Carlos and Viv with their daughter. "They're born one day apart, so that will always be a competition, and until they're old enough to understand that each one has her own party, then you will have problems. But it's not too bad. They *are* only two. Wait until they're old enough to fight like the boys did."

Carlos looked up in shock. "I'm a lover, not a fighter, Mama."

Jenny laughed. "Not once Tomas came along. You were an only child until he came home, and suddenly you had competition for love and affection, and toys and parties. And when Pedro came along, you had *even more* competition to go up against because everyone loved Pedro with his big blue eyes and shock of black hair. You *hated* not being the centre of attention."

Pedro came back to the table with Alena. "Oh, yeah, she's right, bro. Remember that time you broke my toy at Christmas because I got what you wanted, but you didn't get it. You threw a tantrum and made me cry."

Carlos had the decency to blush. "Yeah, well, I was ah, only six or seven. I didn't know any better."

"You made Mama cry. She burst right into tears and ran into her bedroom for hours," Tomas said. Finishing off his piece of cake, he placed the plate on the kitchen counter which he and Roger sat in front of. "She burst into tears and didn't stop."

"Yes, well, that wasn't a good year." Jenny remembered back. "I lost my baby girl a month or so earlier and had spent time with my aunt and uncle in Sydney. I came back to look after my sons, and my eldest throws a tantrum at my youngest and breaks the present I'd brought back for him. You didn't make life easy sometimes, Carlos. In fact, you made it damn hard. I had to get my aunt and uncle to go out and buy another toy and send it to us so it could be replaced. You were punished for a month for that." She put down her plate. "You made life hard *a lot* over the years."

Everyone was silent as they heard what she'd said, and all eyes went to Alena munching happily on another piece of cake on Pedro's legs, completely ignoring everyone around her as she focussed on the food.

"I'm sorry, Mama. Sorry, Pedro." Carlos shrugged, ashamed of himself and his behaviour that year. He remembered it well, and now, wished he hadn't, especially since he now knew what his mother had gone through.

"Mama got me another one, and I still have it at home, so it's okay. I know you can be a jerk at times, but at least you learned to use your powers for good," Pedro joked. "You've grown up in the last few years."

Carlos thought about it. "Yeah. I have. So have you." He gazed thoughtfully at his little brother. "Must be the fact we had our own babies that made us both grow up so much."

"Must be," Pedro agreed, looking back at his brother.

"I'm glad you finally did." Jenny smiled at her sons sitting side by side with her beautiful grandbabies on their laps. "Because look at what we have." She held out her hands to her grandbabies.

"Cay." Alena and Diana held up their cake-filled hands.

*****

"Happy birthday, dear Alena, happy birthday to you. Hip, hip hooray, hip, hip hooray, hip, hip hooray."

They were celebrating Alena Jennifer Stephanopoulos's second birthday. This time the penthouse was decorated in blue and white with streamers, balloons, and lots of presents. She finally got her own cake, a Disney princess, and she ripped into the head of that princess before they had finished singing.

Jenny snapped photos while Spiros recorded film, and everyone laughed at Alena's antics.dear

"Cay," she happily cried out, holding up two hands of cake before shoving both into her mouth and merrily chomping away. Once the cake was gone, it was her presents that she ripped into. Books, clothes, toys, including a huge princess castle the same as Diana had received the day before.

"Cathle," she cried and crawled through the doorway to stand in her own castle.

"Can you say, Princess Alena?" Jenny asked as she snapped photos.

"Pincess A-ena." She banged on the castle window and giggled.

Fortunately, the castle was made of large flat interconnecting plastic blocks and could be pulled apart for transport. Diana joined her inside.

"No, Da-anna, *my* cathle," she said, unable to pronounce her cousin's name properly. "No." Hitting out at her, she tried pushing her out the door.

"*Alena, play nice.* Diana let you in her castle yesterday," Pedro warned

She looked up with her big blue eyes and rosy cheeks. "My cathle, Dada," she whimpered.

"Yes, it is, but you need to share. Diana is allowed to play in it with you," Pedro replied, feeling his heart melt for his little girl. Every time she looked at him from the moment she was born, his heart would swell and melt, and he'd turn to goo. The love he had for her overwhelmed him, more so than the love he had for Angie. He loved her with all of his heart, body and soul, but Alena was different. Maybe it was because she was still a baby, maybe it was because Jenny believed it was his sister reincarnated, but all he knew was, she had his heart. Regardless of what she did. "You can *both* be princesses and play in the castle," he added.

"*My* cathle." She frowned at her father, defying him to say anything more.

"Share with Diana," he replied, making her snub him by turning away with her nose in the air and leaving Diana looking up at them. Sighing, he ran a hand through his hair. "What am I going to do with you?" he asked softly.

"Let her grow up away from Diana," Jenny replied. "Are they together, yes. Will they always be, who knows, but that is why they need their own space and their own time with other family, so they're not always competing for attention."

"I know." Pedro slipped an arm around his mother's shoulders as they stood watching the girls. "Does that mean they shouldn't be at each other's birthday parties?"

"Possibly. Especially after yesterday. They're still learning that not everything is theirs. Maybe they shouldn't be." She shrugged. "Who knows, in this family birthdays are shared with other days, so maybe we just have to let them go through it." Leaving the girls to play, they walked back to the table. "So, when are you boys leaving and where are you going?" Jenny asked Tomas and Roger.

"This week," Tomas replied. "We're going to spend a couple of weeks out on Long Island in the Hamptons, and then we head up to Maine and Massachusetts. We'll visit Boston and Salem."

"Can't wait to visit the witch museum," Roger said. "Spoo-key."

Tomas shuddered. "Ugh, no thanks, you can do that on your own. Then we'll stop off here for fourth of July before heading for Chicago; then it's the Black Hills to see the presidents' heads, then San Francisco, L.A., San Diego, Vegas, and who knows where after that. Roger wants to see Nashville and New Orleans, so maybe we'll end up there."

"That sounds like a very full holiday. I wouldn't mind visiting Hollywood, seeing the sights and visiting that park. What's it called,

Disneyland?" Jenny asked.

"Disneyand," Alena cried out, her eyes wide, her lips in an o shape. She was into all things Disney, toys, movies, books, princess dresses. "Disneyand?"

Diana shared the same expression as they both stood staring at the adults in apprehension.

"Oh, no, I think you've started something, Mama," Carlos said. "You'd better come through, 'cause if you don't…"

Jenny laughed. "I won't get any hugs and kisses from my grandbabies. I say we should go to Disneyland. We're all on holidays, Angie's off school, Pedro, you can get a couple of weeks off can't you? We'll make it a family affair. Tomas, when do you think you'll get there?"

"Oh, it can't be this month," Viv piped up. "I'm busy filming all month."

"That's okay," Tomas told her. "We probably won't be there until July or August. We're taking our time and aren't in a rush. Plus, we're driving, so we get to see the countryside."

"Oh, is that safe?" Jenny asked.

"What? Driving across America?" Roger asked. "Probably."

"More like, *two gay men* driving across America," Jenny quietly said. "I don't want anything happening to you because of your lifestyle. The way you are." Everyone looked from her to the boys, unsure of how this conversation would pan out.

Tomas looked from Roger to his mother. "We've never had problems travelling before, Mama."

"But you weren't driving across the country before," Jenny said. "*On your own.*"

"We'll be fine, Mrs S," Roger said, finishing his drink. "We'll keep the doors locked and the windows up so no one can get in."

But Jenny's worry continued. "Promise me you'll stay in nice motels and not some little backwater hotel where no one will know if you're missing. Like Luiz did with you and then Papadopoulos's man killed him and grabbed you. And take cans of gasoline, so you don't have to stop for any."

Tomas jolted at the mention of Luiz's name and what happened with the double kidnapping and murder that he couldn't even remember. "Mama," he started protesting.

"*No*, Tomas." She resisted. "If you're going to travel by car be safe for God's sake. For *me*."

He relented, sighing at her expression and knowing she was right. While his recollections of his kidnapping were vague, just thinking about it still freaked him out. "Yes, Mama."

Roger remembered their trip to Miami and the sight of his former friends. "I'll take care of both of us, Mrs S. I promise you that."

"Good," Jenny said. "Then you can give me your travel itinerary and Viv, you can give me your work schedule for the next three months, and I will schedule a two-week holiday to Hollywood for all of us."

"Ooh, we can stay at my house," Viv said. "It has four bedrooms and currently has tenants, but I can kick them out in time for the holiday. Then we'll have a place to stay."

"That's good," Jenny said. "We have a place to stay already. It will have to be before Angie goes back to school, so I'll need your schedules."

"I can't believe it will be my last year at Juilliard," Angie said. Mike and Maggie were next to her at the kitchen counter, having been involved in a lot of Pedro and Angie's celebrations. After Leon's death, Pedro and Mike's bond had strengthened, and they all hung out more.

"I can't believe you've made it this far with a baby," Maggie said. She'd had a makeover for summer, a shorter hairdo in style with the current trends, was wearing Viv's perfume and using the cosmetics, as was Angie. And she'd updated her wardrobe after losing weight using Viv's workout videos and getting in shape for summer.

"Neither can I," Angie said. "Could *not* have done it without Mama's help."

"Babies *can* be a handful," Jenny added to the conversation. "And I had absolutely no problem with looking after my grandbabies. We've all had some wonderful times together. Haven't we girls?" She looked over at her grandbabies, and they looked back and waved, screaming as their daddies came running over to eat them.

"Nom, nom, nom." Carlos pretended to eat Diana.

"Dada," she screamed and broke into giggles. Her blue eyes flashed the same colour as her father's, and her golden-brown hair was tied in a pink ribbon.

Jenny watched her boys with their girls and noticed the updated styles they wore. Tight, high-waisted jeans, flared at the bottom, t-shirts and sneakers, the same style Tomas and Roger had been into for a while. The three-piece suits had been delegated to the backs of their closets, as were her clothes from just a few years ago. She and Spiros had new clothes for the summer, and new decade, Vivian was dressed in her runway best as always, and Angie and Maggie had the latest rock chic look, but the major thing she did notice was how abundantly happy her family was.

*****

Jamal sat at his desk sucking on an asthma inhaler while no one was watching. His breathing had worsened, and it was the only thing that seemed to help. It wasn't recommended by a doctor, no, he still hadn't gone to see one, but he had gone to the pharmacist and persuaded him to give him an inhaler. That was almost two weeks ago, but it wasn't getting better.

He stared down at his paperwork, but his eyes blurred. Screwing them up, he rubbed them, trying to clear his vision. It worked, but not for long. "Ugh, fuck it," he whispered under his breath. "Fuck it to hell."

"What's *your* problem?" the new partner said, sitting heavily in his own chair at his desk across from Jamal's, the one formerly owned by Carmichael Burns. He was Stew Babbath, a forty-something meathead with his own issues. He hated blacks, but hated fags even more, and wondered if the cop across from him was a fag. He'd never seen him with a woman, but then he hadn't seen many cops with a woman, not that he'd ever mentioned a date or girlfriend either.

"Been sick, got blurry vision," was all Jamal said, trying to clear his eyes.

"Maybe you should see a doctor," Stew said, eyeing the thin frame of his fifth partner in less than two years.

"Yeah, maybe." Jamal looked at some paperwork. "You up for a trip to Harlem? We got a disturbance."

"Sure, why not, but I'm driving." Stew grabbed his hat from the back of the chair.

"Fine by me." Jamal followed him downstairs to the car, and ten minutes later they were pulling up outside the apartment building.

"Apartment 24B," Jamal read from the paper, and they alighted and went inside, only to find they had to walk up six flights of stairs. "Jesus," Jamal murmured. "I am *not* in the mood for stairs."

"What *are you* in the mood for?" Stew asked as he started up. "Cock?"

"What?" Jamal's face screwed up in distaste. "What the fuck are you on?" He followed Stew up, trying to pay it cool. He'd hidden his sexuality for years and was well practised.

"Just wondering." Stew glanced over his shoulder as he ascended the second set of stairs. "You're puffing already."

"Told you, been sick," Jamal replied. "Doesn't seem to be getting better."

"Yeah, well, I hope I don't catch it." Stew kept going, but Jamal rested a moment, sucking back on the inhaler.

Finally getting to the door, he'd caught his breath and had no problem questioning the woman in the apartment. But as she pointed out that the perp was hiding in apartment 23, the perp bolted out of the door and down the stairs.

Babbath took off in pursuit at full blast, while Jamal thanked the lady and quickly descended, his breath becoming shorter and shorter. He made it to the door and out to the car. Seeing Babbath down the street he started off, stumbling, gasping, his vision blurry, his energy flagging, his throat constricting. He ran, he stumbled, his legs jerked. His vision passed to white; he stumbled, he fell, he collapsed onto the pavement.

"Jesus fucking Christ." Babbath came back with the perp in cuffs and kicked Jamal on the way past. "Get up, you fag," he called and shoved the perp into the back of the squad car. Slamming the door, he went to stand by Jamal and stared down. "What's wrong with you? You dead?" He kicked him again, eliciting a groan. "Ah, fuck it." Getting on the two-way in the car, he called for an ambulance and backup. "Officer down, officer down, I have a perp in the car and a partner flat on the sidewalk. Officer down."

"Ambulance on its way, estimation time six minutes," the female voice came over.

"Roger that," Babbath said, and sat with his leg cocked up on the lip of the door until the ambulance arrived. He barely moved, just enough to indicate to Jamal on the sidewalk.

But their captain arrived as well, and after seeing Jamal strapped onto a ventilation machine and Babbath sitting in the car, he strode over to him. "And what are you doing sitting in the car? Have you been there the whole time, or did you bother helping your partner?" Captain Shield had been Jamal's captain since '75 and knew of his difficulties with partners after Carmichael Burns had retired.

"Ah, no sir." Stew jumped out of the car. "There was nothing *to* do. I caught the perp, put him in the car, checked Jamal, and called for an ambulance and backup. There wasn't anything I *could* do, so I kept an eye on the perp."

"Mmm," Shield mumbled. "I'm sure you did. So, do you know why he collapsed? Were there shots fired?"

"No, sir, no. I ran after the perp, no shots. He'd been complaining about his breathing and blurry vision, but nothing else." They watched Jamal being loaded into the back of the ambulance.

"You'd better pray that's all it is, Officer Babbath," Captain Shield barked before following the ambulance in his squad car.

"His airway was all but shut down when we found him," one of the paramedics told staff waiting at the hospital. "We had to trach him and stick the ventilator on."

"I need chest, head, and throat x-rays, blood samples, and a specialist down here now." The doctor stuck his stethoscope on Jamal's chest and listened. "It's bad. He sounds blocked. Get me that x-ray."

X-rays, bloods, urine. All tests were taken, all x-rays and scans were done, and at the end of the day, they all showed that Jamal did not have long to live.

"Doctor," Captain Shield called as he strode up to him after exiting Jamal's intensive care unit. "How is he?"

The doctor looked up from his chart to see a room full of officers all awaiting news on their comrade. He sighed. "I'm sorry, Captain, but he's dying."

"What?" Shield frowned. "From what? *Of* what?"

The doctor shook his head in disbelief. "His lungs are full of pneumonia and have wasted away. His CD4 T cells are less than 200 microlitres, and he even has cancer. He's on his deathbed, Captain; he doesn't have long." Murmurs went through the group.

"What *do you mean*, cancer and pneumonia? It's summer," the captain said, wondering if he was in some bad movie.

The doctor put on his best explanatory voice as he did with five-year-olds. "His CD4 T cells are below 200 microlitres. Whatever caused that, and at this stage, we don't know, has allowed his immune system to weaken to the point pneumocystis pneumonia has set in. Known as PCP, it's a form of pneumonia caused by the yeast-like fungus pneumocystis jivorecii. It attacks the fibrous tissues of the lungs with marked thickening of the alveolar septa and alveoli which leads to hypoxia. It spread to his visceral organs, liver and kidneys. He has something going on in his mouth and throat, but we're awaiting tests, plus he has what's known as Kaposi's sarcoma, which is a cancer seen in older Mediterranean men, or Africans, which Jamal is. It's affected his lungs as well as the lymph nodes. Both the PCP and KS have probably infected other areas as well, but we can't be sure until an autopsy." He didn't mention the genital ulcers or STDs that were showing, like the candidiasis in his mouth and throat. He hoped to give Jamal some privacy and to save the humiliation.

"Autopsy?" The captain frowned. "Is there *nothing* you can do?"

"Not at this stage, it's too far gone. If he'd come in months ago when symptoms arose, maybe. But not now. The best we can do is to contact his family and priest and prepare for his funeral. If you have any more questions, I'll be around. Excuse me." With a nod to everyone, he went off to do some research on Jamal's condition.

"Jesus, Captain. Was he for real?"

Shield turned around to see half of his squad in the hallway and cleared his throat. "I know you all might want to say goodbye, but I don't think going in there would be a good idea." He glanced around. "But you might want to line up and pass by. Give him a send-off if he's awake and can see you. I'll need to make a phone call, but it can wait a few moments. Let's make this quick."

Walking over to the ICU room window he knocked on it. The nurse looked up and saw him point at Jamal, and then she motioned for Jamal to look. He turned his head slowly, seeing his captain at the window. The captain beckoned to someone beside him, and one by one the officers passed the window to wave, cross their fingers, or make a cross symbol with their hands. They crowded around, and on the count of three from their captain, saluted.

Jamal pulled the ventilator mask from his mouth to say something, but couldn't, so instead, he gave a weak, but official, salute back.

His captain nodded, and wiping away a tear, moved his officers on so he could make the call. He called his assistant for Jamal's next of kin, and then called his parents in Rhode Island. After tears and crying, they were on the next plane down to see their son. As he hung up, the nurse from Jamal's room came up to him to deliver a note.

"It's from Jamal. He asked for a pen and paper and said to give it to you."

"Thank you." Shield looked at the paper. All it said was C Burns.

Carmichael Burns, Jamal's old partner, had retired the year before.

Shield sighed. "Yes, I guess he would want to see him." Knowing Carmichael's number off by heart, he rang and spoke to him.

Burns promised to be there within the hour and kept his promise, going into Jamal's room in mask, gloves and gown. "What the fuck have you gotten yourself into?" he asked his ex-partner.

Jamal smiled, despite his weakness. "Got myself dead," he breathed.

Burns shook his head. "Jesus, Jamal. From what Shield and the doctors said, you don't have long. Why the fuck didn't you get help?"

"Didn't think I needed to. Thought it was a bug." His breath caught, and he sucked in the gas from the mask. It was helping, but not much.

"Well, it's clearly more than a bug," Carmichael said. "Have you done your will?"

Jamal grinned faintly. "Yeah. Not that I have much."

"And your parents?"

"Captain says they're comin' from home."

"Had your last rites?"

"The priest is comin' soon. He'll do it all." Jamal drifted off.

Carmichael wiped a tear away and then saluted. "Goodbye, Officer Jamal Devron. It was a pleasure serving with you," he said.

Jamal came back, just for a moment. "Same here, Officer Burns."

With a gentle squeeze of Jamal's arm, Carmichael left the room and dumped the mask, gloves and gown in the toxic waste bin. "How long's he got?" he asked Shield as they stood side by side at the ICU window.

"A week, days, hours." Shield shrugged. "No one's said."

"So, why'd he ask for me?" Burns was puzzled, but saddened by the whole experience.

"Probably because you're the only partner he ever got along with." Shield gave a half-hearted grin.

Carmichael grinned. "Fought with all the rest, has he?"

"And failed his sergeant's exam five times. Our Officer Devron has anger issues."

"Not that it's going matter now." Burns shook his head. "He always did. But we got along just fine."

"Said your goodbyes?"

"Yeah. Yeah, I have." Burns let out a long slow breath, thinking about his partner's death at such a young age, and what he'd been doing at that age himself.

*****

Jamal Joseph Devron was laid to rest in the Rose Michael Cemetery in Rhode Island. His captain attended, along with his ex-partner Carmichael Burns, and his current partner, Stew Babbath, who had been forced by the captain. A handful of officers that could get away from duty were there, along with Giancarlo Gardo, who had worked with Jamal on several cases over the years.

There was a twenty-one-gun salute, and after the flag was folded, it was handed to his mother and father in the front row.

His parents knew nothing of his lifestyle, always wondering why he didn't bring a nice girl home to meet them. They'd been always asking when he was going to get married, or have children, but that didn't matter anymore. All that mattered was that he was dead and never coming home.

Captain Shield lined up his officers, along with Burns and Gardo, and gave a final salute as Jamal's coffin was lowered into the ground.

July 1980

"Oh, it sounds wonderful. Your father and I went to Long Island last weekend for a look. It's so much like the coast of Australia. How long are you back for?" Jenny asked Tomas.

He and Roger had only come back from their month away on Long Island and up the east coast the day before and were leaving the day after tomorrow. Today, they were battling the crowds at *Bergdorf Goodman*, doing some last-minute pre-Independence Day shopping for the boys before they headed off again.

"Two days. And it's been wonderful," Tomas said, trying to keep up with his mother. "It's summer, and everything is in bloom and beautiful and…and…summery."

Jenny laughed; it was a light sound that tinkled along. "Well…it *is* summer. But are you enjoying yourselves?" She stopped to look at some homewares, admiring a beautiful multi-blue-toned bedspread and matching pillow set before they moved on.

"Oh, we are. It's so…" A smile lit up his face. "Freeing to be able to just do what we want when we want. It's great."

"So, where's the next stop?"

"Chicago, the home of gangsters and—"

"Do you really want to go back there after what happened?" Jenny asked as they travelled down in the lift.

He shrugged. "I never got to see any of it last time. Just the airport."

"Well, I hope you have better memories when you leave. I just have to pop into the beauty department. Is there anything you need?"

"I need to stock up on cologne, so I'll go grab some for Roger and me and meet you in the ladies' section."

"Okay. Don't be long."

They parted ways on the ground floor, and Jenny found herself strolling the aisles looking for Viv's new fragrance. As a major shareholder, she liked to make sure the products were on show. Stopping to look at another range of new beauty products, she glanced up to see a six-foot Mack Truck of a man holding a little boy high in his arms.

"Do you think Mama would like this?" he asked the child.

"Mama." The boy pointed to something. "Dada."

"Yes, I'm your Dada. What do we want to get Mama?"

Smiling at the man, Jenny paused, but couldn't help herself. She walked around the aisle. "You finally got to be a father."

Ex NYPD Detective, Giancarlo Gardo, turned around in surprise. "Ah, uh, Jenny, it's good to see you. We haven't seen each other since—"

"Two years ago." Jenny stepped up to them. "You finally got to be a father. Oh, Giancarlo, he's adorable. How old is he?"

"Ah..." He did the quick calculations in his head. "Seventeen months."

"Oh," Jenny breathed and high-fived the little boy. "He *is* adorable. I'm so glad you met someone and finally had a child. Is she here with you? Did you marry again?"

He lifted his left hand. "Ah, yeah, in '78. This little guy was born Feb '79. Can you believe it, on Valentine's Day?"

Jenny raised a brow. "Well, it's not like that hasn't happened before. I always wondered if it would happen for you again and I'm glad it did. I'm glad you found someone to share a life and family with."

He stared into her blue eyes. Eyes that had once captured him, held him, kept him on a string. But no more. He hadn't had feelings for Jenny with the blue eyes Stephanopoulos for two years. Not when he realised Sheila Manning was the one he'd been searching for. "So am

I," he said. "How's the family? Are you and Spiros…?"

"Still together?" She laughed. "Did you get that big basket of goodies I sent you as a thank-you and token of my appreciation for telling me about my husband? I was so grateful that you found that out and told me."

"Ah, yes," he said gruffly. "I did, and thank you. I ah, didn't think that was information I should keep to myself."

"No. I'm glad you told me because I raced home and phoned Spiros to get back here quick smart, and as I did, Viv went into labour. And then Angie had her baby the day after."

"Yes, I saw the birth notices, both girls. You must be incredibly happy."

"Yes, I am. Can you believe it; they celebrated their second birthdays last month. Rambunctious just like their fathers."

"And how are the boys?"

"Out of the porn business, thank God. Well, Carlos is writing for Harry DeVille still, but at least he's not in them. He's been taking film classes at NYU. Pedro's still DJing, Tomas and Roger have been travelling for the last two years. And last year we all went to Europe for summer, and then Australia for Christmas and New Year. Angie's finished her third year at Juilliard, and I'm a major shareholder in Viv's new company. She's producing perfumes and beauty products as well as beauty and exercise videos. The new fragrance is out next month, but the beauty products and current perfume are over there." She pointed to the display case of Viv's products.

"Yes." He cleared his throat. "I've seen those. My wife uses them."

"Oh, I hope she likes them." Jenny beamed.

"Yes. She says they make her look younger."

Jenny laughed. "That was the plan."

"Dada," the boy said and waved a hand around. "Dada go."

Gardo shifted him higher. "Yes, James, we'll go in a minute."

"Oh, don't let me keep you," Jenny said, tickling James's leg as he rested his head on his father's shoulder. "I know what little kids are like when you stand still for too long."

James giggled and shyly looked away.

"Mama." Tomas was looking in his shopping bag as he came rushing over to them. "I got what we needed and oh…" He stopped when he saw Gardo. "Detective, been a while."

James perked up at the sound of Tomas's voice.

"Mr Stephanopoulos number two." Gardo grinned. "Good to see you well. Your mother tells me you've been travelling."

"Yes, we have, and we're off again day after tomorrow."

James turned his head to see where the voice was coming from.

"This is James, Giancarlo's son. Have you ever seen eyes so aqua blue? I feel like I could drown in them," Jenny said as she took the boy's hand.

Tomas looked into the child's eyes and froze. They were the same. The same aqua blue. Aqua blue eyes such as he'd never seen. Bluer and more aqua than the ocean surrounding them. He breathed in and remembered where he was. In the department store and not Mykonos.

Jenny and Gardo were watching his reactions curiously. "Tomas?" Jenny noticed the faraway expression on her son's face.

"Yes…yes, I have…" He frowned and blinked. "Luiz."

"Tomas," James said and held out his hand toward him.

Gardo flinched, and Jenny frowned.

"Ah…Mama," he gasped, tearing his eyes away from the child. "I'll wait for you outside." He rushed off, gasping for air, to wait out on the street.

Jenny turned from her distraught son to Giancarlo. "It seems Luiz will forever affect him. And I vaguely remember him mentioning aqua eyes." She looked at the child who had an odd expression on his face. Curiosity mixed with wonder, mixed with sorrow.

"Luiz did a lot to him if I remember the reports," Giancarlo said and shifted positions. He remembered all right, and knew that Jenny didn't know he was with Sheila, Luiz's mother, making James Luiz's half-brother.

"Luiz was his first. His first everything, and I've always had a feeling that if Luiz wasn't engaged to Bertha St John and was free and single, that they would have been together as a couple. For how long, I don't know, but Tomas made the decision to let him go and move on. I'm glad he found Roger. He's such an amazing young man and looks after Tomas instead of ruining him as Luiz tried to do. It's affected him ever since. But then Tomas has always been a sensitive soul."

"He has you for a mother. I'm sure he has all the love and support he needs." Giancarlo shifted James to his other arm and hip. "Being poisoned and stalked and kidnapped can take a lot out of anyone. Can *emotionally destroy* anyone. But I know you would have seen to it that he was okay."

She smiled softly. "Yes. I saw to it, and while I believe Luiz was just his test, dipping his toes into the water kind of thing, Roger is definitely his soulmate."

"Just like Spiros is yours?" He gazed at his Jenny. But *not* his Jenny. Not anymore.

The smile brightened. "Yes. Yes, he is. And I hope that your wife is yours, Giancarlo. It's so good to see you again, and to see that you have the family you deserve."

"Ah…" He cleared his throat again. "Speaking of family, did you see that Officer Devron passed away late last month?"

"Yes, oh, that was so sad. I saw it in the paper. Did you go to the funeral?"

"Yes. Burns was there too. He retired the same time I did, but apparently, Devron wanted to see him before he died."

"It was so sad how he collapsed during a call out and died a few days later. Suffering from several diseases, poor thing. But then that seems to be going around with the young men these days."

"What do you mean?" He was intrigued as to what Jenny knew.

"Well…" She glanced around and stepped closer, close enough for him to smell her perfume which was the same one Sheila wore. *Vivian.*

"You knew he was gay, right?"

Gardo frowned. "Why would you ask that?"

Taking a deep breath, Jenny said, "Well, back in February, Leon Talley, who worked at 69 with Pedro, became quite ill with some of the same symptoms and died. And then in March, a photographer friend of Viv's died, and then in May, two of Roger's friends in Miami died. And he said all of his friends looked sick."

His eyes narrowed. "What's that got to do with Devron?"

She stepped closer. "When Leon died in February, he left Pedro in charge of his funeral and calling all of his lovers. And who did Pedro find in Leon's little black book, but Jamal Devron, an officer of the NYPD? He also found the father of an old co-worker of Carlos's back in Mykonos. All gay, Giancarlo. All men. All dying or getting sick from many different diseases. That is too much of a coincidence."

Gardo's frown deepened. He'd never known Jamal was gay, never even bothered suspecting. But he had a feeling Burns would have known, and it was probably why Devron had needed a new partner all the time. "Well." He licked his lips. "I don't know about any of that, so we'll leave it at that. It was good seeing you, Jenny. I'm glad you and your family are healthy and happy, and hope all goes well for you in the future."

At his change of attitude, Jenny knew it was time to take her leave. "Thank you, Giancarlo, the same to you. Goodbye." She departed and found Tomas calmly leaning against the wall on the sidewalk. "Are you okay?"

He smiled sheepishly. "I should have stopped freaking out over Luiz by now. But that kid…he…he had Luiz's eyes."

"What do you mean?" Jenny was worried about her son's mental health. He *should* have gotten over Luiz by now, but if a child could freak him out…then maybe it was time for a counsellor.

"I had never met anyone with eyes like Luiz's, and now what, three years later, Gardo has a kid with the exact same shade." He shrugged. "Is that a coincidence? And did you see the way that kid looked at me? Like *he knew me*. The way he said my name, he homed in on my voice. It was weird, Mama. Like, I don't know, like it was Luiz. Like he knew me and was trying to tell me it was him, and he was back, and he said my name and reached for me."

"Oh, Tomas." Jenny laughed. "I know I believe in reincarnation, but souls generally come back to their own family in some way. Why would he come to Gardo?" They set off for home, still talking as they went.

"I don't know, Mama. But it was weird. I'm telling you, the moment I looked in that kid's eyes it was like I was back on Mykonos in July '77, and he removed his glasses and looked at me. Hell, I even saw him all over again. Smelt the ocean around us, saw the boat, the sky, the…the everything." He sighed. "I was back there, looking into his eyes, and it was like yesterday."

Jenny stopped a block from their building. "He really affected you, didn't he?" She took her son's hand. "Still."

Tomas weakened. "He was my first. My first lover, a man. He made me feel things I'd never felt before. You don't forget that. You don't forget the feelings that wash over you and threaten to carry you away."

"If he wasn't engaged, would you have had a relationship with him?"

"Oh, God, yes," Tomas breathed. "Oh, God, don't tell Roger that. I just…"

"I won't." She smiled at the emotions flowing over her son's face.

"He made me feel things." He stepped closer to her. "I broke it off with him because he was with Bertha. If he wasn't, I would have been with him. I don't know for how long, but I would have been with him." He sighed, and his face fell. "But he wasn't free, and I had to do the right thing. And look how that turned out. Look what he did."

"And you wouldn't have Roger. You wouldn't have the life you have." Jenny gazed adoringly up at her son.

His lips curled up at the corner, and he squeezed her hand. "No. No, I have you to thank for that. And while I didn't love Luiz, I love Roger with everything that I am as a man. I love him. And I didn't feel that for Luiz."

"Then you made the right decision." Jenny kissed his cheek. "Roger is who you're meant to be with."

Tomas's smile brightened up his whole face. "Yes, oh, God, yes. I love him, I want him, I desire him. I am so happy that I met him."

"Good." They started walking. "So, let's get you back to your husband."

*****

Jamal Devron, gay? Gardo thought as he strolled through the department store and out onto the street to head for home. *And what of the others Jenny mentioned. Was it a fag thing going round? Hadn't Devron died of cancer and some pneumonia fungus thing? Burns would know, they'd been partners for five years, and Jamal had wanted to see him when he was in the hospital. Mmm, maybe I should call him.*

He thought about it while waiting for Sheila to come home from her part-time job. She still worked three days a week at the museum and volunteered somewhere twice a week. She was not going to believe this.

"Hello, I'm home," Sheila called as she walked into their house. Two years ago, Gardo had proposed and suggested moving into his home, but she'd put her foot down and demanded renovations which were done in time for their first Christmas as a married couple, two years ago, just before their son was born. "And how's my beautiful baby boy and darling husband?"

Sheila Manning had changed a lot in the last three years. After being a dowdy mousey woman for most of her life, she had changed, all thanks to the five million dollars Jenny Stephanopoulos had given her for her son's death.

She may not have loved Luiz, but he had been murdered, and she deserved compensation. Jenny had agreed and offered one million. Sheila aimed for ten, but Jenny finally settled with five, and Sheila was rich, changing almost instantly. New clothes, a makeover, some new furniture, and within a month a new apartment. She had been seeing Gardo off and on, and they finally worked themselves out, although she had nearly lost him after a stupid moment with Spiros Stephanopoulos. He had hated her, but kept her secret hidden, especially after finding out she was pregnant with his son. Now, she was fit, fabulous, and drowning in all things Vivian Villiers. She figured if she followed the Stephanopoulos family she'd stay ahead of the trends and keep up with the crowd, and she had. She was losing weight with Viv's videos and recipes, and looking fabulous with her cosmetics and perfumes. She was determined to keep up with the times and updated her look regularly. And her husband always took note of what she was doing. He'd even lost some weight recently after packing it on after retirement.

The scent of *Vivian* wafted around him as she kissed him. "We had a bit of fun with a shopping trip today, didn't we, James."

James pointed up at his mother from his place on the lounge room floor surrounded by all of his toys. "Mama."

"And guess who we ran into?" Gardo waited for his wife to sit down beside him on the couch.

"Who?" She removed her blazer and kicked off her shoes.

"Jenny Stephanopoulos." He waited and watched her face.

Her eyes went wide, and her head slowly turned toward him. "Jenny…"

"Yes." He studied her face. "Jenny."

Sheila blinked and swallowed the lump in her throat. "Well…long time no see…" Taking a breath, she looked away.

"Yes, and she looks fabulous." He received a sharp head turn and a scowl for that. "And her son Tomas was with her."

"That fag's still around, is he?" She frowned. How could Jenny love a fag son and accept his fag lover into her family?

"And he saw James and the colour of his eyes was mentioned," Gardo went on.

"They *are* beautiful." Sheila looked adoringly at her son's bright blue eyes.

"And Tomas went and mentioned he'd seen eyes like that on Luiz."

She flinched, just as *he'd* done when Tomas had mentioned her dead son's name. "I told you to never mention him."

"I didn't, Tomas did, and then he ran out of the store. Jenny and I spoke a moment about him and how he had affected her son so much."

"Yeah…well…" She couldn't think of anything to say. Her one and only child until James had been Luiz. When she was twenty-two, she had met his father, Andros Poulos, in Santorini while she was holidaying with friends. He had taken a liking to her, and she had taken a liking to sex with him, finding out she was pregnant three months later. He denied Luiz was his and all but ignored them, sending a lawyer's letter telling her to never contact him again. For seventeen years she lived in a small apartment with her son, working at a small supermarket to earn a living, but after learning that he'd been fucking the neighbourhood kids, the *underage* neighbourhood kids, she'd kicked him out and never saw him again. She'd only learned about his and his father's deaths via the papers, and found out the Stephanopoulos family was involved. Luiz had poisoned and kidnapped Tomas after killing four porn stars and blaming it on Tomas's lover, Roger. And Luiz's father Andros, also Angelina's father, had tried to kill Tomas's brother Pedro for dating his daughter.

And the bizarre part, Andros's one-time stepfather, Stefano Papadopoulos, had ordered all three boys kidnapped and taken back to Greece, and Giancarlo was one of the detectives on the New York case, helping to rescue Pedro from Papadopoulos's man.

And then the morgue asked her if she wanted her son's body for burial. She declined due to lack of funds, but just two months later, she had received five million from Jenny and hadn't looked back. Not wanting to remember Luiz, she had left his body where it was buried and moved on with her life. All she had of Luiz was a couple of albums full of photos and a small box of toys. And that box was safely hidden in the attic. She didn't know how long she'd hang on to it. She was about to celebrate her fiftieth birthday, and with a one-and-a-half-year-old to look after, she didn't want memories of Luiz around. But if anything happened to her or Giancarlo, their son would go through the house and find the box. What then? He'd realise it wasn't him and wonder why his mother had never told him about his brother who had died before he was born.

It was a bittersweet thing. He'd always believe he was an only child, and to a degree he was. Luiz was dead, so what was the point in telling their son when he grew up? She doubted she'd ever have another child. At fifty, it was almost unheard of. They were both too old, and if Luiz taught her anything, it was that second chances *do* come along. She got a second chance at life because he'd gotten himself killed, and she had grabbed it with both hands and run as fast as she could.

She ran for herself, making herself a better woman. A better person. Ran for Giancarlo, because she'd never realised she loved him until it was almost too late. Ran for her new baby boy, because he was the one who would make it all right, make it all better. Give her a second chance at being a mother, a real mother. The mother Luiz never had…when she should have been grateful for a child, she was ungrateful, angry, and resentful at Andros for denying her, and Luiz for ruining her life.

But this time, it was different. Her life was not ruined. It was better; it was beautiful and rich and full of everything she'd always wanted. A man to love her and spoil her, a child to love and be loved by. And she was living life to the best of her ability. Loving her husband, her son, her job and life.

The only thing she questioned above all else was her child. She was a big believer in reincarnation, and when she'd given birth to James and seen his aqua blue eyes, it had left her reeling, freaked her out because Luiz had the same colour eyes and she'd never met anyone else with that colour. And so, she worried.

Worried for her son. Worried for herself. Would he turn out just like Luiz? A fag who loved other boys? Or was that her doing? If it were, she'd vowed never to do it again because, with Giancarlo by her side, she knew this time was different. This child would be different. This time, he would not be Luiz.

*****

Tomas and Roger set out for Chicago the day after Independence Day. Driving across the countryside, they saw Pennsylvania and Ohio before finally getting to Chicago, Illinois where they spent a week seeing the sights, going on boat cruises, enjoying the summer together, and eating at the best restaurants the city had to offer. They gorged on deep dish pizzas and fabulous cheesecakes, and all that Chicago was famous for.

From there they travelled across to South Dakota and the Black Hills to see the presidents' monument, admiring the massive construct that was the Mount Rushmore National Memorial. At sixty feet high, it was mighty impressive, so they stayed for the day and enjoyed the fireworks show that evening.

They travelled across to Yellowstone National Park in Wyoming, and up through the rolling ranges of Montana and the Rocky Mountains. They crossed over Idaho into Washington and spent five days in Seattle.

August 1980

In August, Tomas and Roger made their way down to Portland for a week before moving on to San Francisco. Crossing the Golden Gate Bridge into the city, they marvelled at the structure and the beautiful bay views they had all around them.

Having pre-booked a nice hotel in the middle of the city, which was easy for travelling and walking distance from most of San Francisco, they arrived and settled in.

"Hey, T, what do you want to do first?" Roger asked, unloading his suitcase.

"Rest." Tomas gazed out the window. It was late afternoon, and he could see so much of the city on the ocean side.

"Seriously?" Roger packed his case away and started on Tomas's. They had a week to ten days, and he'd planned everything.

"We've been in the car all day," Tomas said, watching the people walk by on the bustling sidewalk. "I just want to take it easy for the rest of the day."

Roger looked at his watch. "It is nearly time for dinner. Anything in particular you want?"

Tomas was still gazing out the window. "Seafood."

"Okay, Fisherman's Wharf it is then."

Strolling through the city for several blocks, they took a cab the rest of the way to Fisherman's Wharf for a delicious meal of the city's finest seafood before taking a walk along the wharf and a cab back to their hotel.

"Oh, God, what a long day!" Tomas exclaimed as he came through the door. Dropping his bag on the chair, he walked over to the window and threw it open to listen to the late-night hustle and bustle. "It's nice here." He breathed in deeply.

"You've said that about all of the places we've been." Roger turned down the bed before going to stand behind his husband. Wrapping his arms around him, he rested his cheek on Tomas's head and listened to the city. "It is nice."

"It is." Tomas closed his eyes. For gay people, San Francisco and New York seemed to be it, but not for him. His home would always be Mykonos, even though he'd spent the first twelve years of his life in Australia. Mykonos was where his soul was. Nowhere else.

"How about we have a nice hot shower and go to bed?" Roger softly kissed Tomas's neck. "Being in San Fran has gotten me in the mood."

"Being *everywhere* gets you in the mood." Tomas chuckled and turned to face his husband. Wrapping his arms around his neck, he kissed him. "I love you."

Roger rested his forehead on Tomas's. "I love you, too. So, let me show you how much."

*****

The next day dawned bright and warm, and the boys set out to explore the city. They headed up to Telegraph Hill to look at Coit Tower, made their way by taxi across to Nob Hill to visit the cable car museum, then walked four blocks to Hyde Street where they took a cable car down to Beach Street to lunch at Buena Vista café, so they could watch the cable cars turn around. They shopped and bought and enjoyed themselves in the warm summer afternoon, before walking down to the Maritime Museum and Aquatic Park.

Over the next few days, they visited the Walt Disney Museum, Sea Rocks, Alcatraz, Union Square *and* Union Street for antiques and high fashion, The Cannery, Pier 39 and Lombard Street.

With two days to go, Roger had left the important trip until last.

"Where are we going today?" Tomas asked as Roger drove east from their hotel.

"You'll see," was all Roger said, and after fifteen minutes they turned from Market Street into Castro Street. "And we're here."

"Which is where?" Tomas looked out the window to see half naked men cavorting in the street and others just hanging around. "Where are we, Roger?"

"The Castro."

"The what?" Tomas looked at him. "What's the Castro?"

"Do you remember the story from two years ago? The assassination of Mayor George Moscone and Supervisor Harvey Milk by ex-supervisor Dan White. It was all over the news."

"Ah…" Tomas stared out the window. "Not really."

Roger found a park out the front of the store that was Harvey's old camera shop. "Harvey Milk was one of the first gay politicians in the country. Only took him five goes, but he did it. And he was murdered. He was unofficially and affectionately known as the Mayor of Castro Street, which is where we are. Come on, let's walk." Getting out of the car, he pulled a reluctant Tomas with him. "Come on, T. Let's see what the Castro's all about. It's the place to come if you're gay."

"Then why were you in Miami?" Tomas asked as they walked along. The place made him uneasy, but then such extroverted gay sexuality always had. He didn't like Carlos's blatant sex life, so he didn't feel the need to be so open about being gay. He saw a couple kissing in the street, wearing cowboy boots and short shorts that left nothing to the imagination. They were plastered against a wall completely unaware of their surroundings, tongues down each other's throats, hands all over.

Sighing, Tomas looked away and turned to concentrate on the stores and not the people, like the men who eyed him and Roger as they walked hand in hand. They popped in and out of shops collecting souvenirs, munched on pastries, and drank coffee as they crossed the road and started down the other side.

"You know, I expected it to be busier," Roger said. "Everything I've heard and read about the Castro made me think men were always out in droves, but…" He looked around. "This end is fairly quiet."

"People are probably at work." Tomas gazed up and down the street. "Is this all gay?"

"Apparently. Once the gays started moving in the families moved out, so it became the place to be if you were gay, and most store owners are. That's why the place is known for being a gay mecca." They passed another couple. One had purplish blotches on his face, and the other was coughing.

Veering away, Tomas quickly walked on and deposited his rubbish in a bin. Brushing off his hands, he asked, "Is that it? Because I'm not comfortable here." He looked around. "It just…gives me…the creeps."

"Why would it give you the creeps?" Roger asked as they continued on their way. "They're our people." He grinned.

"That's what Willow said to me back on Mykonos when they were trying to convince me to leave and travel the world. She said *that's where your people are.* Just because I'm gay doesn't mean I need to be around other gay men all the time. I like being with my family and you, so why would I need anyone else?"

"Well, you're lucky, T," Roger told him. "Your family accepted you and didn't kick you out of home like a lot of gay men's parents did. You're lucky that you're all still close. For those that get kicked out, this was the place to come for family. People that were the same and didn't shun you or tell you that you were dead to them."

"That's what your family told you?" Tomas asked, reassuringly squeezing his husband's hand.

"Pretty much. That's why I headed for America. Don't really remember why Miami, but the gay scene was just as good as it's supposed to be here." They stepped into a leather goods shop to look at the belts in the window.

"Anything I can help you boys with?" the man behind the counter asked.

"Hi," Roger replied. "I'd like to look at the belts in the window."

"We have more of those right over here." The man led them over to the belt rack. "Any in particular take your fancy?" He eyed the two boys up and down.

Tomas was put off. Put off by the purple spots on the man's lips, and the bony nature of his face. He was uneasy and just wanted to go. Glancing away, he busied himself looking at some other accessories.

"I quite like this one." Roger pulled a black and silver embossed one from the rack to try on. "I like the buckle too."

"You boys new in town? I'm Butch, by the way," he introduced himself.

"No, not new, just on holiday. We've been travelling across the country," Roger told him.

"First time in the Castro, then?" Butch went on.

"First time in San Fran," Roger replied. "And I gotta say, I thought it was going to be livelier than this. With everything I've seen and read and heard, this was the place to be. But walking around today, it seems empty."

"Well, everyone's at work," Butch said, offering Roger a small size. "And then we've got a few off sick."

"Sick?" Roger looked up. "Is it here, too?"

"Is what here, too?" Butch asked, looking at Roger with his pale blue eyes.

Roger studied the man. He was thin, with blotchy lips and looked sick, but must have once been a good-looking six-foot blond surfie type. "We've had friends die. Gay friends in New York and Miami. One minute they're fine, next minute they're sick with some weird pneumonia, or venereal disease then poof, they're dead. It sucks losing friends."

"New York and Miami, huh?" Butch rubbed his chin thoughtfully. "Where are you boys from?"

"We were in Miami in '77 then moved to New York," Roger said. "We've been there since."

"And how come you two aren't sick?"

"Same partner the whole time," Roger told him. "We've been with each other, and that's it."

"The bathhouses don't interest you then?"

"Nope," Roger said and saw Tomas throw a filthy look their way. "Don't interest us. We're together, don't need anyone else." He glanced at Butch again. "You don't look so good yourself."

"Nah." Butch shifted positions. "I'm not."

"So…it's hitting the Castro?" Roger asked, picking up another belt.

"Lost a few friends," Butch said. "A few more are sick."

"Like yourself?" Roger was all knowing.

"Yeah, like myself," Butch said.

"It must be hard," Roger went on. "Watching friends get sick and die. We've had quite a few already this year. It's definitely hard for us."

"Yeah, it is." Butch became suspicious of their motives for being there. "You gonna buy any of these?"

Roger looked down at the belts in his hand. "Mmm, I might take all three of them. You want anything, T?" He looked over at his husband as Butch took the belts.

"There are some nice wallets here," Tomas replied. "Don't you need a new one?"

"Yeah, mine's a bit ragged." Roger looked at the ones on display. "Ooh, that's a nice one." Picking up a black leather wallet, he examined it in detail. "Great workmanship."

"I do it all myself," Butch said from behind the counter.

"Really?" Roger glanced at him. "You're really good."

"Thank you. Don't know how much longer I'll be able to go on, though."

Roger chose a wallet and added it to the belts. "Oh, I'm sure you'll last a while." Noticing the fifty percent off sign in the store he added, "Let me help you out by paying full price for everything. And I'd like to see that small compendium you have on the shelf there." He pointed to the shelf behind Butch. "I've been after something to carry a notebook in." He examined the A5 sized, black leather, zip up compendium. Pockets for notes and business cards, a notebook already in it that could easily slide in and out when needing to be replaced. It had a clear pocket for booklets and other pockets that could be used for other things. "I like it. We need something to keep all our travel stuff in. T, do you want one?"

"No, thanks," Tomas cheerfully said. "You're the one who plans everything and carries it all around. You need it more than I do."

"Okay. We'll take this too, and I insist on paying full price to help out," Roger told Butch.

Butch nodded. "Thank you kindly, that will be a big help." Ringing up the bill, he took the money from Roger and packed everything into a bag. "Thank you for helping a man out."

"You're welcome." Roger smiled and took the bag. They continued on their way down Castro, stopping for a late lunch in a bar before finishing off the street. Making their way back down the other side, they stopped to look at the Castro Theatre with Roger taking photos. Not only of the theatre, but the street. They walked past groups of men, some looking angry, some crying, and Roger heard bits of their conversations.

"...is dead...pneumonia...saw him last week..."

"Richard was fine last week...I was told he's dead..."

"Bob had spots...it's cancer..."

Feeling the creeping chill weave its way down his spine, Roger pulled Tomas along, and they made their way back to their car.

"Did you hear that?" Tomas waited for Roger to open the door. "The same thing we've all been through the last few months. *All* the same things."

"Yeah," Roger murmured. Frowning, he paused at the door and glanced down the street to the group of men. "It's hit here too." Thinking a few moments, he continued, "The Castro is a mecca for gay men, a home for them. What will happen when this thing hits big time? It will wipe out the whole area."

Tomas slowly glanced around. Down to the left and the men they had just come past, across the road, along the other side, back across to their side and down to where they were. All he saw was the same he'd seen everywhere else. A street of shops and a few people here and there. But the people looked sick, sounded sick, acted sick, or talked about the sick, the dying, or the dead. It was depressing. Like being in Miami. Like being in New York. Being gay was going to be a death sentence with the way this was going, and he wasn't sure if he wanted to be a part of it.

It had already hit close to home with Leon and Cabot, even

Devron, and their old friends in Miami. But it was spreading. It wasn't just the east coast; it was the west as well. And while they hadn't really experienced anything everywhere else, just because it wasn't obvious didn't mean it wasn't there. It was here. In one of the biggest gay places in America. The discomfort continued. The same he'd had when they arrived. It wasn't to do with San Fran. More the public display of gay. It wasn't him. He wasn't into being so extroverted when it came to his sexuality. And, just like in Miami or New York, he preferred to quietly walk along with Roger, going about their business instead of so publicly displaying it. He didn't need to.

For him, sex was personal, intimate, private. And with Roger being only his second lover and his last, he wasn't interested in what the gay life stood for. Promiscuity. Fuck as many as possible, wherever possible, whenever possible, and not giving a fuck about using protection. No wonder STDs were rampant among gay men, as so many had them when they died. Leon was full of it, Cabot probably was too, as were most of their friends in Miami. Make that, Roger's friends. He only knew them from meeting them through Roger. Otherwise, he didn't hang out with people.

Being an introvert, he preferred the quiet life. Doing his job, being with family, celebrating life with his loved ones, and Roger had been a part of that for over three years. He was the only gay person he needed to hang out with. A quiet night at home in front of the TV, or in bed, a meal at a nice restaurant, a movie in a theatre, a jog around the park. He didn't need anyone else for all of that. And while Roger had friends all over and they had hung out in a few restaurants and bars at home, he didn't feel overly comfortable.

Greenwich Village was the place for gays in New York, and he thanked God they didn't live near there. He didn't want to be a part of 'the crowd', a part of 'the gay movement' that had happened in the last decade. He didn't need to fight for his sexual freedom because somehow, he'd just slipped into it. And once he'd met Roger, it all seemed easy. Perfect. Maybe a little too easy, a little too perfect. But it was right.

He knew he wanted Roger, knew he was the only guy for him. He didn't need the gay life. Didn't need or want to have sex with every other gay man he came across. Didn't want or need to hook up, or go to a bathhouse, or a gay bar to find someone, because he already found someone and that someone was amazingly incredible.

He came out of his reverie and gazed adoringly at Roger. "I love you. How was I so lucky to find you?"

Coming out of his head after serious thoughts, Roger grinned and leant against Tomas, making him lean against the car. "Because I'm perfect."

Tomas matched his husband's grin. "Yes, you are, Roger Wallace Dencott. Yes, you are."

Roger snatched a kiss and got it. "I love you, Tomas Giorgio Stephanopoulos. There's one thing I want to do before we head home."

"What's that?"

"You'll see." Roger ushered him into the car and slid in beside him. "Let's go." He manoeuvred a u-turn and drove back up to Market Street and turned right. They drove for a few minutes until Van Ness Avenue, where he turned left and continued for three blocks before turning right onto Grove Street. He drove for two blocks, turned left on Larkin Street, and managed to find a parking spot. They alighted and walked down the Civic Centre Plaza to stare at the huge domed building taking up several blocks.

"*What* are we doing here, and *where* are we doing it?" Tomas asked, staring at the building.

Roger led him to the exact place opposite the building. "This is City Hall where Mayor Miscone and Supervisor Harvey Milk were murdered."

"Ew, Roger, that's macabre." Tomas shuddered and rubbed his arms despite the warm afternoon.

"But it's history, T." He took photos. "San Fran's history. The Castro's history. *Gay* history. But bloody Dan White, the murdering bastard, only got four years. The White Night Riots followed that judgement, and I doubt the Castro's been quite the same since. Take a picture of me in front of it." Handing the camera to Tomas, he ran forward to stand in front. "Am I in?"

Tomas looked through the viewfinder then took a few steps back. "Okay, hold it…and done."

"Take a couple," Roger called out, and Tomas obliged. Taking the camera back, Roger turned to stare at the hall. "Man, the history. The *whole* history. The history of the Castro in the last few decades. The history of *gays* the last few years. The history of politics just in two years. Jesus…" He gazed over the huge expanse of city hall allowing himself to soak it all in. What it meant then, what it meant now. What it could *and* would mean in the future. "It all means so much, T."

Tomas watched the expressions and thoughts wash over Roger's face. He could see how their trip to the Castro was affecting him. How being at city hall was affecting him. He vaguely remembered Roger going on about it a couple of years before. But they had been travelling in November '78 when the murders had happened, and Roger had only found out when they'd gotten home at Christmas. He remembered Roger being really emotional and cutting all of the newspaper clippings from the papers his mother had kept for them. But, unlike Roger, he wasn't that into the gay world and all it meant. He went on with his life and hadn't been discriminated against, and for that, he was glad. But Roger *had* with his family, and he supposed that had caused a lot of issues for him. So much so, that he was into any news about gay people achieving anything of importance.

Which, in retrospect, was important in the grand scheme of things. He just wasn't interested. He wanted to live his life on his own terms and not the terms other people set. Not politicians, not other gay men. He would *and did* live his life by the standards his parents had raised him with, and he was happy with the standards he had set for himself, and would continue to live that way regardless of what anyone or anything dictated. And he *would not* be dictated to by other gay men. Even Roger. Glancing at his watch, he looked at his lover. "Ready to go?"

With a deep sigh, Roger finally spoke. "Yeah." Deep breath. "Yeah, I'm ready to go." On their way back to the car, he glanced over his shoulder a few times, even when they climbed into the car. But once they drove off, he stopped looking, leaving the poignant memories behind.

*****

"Yay, Disneyand," Alena cried out as they walked up to the entrance of the happiest place on earth. "Disneyand, Da-anna, Disneyand."

Diana bounced happily in her father's arms as they strode through the gates and into the park. "A-ena, Disneyand."

"Ah," Alena screamed in her daddy's ear.

"Okay, all right." Pedro laughed and held her away. "Yes, it's Disneyland." Everyone was prepared for the day. Between Tomas and Roger, Spiros and Jenny, Viv with Diana's pram, Angie with Alena's, there were bags of baby gear and plenty of bags for all the shopping they'd be doing.

"Cathle," Alena screamed. "Cathle, Dada, cathle." She pointed excitedly to the Sleeping Beauty Castle as they wandered in and they checked their maps, consulting where to go first. They decided to go left, and make their way around the park.

"Cathle, me wanna cathle. Pincess A-ena," Alena screeched, waving her arms, reaching out for Sleeping Beauty's Castle.

"All right, Alena, we'll get back to it later," Pedro said, getting a screaming child in return who would not stop for a full five minutes.

They made their way through Adventure Land, New Orleans Square, Bear County, Frontier Land, took a ride on a boat, walked through a haunted manor, went on water rides, and found themselves in Fantasy Land to see Snow White's Castle which made Alena screech with joy.

"Cathle," she told everyone and toddled forward. Pedro had put her down for a few minutes for her to walk, and now she raced off with Diana hot on her heels and their daddies hot on theirs.

"Oh, my God, they're such a handful." Viv sighed, brushing away a strand of stray hair. She'd swept it all up into a bun to keep cool in the eighty-plus temperature of mid-August. "They're not like this in New York."

"I know," Angie said, wheeling her daughter's pram. "It's like they're on drugs. They just keep going and going." After watching the girls get their photos taken with Sleeping Beauty and the prince, they all went inside to have a look and came out with mini crowns for the girls.

"Pincess A-ena," Alena sang, bouncing up and down on her daddy's hip. "Pincess A-ena, Pincess A-ena."

Jenny laughed. "Clearly gets her musical talents from the two of you," she told Angie and Pedro.

"And clearly gets her princess groove happening because of Grandma," Pedro cheekily replied, putting Alena down once more.

"Pincess A-ena." She ran over to Tomas and hugged his legs, gazing adoringly up at her favourite uncle. "Pincess A-ena an' Unca Tomas."

Tomas laughed and scooped her into his arms. "Yes, Alena is a princess. A pretty little princess." He hugged her tight and kissed both chubby cheeks.

"Pincess A-ena." She threw her arms in the air. "An' Unca Tomas."

"What about Unca Roger?" Tomas asked her.

"Unca Oger, no, Unca Tomas is pince." She managed to get her mouth around the words.

"Pince? What's pince?" Tomas tickled her stomach.

"A-ena is Pincess, Unca Tomas is Pince," Alena explained in two-year-old speak.

Pedro came over and stroked his daughter's hair. "Uncle Tomas *is* a prince," he agreed, watching his brother's expression.

"Mmm, mmm," Alena agreed. "Dat's what I said, Dada. Unca Tomas is pince."

"Yes." Pedro kissed Alena's cheek. "Unca Tomas is a pince." He gazed at his brother. "A pretty damn special pince at that."

Tomas frowned slightly. "You getting all sappy on me, little bro?"

Pedro grabbed Tomas's face with his left hand. "Just a little, big bro. You're my brother, I love you, and you are a damn special pince, bro." He kissed his brother's cheek and wrapped his arms around them both.

"So are you, little brother. So are you," Tomas replied, patting him on the back.

"I know, that's why you can carry Alena for a while." Pedro grinned and backed away.

"Gee, thanks." Tomas grinned wryly and looked at Alena. "I knew there was an ulterior motive. Let's take Princess Alena on some more rides, huh."

They continued to Tomorrowland where they all went on the rides with Jenny and Spiros taking the girls to give their sons a rest. As the afternoon slipped by, they made their way back for the girls to have another teacup ride, and a flight on Dumbo before entering Sleeping Beauty's Castle. They took more photos with Micky and Minnie, all the princesses, and any other character they came across before heading for the front gate at closing time.

"No." Alena reached out over her daddy's shoulder. "Cathle, no, don't go, cathle, my cathle. Pincess A-ena's cathle, Dada."

"I know, my baby, but it's time to go home. The park is closing." He held her tight as she started crying, wailing for her castle. "I know, I know, you want your castle."

"She's tired," Jenny said, watching Diana flake out in her pram with no cries or squabbles. "So different. Diana's out like a light and Alena's still going."

Pedro hung on to Alena's leg as she heaved up and over his shoulder, reaching for her castle as it faded into the distance. "Whoa, Alena, hold on there."

"She'll be out soon." Jenny walked by his side. "It's okay, Alena, we'll come back soon. You want to come back soon?" she asked her granddaughter. "We'll probably come back a few times before heading home to New York."

"Cathle?" Alena asked hopefully as everyone piled into the limo Jenny had hired for them, so they didn't have to worry about cars or taxis.

"Yes, Alena," Jenny told her as she took her from Pedro. "Gamma will bring you back to see your castle, and then Princess Alena will have it all to herself. You've got two to pick from."

"Pincess A-ena has cathle," she tearfully told her Gamma.

"Yes, she does," Jenny agreed, wiping away her grandbaby's tears.

"Princess Alena has her very own castle back home. And we will come here in a couple of days, okay." Jenny held her tight as she climbed into the limo to sit beside Pedro. Spiros got in behind her.

"Okay." Alena tearfully nodded, crawling onto her daddy's legs and curling up in his arms. "We come back to Pincess A-ena's cathle."

"Yes, we will." Jenny tickled her granddaughter. "Yes, we will."

With Diana sleeping in her daddy's arms, and Viv and Angie beside him with Tomas and Roger opposite, they drove back to Viv's house and unloaded. The girls were put to bed, with Alena having fallen asleep on the way home, and the adults showered and met up in the kitchen for drinks.

"Whew, what a hot day it was." Viv poured glasses of iced tea and made a refill before putting the jug in the fridge.

Jenny distributed the glasses, and they all sat in the cool comfort of the lounge room, decorated with fine art and expensive things. The house sat in the Hollywood Hills and had a view of the pool with city views beyond.

"It was certainly a full one," Jenny agreed. "I can't believe Alena. What did you feed her for breakfast? She just kept going and going and going."

Angie laughed. "Must have been the sugar she ate all day. I don't think any of us stopped." She tucked a damp strand of hair behind her ear. "I'm full from everything I've eaten, so I don't need dinner."

Jenny glanced at the clock. "It's nearly seven. The girls will probably sleep through the night and I know I'm tired, so we may as well get an early night ourselves. We've had a busy few days so far."

They had been in L.A. for four days, and Viv and Carlos had shown them the sights, taken them to clubs to see what was happening on the west coast, and showed off his brothers and family to people he knew. They'd lunched at *Le Dome*, co-founded by singer Elton John, and popular with celebrities such as author, Jackie Collins, and *Chasen's*, a popular celebrity restaurant, plus had plans for shopping at the biggest stores Hollywood had. But that would be for the next few days.

"I'd love to head down to the beach." Pedro cocked an arm behind his head. "Haven't been swimming in the ocean for ages, when was the last time?"

"Australia in January," Tomas reminded him. "European beaches before that, and then probably Mykonos in '77."

"Oh, that feels like so long ago," Jenny said. "But it's only been three years."

"And European beaches aren't like Mykonos or Australia. They're not right." Pedro shrugged. "No sand in some places, just pebbles. Yuck."

"And no waves," Carlos added. "Flat as a pancake they were."

"I can't wait to hit the beach." Pedro finished off his iced tea.

"We can make a day of it tomorrow," Jenny suggested. "We need a day off after running around all day. Can we rent a tent or something?"

"A tent! What do you want a tent for?" Carlos asked from his spot on the couch beside Viv. "It's the beach."

"And we have two grandbabies to keep out of the sun and heat, and I have *six adult babies* to keep out of the sun and the heat. I don't want us all to sit there frying."

Everyone smiled at the words, *six adult babies.*

"Guess you're right, Mama," Carlos agreed. "We don't want the babies getting sunburnt."

*****

The next day, they headed for Santa Monica beach, and while the boys set up the tent they rented from the beach supply shack, the others carried the coolers and baskets of food and drinks, plus the girls and their bags, down to the sand and laid out picnic blankets and towels in the shade.

"We all set up, Mama?" Carlos asked, giving everything the once over and ruffling his daughter's hair. "We wanna go for a swim."

Jenny made sure everything was in place, including the girls and their sun hats. "Looks like. Go enjoy yourselves."

The boys stripped off their t-shirts and strode four abreast in their tiny swim shorts down to the water, capturing the gaze of tourists and fans alike. It was like watching a slow-motion movie scene with raunchy porn music in the background. Tomas ran a hand through his hair and held on to Roger's hand with the other. Carlos and Pedro traded glances as well as grins when they saw the stares from the girls on the beach. But once they were in the water, it was on. They reverted to being teenagers in Mykonos, trying to outswim and outplay each other.

Onshore, Jenny shook her head. "Boys *will* be boys." She watched them play, helping Alena and Diana dig in the sand to make sandcastles. Viv and Angie were keeping their delicate skin undercover, even though Angie wore a sleek black suit with cut-outs that showed off her jet-black hair and white skin perfectly. Viv wore a gorgeous iridescent blue one piece with a sarong over it.

"God, it's already warm." Angie put her hair up in a bun and wrapped a black scarf around it.

"They did say the high 80s again today," Jenny said, dumping another bucket of sand before looking out at her sons. "Still having fun, are they?"

"Considering how warm it is, I might join them," Spiros murmured.

"Why don't you," Jenny urged. "It's not often we get down to the beach. Go and join your sons and show them what a real Greek man is made of."

He laughed, removed his shirt and sunglasses, and strode down the sand to the water.

"Jesus," Viv said. "I hope Carlos is in that good a shape when he's in his fifties." She watched her father-in-law. "Damn."

Jenny snorted. "Carlos will be so lucky." Glancing around, she saw other women and a few men on the beach eyeing her husband and felt a surge of pride and happiness that he was hers. Still lean and mean and extremely virile.

"Bloody hell! Is that Papa?" Carlos stopped and trod water. They watched their father walk down to the shore, through the water, and slice his way through to them. "Bloody hell."

Roger laughed. "Oh, come on. How do you *not* know by now he's where you get your looks from, your stamina from, *and* your cocks from?"

"Ew, no, Roger," Tomas said as the others screwed up their faces.

"I've said it enough times, and it's true." Roger laughed as Spiros popped out of the water. "Looking good there, Mr S."

"Why, thank you." Spiros pushed his hair back. "I haven't been in the water for ages. It feels good."

"Seriously, Papa," Carlos said, his face falling. "How are you *still* in good shape?"

Spiros laughed. "From hauling sides of meat around all these years. It takes a lot of muscle to throw an animal on your shoulder…and then there's your mother…" A wicked grin slid across his face.

"I throw Viv on my shoulder. Does that count?" Carlos joked, and everyone laughed.

"Not the same, but if it keeps you in shape," Spiros said.

"You had a lot of stares from other beachgoers," Roger told him.

"Did I?" Spiros replied. "I didn't notice. As long as Jenny was watching, that's all that matters."

"Aw, how sweet's that," Roger said and looked at his husband. "I hope you feel the same about me when we're in our fifties, T."

Tomas smiled. "Of course I will. As long as you feel the same about me." He moved over to Roger and kissed him.

"Yeah, yeah," Carlos said. "All they gays were checkin' you two out."

"Oh, didn't you notice, Carlos," Spiros said. "They were checking *you* out too."

"What!" Carlos growled then saw his father's grin. "Aw, Papa." He splashed and dunked his father like when they were little.

After lunch, the boys stretched out on their towels to get some sun.

"Don't stay in the sun too long. I don't want you getting burnt," Jenny warned.

"Yes, Mama," they murmured.

"Tell us when ten minutes are up, and we'll roll over," Carlos said. "Gotta get a tan."

"Oh, I wish you wouldn't," Jenny fretted. One of her uncles had died from a melanoma from being out in the sun all day, every day, sunbaking. But she kept an eye on the time, and they rolled over and stretched out.

Alena and Diana did the same, giggling together as the faced their daddies, crawling forward on the blanket until they touched fingers with their fathers, and wiggled their chubby little ones on their daddies' big long ones.

Carlos and Pedro looked up, giggled at their daughters, and wiggled their fingers.

But within minutes, the girls were pulled back into the shade as they fell asleep, curled up next to their Gamma and Gampa.

Jenny leant down and kissed both on the cheek, smoothing their hair as they lay sleeping.

After their twenty minutes of sunbathing, Tomas and Roger went for a walk, talking about their plans for the rest of summer and fall.

"Are we still heading for San Diego, or going to Vegas?" Tomas asked, biting into the ice cream they had just bought from the beach shack.

"I'd still like to go to San Diego. We can stay a few days or a week." Roger's tongue slid around the ice cream in his cone.

"Roger…is that you?"

Roger turned to see David Marks come up to him. He was with Adam Zevon and Zack Bryant. All three used to hang out in Miami, and Roger knew them well. "Hey guys, my God, long time no see. When was the last time we caught up?" he asked David. "'78 sometime?"

"Yeah." David nodded. "It's been a while. Hey, Tomas."

"Hey." Tomas shook hands all round, remembering meeting them, but they were Roger's friends from before he had come along, and they hadn't seen much of each other since.

"So, what's going on?" Roger asked. "How come you guys are here and not Miami?"

"Don't you know?" David asked.

"Know what?" Roger replied, quickly finishing his melting ice cream.

"About Judd and Ethan."

"You mean that they're dead?" Roger asked, his insides curling up. "Yeah, Freddy got in touch with my in-laws, who let me know, and I rang him for the details."

"Yeah, sad shit that is," David remarked. At twenty-eight and six five, he towered over all of them. "You didn't go to the funeral, but we did. Jesus, the way everyone looks…" He shook his head at the memories.

"No, we didn't. We were travelling at the time, so couldn't attend, but we saw them at Johnno and Evan's service. They looked like crap, as did everyone else," Roger told him.

"Yeah. We couldn't make that, but I heard you were there." David brushed back his dark hair. "Jesus, what the hell's going on?"

Roger shook his head. "I don't know. But there are gay guys dying in New York. Leon, a co-worker of Tomas's brother, and a well-known photographer friend of my sister-in-law, Viv."

"Yeah, Cabot Conroy, heard about him," Zack said. At six feet and twenty-five, he was still healthy and thanked God for it every day.

"Yeah, but David…" Roger turned to his friend. "So did Jamal Devron." He waited to see what kind of reaction he received.

"Yeah…" David shook his head. "He called me after finding out about an ex-lover dying. He was calling all of his exes. As far as I know, I'm okay. One STD, but that's it."

"You still look okay," Roger said. "All three of you still look healthy, but how'd you manage that?"

David laughed. "I was never one to have too many partners, and when I did, I always played it safe. So far, so good. But I've been tested since Jamal just to make sure."

"And I swore off sex until the surf comps were over," Adam said. "I've had one partner since until recently and have been tested. Only one STD that I've been treated for."

"Then what the hell is happening?" Roger asked. "Between Miami and New York. We've just come from San Francisco last week, and you would not believe how many men are sick there. We went to the Castro to see what it was like and bloody hell, they were either crying about being told to not have sex, or they were gaunt or dead. Some had already died, and the people we spoke to were either very angry, or very sad. It was actually quite an awful place to be, very depressing, so we came here instead."

"Yeah, but have you heard about it here?" David asked, his hands casually resting on his hips. "We've already heard the stories about gays coming down with diseases, and I got out of Miami because of Jamal and what I saw going on. And now we're hearing about it in the gay scene here. There's talk that it's spreading."

"Jesus," Roger murmured. "I'm glad we're married." He took Tomas's hand in his. "At least we know we'll be safer with each other."

"Yeah, but what about all the guys you worked with?" Adam said to Roger. "You were in porn. How many men did you fuck before starting a relationship with Tomas?"

"A lot," Roger replied. "But I always played it safe and told Marcus if it wasn't on, it wasn't on. He agreed, and made us all wear condoms when performing anal, oral was different."

"Yeah, but what about who *they* were fucking on the side, outside of work, and then you all sucked each other off," Zack said.

Roger sighed. "Yeah, that's true, but Marcus also had doctors on call that checked us over every week. If we so much as had a *hint* of a disease, we were out until it was gone. He made our contracts that tight. If we didn't play by the rules and stay safe outside of work, we weren't wanted. He made that *very* clear."

"At least you've got that," David said. "I was safe with Jamal, but it was still a shock that he had diseases and then died from them. I had to read *that* in the paper."

"Yeah, so did we," Tomas said. "We met him when he and his partner were finishing up paperwork with my brother and sister-in-law. He asked us how two fags had gotten married. Roger explained and then mentioned your name. He backed right off, and we didn't see or hear from him again."

"Yeah, he was clearly in the closet," Roger said. "Not ready to admit it, but just the sound of your name made his eye twitch."

"Well, his name, at the end of the day, made *my* eye twitch," David said. "I hadn't seen or heard from him since we'd been together, and I think that was early '77. Then all of a sudden, he's ringing me up and telling me a former lover was dead, and he was ringing all of his lovers to warn them."

"You're still here, so you must be okay," Roger said. "You all look good."

"And we hope to stay that way," Zack said, his arms folded across his chest. "I certainly have no plans to get sick and am sticking to celibacy from now on until it all blows over. No one's come out and actually said anything about it. It's just all gossip and funerals."

"Yeah, but how many funerals do we have to go to before we find out what the hell our friends and acquaintances are dying from?" Roger asked. "How many do we have to bury before someone tells us what the hell this is and how to not get it? How many of us have to die?"

The five of them were silent for a few moments, thinking about the friends they'd lost and those who were sick.

Finally, David sighed. "You're right. But we're not going to know unless someone at some disease centre has the balls to tell us. To find out what it is and then come out and tell us. Until then, we'll just have to keep ourselves safe and cut back on our adventures. You two are lucky that you have each other. And it's cool that you got married on your own terms. But have either of you been tested?"

Roger frowned. "As I said, I was tested all the time at *Seralift*—"

"Yeah, but what about since?" David butted in. "What about former lovers? You gotta be safe, dude. You gotta be as safe as the rest of us."

Roger traded a glance with Tomas. Since being together there had been no one else, and after the testing at *Seralift*, which said they were fine, they'd never gotten another one since leaving. What was the point? "We were clean then, why wouldn't we be now? But I guess it wouldn't hurt to see a doctor. We haven't seen one since last year for our shots to travel overseas."

"We all have to play it safe from now on," David said. "You're right; we shouldn't have to keep watching our friends get weak and thin and no longer be themselves before they drop dead. We shouldn't have to do that."

"No," Roger agreed. "We shouldn't." *We'll get tested once we get back to New York,* he thought. *Put it to rest. We're fine; we don't have to worry.*

October 1980

"Hello, everyone," Carlos said from the stage at *The Pussycat Theatre* in L.A. "I am Carlo Stefan, and this is the annual Porn Star Awards."

The crowd erupted into screams and cheers. After the huge success of the last three years, Carlos had been asked back again. He'd won awards in 1977, hosted with Pedro in 1978 and won most of the awards, and hosted by himself in 1979 and won more awards. This time, he was back once more as host and nominee.

"We have a lot to get through tonight. New entertainment, new awards, old awards, new cocks and old cocks, but thankfully mine is still young."

His tuxedo and open shirt had made the first few rows scream, and they started chanting, "get it out, get it out, get it out."

He laughed and waved his hands to quiet them down. "As you all know, I haven't *been* in movies for two years, and I'm not about to be again. Writing is my forte, and that's what I'm nominated for. My brothers and I probably had the shortest careers in porn that you can get." More screams. "Especially my brother Tomas, who was in it for less time than I was. But he is happy with his partner Roger Dencott," even louder screams, "and my brother Pedro is happy DJing at *Studio 69* in New York. But now, let's get on with the first award, and that is…drumroll please…best male newcomer. Something that I won back in '77, and my brother Pedro won in '78." The crowd cheered, and the screen behind Carlos showed each actor as they popped up.

"The winner is…Jewel Hardcore, congratulations." He handed over the silver penis shaped award to a young, tall blond thing that came on stage in a velvet tux.

"And the next award is…best director." He and Harry won for one of his written movies, followed by the best producer award, which went to both of them.

"Now…we are on to the best cock award which I was nominated for and won in 1977, and which my brothers and I were nominated for in 1978 and Tomas took out." The crowd laughed. "I meant the award, not his cock because he wasn't here. So, the brand-new nominees are…Burrow J. Corner, Macklin St John, Day Hollywater, Bet Michels, and Sinner Lovehead, oh, God, only in Hollywood porn can you get a name like that," Carlos joked, ripping open the envelope. "And the 1980 porn star award for best cock goes to the guy with the Hollywood porn name, Sinner Lovehead." Screaming went through the theatre as Sinner walked up to accept his award. At six feet with long dirty blond hair, he'd been in the business for one year and loved the Stefan brothers.

"I can't believe that the man, Carlo Stefan, not only read out my name and is presenting this year, again, but just handed me a cock." He waved it in the air to hysterical screaming. "Thank you to the Stefan brothers who I learned all of my tricks from, and thank you to those who voted for me."

After a round of applause, Carlos announced best actor and best movie, which Carlos and Harry won for their movie *One Cock Until Midnight.* Next was best gay movie, best gay love scene, best gay sex scene, best straight sex scene, and after a musical interlude and the final four awards, Carlos closed the show.

"Tonight is my last night," he told the crowd to boos and hisses. "I know, I know." He placated the crowd. "It's been fun for four years, I've won every year, hosted for three years, and now my career in porn is over. It's been a ride; it's been fun, I've directed, produced, and written. And the movie *The Greek Gods is still* the biggest seller of all time." The boos and hisses turned to hysterical screams. "I've given you the *Cabana* and *Meat Shop* movies, my brothers have given you their movies, and now my contract is done. I bid you adieu. I've had fun, I've had adventures, and now it's time to hand it all on to the next round of porn stars. Thank you for all you've done for my brothers and me, thank you for buying our movies and going out to see them. Thank you for making them all number one at the box office. This has been the 1980 Porn Star Awards at *The Pussycat Theatre* in Los Angeles. I'm Carlo Stefan, goodnight and goodbye." He threw his arms up in a wave and backed off the stage, blowing kisses and waves until he was backstage taking pictures with Harry DeVille.

"Carlos, my boy." Harry slapped him on the back then slid an arm around his shoulders, directing him to the press room.

"Harry. This is our last night together." Carlos posed with his awards.

"Is it really?" Harry gritted his teeth and smiled for the cameras. "Will I never see you or your brothers again?"

"Probably not, Harry." Carlos waved as they walked off the small platform. "My contract is done. I've fulfilled my obligations. My life is in New York until further notice." They walked outside and met Harriet and Tony. "Hey, Tony, long time no see," Carlos said to the man that was once his bodyguard.

"Stephanopoulos." Tony nodded, on the lookout for would-be harassers.

"So, no chance of you coming back to direct or produce?" Harry climbed into his limo behind Carlos and Harriet.

Carlos shook his head as Tony shut the door and slid into the front passenger side. "Not anymore. My interests lie elsewhere now. Viv's got her own cosmetics company that Mama's invested in. I'm going to be producing and directing her ads from now on, plus all of her other videos. *DeVille* was a good training ground for me, Harry, and I'm eternally grateful that you took a chance on a poor boy from Mykonos when he was in need of help. And you more than came through. I'll never forget what you've done for me."

Harry teared up and slapped Carlos's knee.

They arrived at the same club they had back in '77, and nothing had changed. They went in through the back door and made their way to the roped off area. Alcohol, drugs and sex was flowing. Roller-skating women delivered the drinks, roller-skating men delivered the drugs. He remembered hooking up with Viv that night. He'd backed away from Ackroyd Ackerman and his cock that he'd pulled from his pants, and turned to find himself in Viv's arms. He was so busy remembering that night he didn't realise she was actually standing in front of him. "Viv?"

She laughed. "There was *no way* I was going to let you come home on your own. This is the night three years ago I took you home and realised I didn't want anyone else *but* you."

He picked her up and spun her around to the beats of the music as he had back then. "What about Diana?"

"Your mother, of course. She loves looking after her grandbaby, and her grandbaby loves being looked after by her," she said as he put her back on her feet. She slipped her arms around his neck and tossed back her hair.

He held her close and thrust against her as they swayed to the pounding music. "I'm so glad you're here. It somehow makes it complete. Like we've come full circle from the first to the last."

"And now we can live a life away from porn." She hooked a leg up to his waist and thrust back.

His hands grabbed her and held on tight. "How 'bout coming to my place? We can spend the night together."

She laughed. "Your place happens to be rented out, darling. Whereas mine is free for the week and we haven't had a week alone since Diana was born."

"Ah, how about your place then? I miss being able to just hook up whenever wherever." He twirled her around and slid a hand between her legs to find she didn't have panties on.

"How about here, darling?" she asked in his ear and slid her hand down to unzip his erection.

Under the tribal beating and dizzying lights, they made their way together in a rhythmic beat, all without missing a step, until the music slowed down, and they remained joined through a slow dance, with Carlos massaging her still firm ass, and Vivian clenching her well-trained womanhood. Their tongues entwined and stayed that way for five more songs before they reluctantly parted and walked up to their private party for a drink.

"Viv, my dear, how are you?" Harry stood up to give her a kiss. "We haven't seen you in years."

"Good thanks, Harry. Been busy with the baby and the company."

"I see you've done some sampling of my best cock ever," Harry cheekily replied.

Viv laughed. "I am married to it, Harry."

"Yes, I know." He nodded. "And you are both well-suited."

Carlos came up with two champagnes and heard them. "We're gonna have our drink and go."

"Already?" Harriet asked, twirling her pearls and sipping her champagne.

"I don't need a bodyguard to keep me safe this time," Carlos joked. "We're going to spend a quiet week alone before heading home to the bustling city of New York." He downed his drink and turned to Viv. "Ready?"

"Ready." Viv waved goodbye to everyone and led him by the hand out into the quiet air of downtown L.A. They caught their limo back to Viv's where she led him to the enclosed backyard and pool which was already lit with the spa on.

"Ah, just like that night three years ago." Carlos watched her slip out of her dress to reveal a slinky body still in good shape.

She helped him out of his suit and shirt. "I thought we'd take a trip down memory lane." Her fingers travelled down his chest to his cock.

He picked her up and dipped into her before dipping into the spa. Holding her up over the side, his long even strokes thrust her back and forth.

"Oh, God, oh, God, Carlos, it's so good just having sex again," she gasped as the hot bubbly water slapped against her ass.

He gave one last stroke and lifted her to him, delving into her mouth and tasting the champagne. It was so good to be with her again, without worrying whether Diana was going to cry out, or escape her cot and come running in. He tasted her neck, her breasts, her nipples.

"Ugh," she groaned and tightened her inner sanctum, clenching him, keeping him there, and hardening him.

He sucked harder. She clenched harder. They came together.

Lying on the poolside lounge afterwards, with a towel over them and more champagne inside of them, they stared at the stars.

He stroked her dewy cheeks. "God, I love you so much, Viv."

She gazed up at her husband. "I love you too, Carlos."

"You've always been my dream girl, and I can't believe that for the past three years you've been my wife," pause, "and you still have a crazy incredible body."

She laughed softly. "After all the women you've fucked, so do you."

He kissed her, and she responded, wrapping her legs around him as he rolled on top and entered, sliding in like he owned the place.

And he did. He did own her, every time. This was his place and his alone. Heart, body, and soul.

*****

In the penthouse, Diana was still awake and playing with Alena. Jenny, Spiros, Pedro and Angie were in the sitting room talking and watching the girls with their blocks and teddies that Jenny had bought them before they were born.

"Aren't you girls tired yet?" Pedro asked, yawning as he half lay on the couch next to Angie. "I think it's time for bed."

"No bed, Dada. Pay." Alena still had a problem pronouncing her l's.

"You can't play for much longer, it's getting late." Pedro checked his watch. "God, *it is* late. The awards would be over about now."

"Sad you're not there, babe?" Angie asked, glad it was a Saturday night and not a school night.

"Nah, not really. I miss the adulation, not making the movies. Looking back, I shouldn't've done them, but I did, and now they're in my past." He watched his daughter play with her cousin. "I have more important things to worry about now."

"Exactly," Jenny said, crocheting a blanket. "The girls are what's important and so are your partners. Not those horrible movies."

Spiros was sitting beside her, under the blanket she was making, trying to read a book. He closed it and laid it on the side table. "I've been trying to read the same page for the last ten minutes. Time for me to stop, I think."

"And I think it's time for me to stop for the night." Jenny finished off the row. "Is Diana ready for bed?"

Diana looked up from her spot on the floor, her big blue tired eyes staring at her Gamma. "No. No bed, Gamma."

Jenny smiled. "Are you saying you want to stay up all night?"

"Mmm, mmm," Diana agreed, stacking blocks. "No bed."

"And yet you look so tired, Bubba," Jenny said, watching her eyelids droop. "Come sit with us, Diana. Come on."

Diana obediently climbed to her feet and toddled to her grandmother where she was lifted onto her lap and placed under the bright blanket. "Ah, uh, banket."

"Yes, it's a banket," Jenny said as her granddaughter laid her head on her chest.

"Banket," came softly from Diana before she fell asleep.

"That was easy," Pedro murmured, always surprised at how easy it was for his mama to deal with the babies.

Not to be outdone, Alena stumbled over to her Gampa and was lifted onto his lap. "Gampa," Alena said, snuggling under the pretty blanket and seeing Diana fast asleep. "Da-anna seep, A-ena wake."

"Yes, Alena is still awake and shouldn't be. Alena should be asleep like Diana," Spiros told her, relishing his role as grandpa. It was a role his own father had missed out on due to old Greek stubbornness, and him being disowned by his parents because he wanted to immigrate to Australia in 1950. His father had told him if he left to not come back. He was no longer part of the family. When the boys had started disappearing from home, he'd been angry and readily believed the lies and rumours he'd been told, while his wife had always believed in their sons. And he'd nearly lost them for it. His own Greek stubbornness had almost cost him his only three children. After losing Alena, he didn't want to lose his sons too. So, when Tomas came out and introduced Roger, he knew that he couldn't repeat his father's mistakes. He couldn't disown his son simply because he loved a man. Tomas had never done anything wrong. All he'd done was fall in love with another man, and he wasn't going to take that away from him.

And he was glad he'd had Jenny to pull him into line, because if it weren't for her making him pull his head out, he'd have lost his sons and grandchildren. Just like his father. But there was no way he was going to miss out on this.

He hugged Alena closer, resting his chin on her curly head. He had come so close to missing out on this. So close, especially when he'd exiled himself back in Mykonos believing he'd cheated on his wife of twenty-six years. He'd only just made it back before Viv gave birth. That was all his fault, his own stubborn fault. Arguing with Jenny, nearly hitting her, going out and getting drunk, and ending up in some woman's bed, only to assume come morning they'd had sex. His own stubborn fault for not staying to find out. His own stubborn fault for running out and deciding to leave his wife and family. His own stubborn fault for nearly missing out on the best two things that had ever happened. His granddaughters. Both asleep in his and Jenny's arms.

"I think it's time for bed," Jenny murmured, watching both girls sleep.

"Oh, do we have to? Taking her downstairs will wake her up and make her cry." Pedro jumped into a sitting position.

"We don't have to take her downstairs," Jenny replied. "She can stay up here with Diana. The two of you can have a night alone. We'll take the girls."

"Are you sure, Mama?" Pedro asked. "It's already late."

"Let's get them settled upstairs and then you can go." Jenny removed the blanket, and with help from Pedro in getting up, they carried the girls upstairs to the master bedroom where they had cots set up. The girls always stayed in their room whenever they babysat. Diana stirred. "Shh, Diana, go to sleep now. Time for sleep." Jenny laid her down, and she drifted back off.

Spiros set Alena down in her own cot, getting a cry and grumpy frown.

"Shh, Alena," Jenny soothed. "Time for sleep, time for sleep, shh." Covering the girls with blankets, Jenny stood back. "We'll watch them, you two go and have a rest. Viv and Carlos have the week off; you two have the rest of the weekend off."

"Thanks, Mama." Pedro kissed her cheek then leant down to touch Alena's and Diana's cheeks. "Night girls," he whispered.

Angie bent down and kissed her daughter. "Night, Bubba," she whispered, and they left the room.

"Go down and lock the door, I'll stay here," Jenny told Spiros, and it took all of one minute before he was back staring down at his grandchildren.

"How did we get so lucky?" he asked softly.

"*You* nearly didn't," Jenny reminded him. "If you hadn't've come back to New York when you did, you'd be missing out on all of this."

"I know, I know," he said. "I know you're going to remind me for the rest of my life how I nearly missed it all because of one stupid, idiotic mistake."

"Yep." She kissed his cheek and slid her arms around his waist. "Look at them." They stood staring down at their cherubic angels. "Aren't you glad we did this?"

He smiled, kissing his wife and holding her tight. "Yes, I am. Because as always, you were right, and I was wrong."

"Yes, you were," Jenny laughingly agreed. "But look at what we have."

"Yes. Look at what we have now," Spiros repeated. "Two beautiful, amazing granddaughters."

"Our baby girl came back to us, and we have her cousin, too. Our baby girls," Jenny said.

*****

In Miami, Marcus Seralift sat down in his office at *Seralift Productions*, the huge studio where he filmed his movies. This year, none of them had been nominated for porn awards, so he hadn't been invited. In fact, he hadn't even been asked, out of courtesy, if he'd like to attend.

He was going over his books, trying to find out where it was going wrong. While his movies still made money, it was not like it had been. Not like when Roger was making his movies, and certainly not like when he and Tomas were making theirs. The heyday of *Seralift* was waning. The time they'd made the most money, had the most movies, and won the most awards was '76 to '78. Roger had been working for him for a year and a half before he met up with Tomas, and he'd only done gay movies for about eight months before that. But the chemistry between the two of them was hard to deny, and they had exploded in each scene, and *that* translated to explosions on the big screen with skyrocketing sales, and the knowledge that Tomas was the brother of Carlo and Pedro Stefan, who were already in the business, helped immensely. Those few short months between August and October 1977 and the final two movies in January 1978, well…they had been dynamite, but nothing more until *The Greek Gods* movie which he only received a mention in as former boss. But those few short months, and the months that followed the movie's release, were the most lucrative months of *Seralift's* production life. And now…

Now it was all plummeting faster than the Titanic, award-wise. Their talent was good, but not good enough to win awards, and porn awards meant that people were paying to watch and liked what they saw. But that wasn't happening.

Financially, they were still afloat, having movies in the top ten or twenty at any one time. But they needed new talent. They needed another Tomas and Roger. Another half Greek and Australian.

Sliding his finger down the list of employees in front of him, he stopped to cross out two more. A red line went through their names if they were no longer with *Seralift.* A line that meant they were sacked or dead. And those two made four in two months, eight in the whole year. 1980 was not a good year so far, and thank God it was almost over. All he needed to do was see the year out without losing any more gay porn stars to sickness or death.

Yes, he'd heard rumours about a gay disease crisscrossing the countryside. Heard about it from Greta in New York, and Harry in L.A., plus he kept his ear to the ground in the Miami scene. He'd lost four porn stars to diseases, and four to death, and that was four too many. The diseases could be cleared up with pills, but death couldn't be, and if it continued, he really would be out of business.

His finger travelled down the list, marking off two more with an orange pen. Orange was for 'left of own accord'. And the list was getting smaller. "I'm going to have to find more staff," he muttered, seeing Aiden Head, Jeff Fastwater, Brock Hardwood and Brent Woodcock's names. They'd been killed off by a former worker, Luiz Manning, to get back at Roger for taking Tomas. All four had a red line through it. Luiz's had orange *and* red. Tomas and Roger had orange, but he'd left a question mark next to their names in case they came back. He didn't think they would, even though he lived in hope.

Counting off the names left, he knew he needed more fresh meat. But with disease skyrocketing, and the gay community looking so damn sick, he wasn't sure where to get them from. Maybe Harry could send some his way. Maybe he could get Carlos to write for him. He'd turned out to be such a prolific writer that his movies made millions. And that's what *Seralift* needed. Millions. Millions of ticket sales, millions of watchers, millions of video buyers. But with the changing tide, he wasn't sure how much longer he or the company could go on for. The '70s had been full of life and love and promise. And '77 had given him Tomas and Roger, so what the hell would the '80s give him?

Losing eight stars didn't help, and he needed more. Now. But they had to be clean and young and healthy, not sick and wasting away. Where the hell was he going to get gay guys who wanted to fuck for money and be a star in the making? Where would he get another Tomas and Roger?

He thought about the Greek community in Miami and wondered if he should check it out. *Mmm, two Greeks? What about a Greek and Italian together?* Mediterranean never looked so good as the Stefan brothers, Tomas in particular, but you never know what or who could turn up. Maybe with a bit of a makeover, he could get hot-looking young Greek guys into his movies and brand them with something. Because there was no way anyone would ever get another three brothers on their books.

He thought about it. *Maybe I could find another set of Greek brothers, or Italian, or Spanish, or Portuguese.*

The ideas flooded his head, and after writing them down, he set to work on *Seraliff's* big comeback.

November 1980

"Happy anniversary, my darling wife." Carlos came through the door with a tray of delicious food for breakfast.

"Mmm." She yawned and stretched her arms above her head. "What time is it?" Watching him place the tray on the bed, then fling back the curtains to reveal a dreary day, she saw Diana's head bobbing around in the doorway. "Ugh, what horrible weather."

Carlos adjusted the tray over her lap and kissed her. "Yes, it is, but we are about to make it better." He ran out to the kitchen with Diana waddling behind him and came back with another tray. "Come on, Diana, say hi to Mama." He placed the tray on the bed and lifted her up, climbing next to Viv. "Guess who helped prepare Mama's breakfast."

"Diana," Viv said, ticking her daughter on the tummy. "Diana made Mama's breakfast?"

"Yes, she did," Carlos said and settled his giggling daughter between them. He pulled his own tray over and laid a napkin over Diana's lap. "Is Diana ready for breakfast just like Mama?"

"Mmm." Diana nodded, and her daddy placed a bowl full of fluffy yellow scrambled eggs on her lap. "Eggies." She clapped her hands and took the spoon her daddy offered. "Mmm, eggies." She popped some in her mouth and happily chewed.

"Aw." Viv smiled at her daughter as her husband put his arm around both of them and lay back to eat his own breakfast. It had been quite a week and was going to get busier.

The previous Friday had been Halloween, and they had all dressed up and gone to 69 for the *All Hallows Eve* party. Pedro and Angie went as Mr and Mrs Dracula, dressing Alena up as a little vampire. With their black hair and white skin, they really looked like they could be bloodsuckers.

Viv and Carlos dressed up as Dorothy and the cowardly lion from *The Wizard Of Oz*, with Diana looking ever so cute in her munchkin outfit. Tomas and Roger were both Prince Charming, making Alena scream in delight when she saw them. And Spiros and Jenny went as Lucy and Desi Arnaz. It was the first time they'd dressed up with the girls, or celebrated Halloween. It wasn't celebrated in Australia, or Greece, and '78 had been busy with travel and babies and '79 equally so. But this year they had made an effort and taken a tonne of photos and film. Today was the beginning of anniversaries with theirs coming up first.

"Three years today," Viv said. "We've been married three years today." She looked at her engagement and wedding rings, still sparkling after three years.

"Yeah, babe. Three years ago today, I made an honest woman out of you," Carlos joked and ate some scrambled eggs and bacon.

Viv giggled. "You certainly did, considering I was already pregnant with this one here." She pushed back Diana's golden-brown curls, and her baby looked up from her eggs. "Is Diana enjoying her breakfast?"

"Ah, huh, eggies." Diana held up a spoonful before shoving it into her mouth.

"Yes, eggies." Viv smeared the remainder of hers onto her toast and cut it in half. "What do we have planned for tonight? It's a Tuesday; we're all celebrating during the middle of the week."

"I managed to get us all a table at *Rodriguez*, that new Mexican place you like so much. We won't be alone though; the whole family will be there. Hope you don't mind, but you should know by now we celebrate everything together."

A light laugh emanated from Viv. "I know, I'm used to it. Besides, your mother's already offered to take Diana again, so we can have the day to ourselves. And then when we get home from the restaurant she'll have her for a sleepover."

"That's all right, then. Mama loves her grandbabies. Diana gets to be with Grandma and Grandpa today." Carlos gazed down at his daughter.

"Gamma and Gampa," Diana mumbled around a piece of toast. There was more food around her on the bed than on the plate. But that was okay.

*****

That night, they partied at *Rodriguez*. It had only been open for two months and had a booking list a mile long and months in advance thanks to rave reviews in the *New York Times* and other papers. However, Carlos, being the man he was, had taken notice of Viv's enthusiasm for the restaurant when they'd first visited on the opening weekend and booked in their anniversary. And they were enjoying good Mexican food, good Mexican décor, and good Mexican music. The girls clapped and screamed, with big wide smiles on their chubby faces, and it was everyone else's first time too.

"Oh, I love it." Jenny clapped to the music. "We have to come back," she told Spiros.

"You'll be lucky to get back here before Christmas," Carlos said. "They're booked out like crazy."

"Well, how about we book them for next year," Jenny said. "Valentine's, birthdays, Mothers' Day, Fathers' Day, the girls' birthdays. There's plenty to celebrate in the first half of the year."

"Or the two of you could come back for a nice romantic date for two," Tomas added. "You don't need us around all the time."

"Rubbish!" Jenny exclaimed. "I need my babies and grandbabies around all the time. It's what keeps me young and alive."

"I thought that was Papa," Pedro cheekily said, hiding behind his beer bottle as guffaws went around the table.

"Of course he does," Jenny replied. "Sex with the person you love is incredibly rejuvenating." Casting a glance at her husband she waited for her sons' replies.

"Ew, Mama." Tomas shook his head and turned away. "No."

"Ugh," Carlos groaned, his head going back in disgust. "We *do not* need to know about your sex life, Mama."

"As I keep saying," Roger said. "How do you think they made the three of you?"

"Roger, stop." Tomas gently slapped him on the arm. "You've said that since we were married. You need to stop it."

"Why?" Roger shrugged. "They loved each other enough to get married and have *you* three. That means they had sex. And there is *nothing wrong* with your parents having sex. Just because they're in their fifties doesn't mean a damn thing. Hell, even my parents had sex. How do you think *I* came into this world? And," he leant in closer to Tomas, "if it weren't for *our* parents having sex and having us, *we* wouldn't be here, *together, now.* So *you* should be grateful that your parents *did* have sex. Otherwise, I wouldn't have you. And besides..." His face darkened. "It's not like my parents gave a crap about me. At least you boys have parents that love you and accept you for the way you are, regardless of what you do."

Tomas teared up, his face crumpled, and he reached for his lover's hand. "I'm so sorry your parents don't want to share in your joy," he told his lover. "I'm so sorry your parents disowned you and want nothing to do with you."

Roger heaved a deep sigh. "Yeah, so am I. But your parents have more than made up for it." He glanced at them. "I know it's not our anniversary yet, but considering the conversation, it seems important and needs to be said. I have never experienced such unconditional love in my life. Until I moved to America, I wasn't accepted. In my family, in my town, in my country," he shook his head in retrospect, "but coming here has allowed me to be free, and allowed me to find your son as my lover, as my best friend, my husband. And all of that could not have happened without the two of you accepting me into this family."

Jenny teared up and reached across Tomas for Roger's other hand.

He took it and squeezed. "You're the parents I don't have, but wished I did. And you have been more than accepting. And my siblings…" He turned to his brothers-in-law. "They certainly didn't want me around. But the two of you have welcomed me, and accepted me, and treat me like one of your own, and treat me like a brother. And I am so grateful for that." He sniffed and laughed softly. "But since this isn't *our* anniversary…" He glanced at Tomas then back to Carlos and Viv's teary expressions. "It's yours. I thank you for being the best in-laws possible. Hell, you're not even my in-laws, you *are* my brother and sister, and I thank you for being so amazing in accepting me into your brother's life and into the family. Congratulations to Carlos and Viv." He raised his glass, and the others followed suit. Even Alena and Diana raised their sippy cups. "To Carlos and Viv."

*****

The next night, they were back to celebrating. This time, it was Pedro and Angelina's third wedding anniversary. Ensconced in the *Rainbow Room* in the Rockefeller Center, they snuggled in close around the table with family and friends and Alena between them. Angie looked slick in her blue bodysuit and long silver shirt jacket. Pedro wore a matching blue shirt with his black suit, and Alena matched them in a pretty blue party dress. After organising with Eddie to have three days off, it meant he'd have to work all weekend to catch up. But he didn't mind. Family was important, and he'd been getting a vibe from his mother lately that family was more important than ever.

"Dance, Dada." Alena held her arms up for her daddy to take her.

He laughed and lifted her into his arms. "Alena wants to dance, does she?" He held out his hand to Angie and escorted his wife and daughter to the dance floor where he lifted Alena into the air, getting a giggle out of her, and then set her down to stand on his feet. Holding onto her hands, he moved and danced, and Alena screamed excitedly, looking from her very tall Dada to her dancing Mama.

Angie was getting down in her sky-high black stilettos as she shimmered in the party lights.

"Mama, dance," Alena said, bouncing excitedly up and down on her daddy's extra huge feet. "Dance Dada, dance Mama."

"Dance Alena." Angie clapped her hands. "Dance."

Alena danced her little cotton socks off, shaking her bottom and bopping up and down. "Dance," she cried. "Dance."

Jenny raced over and took a whole roll of photos, laughing as Alena came running over to her.

"Dance Gamma," she cried, grasping Jenny's dress.

"Dance Alena," Jenny replied, and started dancing with her granddaughter as the rest of the family came over and hit the dance floor.

"Da-anna, dance, Da-anna." Alena grabbed her cousin's hands, and they bounced up and down in the circle of parents, aunts, uncles, and grandparents who all stood around the girls, so they stayed safe and didn't stray.

After a half hour, they sat back down and went on with the festivities.

"To my baby Pedro and his beautiful Angelina. Congratulations on your third anniversary. Three years ago, a scared little girl in a sling came to Athens and introduced herself as my son's lover. The one thing I noticed, as with Viv and Roger, is that she loved my son more than anything else in the world." Jenny watched them look lovingly at each other. "And just as with Carlos and Viv, I hope the two of you have an amazing, incredible life ahead of you *and...*" She raised her brows hopefully. "More children?"

Angie laughed. "Not for a while yet. I want to finish school and make it to twenty-five before considering another baby."

"Then I'll remain hopeful," Jenny said, raising her glass. "Angie, you are the daughter I never had, you are the woman that my son clearly loves and adores. I wish you both love and happiness for the rest of your lives. To Pedro and Angie."

"Pedro and Angie."

"An' A-ena." Alena held up her drink cup from between her parents.

Everyone laughed. "And A-ena," Jenny added.

*****

On Thursday night, they celebrated Tomas and Roger's third wedding anniversary at *Santos*, the free and open restaurant bar in the middle of the city. The music was a mix of the '70s and current '80s, mainly disco and pop. The décor was dark yet tasteful, and the boys wore their three-piece suits without the vests, plus matching blue shirts.

"Ah…" Jenny looked around. "Should we be bringing the girls here? Is it safe?"

"As safe as anywhere else in the city, Mrs S," Roger said, watching in amusement as a male couple groped each other. "We've taken the kids to 69 you know."

Jenny gave him a look. "I know. But I haven't been *here* and don't know what it's like."

"Not to worry, the girls have their daddies and their uncles to protect them." Roger leant toward her. "We'll save them if anything happens."

A delicious meal followed, and dessert was a cake that Jenny had made. She'd made sure to have all the anniversary cakes at the restaurants beforehand for her children. This one was a rectangle with an image of Tomas and Roger on it.

"Aw, cute cake, Mrs S." Roger picked up the knife.

"Cay," Alena squealed, her eyes going wide. "Cay, Dada, cay."

Pedro laughed. "Yes, Alena, Uncle Tomas and Roger's cake."

"T, shall we?" Roger held his hand out.

Tomas grinned back and laid his hand over his husband's. "And we cut," he said, and they sliced through the chocolate cake. They cut the first piece and handed it to Alena who squealed with joy.

"Cay." Her eyes were as wide as saucers, and she clapped her acceptance.

"You have an obsession with cake, Alena." Tomas laughed. "And I think you two need to put a stop to it," he told Pedro and Angie and made another cut.

Diana looked at her uncles for her piece and got it. "Ta, Unca Tomas."

"It's hard not to eat cake in this family," Angie replied. "We're celebrating something every month, and most of those celebrations require cake."

"That's true," Jenny said and passed plates of cake around the table. "The first half of the year is always busy; the problem was, we were celebrating from December through June, now we're celebrating Halloween in October, and anniversaries and thanksgiving in November. We're now going *October* through June. That's eight months of a year, and most of it requires cake."

"Cay," Alena cried between mouthfuls of yummy chocolate cake. "Yummy cay."

After snapping photos of Alena and Diana, Jenny turned her camera onto their parents. Vivian and Carlos were happily laughing and watching Diana eat her cake. Pedro and Angie were smiling, cracking jokes and cleaning up Alena's cake-covered face. And then there was Tomas and Roger, true soulmates in every way, feeding each other cake and laughing, having the best time of their lives. They'd travelled the country and world, visited everywhere they wanted to go, shown each other where they were born, and grew up, and went to school. And they accepted everything about each other.

Jenny's boys were different from Carlos and Viv, and Pedro and Angie. While both of the couples loved each other and knew they wanted to be together, to have their babies, and love and support one another, Tomas and Roger were different. They'd never be parents; gays were not allowed to get married let alone adopt, so the only way they could make it happen would be to get a woman pregnant. But that wasn't in their plans. In fact, Jenny didn't know if they'd even thought about it. Maybe they didn't need kids, at least not yet. Clearly, being together and so totally, completely and deeply in love, was enough for them. The way they moved, the way they talked, it was evident they were one. One couple, one true love. *Each other's* true love. She saw the love radiate from every pore as they stared into each other's eyes. Feeding cake, laughing, smiling, not tearing their gaze from each other. They were in love and complete.

She snapped photos without them noticing and felt Spiros's hand on her leg. Glancing from her sons to her husband, she saw his happiness reflected hers as he looked from her to their son.

Clearing her throat, she picked up her glass. "I want to make a toast to my son and his husband." She waited while everyone raised their glasses, and even the girls raised their drink cups, looking from parent to parent to see what they were doing.

Smiling at her grandbabies, she turned her attention to the boys. "This is your third wedding anniversary, and I'm sure that three years ago neither of you even dreamed of finding each other and getting married. But, after a troubling start to life, Tomas was on his way to meeting Roger and the love and happiness that came with it." She took a breath. "Planning all three weddings was one of the happiest times of my life. Knowing that I was going to give you something that no other gay person has been given. A ceremony, a wedding, a marriage. And while it may not be technically legal, as long as it is in your hearts and souls, it is."

She watched them look at each other and entwine their fingers together. "The way you two look at each other, the way you love the other, the way you are together it's like you *are* one. All I see are true soulmates who adore each other, love one another, and *want* no other. There will never be anyone else for either of you. *You are it. You* are each other's, and I pray that you will spend the rest of your lives happy and healthy, loving and rejoicing in each other's love, passion and adoration. Congratulations on your anniversary. May you have many, many more. To Tomas and Roger."

"Tomas and Roger."

"Tomas an' Oger," the girls chimed in, getting giggles and laughs from the family.

Seeing she had the adults' attention, Alena raised her voice. "Tomas an' Oger."

"Okay, little one, we know what you mean, hush now," Pedro told her. "I want to say something." Clearing his throat, he raised his glass and stared adoringly at his older brother. "Everything I said at your wedding is still true. We missed your first anniversary because you were off travelling through Europe on your fancy holiday." Tomas and Roger laughed. "But ever since you found each other and have been together, it's like you've found your best self. You've become the man you were destined to be. And I know we've all said this before at other celebrations, but it's true. Every time I look at the two of you, you're gazing into each other's eyes and doing all this kissy, kissy stuff—"

"Kissy, kissy," Alena said, drinking from her sippy cup as the others laughed

"Yes, kissy, kissy," Pedro repeated, grinning at his daughter. "But seriously, you have become an amazing man, an amazing brother, and I cannot believe that I am so lucky to be related to you. I love you, you're my best friend, my brother, my champion, and I am so glad you found Roger because he is an amazing man himself." He watched them trade smiling glances. "He'd have to be to take on this family." That elicited laughs. "To my brother Tomas, and my brother-in-law Roger, happy anniversary, happy life, happy love. I hope you have many, many more. Tomas and Roger."

"Tomas and Roger."

"Guess it's my turn now," Carlos added, becoming serious. "As the *eldest* Stephanopoulos in the family—"

"I think that would be Papa," Tomas interrupted with a grin.

"Yes, I should say so," Spiros quipped, looking at his eldest son with raised brows and a grin.

Carlos blushed. "You know what I mean. As the *eldest* Stephanopoulos brother, stepping up two years ago made me realise a lot of things. One, that I *am* the eldest and have to take over when Papa can't, and two, that I have more than myself and my brothers to look after. I have a wife and sister-in-law, we have babies. But Tomas has you, Roger." He looked at his brother-in-law. "And if it's one thing I've seen since meeting you three years ago, it's that no matter what, you'll look after my brother. And that means a lot to me, as I'm sure it does to Mama and Papa. To know that my brother has you in his life to love him, come home to him, support him no matter what, means the world to me. And like Mama, I saw from that first meeting that you were going to be someone we could all trust, all love like another brother, and in whose safe, protective arms we could leave *our* brother."

He watched Tomas wipe away his tears and teared up himself. "Another thing I've learned since becoming a father, and since you were poisoned, is that family matters more than anything else in the world. To know, and see you go through that hell, made me sick with fear that something was happening to you. And while I didn't truly understand it, Mama did, and she told us to love you, and support you, and make life count. All of us living here in New York the last three years has been an incredible experience I can't even begin to describe. We all grew up in Australia together with aunts and uncles and cousins. And then we were moved halfway around the world as teenagers, and I saw you blossom. You loved the sea, and the place, and our new life, and I saw you be happy. And now, after what we all went through back in '77, being separated from our parents *and* each other, the last three years have been so incredibly important to me."

He looked at his parents, to Pedro and Angie, to Viv, then back to Tomas and Roger. "All of us being together again, sharing Christmas like we always did, new years and our birthdays, our parents' birthdays and anniversary, it all means so much, and I'm glad that they've happened and we've been together to celebrate them. Our birthdays always mean so much to me. All three of us together—"

"You resented sharing your birthday," Pedro cut in.

Carlos grinned. "I did when I was a kid, but the last three years they've meant the world, especially seeing my two little brothers with the people they love, and sharing in that love. And I thank you, Tomas, for letting us, Pedro and me, share in your relationship and love for Roger. That you weren't afraid to be yourself in front of us, to love a man instead of a woman, and that you chose a really great guy to be with and bring into the family. I love you, you are my brother, and I wish you and Roger all the best until your last day on Earth, which I hope is a very long time away." He raised his glass, wiped away his tears, and saw his family do the same. "To Tomas and Roger."

"Tomas and Roger."

"Oh, my God," Tomas cried, wiping away his tears. "I can't believe you guys." He jumped up to hug Pedro and pulled Carlos into it. "All the things you said at my wedding. All the things you say every birthday and anniversary and Christmas. I've never felt more loved in my entire life. You guys are amazing."

"Yes, we are, and don't you forget it." Carlos gave him a thud on the back. "We *are* amazing, and so are you. 'Cause that's the way Mama and Papa made us." He pulled back and slung his arm around his brother's neck while the other was around Pedro. "You are an amazing man, Tomas, and I am so proud to call you my brother." He kissed him on each cheek. "I love you too, Roger, get in here."

Roger moved around the table and joined in on the hug.

"You take care of him because when we can't, it's up to you."

Roger grinned. "You know I will." He gazed down at Tomas, his life, his love, his husband.

"Good." Carlos clapped him on the back. "Let's eat more cake."

*****

It was a week before Thanksgiving, and the Stephanopoulos family were preparing for a feast in their apartment building. In the penthouse, Jenny strung turkey ornaments around the dining and lounge rooms, and wrote out a list of the ingredients she would need for the meal. Plus, she had lists of Christmas goodies to get. She had no idea what presents to get her family; they had pretty much everything they could want already.

Downstairs in Apartment 2, Tomas and Roger were on their way out the door when the phone rang.

"Oh, leave it." Tomas encouraged him. "Let the machine get it."

"No, no, it could be important." Roger ran over and picked up. "Hello."

"Hey, Roger, glad I caught you. It's Freddy."

"Hey, Freddy, how are things in Miami?" Roger saw Tomas creep back into the room.

"Not good, man. We've lost four more this month alone. An' five between September an' October."

"Jesus, Freddy." Roger sagged and went into shock. "Who? What? When? Ah, how?"

"The disease, man. The disease eatin' up gay folk. Men in particular."

"Jesus…bloody…" Roger stared at Tomas and swallowed the lump in his throat. "Have they all been buried?"

Tomas frowned and inched closer.

"The ones from September an' October have. The others are bein' buried this weekend. They're droppin' from everywhere."

"Jesus," Roger repeated. "All the local haunts…local hangouts. What the bloody hell is happening?"

"Don't know, but I thought you'd like to know. We lost Caden, Sam, Chris an' Nathan. They're the ones bein' buried this weekend in a joint service."

"Jesus, Sam, Chris and Nathan, bloody hell. They were so healthy just a few years ago when we saw them. What sort of fucking disease is this?"

"Dunno man, but it's ravagin' the community. A lot of places aren't frequented as much as they used to be. People are stayin' away."

Roger sighed. "I'd really like to attend the funerals. Can you put us up?"

"Course I can. When are you comin'?"

"Tomorrow. Just like last time. We'll attend the funeral and fly home Sunday."

"Okay. I'll see you tomorrow."

"Roger?" Tomas watched him slowly replace the phone. "More deaths?" A sickness washed over him. He didn't want to return to Miami, not for funerals.

"Yeah." Roger breathed out. "Four this month, five more since September." He stood still, his fingers lingering on the phone handle. He couldn't move. He could barely breathe.

"Roger?" Tomas reached out a hand and touched his arm. "Roger."

A single lone tear slid from Roger's eye and rolled down his cheek as he stood silent, still in the moment.

"Oh, Roger." Tomas gently kissed the tear away. "I'm so sorry you're losing your friends."

Finally, Roger blinked, and two more tears fell. "So am I, T, so am I."

"You want to go?" Tomas softly wiped his lover's tears away.

"Yes. We can leave tomorrow."

"Ah…" Tomas breathed.

"What?" Roger took his husband by the arms. "Tell me, Tomas. What?"

"Ah…" Tomas looked down, took a deep breath, and looked into his lover's eyes. "I…don't…*want* to go. Last time was horrible, and I have a really sick feeling about going back to Miami. *But…*if you want me for support; then I'll suck it up and be there for you."

Roger lovingly brushed away a lock of Tomas's hair. It was long on top, but he'd trimmed the sides and back. "I love you, Tomas. Always putting others ahead of yourself. I know after last time it wasn't right anymore. It wasn't the place it used to be, and that sucks." He shook his head and collapsed onto the sofa. "They're all dying." His hands went to his mouth as he sobbed. "They're all dying. From *Wood, The Bat and Balls*, even *The Joy Stick* where we met. They're all dying. I just…" His head moved in slow motion. "I just…"

"I'm so sorry," Tomas said softly, sitting beside his man. "I'm so, so sorry."

Roger sobbed. "Nine dead in the last three months. Judd and Ethan, and Johnno and Evan before that. What the hell is going on?"

"Not to mention Leon, Cabot and Devron," Tomas added, rubbing Roger's back. "Whatever the bloody hell this thing is, it's horrible."

"That's not even the word for it," Roger gasped. "Horrible is definitely *not* the word for it."

"You want to leave tomorrow?"

"Yeah." Roger wiped his face. "Yeah, I do. We'll attend the funeral and then stay for the service long enough for one drink and then leave. Jesus bloody Christ." He breathed in. "I knew these people for two years, and while I haven't seen most of them in the last three years, they were a huge part of my life. We hung out, looked out for each other… What the hell is going on?"

Tomas shook his head. "I don't know, Roger. I don't know."

*****

They flew into Miami the next day and went to Freddy's. "Jesus Freddy, you're looking worn out." Roger greeted his old friend.

"You would be too if your customers were dyin' off an' business was down. I'm strugglin' to stay afloat."

They sat in *Love Stick* at the bar and ordered drinks.

Looking around, Roger saw it was only a quarter full even though it was lunchtime. "Business is definitely low. Is it always like this?" He spotted a couple of familiar faces and waved. At least they still looked healthy.

"This is the norm now," Freddy said. "I'm workin' double shifts just to stay in business."

Roger sighed and faced the bar. "That's thirteen this year alone, and we're only in November." He swigged back half his beer. Miami was *not* the place to be anymore.

"Yeah, man, thirteen this year, but you know, there's been more."

"When?" Roger asked in surprise. "I thought it was just this year."

"Nah. At the last service, we tried to make a list. Everyone remembered someone else that wasn't in Miami anymore, or who'd disappeared. It started with those four porn star friends of yours back in '77."

"What! Are you serious?" Tomas demanded. "This thing could *not* have started back then. We've only heard of it this year."

"Wait!" Roger put his hand up. "You mean Jeff Fastwater, Brock Hardwood, Aiden Head and Brent Woodcock? They were killed by Luiz Manning, not some disease."

Freddy shrugged. "We made a list, an' it came back to those four. We tried to figure out who'd slept with them, an' who slept with them, an' so on, an' it seems that those boys fucked half of Miami. An' now all of those boys are either dead or sick. Three years is a long time."

"But surely they couldn't have all slept with each other? That seems absurd," Roger said. "I certainly didn't." He finished that sentence knowing full well it was a lie. He'd had a quick night or two with all four men outside of work. They'd done their movies, continued long after the cameras rolled, but always played it safe. Once Tomas had come along, it all changed, but he couldn't tell Tomas what he'd done. He'd denied it from the get-go when Barden accused him of their murders, and he'd deny it until his dying day. But if they'd passed some filthy vile disease along, he'd better find out.

"Yeah, well, man." Freddy knocked back a shot of whiskey. "We've all slept with someone who's slept with someone who's slept with someone. An' half of the Miami gay community is sick or dyin'."

"Has everyone stayed? We saw David Marks, Zack Bryant and Adam Zevon back in August in L.A. They said they'd gotten out to stay healthy, but had heard the buzz about the disease being there as well."

"Some have up an' left. God knows if they're takin' the disease with them to wherever they're goin'. But most stayed. Now I bet they wish they hadn't," Freddy said wistfully.

"Because they're sick or dying?" Tomas asked.

"Yep." Freddy cast a long look at them "Bet you're glad you got out?"

Tomas smiled sadly. "I was barely here two months, and then a whole bunch of shit happened for me to leave and stay gone. I've… we've…" He took Roger's hand. "Been in New York with my family since. We get to travel and see new places, meet new people. Spend time with our nieces."

"That's good." Freddy raised his glass to them. "Cheers to you for gettin' out when you did."

*****

The next day, they attended the church service for Roger's four dead friends. Caden Colby, Sam Underwood, Chris Vine, and Nathan Brander. All gay men under thirty who had found solace in Miami's bright lights and gay community. No family members attended, just gay friends, and former gay co-workers.

"Jesus, I hate funerals," Tomas whispered as they sat in their seats. Four coffins lay side by side at the front. Large blown up pictures of the boys stood by each casket showing them in their healthier, happier days.

"I hung out with them for two years. I was here before I met you," Roger whispered back. "We all hung out. We rotated between *Wood, Bat and Balls, Joy Stick, Love Stick.*" He sighed. "We all hung out. Life was fun and carefree." The crevice between his eyes deepened as he frowned in remembrance. "We all hung out."

Tomas squeezed his hand. "I'm so sorry," he whispered before the service started.

Friend after friend, and co-worker after co-worker, stood up to speak. Out of the forty or so, only three or four still looked healthy and normal. They spoke of how great the boys were, so friendly and welcoming to new people in Miami, and how everyone had gotten along with everyone else. But times were changing, and they were losing their friends.

Roger stayed where he was. As much as he wanted to get up and speak about his friendship with the four of them, his throat was too constricted from choking back sobs and tears. At the end of the service, there were prayers and hymns as the caskets were rolled away, and they all stood to pay their last respects.

At *Love Stick* the party was sombre. Thirteen dead in one year was thirteen too many. After toasting to them, Roger led Tomas over to the board that was leaning against a wall. It had thirty-six pictures of their fallen friends, all the way back to Jeff, Brock, Aiden, and Brent, plus four more *Seralift* porn stars from the last few months. "Jesus, there's Braden," Roger said, pointing to the tall, dark, African American man he'd done his last movie with before hooking up with Tomas.

"He was the one I watched you work with?" Tomas asked, shock raining down over his face. "Before we started?" His eyes wandered over the rest of the board, seeing a few people he remembered.

"Yeah…yeah…that's him…yeah…bloody hell." Roger sighed deeply before knocking back the rest of his beer. "Bloody hell. Look at them all."

"There are a lot of them." David Marks came up behind them still looking healthy.

"Hey, David, you still good?" Roger shook his hand. "Is this all real?" He pointed to the board. "Are they *really* all dead?"

"Yeah, man. We figured it all out at Judd and Ethan's wake. It's like a very complicated family tree. Who slept with who slept with who. We traced it back to your boys even though they had been killed and not died from some disease."

"But that just seems so…bizarre." Roger stared at the photos. "I *know* we were all known around the traps, but—"

"There are more *Seralift* members on there," David pointed out.

"Yeah, yeah, I know." Roger swiped his hand over his mouth. "But four then, four now, five in between…and that's just *Seralift* stars from '77 through '79."

"That's thirty-six people in three years." Tomas was astounded. "Three full years and thirty-six people are dead."

"And quadruple that are sick." David nodded behind them.

They turned and looked at everyone. Thin, gaunt, sick, in wheelchairs, or barely able to walk.

"Do they know?" Roger asked forlornly.

"What?" David asked in return.

"That they're dying," Roger said. A deep sad sigh rose up from his diaphragm.

"I think so," David replied. "I think they know they don't have long, and that before they know it, they'll have their own photo on the board right next to this one." He glanced back to the board of thirty-six familiar faces. The blond Aussie bartender from *The Bat and Balls* was gone, and *his* partner was still hanging on, but didn't have long. A couple of bartenders from *The Joy Stick,* and waiters from *Wood.* "It's sad, and it sucks. Death always does, but when it's all your friends or co-workers…"

"It sucks fucking shit balls," Roger finished, wrapping his arm around Tomas and thanking God they were still safe. He hoped.

"Zack and Adam didn't want to come, but both of them are still okay." David gave one final glance over the crowd. "I'll let them know you guys are too. I'm gonna head out."

"Okay, yeah, tell them to be safe," Roger said, hugging David. "You too, man, be safe."

"Same goes for you, although from the sick looks on your faces, I'd say you've had enough of this place."

"Yes," Tomas said quickly. "Can we go? It's too miserable and depressing."

"Of course, my love." Roger slid his arm back around Tomas. "Let's get out of here."

The three waved goodbye to Freddy and walked out into the midday sun, parting ways as they went.

"Where do you want to go, T? We have until tomorrow." Roger pulled their car into their favourite beach spot and cut the engine.

Looking out over the cool sunny day, the light winds whipping up the water, Tomas sighed. "You brought me here on our first date."

"Really? I remember you freaking out when I called it a date, and I had to rename it 'just two guys hanging out'." He smiled, remembering back just over three years ago.

Tomas glanced at his lover, a small smile on his face. "Yeah, it was our first date, and I seem to recall what we did on our second."

Roger's smile spread across his face. "Yes, we did fall hard and fast for each other."

"We fell into bed on our second date, so yeah, we did." Tomas grinned.

"So, where do you want to go in case we don't come back?"

Tomas let his gaze wander as he thought. "To see the girls."

"Girls?"

"Bette, Bertha and Willow."

"Okay, it will take a while to get there. We'll need gas."

"Wait." Tomas looked around and saw a public phone booth. "I'll call in case she's not home." Dashing over, he dialled Bette's number.

"Hello, Olander residence."

"Webster, is that you? It's Tomas Stephanopoulos. I stayed with Bette in 1977."

"Oh, Mr Stephanopoulos, yes, I remember you. How are you?"

"Good, Webster, is Bette in? I'd like to see her while I'm here."

"Oh, no sir, she's at the Coral Gables Country Club. Some fundraiser do."

"Are the other ladies with her? Bertha St John and Willow Bertran?"

"I'm sure they are as they all belong to the club and fundraise often."

"Okay, thanks, Webster. I'll catch them there."

"Good day, sir."

Tomas ran back to the car. "To the Coral Gables Country Club, Jeeves," he joked. "They're having a fundraiser."

"Okay, let's go." Roger reversed and set off. Fifteen minutes later they pulled into the car park of the club and made their way inside.

"May I help you?" a staff member with a clipboard stopped them.

"Yes, we're here for Bette Olander's fundraiser," Tomas said.

"Of course, down the hall and on your right."

"Thank you." Tomas and Roger strode down the hall, hearing Bette's voice grow louder and louder. They came to a stop in the doorway and saw at least a hundred women and some men seated at round tables. Bette was on stage in a fluffy chiffon creation.

"And so we come to the giveaway part of the day." She gazed across the crowd. "Where we give away…" She spied the two boys. "Tomas," she cried. "Oh, Tomas, my dear boy, you've come back to us."

He grinned and waved at everyone who turned around.

"Oh, come in, come in," she said, and quickly made her way to them, the giveaway forgotten. "Oh, it's so good to see you two." She hugged him fiercely. "Oh, it's so good to see you, young Tomas." Taking his face in her hands, she moved it back and forth. "Still healthy and good. And Roger, how are you? It's been far too long." She hugged him too. "Come, come, come and tell us everything." Leading them back to the stage she ushered everyone else away. "Get back to your seats; I'm bringing them up on stage."

"Oh, you don't have to," Tomas said. "We don't want to interrupt." He let Bette take him on stage and Roger followed.

"Nonsense." She handed her microphone to Tomas and picked up another for herself. "Quiet down, everyone, Tomas and Roger are going to tell us what they've been up to the last three years. Settle back in your seats."

Tomas and Roger traded grins and looked at the crowd of women they knew. Marcus Seralift was also in the audience with his ex-wife and business partner, Violet. Roger nodded at him and received a nod in return.

"Okay now, Bertha St John, Willow Bertran and I all scored a trip to Greece when young Tomas was found three years ago after being kidnapped. So, we got to meet the rest of the family including those two incredibly gorgeous brothers of his. And we know they became engaged that day and had babies on the way, but tell us what happened."

"Ah, well," Tomas spoke into the microphone. "My mother organized everyone's weddings, and Carlos and Viv were married on the fourth of November, Pedro and Angie on the fifth." He looked at Roger and grasped his hand. "And, which was an amazing surprise, Roger and I were married on the sixth."

Gasps went around the room. "Wait!" Bette exclaimed. "The two of you got married…how?"

Tomas blushed. "Yes. Mama organized a service in the church, and she and Papa did it all. My brothers were our best men, we exchanged rings, we walked down the aisle, and Mama stole a marriage certificate for us to sign. So, to us…" He and Roger flashed their hands to show off their rings. "We *are* married." They received a round of applause.

"Oh, how delightful, go on, what then?" Bette asked.

"Well, after a honeymoon we had our last dinner with my great-grandfather, Giorgio. He died a few days later." Murmurs went through the crowd. "Don't worry," Tomas hurried on. "He was a hundred and one, so it was old age."

"Where have you been for the rest of the time?" Bette asked.

"We flew to New York to settle Pedro and Angelina in. She's still at Juilliard, and he's still DJing at *Studio 69*." A few claps went around the room. "We celebrated Thanksgiving, Christmas, New Year, our birthdays at 69, and then Roger and I toured Australia for three and a half months. We came back to Viv and Angie giving birth, and then spent the rest of the summer and fall travelling through Europe. Oh, my God, it's so beautiful."

"Oh, so lucky to be travelling," Bette said. "Europe is so beautiful in summer."

"It certainly is," Tomas replied. "We came home for Christmas, New Year's, and our birthdays, then Mama took the whole family back to Europe for summer, then we were back in New York, then Mama took us all to Australia for Christmas and New Year. Then we were back in New York for birthdays. Then Roger and I travelled across America over the summer, and now we're here for one day. We'll be in New York for Thanksgiving and Christmas and do it all over again."

"Oh, why are you here for only a day? You should stay and see us again. Although I do miss those clothes you used to wear. You look like you've been to a funeral." She looked them up and down, taking notice of the black suits, shirts and shoes.

Roger and Tomas gravely exchange glances. "We have," Tomas said softly.

"What?" Bette's face fell as murmurs once more spread through the crowd. "Oh, I'm so sorry. I didn't know. Friends of yours?"

"Of mine, yeah," Roger said, pointedly looking at Marcus.

"Oh, well, that's just terrible," Bette said. "Is it the gay disease that all of you are getting? It's affecting everything. Even *Sexe et Faveurs* has suffered. *The Joy Stick* where we took you, and you met Roger. Everywhere is suffering."

"Apparently," Roger said. "It's in New York, San Fran, and L.A. as well. We've lost thirty-six friends, or co-workers, in three years, and a whole bunch more. Looks like more will add to the tally in the next year. It sucks."

"Oh, well…the two of you look happy and healthy, so let's mingle," Bette told everyone. "Come on." She grabbed Tomas and Roger's hands, leading them into the crowd that rose as one. Ladies that Tomas used to train came over. Beatrice, Marie, and Violet Seralift, Bertha and Willow, plus all of the other fifty-plus women he'd worked with. They all kissed and hugged and congratulated while Bertha stopped to talk.

"I'm so glad you found Roger," she told Tomas. "And that Luiz is dead for what he did to you. I read about it in the newspapers. He was the half-brother of your sister-in-law, Angelina Poulos."

"Yes." Tomas nodded. "We didn't know at the time. Not until the cops told us at Chicago's airport. Then we flew home and sorted it all out, then went back to New York."

"I'm glad you're happy," she went on. "And still healthy. You two *are* healthy, aren't you?"

"So far, so good." Tomas laughed lightly. "As far as I know, we're fine."

"That's good. And it's good to see you again, young Tomas." She kissed both cheeks, leaving lipstick marks behind.

Bertha St John had been Luiz Manning's fiancé back in '77 when he'd met Tomas. A short affair happened before Tomas found out who he was and apologized to Bertha for sleeping with her fiancé. She'd said she'd always known he was bisexual and forgave Tomas, taking him back to Miami with Bette and Willow. And they had come through when Tomas was sick in the hospital, and she had seen Luiz taking him out the door, for which she had alerted the police.

"Bertha..." Tomas faltered and took a slow breath in. "Do you have a photo of Luiz?"

Her brows rose. "Whatever for?"

"I never had one and ah..." He paused. "I'd like to show my mother what he looked like. She's always been curious and..." His head twitched. "I just..."

"I'll have my butler dig one out and bring it over." Bertha grasped his hand and squeezed. "Sometimes it's nice to have a picture of our past loves, even if they did do us wrong."

"Yes," Tomas murmured, not even sure why he was asking. "Yes."

"Marcus." Roger shook hands with his former boss. "How's business? I hear it's falling apart."

Marcus sighed. He'd aged ten years in two and looked it, not just felt it. "It is. With everyone dying on me, or getting sick, it's hard to keep up with good stock."

"You can't get them from anywhere else?" Roger asked, glancing at the ladies nearby and nodding at Violet.

Marcus sadly shook his head. "I had to fire four stars this year from being full of STDs. If they can clean up, I might re-hire them. I've got eight dead in two years, but with whatever this gay disease is, it's rampaging through everything. Ah…" He paused. "You two wouldn't…"

"No, Marcus, we quit two years ago. We're not coming back."

Marcus nodded. "Fair enough. It's good to see you again, Roger."

"Same here, Marcus."

*****

After spending a sombre week at home reminiscing about past friends, the boys walked into the penthouse on Thanksgiving Day.

Tomas looked around for his mother and saw her coming from the kitchen. He paused while Roger closed the door and waved to the rest of the family in the lounge room.

"You're back." She kissed both cheeks and hugged him. "Are you okay after last weekend?" Studying his face, she saw something. "What is it? What's wrong?"

"I…ah…" he started, looking down at the photo in his hand. "We went to see Bette and spoke to Bertha. I asked her for a photo." Glancing up, he took a deep breath. "Remember when we saw Detective Gardo with his son, and you asked if I'd ever seen eyes so aqua blue, and I said…Luiz?"

Jenny frowned and glanced over her son's shoulder to see Roger smile slightly and nod. He moved over to the rest of the family, leaving them alone. "Yes, why?" she answered.

"Well…" Tomas licked his lips. "She gave me…a picture of Luiz." He handed over the photo, knots in his stomach.

Jenny took the photo, her breath taken with the young man in it, and she noticed the eyes straight away. "Oh, my, they *are* uniquely aqua blue." She studied Luiz. "He's a very good-looking man, no wonder you fell for him."

Tomas smiled sadly. "Bertha said that was taken on Mykonos after he met me. So the time is right…"

"What's going on?" Carlos asked Roger and watched him sit next to Angie. "We haven't seen you since you got back from Miami.

Figured you'd want some time alone." He was on the couch opposite next to Pedro.

"Yeah, what's he showing Mama?" Pedro asked, looking from Roger to his mother and back.

"A photo." Roger stared at them and sighed. "Of Luiz."

Going into momentary shock, both boys were out of their seats and over to their mother to see the man who'd taken their brother.

"Jesus, bro," Carlos breathed, looking at the photo. "No wonder you fell for him."

A blush reddened Tomas's cheeks.

"He's gorgeous," Pedro added, standing on the other side of Jenny, studying the man who'd kidnapped his brother, and who was also his half-brother-in-law.

Tomas's sad smile came back. "Yeah, yeah, he was."

"His eyes are unusual. I don't think I've seen eyes that colour," Carlos said, taking in the tanned, muscular man with the dark brown hair and teeny tiny briefs. "Looks like he packed a punch himself."

"Luiz," Angie whispered, frozen to the spot. They barely talked about him except when Tomas mentioned him in anger or sadness.

Spiros went over to his son and put his arm around Tomas's shoulder. "May I see the man that stole my son's heart the first time he fell in love?" He held his hand out to Jenny.

"He didn't..." Tomas faltered, and looking down at his hands he twirled his wedding ring. "It wasn't...love, just lust..."

Spiros stared at the photo. "He's a *very* good-looking young man. If I were younger and gay, I'd probably—"

"Ew, Papa!" The boys all stopped him; faces screwed up in disgust.

Spiros grinned and looked at Tomas. "He was a very good-looking young man. It's just a pity he became obsessed and wanted to ruin your life."

"What does Roger think about you wanting a photo?" Jenny asked.

Tomas shrugged a shoulder. "He says he understands. Luiz is dead; we're married, it doesn't matter."

"Can I see it?" Angie asked from behind Spiros. They turned. "He...ah...was my half-brother and...all... I've never seen him." She looked from Tomas to Spiros and back. "Please?"

Tomas nodded to Spiros who handed it over. "Just don't," he paused, "get angry and rip it up."

Angie took the photo and stared at the man in it. "Well, he has our father's tanned complexion and dark hair, but those eyes are definitely not ours. Are they Sheila's?" She looked at Jenny.

"No," Jenny replied. "Although she does have blue eyes like mine, they're not like that."

"No. But they're like Gardo's son's eyes. Remember, I told you it was like he was Luiz and he was reaching out to me, and he said my name like he knew me," Tomas told his mother. "Two different people, twenty-six, twenty-seven years apart, with the same aqua blue eyes. That *can't* be a coincidence?"

"But Sheila is not in the picture, so why would Luiz come back to Gardo?" Jenny asked.

Viv came over for a look and peered over Angie's shoulder. "Oh, my God, he's gorgeous."

"Yes, he was." Roger walked up beside them. "He was *very* gorgeous, and it's no wonder Tomas fell for him. I probably would have to." A twinkle came to his eye.

"Roger!" Tomas stared at his lover in shock then saw the twinkle. "Oh, God, don't scare me like that." He moved into his husband's arms. "I chose *you, not* Luiz."

"Just as well you did." Roger kissed Tomas's forehead. "When's dinner?" he asked over his lover's head.

"In another hour or so," Jenny said, taking the photo from Angie and looking at his eyes. *God, they do look like Gardo's son's eyes.*

"I don't need the photo," Tomas told them. "I just wanted something for all of you to see. I have more. Bertha gave me several, but that was the only one on his own. You can keep them, Mama. I don't want them."

"You sure?" She saw her son snuggled in his husband's arms.

"I'm sure, Mama." Tomas looked up and kissed Roger before they made their way into the lounge room and settled on a sofa with the girls.

Jenny continued gazing at the photo while she walked into the kitchen and opened the hidden safe in the wall. After placing it inside, she locked the door.

It being Thanksgiving, they sat around the table an hour later giving thanks, as each dug into their turkey.

"I give thanks for my amazingly talented husband and beautiful baby girl," Angie said, wiping cranberry sauce from Alena's face.

"A-ena," Alena replied, waving her hand in the air.

"Yes, Alena." Angie rubbed her nose to her baby girl's. "I love, Alena."

"A-ena wuvs Mama," she replied.

"Well, *I* give thanks for my amazingly talented and incredibly beautiful wife, and my beautiful baby girl," Pedro said, leaning over Alena's head to kiss his wife. "I love you," he added quietly.

"I love you," Angie replied, beaming up at him.

"A-ena." Alena reached up to both of them.

"Okay, my turn." Carlos turned to Viv. "I give thanks to my incredibly talented and amazingly beautiful wife, Viv. Without you, I wouldn't feel complete. I wouldn't feel like my destiny was right. You gave me our beautiful baby girl, and I am so grateful for that, and for Diana." He gazed down at her smiling face and brushed her hair back with his hand. "I love you, Diana, and I am so grateful for you and Mama."

"Da-anna," she said. "Dada, Mama."

"Yes, we are." Viv smiled at her. "And I am so grateful for my beautiful baby girl and the fact that she was given to me by the almighty universe. And that she wouldn't be here if I hadn't met her beautiful father." She leaned over Diana and kissed her husband. "I love you, Carlos Stephanopoulos."

"I love you, Vivian Villiers," he replied, kissing his wife back.

Jenny had studied her children as each gave their speech. She saw many, many years ahead for Pedro and Angie, Carlos and Viv, and saw the love they had for each other that would last a lifetime. But not so where Tomas and Roger were concerned. She didn't see a future lifetime for them, and that scared her. News of this disease scared her.

She scoured the papers from the east coast to the west, and not one of them had any news of a disease amongst gay men. But she'd read the obituaries habitually, and saw the death notices for many young men week after week. She worried for her son and son-in-law and whether this disease would affect them. Whether they were safe from it, or still had it coming. One thing she knew, from what they had told her, was that it seemed to be sexually transmitted. Too many partners, not being safe enough. And while the boys had been together for three years, that didn't guarantee that they *were* safe. And since they couldn't guarantee their own safety, she fretted.

Because neither could she.

"Well, *I* am grateful that our ancestors got together to bring Jenny Marsh and Spiros Stephanopoulos into the world, so they could come together and have us." Tomas raised his glass and looked from his father to his mother, seeing tears well up in Jenny's eyes. "I am so grateful to have the parents I have. The two people who brought me into this world, who raised me, loved me, taught me right from wrong and gave me the values, morals and principles I live by. I am so eternally grateful to the both of you and am so glad I picked you as my parents. I've had the most amazing twenty-five and a half years on this planet, and without the two of you, that would not have been possible. *My life* would not have been possible. I would not have travelled to the countries and places, and seen and done the things I've seen and done, and experienced life on all levels without the two of you. You brought me into this world as you did my brothers, and I would not be the person I am without all of you. Without my two incredible brothers to stand beside."

He glanced from a teary-eyed Pedro who was sitting across from him, to Carlos who was beside Roger. "I have learned so much from both of you, and am proud to call you my brothers. Mama and Papa raised three fine young men. And if you hadn't've had me, then I would not have been able to meet the man beside me."

He turned to Roger who smiled back. "I would not have had the most amazing experiences that I've had, felt the explosion of unconditional love that I felt, or been with the most amazing man ever.

Three years ago, I was single and trying to find my way through life, and then I met you, and my life changed in so many amazing ways. For the better, believe me. I am so eternally grateful and thankful for the love you gave me, the support you give me, and the undying love you show me. Mama says we're soulmates, and I believe her because I can't imagine my life without you, without the support that you give to me, or show me. I am so eternally grateful for you, Roger. I love you; I thank you, I can't wait to spend the rest of my life with you."

"Oh, Tomas," Roger cried and wiped his face, as did the others.

"I'm not done," Tomas said quickly. "I am grateful and thankful to the two women who fell in love with my brothers, and loved them enough to marry them and make honest men out of them."

"Aw, bro." Pedro blushed, and Angie and Viv wiped away their tears.

"I love you both, Angie and Viv, you are my sisters, and you have given my brothers two amazing daughters of their own, and me and Roger two amazing nieces to love and adore. Alena and Diana."

"A-ena an' Da-anna." Alena nodded in agreement.

That brought an even bigger smile to Tomas's face. "Alena and Diana, the cutest, most amazing little girls I've ever met. Your Uncle Tomas loves you so, so much as he does your mamas and papas. Thank you, all of you, for being the most amazing family that a person could have. To be so loving and accepting, and kind and caring, is more than one person could ever hope to have."

He looked at his mother, but couldn't read her expression. "I know I'm loved, and accepted for who I am and who I want to be with, and I will be eternally grateful for that. Because you are my parents and I love you, and I know you love and accept me for who I am. The man you raised to be amazing." He raised his glass higher. "I love you, Mama and Papa. Thank you for having me."

Jenny covered her face with both hands as the tears flowed forth. She so desperately wanted a future for her son, but had a deep-seated sick feeling in her gut that there wouldn't be one. Not with all of the disease going on among gay men, and while Tomas had only discovered his sexuality three years ago, she knew there was a very real possibility he'd end up like them.

"Aw, Mama, I didn't mean to make you cry, no." Tomas left his seat and pulled her into his arms where she sobbed harder. "Mama, no." He looked at everyone else and saw them crying, or trying to quickly wipe away tears. "No, I didn't mean to make everyone cry. God no."

"Oh, my baby." Jenny wrapped her arms around his neck. "I so desperately want happiness for you, for you and Roger. I do. I am so, so glad I have all three of you. I love you." She kissed his cheek. "I love you so, so much."

"I love you, Mama." He felt his father's arms wrap around both of them from behind.

"That was the most incredible thing I think I've heard any of my children say," Spiros said beside Tomas's ear. "I love you, Tomas."

Tomas looked over his shoulder and saw his father's tears. "I love you, Papa."

Pedro came up to the front. "I love you, Tomas, so much. You're my big bro, and I love you."

Tomas laughed. "I love you, too." He grabbed his brother the best he could, but Carlos came into the crowd.

"Jesus, little brother, that was some speech."

"I made it from the heart," Tomas replied as Carlos slid his arms around him and their father and pulled them close.

"I love you, little brother," Carlos said in his ear.

"I love you, too." Tomas smiled and stared into his brother's bright teary eyes.

Alena, not to miss out, crawled from her high chair and toddled over to the hugging group. "A-ena hug an' kiss." She bounced up and down. "Hug an' kiss." She tried to get between the legs of everyone, but they were all too tall. "A-ena hug an' kiss."

"All right, Bubba." Pedro stepped back for his daughter to come into the group.

Tomas let go of his mother to pick up Alena. "Alena wants hugs and kisses does she?"

"Mmm, mmm." She nodded and was bombarded with kisses on her chubby cheeks by her daddy and two uncles, making her burst into a fit of giggles. "Stop," she cried, so they did. She looked at everyone staring back at her and said, "More." And was promptly smothered again.

Settling back into their seats and wiping away tears, they had more thanks to go.

"Roger, your turn." Tomas refilled his glass.

"Jesus, T, I don't know how to compete with, or top that." Roger wiped his face.

"Neither do we," Carlos said dryly. "And compared to that, ours sounded positively selfish."

"No, they didn't," Jenny said. "You're thankful for your wives and daughters, that's what matters and is most important." She watched her sons look lovingly at their wives. "Go on, Roger."

"Well, ah…" He cleared his throat. "I don't think I can get anywhere near that, but I have an idea that it's come off the back of all the loss we've suffered." He saw Tomas nod slightly in agreement. Sighing, he felt the pain. "I love you so much, Tomas. And this thing is starting to scare me. I can't even begin to express how I feel for you because just saying I love you isn't even enough. Just *showing* you isn't even enough." He turned in his seat to face his lover. "Everything that we've done together is because of your mother in part, and I thank you, Mrs S." He raised his glass to her, and she nodded her acknowledgement. "We've travelled the world," he told his husband. "We've explored towns and cities, and museums and art galleries, we've gone on rides at Disneyland."

"Disneyand," Alena cried and threw her arms in the air.

Roger chuckled and turned his attention back to a smiling Tomas. "We've done so many things together, been lucky enough to spend time together and not have to work. And I am so eternally grateful to your parents. For not only supporting our lifestyle, but for encouraging us to do what we want and be what we want. Words are not enough to express how I feel about you, Tomas Stephanopoulos." He touched his fingers to his husband's cheek. "So, I hope that my actions speak louder than my words. I hope that my actions show you every day how much I love you and appreciate you, and am *so* grateful to have you in my life,"

"Oh, Roger." Tomas teared up. "I love you."

"I love you, Tomas, always and ever, for life, here and beyond into the next."

Jenny looked up sharply, and the rest of the family noticed, except for Tomas and Roger who were engrossed in each other.

"I am so glad I have you, Tomas. So, so glad." He kissed him. "I love you."

"Oh, Roger, I love you, too." Tomas took his face in his hands. "I love you so much. I do, more than life itself."

Jenny frowned at his choice of words, and her husband and sons read her expression, with Carlos staring back as if knowing. Blue eyes staring into blue eyes, knowing exactly what the other was thinking. That's the connection Carlos had been developing with his mother the last few years. They were on the same wavelength emotionally and business-wise, and he knew she still feared for Tomas's health and safety. And with all of their friends dying off... He shuddered, thinking about the loss Tomas's death would bring.

"And to the rest of the Stephanopoulos family..." Roger turned back to the table, his left arm around Tomas. "Everything I said on our anniversary is true. I'm grateful that you've accepted me into your brother's life, and have accepted me as a brother. I see how much you love him, and each other, and I'm so grateful and proud to be a part of it." He raised his glass, his tears falling freely. "Thank you."

Tomas buried his head in Roger's neck. "Oh, Roger."

"Oh, Tomas," he laughingly replied, kissing the top of his husband's head.

"That was beautiful," Jenny managed through her tears and looked at Spiros. She knew she wouldn't be able to talk much at that moment, so left it up to her husband.

He cleared his throat. "When I immigrated to Australia, I never imagined that I would find the woman of my dreams waiting for me at the end of the walkway down to the dock. But there she was, little Jenny Marsh in her bright pink dress and blue accessories." He stared lovingly at his smiling wife. "She captured my attention and never let go. And when she accepted my marriage proposal two years later, it was the happiest day of my life. Or so I thought, because it kept being topped every year or so. The day we were married, the days you gave birth to our sons. The day you said you were going to pack up our family and move halfway around the world to a country you didn't know. They were the happiest days of my life, and yet they keep being topped all these years later, time and time again. With my three sons getting married, and then bringing our beautiful granddaughters into our lives." He sighed and choked back a sob. "Every Valentine's day, birthday, anniversary, Christmas and new year, it keeps being topped. And every day is more amazing, more incredible, more filled with love than one could ever imagine."

He wiped his face. "Ah, listen to me." He looked around the table, and his gaze landed on Jenny. "I love you so much, Jenny Marsh, and I'm so grateful that you said yes to me twenty-eight years ago, and so grateful that you made me come here and gave me the kick up the butt I needed to see that it was time *I* sacrificed for the family. I love you, I love our sons, our daughters, and our grandbabies, and I'm so forever, eternally grateful that I have you all. Happy Thanksgiving."

"Happy Thanksgiving," everyone cheered.

"My love, you're lucky last," Spiros said.

Jenny took deep breaths and had no idea how she was going to get through this without crying. There was nothing lucky about going last when you were already overly emotional. "When I saw you," she told Spiros, "come off the boat, I fell head over heels. I was crushing on you so badly, and then I found out that your relatives lived right next door to me and I was over the moon. You looked so different to the other boys. You were the exact splitting image of what Tomas is now. You were young and gorgeous and dark and exotic."

She reached out and grabbed her son's hand, and he squeezed back. "You so take after your father when he was your age," she told him before turning back to her husband. "And I fell in love with you, so much. There was no one else for me. You were it. The only one I wanted. The only one I would ever say yes to. Once I married you, that was it. For better for worse, for richer or poorer, in sickness and in health, you were it. There was no going back, only forward, and look what we have now, twenty-eight years later. Three healthy strapping sons by blood and one by marriage." She glanced at Roger. "Two amazing, incredible daughters, and two even more amazing granddaughters."

Alena and Diana took that moment to yawn.

Jenny laughed softly. "Who are clearly tired and in need of sleep. And all of this would not have been possible if you hadn't immigrated to Australia in 1950. We wouldn't have all of this." She held out her hands to her family. "We wouldn't have each other. And even though we've had several bumps in the road along the way, we managed to make it through, come back together in one piece, stronger than ever. Because our bond will not break. I won't allow it to. Ever. Never ever."

Everyone chuckled at that.

She smiled lovingly at her family. "To my eldest, Carlos Spiros Stephanopoulos," she looked at him, "you were a handful from the moment you were born. You yelled and screamed for attention—"

"He still does," Pedro quipped.

"And you wanted it all to yourself," Jenny went on, hiding her smile. "You wanted everyone's attention even if you didn't know them; you had to have them watching you. Mum said to me once," Jenny frowned slightly, "that she thought one day you'd be in movies. That your attention-seeking ways would get you into movies."

"It did," Tomas said before sipping his drink.

"Yes, it did," Jenny agreed. "You were always boisterous, loud, obnoxious, annoying, attention-seeking, and wanting it to be all about you."

"He still does," Pedro and Tomas replied at the same time then laughed.

Jenny joined in, seeing Carlos smile at their words. "Yes, he still does. But that's what made him the man he is today. Regardless of how he got here, it has made him the man of twenty-seven that is right here in front of us. And I'm glad that for all of your attitude, you remembered *exactly* what we taught you, and you stepped up when the time came. I absolutely adore the person you have become, and I think you chose an incredible woman to match you. And now we have the beautiful Diana who's fallen asleep in her high chair to love as well."

Carlos bent down and kissed his daughter on the top of her head.

"Vivian, you are the perfect match for my son. You've helped tame him, he has become relaxed and calm because of you, and I'm grateful to you for that. I'm grateful for both of you. I love you all."

"We love you, Mama," Carlos said as Viv wiped away her tears and smiled her appreciation at being included in Jenny's thanks.

"I love you too, my baby, now…Pedro Matthew Stephanopoulos." She turned to her youngest. "You were a slippery little sucker as a kid, but I loved and adored you. You took after both of your brothers, and that made you a handful. When you were with Carlos, you were like him. When you were with Tomas, you were like him, and that made it hard to keep up with you. You wanted to be like both of your big brothers, and you just couldn't be because you had to find your own way into being yourself, and you have turned into an amazing man. Although you're only twenty-three, you are the most amazingly talented DJ I have ever seen, and I'm so proud that you've found that love of music. You were raised on it, you danced to it, you lived by it, and you still do. It's your career, and I hope it's a long and fruitful one. Much better than those horrible movies."

He grinned at her and squeezed her hand.

"You have your father's black hair and my eyes, and you are a lethal combination. Just look at you, you're gorgeous."

"Now, now, Mama, don't give him a big head," Carlos joked.

"You can talk," Tomas retorted back to his brother.

"Yes, yes." Jenny laughed lightly. "He *is* gorgeous and *my* baby boy. You are my baby and always will be, and you have found your perfect match in Angelina. Although both so young when you got together, you have proved you can be adults. And I see the love you have for each other. And Angelina, you came into this family at a time when it needed a daughter, and you needed parents and love and support."

Angie dabbed at her tears with her napkin, her heart overflowing with love.

"And I have watched you grow into an amazing young woman over the last three years. A fourth-year student at Juilliard, a mother, a wife. You have blossomed into a woman who doesn't need her Mama as much anymore. And I feel I have done my duty to *your* mother, who I'm sure is looking down on you and is grateful that you found a family to love you and support you in all you do. I love you both; you are my babies."

"Aw, Mama." Angie wiped her face. "I'll always need you."

"And I hope you will," Jenny said and smiled before looking at Tomas. "My baby, Tomas Giorgio Stephanopoulos." She took his hand in both of hers. "My middle baby. Always the quiet one, always the studious one. Always the one who looked *up* to Carlos and looked *after* Pedro." He smiled at her. "The one I could rely on to be there when needed. But I saw what their departure did to you back in Mykonos; it left you lost and alone and lonely and frightened. What was left for you without your brothers there? I saw the pain and knew what was coming. I saw you fall for a man and have your first experience. I saw you falter when it came to what to do. Stay or go. I saw you decide to take the bull by the horn and go and live life and have an adventure. And that adventure led to Roger, the only man to truly capture your heart, your soul, your mind. You are two peas in a pod, true soulmates, true lovers, true friends, and I have a feeling you've both been here before and will be again. You will get another go-round at life, as I hope all my babies do."

She glanced at Alena who was nodding off. "And I hope it's in my lifetime…" she trailed off, before looking back at her puzzled son. "I love you so much, Tomas. What happened to you scared the life out of me, and I so hope there are no long-term repercussions from it. I want you and Roger to have a long healthy life together and be happy in love. I want that for the two of you so much. Just like with all of my babies. You are so special, Tomas. So, so special I can't even begin to list how many ways you are. But regardless, I love you, I will always love you, and you will always be the one I look out for most because you're different to your brothers. Carlos can handle himself, and

Pedro has his music, but you have Roger, and that's what matters."

She squeezed his hands. "That you have each other, because that's all that matters for the two of you. That you love each other and are together, when and where it counts. And Roger…" She looked at him. "You are a fourth son to us, you have taken care of our baby and look after him when we can't, and thank God he found love and happiness with you. *True love* and happiness. I hope that it continues for the rest of your lives. And that you all," she raised her glass to the table, "live very happy lives like your father and me. We love you, you are our babies, and you mean the absolute world to me. It would *destroy* me if I lost one of you and I already did, twenty-one years ago. But we've been given a second chance at that happiness, and I am forever grateful for that." Her face crumpled, and she smiled at Alena asleep in her daddy's arms. "I am so forever grateful for my family. I love you all, happy Thanksgiving."

December 1980

It was Christmas Eve, and everyone gathered in the penthouse to watch the festivities on TV and sing carols. Pedro had managed to get the time off work, and the girls were trying to grab at the lights on the tree that was decorated with the family baubles, with Alena's next to Pedro and Angie's, and Diana's next to Carlos and Viv's. They also had their matching stockings hanging on the mantel.

A Christmas train filled with small candy and popcorn was set up around the tree that sat in its usual spot in the corner of the lounge room. The girls squealed and grabbed at it every time it came around and made a mess. But it didn't matter; it was Christmas; it didn't matter at all.

Jenny ran around taking photos, Spiros recorded film, and everyone sat around the fire, relishing in their time together.

"Six more months and I am free," Angie squealed, double fist pumping herself.

"Goodness, already." Jenny laid a tray of Christmas cookies on the coffee table. "It just seems like yesterday you were starting."

"Yeah, it does." Angie grabbed a cookie and nibbled on it. "But I started amidst that mess with my father and us running away to come here. And then I got married and had a baby, and two years later here we are."

Jenny smiled. "Yes, here we are. Girls, biscuits," she called, still using the Australian term for them that she had taught the girls.

"Bickies," Alena cried, running around the couch and tripping over her father's long legs. She still managed to get to her feet and to the coffee table before Diana did and score a Rudolph biscuit. "Wudoph." She held it up for all to see before she bit his antlers off.

"I want Wudoph." Diana landed on the coffee table and reached for the last reindeer biscuit. "Wudoph." She too bit the antlers off before she and Alena pretended their reindeers were running along pulling Santa's sleigh.

"Easy girls," Pedro said. "There's enough biscuits to go around." He munched on a bauble while Carlos and Viv had Santa's, and watched the girls run back to chase the Christmas train. "How are the videos going, Viv?"

"Well," she replied. "We're doing one set a month and getting them ready for release. Photo shoots, make-up, perfume, cosmetics, it's all going ahead."

"And the new perfume?" Jenny asked. She was all over the business as financier and was thrilled at having something to be involved in. "The new one that came out on November first."

"Yes, *Angelina*." Viv smiled at her sister-in-law. "It's selling well."

"It had better," Angie laughingly retorted. "It's got my name on it."

Viv laughed with her. "I know, but all perfumes are selling well, and *Vivian* is *still* a sell-out."

"I'm glad." Jenny bit into a snowman. "And the videos are going gangbusters."

"Mama," Carlos said. "No one uses that phrase here."

"I do," she quipped. "Besides, *I'm* not from here, so I'll use whatever phrase I want to." She eyed Tomas and Roger sitting quietly on the other couch. Tomas was slowly nibbling his biscuit, but had barely eaten any. "Not in the mood for Chrissy bickies?" she asked him.

"Still full from dinner." He sighed, and a soft smile touched his lips. "Awesome as always, Mama, but I guess I didn't really need a biscuit." He offered the rest of his Christmas tree to Roger who took it and bit it in half.

"Except you didn't eat a lot of dinner either," she said quietly.

He glanced at her. "No. Not really hungry."

"Are you okay?" she continued, the dreaded fear creeping up from her stomach.

His eyes moved down. "No, not really."

Jenny's eyes narrowed, and she went to his side. "Are you not feeling well?" She felt his forehead. "Are you coming down with the flu again?"

"I don't know." He moved his face away. "Mama, stop." Gently pushing her hand back, he looked down at his lap.

She froze, for something was definitely wrong. "Tomas," she said firmly. "What is it?"

He didn't say anything, just stared down at his fingers fidgeting in his lap.

Roger looked at his husband. "T?"

"Tomas." Jenny gripped his hands. *"What is it?"*

He gasped a ragged breath. "It's Christmas," a breath, "and all our friends are dead."

"Aw, T." Roger put his arms around him. "Yeah, I know."

Tomas laid his head on Roger's shoulder. "They don't get to spend another Christmas with family or friends, and yet we do," he sobbed, eyes screwed shut as tears flowed. "They're all gone."

"Not quite," Roger said. "There's still some around. Not many, but there's still some around."

Jenny's eyes watered, and she looked at her family, seeing Pedro's tears for Leon, and Viv's for Cabot.

"Not many," Tomas told Roger. "You saw how many of them were sick. How many have died this month since we were there?"

Roger sighed. He'd received three phone calls from Freddy, telling him more had died in the last month. He and David had been right at the last funerals. With so many sick, it wouldn't be long before their photos were added to the remembrance board. "Ten," he finally murmured. "This month."

Shocked murmurs went around the room and tears fell freely.

"Jesus Christ." Jenny made a cross symbol with her fingers. While raised a Catholic, she'd only gone once a week on a Sunday, but didn't feel the need to go anymore, not since being in New York.

"So, how many of your friends have gone?" Pedro asked, thinking about Leon.

"Forty-six in three years. Twenty-seven this year alone," Roger replied.

"Oh, my God," wafted through the air, everyone in shock at the death rate.

Pedro let go of a deep sigh. "You know, I haven't seen a few regulars in months. But I haven't seen or heard anything either."

"Have you read the obituaries?" Jenny asked.

"No." Pedro shook his head slightly. "I don't know if I could."

"I do," she said quietly.

Tomas looked up and wiped his face. "Why?"

Jenny lightly shrugged a shoulder. "I don't know…" pause, "maybe I'm looking for people you know, I've met, counting how many…" Taking a deep breath, she squeezed Tomas's hand. "You're…" another breath, "gay…and I worry for you. For *both* of you."

"Mama." He hugged her. "We're okay. We both are."

"Are you? After what Luiz…"

"No more, Mama." He pulled back and shook his head. "No more of him. That was over three years ago, and he's been dead that long. It's over; we need to let it go. This isn't about him anymore; we're fine."

"Are you?" Jenny stared into her son's dark eyes, looking for some sort of confirmation. "Are you?" she repeated softly.

"Yes, Mama." He stroked her face. "We are."

"Promise me you'll stay that way," she said, not believing him.

"Yes, Mama, we will," he promised. Of course he would, he had no reason to believe they wouldn't be.

"Pedro, do you know what Leon's family are doing?" Jenny turned her attention away from Tomas.

"Probably having it together," he replied, having not stayed in touch.

"And for the first anniversary next March?"

He shrugged. "We'll probably do something to celebrate him."

"Good." Jenny nodded. "That's good. Viv, what about Cabot?"

Viv shuddered delicately. Just the mere mention of her friend's name made her weepy. "I'm sure some of us will do something."

"I'd like to participate in both services, whatever they will be and…" she paused and glanced at Spiros, "I would like the two of you to invite their family over for Christmas dinner."

"What?" Pedro and Viv said in unison. "Here?"

"Yes," Jenny said. "Invite Leon's mother and grandmother, and if Cabot's parents or siblings care, invite them."

"I don't think he had any," Viv replied. "Not any that cared," she corrected. "His parents didn't come near him, and I don't even know if he had siblings."

"Do you know where his parents live?" Carlos asked from beside his wife.

She thought back and took a breath. "No."

"Then we'll invite Leon's family," Jenny said and glanced at the clock. "It's still early, why don't you ring them and find out if they'd be interested in coming. I can send a car for them."

"What! Now?" Pedro exclaimed.

"Yes." Jenny laughed. "Now." She watched her son leave for his own apartment for Leon's mother's number, then turned her attention back to Tomas. "Anyone you'd like to invite?"

"To what? Christmas?" Tomas asked from Roger's arms.

"Yes." Jenny raised her brows. "*Of course* I mean Christmas."

Tomas looked at Roger. "Do we know anyone in New York at the moment?"

Roger shook his head. "No. Freddy's in Miami. I think David, Zack and Adam are in L.A."

Tomas looked at Jenny and gave a limp shrug. "There's no one, Mama."

"That's okay. Just thought I'd ask." She patted his hand.

Pedro came through the door. "She said she'd love to come once I reminded her of who I was and what I'd done."

"The papers are in the office. Newest on top," Jenny told him.

"What?" He stopped at the couch.

"The newspapers are in the office, already folded at the obituaries. Newest on top."

"Oh." He hesitated, looking from the office to his mother, and then he moved. Finding the newspapers in piles, he started with the one on top. His finger moved down each column, stopping at photos, and if he didn't know them, he moved on. Feeling the heavy stone-like lump rise from his chest, he was three papers in when he spotted a familiar name and picture, then found three more in papers further back. Slowly, he walked into the lounge room with the papers in his hands.

"You found some?" Jenny still sat beside Tomas, holding his hand.

"Yeah…" slowly came out of his mouth. "Four regulars, they…" He swallowed that stone-like lump that now sat in his throat. "They would come every night. I haven't seen them since…" He thought back. "Summer. August, September maybe. They used to come every night I was there, and then every few nights, then maybe twice a week, once a week, then not at all." He looked at the four faces, read their names. He'd only ever known them by their first names and never knew their last. "Ah…" His head moved slowly. "I…"

"Yeah…that's how we feel," Tomas said, seeing his brother's sickened expression.

Pedro sat on the couch arm and looked up. "Jesus, Mama. I know these guys."

"As I'm sure many, many more did," Jenny replied. "It's happening to a lot of people." She glanced at Carlos and Viv. "Lost anyone else?"

"Harry," Carlos paused, "he said he's lost a few guys this year, some actors, some staff. Five in total so far. He's not sure what to, though."

"Well…" Jenny reassuringly squeezed Tomas's hand. "Let's give our thanks that we are all still in one piece, and are still with each other and love each other. So, let's get some cheer happening. Who's up for more carols?"

*****

On Christmas morning, Alena woke her Mama and Dada by running into the room and climbing on the bed. She may have only been two, but Mama always left a step stool by the bed so she could climb up. "Mewwy Chwismas," she cried, bouncing up and down. "Pwesents, can we open pwesents?"

"Oh, Alena, stop bouncing," Pedro complained. "What time is it?"

Angie grabbed her alarm clock. "Oh, God, 6:10 in the morning. Alena go back to bed."

"No wanna go back to bed, wanna open pwesents." She bounced some more.

"Alena." Pedro reached out and grabbed her arm. "Enough. Come snuggle with Mama and Dada." He pulled her under the covers. "Grandma and Grandpa aren't up yet, so you can't get to your presents."

"Aw." She pouted. "Me wanna pwesents." Pressing her nose into her daddy's cheek, she repeated herself. "Me wanna pwesents."

"Oh, for God's sake," Angie groaned. "Be quiet, Alena."

"No, Mama be quiet, A-ena no be quiet."

Pedro laughed. How could he not? His daughter was the apple of his eye. "You know, Angie, this is what it's going to be like for the rest of our lives. Alena and any other children we have will be hounding us to get up and have presents." He tickled Alena's stomach, and she giggled.

"I know. But at least now you know what you put your mother through." Angie sighed. "It's still so early."

Pedro grinned at the memories Angie's comment stirred up. "Mama did say by seven-thirty."

"It isn't seven-thirty," she replied.

"By the time we shower and dress and get this one cleaned up, it will be. Come on, Alena, let's get you bathed and into a pretty outfit for Grandma." Flinging back the covers, he bounced out of bed and flew his daughter into her room, pretending she was an airplane.

*****

"Pwesents, pwesents," Diana cried as she bounced on her parents' bed. "Chwismas, Chwismas."

"Oh, for the love of…" Viv started, but burst out laughing instead. Diana's hair was sticking up all over the place, and so was Carlos's when he poked his head out from under the blankets.

"What's going on," he mumbled. "Too early to go upstairs."

"But your daughter wants her pwesents," Viv told him.

"Pwesents, Dada, pwesents." Diana jumped on her father.

"Oomph, watch the goods, Diana. Otherwise, I won't be able to give you brothers or sisters."

"Brovers an' sisters?" Diana's lips quivered. "I want pwesents."

Vi's laughter continued. "Oh, that's a good one. Even she's not interested in more kids. That's two to one Carlos; you're out of luck."

"That's what you think." A wicked look appeared in his eyes.

"Oh, you…" Viv caught the look. "You can't…we can't…you-know-who's here."

"Sooo…? Vivian…" Carlos sang and lunged for her.

"Ah," she cried leaping out of bed and grabbing Diana. "Oh, no you don't."

*****

Tomas sighed deeply. He loved waking up in Roger's arms. There was no other place he wanted to be. No other place he could imagine himself in. It was Roger, or nothing, and he was not about to have, or accept, nothing. This disease was ravaging the gay community, and he didn't want to be a part of it. Didn't want to attend more funerals, more services. Didn't want to lose one more person he knew personally. Didn't want to lose the man he loved.

Roger was it, as Mama had said. His one true love, his one true lover. He didn't want, or need, anyone else to be happy, didn't want, or need, anyone else to love him. Just Roger. He just wanted Roger, and he hoped and prayed every night when he went to sleep, and every morning when he woke up, that he and Roger had a long and happy life.

*****

Upstairs in the penthouse, Jenny rose at 6:30. With the girls old enough to come screaming into a room, it was time to get up just like in the old days of the boys tearing into the lounge room to rip open presents.

After showering and rousing Spiros, she went downstairs and preheated the oven, putting the six small turkeys in at seven. Preparing the vegetables, sauces, and other goodies, she was done by seven-thirty when the kids came screaming into the room.

"Pwesents." Diana and Alena bolted for the tree.

Jenny laughed. "Hold on there, missies. I need to get the camera, and not everyone is here yet."

Pedro and Carlos grabbed their daughters as they ripped open the first presents they came to.

"Hold on, Alena, that may not be your present," Pedro chastised his daughter as he held her to his waist and bent down to read the tag. "It's actually for Diana, so no, you don't get this one."

"Aw, Dada, pwesents." Her bottom lip extended and quivered. It was a look she gave everyone when she wanted her own way.

"You can wait, Alena," he said firmly. "Not everyone is here, and that is *not* your present. You will wait."

"Aw." Her chubby little face screwed up and she burst out crying.

Pedro carried her to the lounge room, where everyone gathered, and handed her to Jenny. "See what you can do, Mama. I'm over this."

Jenny laughed and took her granddaughter. "Just wait until you have more children. It will be worse."

"Ah-ah no way, not if they're all like that," Angie said, rubbing her eyes.

"What's Alena crying for, huh?" Jenny walked over to the mantel where the stockings were hanging. "Let's see what's in Alena's stocking. What did Santa put in Alena's Christmas stocking?"

The tears stopped. "Chwismas stocking?" Alena asked through gulps of air. "Pwesents?"

"Maybe," Jenny said and pulled the stocking from the mantel. "Does

Alena want to see what's inside?" She held it up for her to dig around. "Oooh, what's that?"

"How the hell does she do that?" Angie murmured to Pedro, both amazed that Jenny had gotten Alena to quieten down.

Spiros leant over the back of the couch behind them. "She had three boys to deal with, how do you think she does it?"

They smiled and looked on as Alena pulled out candy canes, and bags of biscuits and popcorn, small story books, and lollipops.

Diana, wanting some of what her cousin was getting, toddled over to her grandmother. "Stocking for Da-anna, Gamma?"

"Of course there's a stocking for Diana." Jenny set Alena down on the couch with her parents. "There's a stocking for everyone. You want to help me hand them out?" Pulling Carlos's, Viv's, and Diana's down, she gave them to Diana. "Can you carry these to Mama and Dada?"

"Ah, huh," Diana murmured and carried them to her parents. "Stockings."

"Yes, stockings." Carlos lifted her up into the couch between them, and they went through theirs.

"And Pedro and Angie." Jenny handed them over. "And Tomas and Roger."

"Thanks, Mama."

"Thanks, Mrs S."

"And Spiros and Jenny."

"My love." Spiros kissed her as she handed his over.

Amidst candy canes and lollipops, presents were handed out. Clothes, books, toys, cologne, whatever anyone had wanted they'd received. And by the time Leon's mother and grandmother arrived at eleven, the room had been cleaned and presents put down in apartments.

"Hello, welcome to our home." Jenny held the door open and ushered them in. "Spiros, take their coats." She looked at the familiar-looking fake fur one Leon's mother was wearing. "Is that—?"

"Yes, it is." Leon's mother grinned. "He left us his clothes, and we've been wearing these ever since. Aren't they delectable?"

Jenny laughed. "They certainly are. Come in." She introduced her family.

"I'm Betty, and this is my mother, Winifred," Leon's mother said.

"Welcome, come and sit in front of the fire." Jenny led the way as the girls looked inquisitively on. "We have Christmas cookies, freshly baked yesterday. We have an assortment of drinks, and lunch will be ready in an hour or so."

"Oh, this is delightful," Betty said, taking a spot by the fire and looking at the goodies on the coffee table. "A nice bit of sherry would be lovely." For the next hour, she regaled them with stories of Leon. "He was an ambitious child. Always wanted to do everything and go everywhere. He always said nothing was going to stop him from what he wanted to do, and he wanted to do everything. And he did it in the most flamboyant fashion he could."

"He certainly did," Pedro said. "I met him the week *Studio 69* opened. We were both new staff and hit it off as friends. He was always talking about wanting to be in movies and be an actor. He always encouraged the rest of us to try new things, and he did it all in the most amazing clothes."

Betty laughed. "That's my boy. He always did have a flair for the dramatics and great clothing. We kept most of it, but obviously, some had to go. I mean, we just weren't going to fit into lime green hot pants. Not at our age."

Everyone laughed, and the stories went on through lunch. Before the roast turkey and vegetables, they paused to hold hands and murmur a small prayer before saying Amen.

"One time, he called me up and asked me if I wanted to go to that new musical *Love Machine*. I said, child, why would you even need to ask, you know I love stories about love, and he said, but Mama, it's a *gay* love story, and I said, what's wrong with that? I love bright and cheerful love stories."

"Oh, no." Jenny laughed, knowing full well she was referring to another meaning of the word gay. Betty and Winifred were sitting to her right with Carlos and Viv next to them, and Tomas and Roger across from them, with Pedro and Angie to their left.

Betty studied Tomas and Roger. "Speaking of gay, you two are, aren't you?"

Tomas and Roger traded glances before replying. "Yes, ma'am."

"Mmm, mmm," she murmured as if she knew she was right. "Don't you boys let this disease get you like it got my Leon. His father up and left when he was two, and I had to move in with Mama to survive. Being raised by two women, it's no wonder he turned out with such a flair for the dramatic, but no matter what lifestyle he chose, he was my son, and I loved him. Make sure your mama loves you and looks after you."

"Oh, I do," Jenny said while staring adoringly at her boys. "Absolutely I do."

Over dessert, they learned about Leon's life, and come five o'clock they bade Betty and Winifred adieu. They needed to be home by six, and it was a way to go.

"You don't know how much this means to me, child." Betty grasped Jenny's hands as they stood in the doorway of the penthouse. "Leon always came home for Christmas if he wasn't working, but this is the first year without him, and talking to people that worked with him and knew him has helped immensely." She grabbed Pedro's hand as well.

"I'm glad," Jenny said. "I'm glad that we could help ease that grief."

"Thank you, child," Betty replied. "Thank you so much for thinking of our Leon this Christmas. He always spoke highly of you," she told Pedro.

"And I always thought highly of him," he said sadly. "I miss him."

Betty nodded. "So do I, child. So do I."

"We need to get going," Winifred reminded her daughter. "Come now; we'll miss our church service."

"Goodbye." Jenny walked them out to the lift. "We'll be thinking of you both tonight. All three of you."

"Thank you, child, and I'll be praying for yours." She gave Jenny a knowing nod.

Jenny knew what she meant. "Thank you, so will I."

*****

On New Year's Eve, Pedro did the first shift at 69. He'd be working from 6pm until midnight when Master Z would take over for the next six hours. The whole family was there with the girls wearing their noise cancelling headphones. Carlos and Viv caught up with new friends from her business ventures. Angie was hanging out with Maggie as Mike was working too. Jenny and Spiros were with the girls and dancing with them, and Tomas and Roger were surprised by their old Miami friends.

"Hey, you guys are still here." David, Zack and Adam came up behind them and slapped them on the back.

"Hey, guys." Roger gave them man hugs. "What are you doing here? Thought you were in L.A."

"Yeah, we were, are, just thought we'd pop over to The Big Apple and check out your brother-in-law play." He glanced up at the stage. "Glad we came." They watched Pedro dance, flip records, and wave the crowd on. "Figured with everyone dying we'd better get a look-in, in case something happens," David said.

Roger turned his head to look at him. "How is it in L.A.?"

"There are a few death notices, obviously no one we know, or knew, but when you know what to look for, it's hard not to see it glaring right back at you. I heard ten more had gone from Miami."

A deep sigh left Roger and he flagged. "Yeah. This month alone."

"Yeah." David sadly shook his head and looked around the club. His friends were silent, but the place was still jumping. "And a whole lot more are going to go. There have been quite a few in San Fran I hear."

"I know. My mother-in-law gets all of the major papers, hundreds of them are gone."

"The Castro *is* a gay neighbourhood, it's going to hit it hard," David said.

"Harder than Miami, clearly," Zack said above the noise. "How many more are we going to lose?"

"Judging from how ill everyone looked when I was there in

November, I'd say hundreds. And there will also be ones we don't know personally, but others do," David told him.

"That sucks." Roger swiped a hand through his hair. "This whole bloody thing bloody sucks. Why just gay people for fuck's sake?" Slamming his hands onto his hips, he looked around. "Why not women, gay or straight, why not straight men, why not old people? Why do we all have to be young? Why is it only *young, gay men* getting this thing?"

"Don't know," David replied sadly. "But we're looking out for number one and sticking with each other. Staying celibate for a while until it all blows over."

"And if it doesn't?" Tomas asked from beside Roger. "What if it doesn't?"

No one had thought of that. This disease not blowing over. Not stopping, not leaving them alone. They had no idea what it was, or why it was affecting them, but they had all hoped it would blow over at some point.

Sitting on the sidelines was Stan Kosnov, a 69 regular since it opened, and he knew it would be his last visit. He'd struggled to get there, having a lover come along for the party, and while Stan sat on the side, he danced up a storm. But Stan didn't mind. He'd just needed help getting there and then getting home. He was too weak to do it himself; but was still able to sit, drink, and have a good time.

The music was what it was all about. The freedom to express himself as his real self was thrilling, to say the least. It was something he couldn't do during the day. As a businessman for nearly twenty years, he'd worn suits all day and partied all night. His co-workers had no clue about his nightlife, and had no clue why he'd up and quit his job two months ago. But he'd been told he had cancer, something called Kaposi's sarcoma, and it was killing him. And unfortunately, because his immune system was down, he'd developed other problems as well, like CMV, Cachexia, and some sort of pneumonia.

The doctors had bombarded him with every medicine they had, but it barely touched the surface, and the cancer had spread too much. So, he'd quit his job and spent the remainder of the time seeing the sights and travelling with his partner who was sticking around. He'd loved him even more for that, and paid for everything to show his thanks. After all the years he'd worked, he had quite a fat bank balance and could afford to blow it the last few months.

He was weak, thin, unable to eat much, was wasting away, but could still love music, still love 69, and still love the spectacular DJ, Pedro Stefan. He'd watched all of the boys' movies with his lover, and even re-enacted some. But the one thing he wished was, that he'd had a night with Pedro. Even if it was just sucking his cock.

Gently swaying to the music, he dreamed of nights he'd danced and nights he'd loved. His days didn't matter; they were just work. It was the nights that meant everything to him. The music, the dancing, the feeling of being alive and free to be whoever he'd wanted to be. Even to the point he'd fucked a couple of the waiters and other partygoers. They didn't care, it was the '70s, and they *and* things were all free and easy. He missed them, though. Leon the roller-skating waiter, the hot hunky moustached construction worker who'd taken his fancy, the hot African American who was a cop by day, and he'd even had a gorgeous older Spaniard who'd dropped by once or twice. And none of them ever said no. None of them ever turned down a quick fuck, or suck in the toilets, or even a three or foursome in the hallway.

Sex and drugs and music made them alive, and they did whatever they wanted, whether it was in the toilets, out in the alley, or even on the dance floor. Not to mention the secret party room Eddie had downstairs, where only the most privileged attendees got to go. If you were a regular, you received a gold-embossed invitation to the party room, and party they did, into the wee hours and then some. But attendance to the room had waned. The regulars had disappeared, and new invitations had to go out. And being as sick as he was, he knew he'd never visit the room again after tonight. Eddie had agreed to let him watch and only participate in the drugs and music. The fucking was no longer possible, and with word on the street of fags dying off, things were getting a little tighter. Not that it mattered; he wouldn't be there for too much longer. He'd say goodbye to everyone tonight. He spied the other porn star brothers across the room and imagined fucking every one of them. And he didn't mind the boys Roger was talking to either.

"I hope you stay as safe as possible," Roger said. "Wherever this thing goes, get the hell away from it and stay away from sex."

"Is that what's really causing it, though? So many have cancer, pneumonia, hell," Adam looked around, "I've heard of guys getting STDs in their mouth."

"Well, that just goes to show how sex is transmitting diseases, doesn't it," Roger said. "But whatever this thing is, whatever's causing it to only happen in gay men, it's better to be safe than sorry. I just thank God I've always been safe." He ran a hand through his hair. "I've got my fingers crossed that this doesn't happen to us." He glanced at Tomas and pulled him close, his arm going around his shoulder. "'Cause it's scaring the absolute hell out of me, and I don't know how many more friends I can bury."

"Yeah, I hear ya," David said. "We'll keep you in our thoughts and hope it doesn't affect you guys. You're the first gay married couple we know, and we live in hope that one day it can happen for the rest of us, but," he let out a sigh, "if this thing keeps happening, we may not ever get to experience being married. I really hope you two survive this, whatever the hell it is."

"How's everyone doin' tonight?" Pedro asked over the microphone. Screams and cheers thundered through the place. "It's an hour until midnight and it's 1981, so get your groove thing on and party till we count down the clock. Here's *Celebration* by Kool and The Gang." Once the song started playing, he took a few minutes to towel down and knock back a litre of fluid. He would have sweated out ten times that, but his stomach couldn't hold much more at any one time. Only an hour to go.

He saw his parents on the dance floor with Alena and Diana, Angie and Maggie egging the girls on to dance, and they did, jumping up and down and clapping their hands. Watching Angie swing her hair around, they tried to imitate, but made everyone laugh instead. He watched Roger and Tomas say goodbye to their friends and walk over to their booth at the side of the room, and watched Carlos and Viv dance over to their daughter.

He spied Bev, Sara, and Martine. They'd been regulars from the day 69 had opened and had stayed loyal and faithful since, regardless of the number of other clubs that had opened up that year. They always came to 69 during the week. And then there was Stan, another regular, who wasn't dancing. Pedro hadn't seen him in weeks, but there he was on the sidelines looking like a shadow of his former self, sipping cocktail after cocktail and swaying along to the music. He knew it. He could see it. See how ill Stan looked, how weak, how… skeletal he was. And Roger and Tomas had told him that's how all their friends had looked before they died. So he knew, knew Stan didn't have long, and soon he'd see his name in the obituaries that his mother collected. He'd also noticed there were a few more missing, but they could have moved on to another club…or they could be dead.

Finishing his break, he hit the decks.

Tomas watched his brother come back from his break before turning to his husband. "I can't believe we're still here," he told Roger as they quietly sipped their drinks in the family booth that Eddie had reserved for them year after year.

"Why's that?" Roger asked, a slight frown on his face.

"Considering everyone we know is sick, or dead, so many from *Seralift*, including that black guy Braden. Jesus, I watched you make that movie with him, and just days later we're hooking up. Now he's dead. So are the other stars from *Seralift*. So are your friends. Why aren't we? Why hasn't something happened to us? *We're* gay." Tomas sighed, sickened with fear of catching something, *anything,* that all of Roger's friends and ex-co-workers had gotten.

"Because we've been careful, T." Roger put his arm around his husband's shoulders. "Everyone I did a movie with we used condoms, we were continually tested, *we* have been safe every time."

"Yeah…but…" Tomas trailed off. "Did you see Mama's face at Thanksgiving and Christmas? There was *something* in her eyes. There always has been, ever since Luiz poisoned me. And she keeps talking about the ramifications of what he did. What if she's right? What if what Luiz did has somehow made me susceptible to getting *this thing, this gay man disease*, whatever the hell it is?"

"We can't think like that," Roger chided. "We have to stay positive. As long as we're safe, we're okay."

"But what if it's not sexually transmitted?" Tomas went on. "What if it's a disease that you can catch from sneezing on someone, or touching their hand, or hugging or kissing them? God Roger, the amount of hands we shake and people we hug. What if we have it? What if we have whatever this disease is? What if it kills us? What if it kills you or me? I don't want to live without you, Roger, I love you. I want to grow old and grey with you and celebrate birthdays and anniversaries. What if—"

"Enough," Roger cut him off. "Tomas, you are working yourself into a frenzy of what ifs. Look at you; you look freaked out. Are you on something?"

Tomas stared dazedly at him. "No," he said tearfully. "I'm scared. I am *so* scared, Roger. I don't want to die, and I don't want to lose you."

"Aw, T, come here." Roger pulled his husband into his arms. "I love you. Nothing's going to happen to us."

"I bet that's what they all said, and now they're sick, or dead," Tomas replied, buried in Roger's shoulder. "I'm so scared, Roger."

Roger sighed. "So am I, T," he finally said, rubbing his lover's back.

"Okay everyone, thirty minutes left until midnight and it becomes 1981," Pedro called out. "Make sure you know where your partner is because time will go quickly. Make sure you have enough drink to cheer the New Year in. Make sure you've got your party poppers and streamers."

Carlos only vaguely heard his brother as he swung Viv around, then he grabbed Diana and swung her too, to her delight. "Diana wants to dance," he sang, sitting her on his hip and taking Viv into his other arm. "Diana wants to dance with Mama and Dada?"

"Da-anna dance." She bounced happily on her daddy's hip, clapping her hands, and being hugged and kissed by her parents.

"And there's Gamma and Gampa." Carlos pointed to his parents in each other's arms dancing up a storm. Definitely not something they used to do back on Mykonos. But then, they'd all done a lot of things they wouldn't have done back on Mykonos. Get into the porn business, move to America, get married and have kids. *Hell, if I was still back on Mykonos I would definitely not be married with a baby,* he thought. *I'd still be making my way through all the women, and I wouldn't be happy and settled and in love with the most amazing woman on the planet.*

Jenny glanced over at Carlos and saw the love emanating from his eyes as he gazed at his wife and daughter. *God, they're such a beautiful couple,* she thought looking at Diana in their arms. *And look at my beautiful grandbaby, she looks like both of them.* Such a gorgeous golden-haired family. She smiled, happy that Carlos had found a woman to love and be loved by. *Considering his antics back home, I'm surprised he's found someone. Maybe her being sixteen years older was what he needed. An older woman to pull him into line, and he proposed before finding out she was pregnant, so it was for love, not for a child.* But just one look at them and she knew they were meant for each other.

"When are you and Mike going to get together?" Angie yelled over the music to Maggie. "It's been three years."

"I know," Maggie yelled back. "But with the way my parents raised me, I won't be having sex until I'm married. Besides," she spun around, "Mike knows I want to finish school and get a job. And he wants to get a better job than this one. We're both saving up for an apartment."

"You're moving in together?" Angie asked.

"Maybe." Maggie shimmied up and down. "Once school's over, and we both have jobs. We might be living together by this time next year."

"Only one more year to go then." Angie giggled.

"And I can't wait to be out of school, yeah." Maggie threw her arms up in the air.

Jenny saw the girls laughing; Alena between them, hanging on to her mother's hands, dressed in the little sparkly party dress that Jenny had given her for Christmas. There was *no way* she wasn't giving out pretty little party dresses hand over fist to her granddaughters. She'd missed out on it with her Alena, and was making up for it with theirs. If she was going to blow the Papadopoulos estate, it would be on her babies and grandbabies.

Her attention caught hold of Tomas and Roger over at their booth, sitting in each other's arms. They were passionately discussing something with Tomas looking as if he was in tears, and Roger close to it. She fretted, knowing they had caught up with old friends earlier, no doubt talking about lost friends and co-workers. She prayed every night that her babies stayed safe, and every morning thanked God that they were still with her, cherishing every moment she could with them, loving seeing them so happy and in love. But not now; now they looked depressed.

"We have five minutes to go until midnight everyone," Pedro called out. "Get your partners, get your streamers, get your drinks now, we are counting down in four minutes and thirty-eight seconds."

"Whoo," screamed through the crowd and Jenny headed for her boys.

"Tomas, Roger, everything okay?" She sat beside her son and slid an arm around him. "Everything okay?"

Tomas quickly wiped his tears away. "Not really. But it's New Year, so let's leave it, okay, Mama."

"Is everything okay between the two of you?" She didn't take a brush-off from anyone, let alone her family.

"We're okay, Mrs S," Roger replied. "Just scared about this gay thing."

"So am I, my baby boys, so am I." She patted Tomas's hand. "Let's get ready for the countdown. Come on, if you have friends, invite them over." Standing, she led them over to Spiros and corralled the rest of the family in, telling Carlos and Viv to bring their friends over. They went in search and came back two minutes later just in time to get glasses of champagne from the waiters rolling by.

"These are my in-laws," Roger introduced his friends. "Jenny and Spiros Stephanopoulos. Mr and Mrs S, David, Zack and Adam."

They all shook hands. "Pleasure to meet you boys," Jenny said. "Happy New Year. I hope it's better for you all."

"Thanks, Mrs Stephanopoulos," David said. "Happy New Year to you, too."

"Okay, here we go, people in the house, *Studio 69* is on the countdown. 10, 9, 8, 7, 6, 5, 4, 3, 2, 1 Happy New Year," Pedro yelled and left the mic to Master Z to jump off stage and kiss his wife and daughter as the first strains of Auld Lang Syne wafted across the room.

The kissing and hugging went on for five minutes before Pedro departed to shower and change. His shift was over, and it was time to leave.

"You boys have a place to stay while you're here?" Roger asked David as they gathered coats and bags.

"Yeah, managed to bunk into a friend's place for a couple more days, but then we'll be going back to L.A. Wanna catch up before we go?" David asked.

"Sure. I'll give you our number." Roger dug out his compendium from his bag and scribbled down their details on the notepad before ripping the page off. "Our address and number. Let us know when you want to get together."

"Will do." David slapped him on the arm. "We're gonna go hit the streets; see how The Big Apple celebrates New Year. Night everyone." He waved a hand at Jenny and Spiros and all who stood near them.

"Goodnight boys, be safe," Jenny called.

Pedro came out from his quick shower. "Babe, I gotta talk to someone before we go. Do you mind?"

"What? No, go right ahead. Alena still wants to dance."

"Okay, back in a minute." He strode across the dance floor, getting new year's wishes and hugs from the partygoers before reaching Stan's booth. "Stan."

"Pedro, my darling boy." Stan's eyes lit up when he saw the Greek God stop at his seating area. "Good show as always, sit, sit." He motioned to the seat beside him.

Pedro sat and got to the point. "Are you dying, Stan?"

Stan blinked, and the music faded into the background, leaving them in a silent bubble. "Yes."

"How long?"

"Not very."

"Do you have the gay disease?"

Stan sighed. "I don't know. I don't *think* so. I have cancer, low blood cells, and a couple of opportunistic infections because of the cancer."

"Oh." Pedro looked down. "I'm sorry."

"So am I, my dear boy. It's not nice having your life cut short."

"No, no I guess it wouldn't be. I'm sorry."

Stan squeezed Pedro's hand. "I had my fun and believe me, most of it happened here. You've been the light that drove me, my darling boy."

A sad smile lit across Pedro's lips. "That's sweet, Stan. Are you here with someone?"

"Yes, my lover, Gary." He pointed to the African with the dreadlocks in the crowd. "I tend to go for the black men. Had a thing with Leon, the waiter, and that black cop that was still in the closet, but, of course, there was the Spanish bullfighter..."

Pedro slowly looked at him, his brain ticking over, his eyes narrowing. "You what?"

Stan laughed. "Oh, my dear boy, didn't you know people were hooking up with people every time we came here?"

"Wait..." Pedro sat straight. "You hooked up with Leon, *our waiter.* And which black cop and Spanish bullfighter?"

Stan thought wistfully for a moment. "Jamal...I think the cop's name was, and the delicious bullfighter was an older man. Jet-black hair, what was his name...oh, that's right, DeLuca, but I called him de luckiest man on the planet. Get it, DeLuca, de luckiest..."

"Yeah, Stan, I got it. Great joke," Pedro managed, disgust crawling up his insides at the catastrophe that was this disease and the rampant free sex at the club. "Take care of yourself, Stan."

"Not much point to that now, my dear boy, is there?" Stan sipped his fiftieth cocktail, planning to be thoroughly intoxicated before sunrise.

"No...well...still...it's been good knowing you, Stan." Pedro squeezed his hand. "And I'm sorry about all of this. Life's a bitch sometimes."

"And then you die, my darling. Now go and join that beautiful family of yours." He shooed him away. "Go."

Standing, Pedro glanced down, hearing the music come to life again as their bubble disappeared. "Goodbye, Stan."

Looking up, Stan smiled. "Goodbye, my darling boy, and Happy New Year to you and your family."

With a sad nod, Pedro made his way back to his family and told them the shocking news. That Stan had been with Leon, Jamal, and Stephano, and now he was sick and dying too. He pulled his coat on, shaking his head. "Whatever this is, it's spreading, and everyone's screwed everyone else."

Jenny shook her head in disappointment. "How appalling that people can't be careful when it comes to sex," she said. "Why can't people just be safe?"

They made their way outside and gazed up and down 54th Street. People lined the sidewalks to get in; people roamed the street to celebrate. Leaving their cars, they decided to go for a walk to see how everyone else was celebrating the beginning of 1981.

January 1981

In the morning edition of the New York local paper, Pedro found Stan Kosnov's obituary. It was the fifth day of January. Five days since Pedro had seen Stan at 69 for New Year's Eve. Five days since he had heard anything.

Stan was forty-four years old, a banker by day, and there was a notice from his firm, thanking him for all the years he'd worked. Friends and family gave their prayers. There would be no funeral or service; Stan had been cremated. There was a loving tribute from his partner Gary, and a picture of Stan in one of his suits.

That night, when Pedro went to work, he showed Mike and his other colleagues the paper. "You guys remember Stan? He's gone, just like that."

"Yeah, he was here for New Year's, wasn't he?" Mike was wiping out glasses ready for the night. "He *loved* you. Used to hang out at the front of the stage just to watch you play."

A sad sigh escaped from Pedro. "Yeah. A lot of people did. But now they're gone. Where are they all going? Are they hitting up another club, or dying off like my brother's friends in Miami?"

"How many are gone now?" Mike asked, lining the glasses on the back counter. "As many as here?"

"Forty-six in three years alone," Pedro replied, staring at the paper. "And look at how many more men are dead. There are more men than women in here. Almost four times as many."

"That's rough, man," Mike said, watching Eddie walk up to the bar. "See the obit for Stan?"

"Yeah, yeah, poor bastard. Took his life by going out the only way he wanted. With an overdose. It was his way or the highway."

"Wait…what! *How* do you know that?" Pedro's head swung in Eddie's direction. "How do you know that? It says nothing about drugs, just that he had cancer and pneumonia."

"Ah…well…" Eddie blushed. "He may have wanted to go out his own way here at 69 and ah…I may have helped him out…a little."

"How did you help him out, Eddie?" Pedro straightened. "Did you give him drugs? Did you kill him?"

"I didn't." Eddie put his hands up in defence. "Stan came to me with a proposition. He knew he was sick and dying and wanted to know if he could spend his last night here seeing in the New Year. When I questioned him, he asked if he could overdose. He'd bring his own drugs, but he wanted to spend his last night partying and high, and end it all in the place he loved most. So, I let him down into the party room about 6 a.m. because the party was still going on down there and he OD'd on his own drugs. Then that partner of his carried him out to their car and took him home where he reported the death. That was in the paper a few days back. Sick man takes own life. They left his name out of it."

Pedro stared, dumbfounded at what he was hearing. "You what?"

Eddie was shamefaced. "I was just doing a regular a favour. He was sick and dying, Pedro, he wanted his last night on Earth to be at a place he loved, surrounded by people he knew. I just helped him achieve that."

"Jesus fucking Christ, Eddie," Pedro spat. "It's bad enough what already goes on here, the sex, the party room, but helping someone to kill himself."

"He was already dying," Eddie argued.

"And so did Leon, and Devron and God knows how many other 69 partygoers who all had sex with each other and are now all dead or dying. This has become a cesspool of debauchery, Eddie. Jesus, have *you* been fucking them too? Are *you* going to die next?" Pedro was incredulous at all going on around him.

Some of the staff crowded around to hear the argument. No one went up against Eddie Monteif, especially if you valued your job.

"Now, hang on a minute, Stephanopoulos." Eddie put a hand out to stop him. "You've been here since '77, and I've been quite generous in letting you have time off over the years, but what I do to help my patrons is nobody's business but mine."

"Well, maybe I don't want to be a part of it anymore," Pedro yelled. "All this death and dying. How many more are we going to lose? How many more will get sick because of the sex and drugs you allow here down in that party room of yours? The filth, the germs, the disease that's spreading. Have *you* got it, Eddie? Are *you* going to get sick and die next? Are you a part of it? Because I don't want to be. My brother's friends are dropping like flies, friends of Carlos and Viv, people my family knew, Leon, Stan. Jesus, how many more people have to die because none of you can keep your fucking dicks in your pants? It's either up each other's ass, or down each other's throat. It's disgusting, and I don't know how much longer I can tolerate it. If you don't clean up, Eddie, I'm done." He stormed out of the room, down the hall, and smashed through the back door into the alley where his tears fell for Stan, for Leon, Jamal, Cabot, and all of Tomas and Roger's friends. And then fell, out of fear, of losing his brother and brother-in-law.

"What are you looking at?" Eddie barked at the staff watching on. "Get back to work." He took the same path as Pedro and found him sobbing against the trunk of his car in the alley. "You think it doesn't scare me too? I've got regulars dropping like flies, new clubs competing for the celebrities, people always asking me to get them any kind of drug they want. How could I say no to Stan? He was already dying. He wanted to go out his way while he still could. While *he* was still in control. While *he* could still make his own choices, and tell people what *he* wanted to be done after his death." He stood with his hands in his jacket pockets, rocking from one foot to the other.

Pedro wiped his face and looked up. "Doesn't make it right, though."

"Yeah." Eddie shifted his foot. "I know. Neither does death. Don't you want to go out on your own terms instead of letting some non-existent thing called God decide for you? God gave Stan cancer and other diseases, just like God is killing off all our regulars and your family's friends. God doesn't care, so why shouldn't you do it your way? Stan made everything official right down to the letter. He did it his way and didn't leave it up to anything or anyone else. And as for you leaving, what is it you want? More money? I already pay you two grand a night."

Pedro sadly shook his head. "I don't know what I want, Eddie. Not when it comes to my life. What I *do* want is for my brother and brother-in-law to be safe, and for friends to stop dying. How many more? How many more have to die? How many more do we have to lose? I don't even know if…"

"What?" Eddie asked, concerned for his star DJ's welfare. If he lost Pedro, he'd lose the club.

"I don't even know how long I can go on in this job, at this club. I love music, but I just can't…" Pedro sighed, and his body sagged against the car. "I don't know how long I can keep doing this…maybe once Angie finishes school we can…" a shrug, "I don't know…travel more, see the world again, visit Mykonos again." He finally looked at Eddie. "I'm grateful for the opportunity you've given me. But I just don't know how much longer I can do it. Not with friends and co-workers dying off. And how long is disco going to last before the next wave of whatever comes along? How long is the club going to last? We've already been shut down three times, Eddie. You've gone to jail for tax evasion, how much longer can we last?"

"Dunno, Pedro my boy, but I'm not giving up. So, look, we're gonna work hard for however long we need to, and keep making it a success until we can't do it no more. You got that?" Eddie pointed his finger in emphasis.

Pedro shook his head. "Sorry, Eddie. You have me until Angie graduates, and then I'll decide if I'm staying. Because I don't know if I can or not."

Eddie sighed and brushed a hand through his thinning hair. "Well, at least you've given me advance warning."

"And that's all I can give you, Eddie, because," pause, "I don't even know what's going to happen after that. Life is too short, and I have a wife and daughter to worry about. My family, my brother…"

"Have they been doing okay?" Eddie asked. "They didn't really look happy the other night."

"They're scared, like the rest of us. Their friends are dead; they're worried they'll get it. It's damn frightening."

"Yeah…yeah. I know what you mean." Eddie took a breath. "Listen, kid, what's happening sucks, especially with it hitting so close to home, but I need you here, and now you've told me about all of this, I'll keep it in mind. But since you're here, can you get dressed and get on stage? We're still relying on you, kid. You're the life of the ball. You're what draws in the crowd, for what crowd there *is* left. So, get in your gold shorts and get ready to wow the people that do come in."

With a sad smile and a deep sigh, Pedro went to change.

*****

A week later, Carlos walked into his apartment, shrugged off his coat, and dumped it on the side table along with his bag. He'd been attending film classes off and on for over a year, learning the ins and outs of movie making. He'd also done short courses in business, accounting and managing, as well as learning about the law where running a company was concerned. Now that Viv was in business for herself, ideas had flowed thick and fast. And with a renewed interest in filming Viv's ads, he'd been talking to Jenny about setting up a company to run Viv's business, and manage the family's careers, plus keeping the apartment building as an investment if they ever went back to Mykonos.

"Hey, babe." He kissed Viv hello then swung Diana into the air. "And how's Diana today?"

"Good, Dada, Mama read book," she said as her Dada kissed both of her cheeks.

"And what book are we reading?" He gently placed her back on her mother's lap and sat beside them.

"*The Cat Sat on the Mat,*" Diana said, rugged up in a warm snuggly jumper that Gamma had knitted for her, a turtleneck top, blue jeans, and little sparkly pink shoes.

"There's a pile of mail on the kitchen counter," Viv said, kissing Diana before setting her on the couch between them. "And the kettle's about to boil for coffee."

"Oh, great, I could do with something warm." He wandered over to the kitchen and got two mugs ready, then poured the boiling water over the heaped coffee and watched it melt. Giving it a mix, he added sugar and milk to Viv's, and a touch of sugar to his. Tucking the mail under his arm, he carried the mugs over and handed Viv's to her. "Careful, Diana, mugs are hot."

"Me, Dada?" she asked, looking at the steaming mugs of liquid goodness. "Me drink?"

He placed his mug and the mail on the coffee table in front of the couch. "Diana want a drink? Some milk?"

"Mmm, mmm," she agreed with a nod of her curly head.

Back in the kitchen, he poured some milk into her sippy cup and returned to the lounge. "Here you go, Bubba, some milk."

"Ta, Dada," she thanked him and took her cup, only sipping when her mother or father did, her blue eyes going back and forth to them, watching for when they drank.

"Ah, let's see what we've got here." Carlos picked up the mail and flicked through it.

"There's one from Harry I see." Viv slipped her arm around Diana.

"Really? Why would he be sending me mail? Usually, he just calls." Finding the bulky envelope, he ripped it open and pulled out several sheets of paper, one of which was a letter, the others were full-page newspaper sheets.

"*Dear Carlos, how are you my boy, staying safe in this time of a new year I hope. I'm sending my condolences to you and Viv because Connie DeLuca has died…*"

"What?" Viv looked up from Diana's book to see Carlos silently reading the rest of the letter. "What does it say?"

He finished reading in shock, and his head shook slightly, barely moving. "What the hell…when…what the hell…?" Glancing over the other papers, he found obituaries. "Jesus Christ," he breathed. "Jesus bloody Christ."

"Carlos, tell me. Let me read it," Viv said, touching his arm. Connie had been a friend, along with Harriet DeVille, and while they'd known each other for many years, had recently lost contact except for the odd letter here and there.

In a daze, he looked at Viv and silently handed the paper over. He watched her read it silently, her eyes widening, before her face crumpled in tears.

Diana sat silently, her head going back and forth to her parents, worry creasing her beautiful face, tears filling her beautiful eyes.

Turning the letter over, Viv looked at Carlos, unable to speak. What she had read was one of the saddest most painful things. And she'd lost a good friend because of it. Seeing the other papers in his hand, she reached out for them, and he gave them to her. All were incredibly sad, incredibly touching, and almost a page each.

"What have I done?" Carlos whispered. "What have I done?"

Viv looked up. "What do you mean, what have *you* done? You haven't done anything. This is nothing to do with you; it's not your fault."

"It is, it *is* my fault. I could have stopped it. I could have done something." The panic rose from his gut and made its way up his insides until it choked him. "I could have done something. I could have told her. I could have…" He was on his feet, prowling around the room, hands on hips, tears falling. "I could have stopped this. I could have told her."

"Told her what?" Viv was on her feet and walking beside him as he moved. "This had nothing to do with you."

"It has *everything* to do with me. I let all of you talk me out of telling her. When we found out DeLuca was in Leon's black book I wanted to warn her. But no, I listened to you and now look. This is your fault, my fault, everyone's fault. I—" He became flustered, his breathing rapid, his head crazy. "I need to see Mama." Snatching the papers from Viv's hands, he raced upstairs and into the penthouse to find the rest of the family getting ready for dinner.

"Unca Carwos." Alena ran over to him, expecting a hug.

"Ah, not now Alena. Angie, can you take her down and stay with Viv? I need to talk to my family. And keep Viv there too."

Angie hurried over for her daughter. "Why do I need to—"

"Just do it," he snapped as she picked up Alena.

"Carlos," Spiros warned.

Carlos softened, seeing the fear on his sister-in-law's face. "Please, it's important. Viv will tell you. She'll need someone to talk to."

"Okay." Angie swallowed, a little scared at having been told off, and carried a teary-eyed Alena out the door.

"I don't appreciate you talking to her that way, Carlos," Pedro told his older brother. Tomas was by his side, Jenny and Spiros by their sides, while Roger was across the table getting it ready for dinner.

"And *I* don't appreciate being talked out of something I want to do that I think is *vitally* important," Carlos said darkly, walking over to his family. "I told you, little brother. I *warned* you that Connie had a right to know what her husband was getting up to but *no*," he waved a finger at his brother, "you all convinced me it was none of my business and to keep out of it. And *now* look, everything is ruined because I listened to you, and Mama and Papa." He glanced from his father to his mother. "*This* time you were wrong, Mama. It *wasn't* the best thing to do. Staying out of other people's business *was not* the right thing to do." His voice grew louder, "it's all *your* fault, it's all Pedro's and Papa's fault," he yelled. "It's *my* fault for listening to you and not going with my gut instinct. Not doing what *I* thought was right. What I knew to be best."

"Carlos your mother's not to blame," Spiros interjected.

"We're all to blame." Carlos whirled on his father, waving the papers in front of everyone. "We are all to blame for what happened because we were the ones who knew better and did nothing about it. Here," he shoved the papers at his mother, "read all about what *we* did. What *we* caused. And I hope you feel as damn guilty as I do because *we* did this."

Jenny took the papers and quickly read the letter. "Oh, my God." Her hand flew to her chest. "Oh, my God, no."

"Yes," Carlos spat. *"That,"* he thrust his finger at the papers, "is what *we* did." He turned away, stalking, moving away. "*That* is what *we* did. *That* is what happened because *I* allowed myself to be talked out of telling her, of *warning* her." He moved into the sitting room, prowling, moving on the spot, turning, and not really going anywhere because his brain was focussed on spitting out words. "It's all my fault, all my fault." He was crazed. "All my fault for listening to you, because if I didn't, they wouldn't be dead. *None of them* would be dead, and I wouldn't be feeling so goddamn fucking guilty. So guilty, so guilty…"

Jenny looked from the papers to her son, seeing him grow more frenzied. She sent a worried look at Spiros, who knew instinctively what to do and went over to his son.

"Carlos, nothing is your fault," he said, wanting to calm his son.

"*Of course it's all my fault,*" Carlos screamed, spit flying from his mouth, hands clenched by his sides. "It's all my fault for listening to my family and not telling Connie when I should have. She'd still be alive if I'd told her. All I had to do was ring her and tell her that her husband was screwing men, and at least two of them were dead or dying. That's all I needed to do, and I let you lot talk me out of it. And now they're all dead because of you lot and because of me, and now his baby boy doesn't have a father. He's lost his father because of me…" He ran out of steam and fell into his father's arms as Spiros pulled him into them.

Watching her son fall apart in his father's arms made Jenny's heart ache. The loss was too great, and after her son's words, she felt the guilt. Looking at the paperwork, tears fell down her cheeks. Hindsight was a wonderful thing. You could look back on your mistakes and know not to do them again next time, know better *for* next time. But there would be no next time for the DeLuca family. There would be no better. Life was over, and Jenny felt the heavy burden of guilt. Knew what Carlos was saying. Knew what it meant, and it hurt deeply because, in hindsight, they could have stopped most of the bloodshed from happening. Could have stopped the diseases from spreading.

With a glance at her two younger sons standing in front of her and seeing them mouth 'what's wrong', she handed Harry's letter over to Pedro.

With Tomas looking over Pedro's shoulder, they read it. A hand flew to Tomas's mouth, his face crumpling at the news.

Pedro came to the end and silently handed it back to his mother, staring at Carlos still sobbing in their father's arms. Connie had been one of his ladies. The woman that helped him get away from the shooting in Mykonos to Athens in her Louis Vuitton trunk. Her son had worked with Carlos at the resort bar on Mykonos, but they'd lost contact after Greece and the wedding, and once they'd moved to New York, except for an odd phone call or letter that Viv received.

Letting out a shuddering gasp, Pedro looked from his brother and father to Tomas, pulling him into his arms, shocking him with the ferociousness of his love. "I love you, Tomas, don't ever forget that." He held on fiercely, not wanting to let go as Tomas hugged back.

Jenny watched her boys as Viv silently came through the door and hurried over to her husband. She took him into her arms, and they both sobbed, collapsing onto a couch. Looking back at the letter, she re-read the heartbreaking words.

Dear Carlos,

How are you, my boy? Staying safe in this time of New Year I hope. I'm sending my condolences to you and Viv because Connie DeLuca has died. It's a long story, so I hope I have all of the details.

Stephano DeLuca, Connie's estranged husband, died on October 27th last year. He was in the throes of passion with his twenty-two-year-old toy boy when he lost his breath and basically dropped dead right there, up the ass of his current fling. The toy boy panicked, screamed, and tried to get out from under DeLuca which brought it to the hotel's attention, and the cops were called. They called the doctor who announced DeLuca dead, and the cops arrested the toy boy. But Connie, as next of kin, still his legal wife, was unbelieving that Stephano had a male lover, let alone a twenty-two-year-old Filipino housemaid, and demanded an autopsy to find out what had killed her husband.

She had only been with him back in February, and except for a few blotchy skin lesions, he'd been fine. So she said. It took two months for her to receive the autopsy report from the Madrid morgue, and when she read it, she was still in denial, demanding new tests. So, they had the body transported to another doctor and new tests done. But when she received those they said the same thing. That Stephano had Kaposi's sarcoma, genital ulcers, a variety of sexually transmitted diseases, pneumocystis pneumonia, a low blood cell count, and was dying in any case.

Terrified of what she'd learned, she called us to get advice and told us the whole sordid thing. We immediately advised her to get every test on herself that she could and be tested for every STD, as there was a gay disease going round. She said she would. We heard back two weeks later when she told us that he'd given it all to her. Every STD he had he'd passed on and that she was violently ill from it. She hung up before we could give any more advice.

It was a few days before we heard from her son, Antonio. Connie had gone into despair and thrown herself from the parapet of their Spanish home, connecting with the stone driveway below. She died instantly. Antonio was the one who found her and said she'd been unable to bear what had happened, what his father had done, and the fact he'd had many male lovers as stated in all of Stephano's paperwork. Being unable to get past it, she had decided to end her life.

We got a call a week later from the DeLuca lawyer saying that Antonio had dealt with his mother's death by finding his father's old gun in the desk drawer and shooting himself in the head, apparently being unable to live without his mother. Only an hour beforehand he had left a huge envelope full of paperwork for the lawyer. Wills, letters, house deeds, and a note about what to do with everything else and their bodies. It all went to his two-year-old son by his young wife who is living in England, in a trust fund until he turns twenty-five. I know you worked with Antonio at the bar in Mykonos, Connie joked about it a couple of times back in '77. She thought it was a real hoot that her son worked with her 'masseur'.

Harriet and I are heartbroken about the loss, and we pray you and

Viv can deal with it too. I've enclosed the Spanish and American obituaries for all three of them, so you can see how loved the DeLuca family was. Unfortunately, poor Connie suffered because of her selfish ass of a husband, and Antonio couldn't cope with the loss even though he had a future to live for.

I hope you and the family are doing well, including your brothers, if you know what I mean. I hope to see you before I end up dead.

Love, Harry and Harriet.

February 1981

"I can't believe the three of you are another year older," Jenny told her boys at dinner on Valentine's Day. "You're all so much older than when you left Mykonos."

"We're only four years older, Mama. That's not long." Pedro dug into his favourite birthday cake that Jenny had made. She always made them the same cake year after year. A triple layered, rectangular chocolate sponge cake, with jam and cream filling, and chocolate cream on top, with berries and flaked chocolate.

"I know, but four years is a long time when you see your babies grow up. Just look at what's happened in those four years. You all left home, got into movies, got married, had babies, and are setting up your own businesses." She waved a hand at Carlos. "So much has happened."

"Technically it's about three and a half years, but we're getting there," Carlos said, smiling at his mother whom he knew loved him so much.

"Whatever it is, it's gone by so fast. And I'm glad we finally get to spend Valentine's Day away from 69."

"Yay!" Cheers and clapping went around the table.

"Unless you want to go tonight," Jenny cheekily continued.

Cheers turned to groans.

"Eddie offered to double my wage for the night if I played," Pedro said. "But, being a Saturday, and being my night off, I had to say no.

My job is five nights a week, not weekends."

"He offered to double your wage?" Carlos asked, astounded. "Geez, I know you're good, but come on, he can't be *that* desperate. Although, four grand would have been a nice little earner."

Pedro shrugged nonchalantly. "I know, but as Mama pointed out, we've been there the last three Valentine's and today is Saturday. So it's *our* time. Besides, I don't know how much longer I'll work there. Once Angie's out of school, I'm not sure I want to stay. It's been an amazing job with great pay, but with everything else that's happened in the last four years..." He shook his head. "I just don't know if I want to do it anymore."

"You've been saving up your money and paying your taxes, I hope." Jenny aimed a pointed look at Carlos knowing full well he would never admit to all of the money he'd earned in Mykonos. She received a blush in return. "And with Angie's inheritance, you should be able to support yourselves and your children well into the future. What's to stop you spreading your wings and seeing the world again, or investing in property, or taking the time to look for another job you might want to do? Or you could even study, like Carlos."

"Yeah." Pedro took a sip of beer. "I have thought of learning more about DJing, not that I'm sure if there's any more *to* learn. But maybe I'll take some classes from the experts, maybe get into radio, or, maybe Angie and I could make music of our own." He glanced at his wife sitting on the other side of Alena. "Ooh..." His head turned to his mother as an idea came to him. "Or, I could learn about making records."

Jenny's eyes lit up. "You could become a hit maker."

That made Carlos snort. "Oh, for God's sake."

"No, *for God's sake*, Carlos," Jenny chided. "I've always encouraged you boys to do what you wanted when it came to careers, except for *those* movies. And I think this would be the next natural step for the two of them. A DJ and a Juilliard-trained pianist and violinist. *You're* working behind the scenes of film now, why shouldn't Pedro get behind the scenes of music?"

"Yeah, bro." Pedro grinned. "Angie and I could make the music for your films…if you ever get around to making them."

"An' A-ena can sing, Dada. A-ena, A-ena," their daughter suggested, singing as she spoke. "A-ena can sing for Dada an' Mama." She waved her chocolate-covered fingers in the air.

"Oh, Bubba, look at you covered in cake." Angie wiped Alena's mouth then attacked her fingers with a napkin.

"She can carry a tune," Jenny said. "That sounded on key."

"It certainly was." Pedro ruffled his daughter's jet-black curls. "Looks like we have a budding singer on our hands."

"A-ena, A-ena," she sang, wriggling in her seat and scrunching her nose up. "A-ena, A-ena."

"Can you say L?" Pedro asked her.

"Elw," she replied.

"No, L," Pedro repeated. "For A-*lena*."

"A-ena." She looked inquisitively at her father.

"No, A-*lena*."

"A-ena, dat's me, Dada. A-ena."

The family laughed. "Yes, *you are* A-lena," Jenny said, smiling at her baby girl. "And clearly musically gifted. Maybe we should put her in some sort of music class for children. There must be some in the city somewhere."

"Oooh, that's a good idea. We can put the girls in together," Viv said. "Would Diana like to do some music?" She looked at her daughter sitting between her and Carlos, but she was busy eating her daddy's cake.

"Ha! Doesn't look like she's interested." Carlos grinned. "Loves cake too much."

"Maybe she can be a chef, or run a restaurant," Tomas suggested.

Carlos glanced over his shoulder at his brother. "Cute bro, real cute."

Downstairs, a black stretch limousine pulled up to the apartment building. Inside were Greta Von Burro, Carson Trumack, Stephanie Martison, and Thomas Derbon.

"I'll just be a minute." Greta alighted and entered the building.

"Can I help you, ma'am?" Martin Brewster, the doorman asked. He'd been with the Stephanopouloses from the beginning and didn't know this woman.

"Yes, hello." Greta loosened her scarf. "Is Pedro Stephanopoulos in? I'd like to talk to him."

"And your name, ma'am?"

"Greta Von Burro." She glanced around the lobby while waiting for Brewster to call Pedro.

"He doesn't seem to be in, but I know he didn't go out. I'll just ring the penthouse for you," he told Greta.

After five rings Jenny answered. "Yes, Brewster."

"Mrs Stephanopoulos, is Pedro there? There's a Greta Von Burro here to see him."

Jenny frowned, wondering why Greta was there to see her son. With a quick glance behind her, she asked Brewster why she was there.

"Ah, Mrs Stephanopoulos would like to know why you're here," Brewster said to Greta.

"May I speak to her?" Greta asked. "It's important."

Brewster frowned. "She'd like to speak to you, Mrs Stephanopoulos."

"Put her on, Brewster," Jenny said.

Brewster handed the phone over and stepped back.

"Mrs Stephanopoulos," Greta said. "We need to speak to Pedro."

"And why's that?"

"Ah...because a colleague of mine would like to say his goodbyes to him."

Jenny frowned. "What do you mean...goodbyes?"

Greta sighed. "We...ah...think that he has this...disease...and he hasn't long to live according to the doctors. Since we worked together, he'd like to say goodbye to Pedro. We went to 69 tonight to see him, but found he wasn't there, so we came here, hoping to catch him."

Jenny carefully went over Greta's words. "And what's this man's name?"

"Thomas."

Jenny froze. The same name as her baby. Biting her lip, she quietly asked. "Is he gay?"

Silence.

"Ms Von Burro."

"Yes."

Jenny breathed in. "So…it's the disease that…*certain men* are getting?"

"We think so."

"Ah, okay, just let me speak to the family and I'll ring back down." Hanging up, she took another breath. "Jesus Christ."

"Hey, Mama, who's downstairs?" Pedro called, launching into another piece of cake.

Finally turning, Jenny slowly walked back to the table and stood beside Tomas, laying a hand gently on his shoulder and getting an inquisitive look in return. "Greta's downstairs."

Pedro frowned. "Von Burro?"

"Yes."

"What does she want?" He was as puzzled as everyone else was as to why his ex-boss was there and wanted to see him.

"She…" Jenny started before looking down at her hand. "She has a young man with her who'd like to see you."

"Who?" Now he was really confused.

"A…Thomas…" She glanced at her own Tomas whose eyes widened in surprise.

"Derbon?" Pedro asked, his frown deeper.

"She didn't say a last name," Jenny told him.

"Why would he want to see me? We didn't really get along, and I got a bit sick and tired of him hitting on me." Pedro finished off his beer.

"He's gay," Jenny said.

"Yeah." Pedro shrugged. "Why?"

"Because he's sick," was all Jenny said.

Silence blanketed the room before Roger caught on. "Oh."

"Oh, my God." Tomas buried his head in his hands, elbows on the table.

Pedro glanced at them and realised what they meant. "Oh…my God…you're kidding?"

"Apparently not," Jenny said, squeezing Tomas's shoulder. "He'd like to say his goodbyes. Thought he'd see you at 69, but when you weren't there, they took a chance on you being here."

"So, what do I…we…do?" Pedro asked, looking up at her for the answers.

"I suggest we let them up and offer tea and coffee and cake, and since this really has nothing to do with the rest of you, you can go to your own apartments, or over to the lounge room. We can entertain them here at the table. I doubt they'll stay long."

Pedro gulped and looked at everyone at the table, almost in a panic. "What…I…don't know…" He saw Tomas's sick look. "You don't have to stay, bro."

"I think I'll go and sit near the fire." Tomas quickly stood and moved over to the lounge room with Roger following.

"Can the rest of you quickly clear up and get clean plates and cups, and get the girls out of here. I'll see if they need help." Jenny rang downstairs. "Do they need help getting him up?" she asked Brewster.

He relayed the message and Greta shook her head.

"We have a wheelchair; we'll get him out." She quickly went outside and asked the driver to open the trunk. He set up the wheelchair and helped Carson get Thomas out of the car. Ten minutes later they were at the penthouse door.

Jenny opened it, took one look at Thomas, and knew he didn't have long. "Jesus Christ," she said quietly, before seeing the others. "Come in."

Pedro moved to her side and looked down. "Jesus, Thomas."

"Hello, my gorgeous porn star," Thomas breathed. "I wanted to see you one last time." He was gaunt, jaundiced, with a breathing tube down his nose, a gas tank on the back of the chair, his eyes and cheeks sunken, his hair thin, his body frail.

"Please, come sit at the table, and I'll get everyone something hot to drink." Jenny led the way to the dining table where they'd removed a chair for the wheelchair to fit. "Everyone, please take a seat; we have tea, coffee, cake."

"Coffee will be fine." Greta sat next to Thomas with Carson next to her, and Stephanie took the seat next to Pedro.

"Thomas, what can you have?" Jenny asked as she poured three coffees.

"Not a lot," he rasped. "But I'd love a mouthful of that delicious-looking birthday cake."

Jenny cut a small corner off, placed it on a plate, and put it in front of him. "Is this enough?"

"More than enough," he replied, picking up the fork and trying a small piece. Swallowing, he sighed. "That is even more delicious than it looks."

"Thank you. I make it every year for the boys," Jenny told him.

"You made it?" he asked. "You are an amazing cook, Mrs Stephanopoulos."

"Thank you, Thomas," she paused, "Greta said that…you don't have long and wanted to say goodbye to Pedro." Her eyes flickered to her son who sat in his usual spot, looking curiously at Thomas.

"Yes." Thomas laid down his fork. "I've been saying goodbye to everyone I've worked with, or know. It's been a rough few months. I became sick very quickly. One minute I was fine and healthy and helping Greta make movies, and the next I had blotchy lesions all over my body, and all kinds of diseases cropped up, and now I have a breathing tube down my nose because I have some fungal pneumonia."

"Did you get it from being promiscuous?" Pedro asked bluntly, getting a sharp look from Jenny.

Thomas smiled. "Probably. Apparently, this gay thing is going around and no one knows what it is. I wasn't always careful, unfortunate for me now. Look where it's gotten me."

"And ex-lovers?" Pedro asked. "Do they have it? Are they dying, or sick, or dead?"

Thomas looked down with a deep sigh. As deep as he could manage. "A few are quite sick; others only have STDs. Two are dead in the last six months. I can't say how many more will die. I certainly didn't expect to so young."

"How old are you?" Jenny asked softly.

"Forty-two," he replied and placed another piece of cake in his mouth.

"From what we've heard, no one knows what this is. But the gay community is dying and worried, and no one is doing anything," Jenny said.

"Seems so," Thomas replied. "All I knew was that a couple of ex-lovers were sick, and then I became sick, and suddenly the community's worried."

"But is it stopping you?" Jenny asked, concerned for her son who'd gone downstairs to his apartment with Roger and the girls, not wanting anything more to do with death. "Is it stopping you from having more than one partner, is it stopping you from being unsafe?"

Thomas smiled sadly. "Clearly not, Mrs Stephanopoulos. From the people I've spoken to, all of the deaths are freaking us out, but none of us wants to believe it's to do with sex, or having sex with each other. We've just come out of the free-loving '70s, after fighting for our rights in the '60s, to be out and free to love who we want when we want."

"And now this disease is taking that away from you," Jenny said.

"Is it?" Thomas asked. "Some of my friends believe it's the government's way of controlling us gays, telling us what to do and how to do it, trying to take over our sexual freedoms after we fought so hard for it."

"Do you seriously think the government is making this up?" Jenny asked, incredulously. "Look at you." She waved a hand in his direction. "Did the government do *this* to you? Did *they* make you sick? Did *they* give you a disease, or any of the diseases you have? Why would *they* bother wasting time and money killing off gay men? Why would they make you so sick that you'd end up in a wheelchair? This disease is freaking me out too. I have a gay son and son-in-law, and I worry for them every single minute of every single day, and it scares me to absolute death. If this disease is more than from having multiple partners, who's to say that straight people won't end up getting it? Who's to say women or children won't get it? It worries me every goddamn day because I don't want to lose my son. All of my children mean the world to me, and my grandbabies mean even more, and I don't want to lose them. America is a far cry from where Spiros grew up, where I had my sons and raised them, and now this…this *thing*," she waved a hand, "is taking the lives of so many people. And it's horrible. We just don't know where it's going next. *Who* it's going to affect next. And I'm sorry for you, Thomas, just as I'm sorry for

Pedro's friend Leon, and Viv's friend Cabot, and all of Tomas and Roger's friends. I'm sorry this is happening to all of you, but I'm even sorrier that no one even knows what it is." She looked at him and shook her head sadly. "I really am very sorry this is happening to all of you, and that no one seems to know what it is so they can save you."

"Thank you, Mrs Stephanopoulos," Thomas said. "That's more than what anyone else has said to me." He looked at Pedro. "I wanted to see you play one last time. But I was there at New Years, and I've been to see you a lot, including the last three Valentine's. Besides the movies, you are an incredibly talented young man, Pedro. And whatever it is you do in life, I really hope you are successful."

"Thank you, Thomas," Pedro said. "It's a pity I can't wish you the same."

Thomas's sad smile slipped back into place. "Yeah, it is. But I can at least say I tried to live my life the way I wanted. I partied, I did publicity and management, and got to see some of the hottest stars and celebrities; those in the making and those already made. I've seen them rise, I've seen them fall, but most of all, I had the time of my life doing it. Parties, holidays to the Caribbean, lovers, friends, partners. I've done everything I wanted to do, and I just wanted to thank you for being a part of that."

Pedro nodded. "I'm glad I could help make your life great," he said in all honesty.

"Yes, thank you," Thomas said wistfully before a dry hacking cough took over.

"Easy." Greta patted his back, and Jenny retrieved a glass of water.

"Thank you." Thomas took it and quickly sipped until the coughing subsided. "I think it's time I went home now, Greta." He placed the glass on the table as Greta stood. "Thank you very much for your hospitality, Mrs Stephanopoulos. After you tore Greta a new one in '77, we didn't think you'd let us in."

Jenny looked from him to a guilty-looking Greta standing behind him. They were all standing now, ready to go. "That was a long time ago, Thomas, and Pedro and the boys are all out of the business, so I'm happy."

"I'm sure you are." He smiled, and Carson turned the wheelchair for them to go to the door. He saw Spiros open it and stand waiting for them. "Mr Stephanopoulos." Thomas lifted his hand for Carson to stop. "You must be very proud of your sons. They are incredible men, incredible people."

"I am, Mr Derbon. Very much so." Spiros held out his hand and gently shook the hand Thomas offered.

Thomas noticed Angie, Viv, and Carlos standing in the lounge room. "Goodnight, everyone."

"Goodnight," the three of them called.

Carson wheeled Thomas into the foyer and rang for the lift.

"Thank you, for letting us come up, Mrs Stephanopoulos," Greta said. "I didn't know if you would…considering our last meeting." They stood waiting for the lift.

"This wasn't about you, Ms Von Burro," Jenny replied, looking at Thomas. "It's about a dying man's wish to say goodbye."

The lift opened, and Carson backed into it, so Thomas was looking out. Stephanie piled in behind with a longing glance back at Pedro.

"Yes," Greta murmured. "Yes, it is, Mrs Stephanopoulos." She entered the lift. "Thank you, thank you very much for this."

"You're welcome," Jenny told them. "Goodbye, Thomas. I hope it's peaceful at the end and you have all you need."

"Thank you, Mrs Stephanopoulos." He saw Pedro lift a hand in a sad wave goodbye. "I do. I do."

The door closed, and Jenny heaved a sigh, her body sagged, and she fell into her son's arms.

"Oh, Mama, how many more?" He hugged her tightly and kissed the top of her head. "How many more people that we know?"

"I don't know, my baby. I don't know."

"Come back inside," Spiros called from the doorway. "Come back in and sit by the fire. Sit, and I'll finish cleaning up." He watched them walk inside, arms still around each other, closed the door, and headed for the dining room while they joined the others and stood around the fire for warmth.

"He's dying of that disease, isn't he?" Carlos asked, frowning at the despair of it all.

"Yes," Jenny said. "As so many have."

"Way too many," Viv murmured. "A few more photographer friends of mine are sick now. I don't know if it's the same thing and they'll die, or if they just have the flu or normal pneumonia."

"Yes," Jenny mumbled. "So many, so, so many. I hope Tomas and Roger aren't added to the list."

"Mama," Pedro said. "Don't go there. Please don't go there." He shook his head and closed his eyes. "I can't bear to lose him. I can't bear to lose any of my family."

"I know, baby." Jenny rubbed his back and leant her head on his shoulder. "I can't bear to lose any more of my babies. I've already done that once, and it was absolutely horrifically heartbreaking." She sighed as Spiros turned up at her side. "I can't bear to lose any more of you, especially Tomas, to this awful disease."

"We won't." Spiros took her into his arms. "Be positive. We won't."

"I'm trying," she said. "But all of our children's friends are getting sick and dying, and the one thing they have in common is the fact they're gay. Tomas is gay, and since he has a husband that's *two* children we have to worry about, and I won't stop worrying until doctors find out what this disease is, how people catch it, and how it can be treated or cured. Until then, until I know my babies are safe, no matter what, I *will not stop* worrying."

"How about you stop worrying for now since it's our sons' birthdays, and we'll call Tomas and Roger back up to continue celebrating the day. Especially since it's also Valentine's Day and I have a special present for you..." Spiros told her, trying to comfort her the only way he knew how.

March 1981

The obituary for Thomas Derbon appeared in the paper one month later. Many people, ex-porn stars of Greta's, paid their respects by leaving notices, thanking him for being a great guy and helping them with their careers. They were glowing compliments, from young and old, including some ex-lovers.

Greta called Pedro to let him know how much Thomas had appreciated that night, how he'd passed comfortably in his home with friends around him, and that he was glad he'd had the opportunity to say goodbye and see him one more time. She was taking care of his effects and personal affairs, but he'd left a hole at *Von Burro* that she wasn't sure she wanted to fill. She just wasn't sure she'd ever be able to replace him. His eagerness, his expertise and experience, the way he could publicize the hell out of anything, even a paper bag, to make it believable. That was a gift she just didn't know if anyone else had.

Pedro thanked her for calling and that he was glad Thomas had a comfortable end. Replacing the phone, he paused and thought about his own Tomas and how he desperately didn't want to lose him. Taking a deep breath, he finished reading the obits and saw a familiar name. Heading up to the penthouse, he found everyone already there. "Hey, Carlos, didn't you tell us years ago about an old guy named," he looked at the paper, "Leon Spenter?"

"Yeah, why?" Carlos looked up from his spot on the couch. It was still cool out, and the fire was crackling merrily away.

"Besides Thomas Derbon's name being in the obits today, so is a Leon Spenter, late 60s, American, loved spending summers on Mykonos."

"Jesus Christ," Carlos muttered. "I knew that fag was up to no good."

"Carlos," Jenny chastised.

"What?" Carlos looked up from the toy on Diana's lap, glancing from his mother on the couch to his right, to his brother and brother-in-law on the couch to his left, who all stared almost accusingly at him. "What? I didn't mean it in a bad way, but he was. He was slimy and creepy and always hit on me. It was gross."

"Yeah, but you don't need to use that word," Roger said.

"What word? Fag? I didn't mean it in a bad way. It's just another word for gay, isn't it?" Carlos stared at both of them.

"Not quite," Roger told him.

"Well…" Carlos shrugged. "I didn't mean it in a bad way." He didn't see what the big deal was over one little word. "So, what about him?" He turned to Pedro.

"He's passed away." Pedro handed the paper over.

Carlos took the paper and looked at the picture. "Yeah, that's him. *Leon Spenter, American-born fashion millionaire, passed away on March the 10th, 1981. He was 67 years old and leaves behind no heirs.*" He read a few notices from friends and co-workers who all loved his sense of style. "Style!" Carlos exclaimed. "Is that what you call too-small leopard print swim briefs that barely covered his package. Even back in '77 he looked like old withered leather and had thin hair. He thought he was shit hot and that I'd do him. Gross."

"He thought you'd…*be* with him?" Jenny was shocked. "In…bed…"

"Yep. Kept propositioning me regardless of how many times I told him I didn't swing that way. He didn't care, just kept on and on and on. I got so goddamn annoyed and ended up sick of him. He was there before I left. Came back day after day for a spray even though his skin was like old leather, and he kept popping up at the bar when Antonio and I were…there…" His voice trailed off as he thought about his ex-co-worker. "We used to joke…" he reminisced. "About which one of us he hit on most." Sadness flowed over him. "Antonio used to joke about taking him up on his offer because he wasn't getting any girls. They all wanted me and weren't interested in him." Wiping away a wandering tear he went on. "He was at my wedding, sitting with Giorgio. Now they're both dead. Jesus." He thrust himself up and around the couch and strode out the door, coming to a stop against the foyer wall. He needed air; he needed to breathe.

"I'll go," Jenny quickly said to everyone's shocked expressions, and put down her knitting and followed. "Carlos." She closed the door behind her, seeing her son bent over, leaning back against the wall.

"Mama, he's dead. They're all dead," he sputtered through his tears. "Antonio, Connie…"

"I know." She rubbed his back. "It's horrible, and you were right. We should have told them. But we didn't, and Antonio chose to do what he did, and obviously, nothing was going to stop him."

"But he was young, Mama, just a bit older than me, we bartended for three years over the summers. He came to my wedding." He couldn't stop the tears no matter what.

"I know," Jenny said softly. "This disease is taking almost everyone we know, and it's foul and horrible and won't stop until it's desecrated the human race. But there's nothing wrong with grieving, my baby. You grieve all you want. It was a horrible way to die, but he made a choice."

"It doesn't make it any easier," Carlos sobbed, swiping the back of his hand over his face as he stood. "It doesn't make it any easier."

"I know. It never will," Jenny murmured, holding her son. "It never will."

*****

"Happy birthday, dear Vivian, happy birthday to you. Hip, hip hooray, hip, hip hooray, hip, hip hooray." They cheered as she blew out the candles on the huge perfume bottle cake that looked like her perfume, *Vivian*. Jenny had shown the cake maker what she wanted, and it had turned out perfectly.

"This is an awesome cake, Jenny." Viv sliced the first piece and bit into the creamy vanilla sponge with a light orange and chocolate cream cover. "Oh, my God, this is amazing."

"Cay?" Diana and Alena looked up with urgency in their eyes and wiggling fingers, desperate to get themselves onto it. "Cay?"

Everyone laughed. "Of course you can have some cake, my darlings." Viv cut slices for both of them, and they dug in with both hands, soon smearing it all over their faces. She passed around plates, and they all enjoyed the delicious delight.

They had reserved tables at *Windows on the World* atop New York's North Tower of the World Trade Center. It was a hard restaurant to get into as it was always booked out, but they'd managed, and had enjoyed a mouth-watering dinner followed by the equally mouth-watering cake.

"I can't believe I'm another year older," Vivian joked. "Where has the year gone? Weren't we just at *Santiago* yesterday celebrating my birthday?"

"Babe, where have you been?" Carlos joked back. "That was a year ago, not yesterday. But here, here's another present to add to the list of many." He pulled out a velvet box and presented it to her.

"Pwesents?" Diana and Alena stared wide-eyed. They loved getting presents. "Pwesents for me, Dada?" Diana asked her father.

"No, Bubba," he told her. "It's *Mama's* birthday, so she gets the presents."

"Oh, Carlos, it's beautiful." She pulled a gold necklace from the box with a two-centimetre, diamond encrusted, gold V pendant. "It's," she blinked back tears, "it's beautiful."

"Let me put it on for you." Carlos took the necklace and carefully clasped it around her neck as she lifted her hair.

She fixed it to sit straight, and it glinted in the soft lighting of the restaurant. Oohs and aahs went around the table. "It's beautiful." She leaned over Diana to kiss her husband. "And it goes with all of the other jewellery you've given me."

"I try to be careful with what I buy. I did have my eye on something spectacular, but you'll have to wait until our anniversary." He cheekily grinned.

"Oh, but that's so far away," she cried. "Why do I have to wait that long?"

"I could give you everything now, but then what else would I give you for every other day? We already have lots of presents to give out through the year, birthdays and Valentine's, anniversaries and Christmas, Mothers' and Fathers' Day," Carlos rambled off the list.

"It's a pity we have those days in Australia and Mykonos," Jenny said to Spiros with a twinkle in her eye. "Just think of all the presents we *could* have missed out on."

"Yes," Spiros agreed. "*Think* of all the presents we could have missed out on because the boys really weren't that good at making things."

Jenny laughed as the boys looked on in horror. "But all the paintings and horrible art and craft we *could* have missed out on. They would have been so treasured." Oh, how she loved to tease her boys.

"Relegated to a box in the laundry room, you mean." Spiros chuckled.

"That is *so* unfair," Pedro whined. "You mean all the stuff *I did* make you got dumped in a box in the laundry?"

"No, no," Jenny placated him. "It's in a box being kept out of the dust, so it's basically in storage for you when you want it."

"But we made all of that for you," Tomas said, shocked that his mother could throw out all the things they'd made for her.

"Yeah, like the clay ashtray we made in art class," Carlos added, scowling in mock anger at his parents.

"Even though we've never smoked?" Jenny smiled.

"Well...so..." Carlos complained. "Does that mean you chucked it all out?"

"We've kept everything," Jenny told them. "All neatly piled into boxes with your names on it. It's all safely stored away. Besides, you didn't want it as you were growing up, and we had no room in Mykonos. And even after you got your own rooms there wasn't much space to keep it all. It's in the laundry on the storage racks."

"Yeah..." Carlos muttered thinking about the ashtray. "Not that you really needed to keep that thing. It was pretty ugly."

"Oh, it certainly was," Spiros replied.

April 1981

On April first, they celebrated Roger's thirty-third birthday at *Castro*, the hot and happening restaurant bar in Soho. Unlike the year before, where they'd spent it at home, he wanted to go out after hearing about the new place in town. It had provided good home-cooked food and wine, while Jenny supplied the cake. A three-piece band on the stage at the far end of the restaurant played a resounding rendition of Happy Birthday, getting all the other guests and staff to join in and sing along.

Digging into the delicious marble cake covered in chocolate icing, they listened to the band some more. Pedro had the night off from 69, and everyone was in good spirits as cake, wine, and presents were handed around.

But the next day was a different story…

Roger stumbled into the penthouse just shy of five o'clock. The phone had rung, and he'd hung back to answer while Tomas had gone upstairs. After the call he'd sat for a few minutes, just thinking, crying, falling apart. Finally, he faced his family who was all standing around looking at him.

"There you are," Tomas said from the table where he was getting it set for dinner. "I was about to call out a search party." He looked at his lover's face, and his stomach fell. "Roger…what is it? Who was on the phone?"

Roger hadn't moved, he couldn't. His hand still clung to the door handle for support as everyone stood staring at him.

"No." Tomas tilted his head in despair. "No, no, no more." His breathing became laboured, and his mother put her arms around him. "No more."

Roger finally closed the door and tried not to fall apart.

"Who?" Jenny asked, holding her crying son as Spiros came over to them both to comfort and hold them.

Blinking, Roger took a breath. "Freddy."

"No," Tomas wailed, almost collapsing.

Jenny pulled him into her arms. "There, there, my baby. Shhh." She comforted him, and he clung to her, wailing.

Roger slowly made his way over to them, awkwardly putting his arms around them both. "He…" Clearing his throat, he started again. "He held on for as long as he could. He was okay until last month… and then it just attacked, and he was gone." Roger hugged both Tomas and Jenny who was also in tears.

"Was he the friend you've been staying with?" she asked.

"Yeah." He nodded. "Yeah."

"I'm sorry," she added. "I'm so sorry." Clinging to her son, she couldn't let go. She knew if she did he would fall apart more, and felt that right now he needed her more than ever.

"No," Tomas sobbed. When the hell was this going to end? When the hell were people they knew going to stop dying?

"Was he a good friend?" Jenny asked Roger as she stroked Tomas's head.

"He ah…" Roger rubbed his hand across Tomas's shoulder. "He owns…*owned Love Stick*. The restaurant bar where I took Tomas the first time we…dated. We've been staying with him every time we've gone back, but I guess we can't do that anymore." He sighed from the pit of his knotted stomach. "*Love Stick* was so hip and happening, like *Castro* last night. It was the place to be for gay men, but the last year, with everyone gone, or leaving, no one was left to frequent the place. He told us last time he was working double shifts to stay afloat. Clearly, this was all too much for him."

Viv approached the group from the lounge room where she had

been with the girls. "Was the disease what killed him?"

"They think so," Roger told her. "Over the last few years his health had declined with all the hard work. He looked tired and worn out in November. But in the last month, he really went downhill, became bone thin, blotchy skin, couldn't breathe. They said he went very quickly."

Tomas pulled back and sniffled. "So, he was sick when we were there?"

"I don't know, T." Roger shook his head sadly. "No one really knows how long he's been sick, or whether it was this disease at all."

"Will they do an autopsy?" Jenny asked.

"Probably," Roger said. "Funeral's about a week from now. Whenever they can get the body back. They'll call and let us know."

"I can't do this anymore." Tomas's head moved mechanically from side to side. "I can't. I can't do this anymore. I can't do death; I can't do funerals. I just can't."

"You don't have to," Jenny soothed him. "You don't have to." She knew what a sensitive soul Tomas was, he always had been, especially as a child. As he'd grown older, that waned a little, and he toughened up when they lived in Mykonos. But the last few years, since coming out, that sensitivity had come back, and she knew that this must be depressing him. "Roger." She looked from Tomas's agonised expression to her son-in-law. "If you want to go to Freddy's funeral then I'll get you a private jet. But I don't think Tomas will be making it."

Roger sighed, seeing the determination in his mother-in-law's eyes and the depressed desperation in his lover's. "Thanks, Mrs S. I'll be able to get there and back faster. Don't worry, T." His hand stroked Tomas's face. "You don't have to, or need to, go. This is killing you, and I can do this by myself."

"I can't." Tomas sniffled.

"I know, my love." Roger took Tomas into his arms. "I know."

*****

They celebrated Angelina's birthday ten days later by going to *Spade,* a new dance club restaurant. Since the kids were always in tow, they had to make sure all of the places they celebrated were child-friendly. They also had Maggie and Mike along.

"Whoo twenty-two today and almost free from school!" Angie exclaimed, throwing her arms in the air as they danced in the club room.

"And then what will you do?" Maggie asked over the music.

"Don't know," Angie replied. "I'll think about it when I graduate. Maybe I'll take summer off and just have fun."

"Isn't that what you do every summer anyway?" Maggie asked.

Angie laughed. "Yeah, pretty much. I'm still very surprised I managed to get this far without being kicked out for all the time I've had off. I had to sit exams either before I left, or after I got back just to keep up. And now we have final exams in the next few weeks."

"But we graduate next month," Maggie squealed. "And then we're free. Whoo!" They held hands and bounced around in circles.

Jenny watched from the restaurant section where the family were watching the girls and having a relaxing wine.

"A-ena go dance wiv Mama." Alena looked imploringly up at her father then pointed at her Mama having fun on the dance floor.

"Alena wants to go and dance with her Mama, does she?" Pedro asked his daughter, looking into her big blue eyes so much like his. He smiled. He couldn't help it.

"A-ena dance wiv Mama," she repeated, her big blue eyes never leaving her dancing mama and aunt Maggie.

"I'll take you, Alena," Viv said. "You and Diana come and dance with your Mamas."

"Okey-dokey." Alena slid off her chair and ran around the table to Diana, grabbed her hand, and they raced towards the dance floor.

"Whoa, wait up." Viv laughingly followed and pushed open the door that separated the two rooms. The girls took off for Angie and Maggie, dodging the other people on the floor. Viv danced her way over and joined in.

Jenny heaved a big happy sigh. "If it's two things those girls love, it's music and dancing."

"You forgot cay." Pedro grinned.

Jenny laughed. "Yes, who can forget about cay? Make that *three* things they love."

"And the cays are always excellent, Mrs S," Roger said from the other side of Tomas who was between him and his mother.

"Thank you, Roger, I learned a lot from my mother about cay baking and managed to perfect it fairly quickly." Jenny smiled at the memories.

"You would have with so many brothers and sisters," Spiros said.

"True," Jenny replied, watching Pedro sneak another piece of Angie's piano cake. "Taste good, does it?"

He looked up, thinking no one had seen up. "Ah, yep." Everyone laughed. "Your cays are always awesome, Mama."

"We all saw you, bro," Carlos said.

"Well, while she's not here." Pedro shrugged. "Help yourselves to another piece."

"Oh, I think we've all had enough." Jenny groaned and turned her attention to Roger. "When do you go to Miami?"

His face fell, and he let out a deep sigh. "Not for another two weeks."

"Why so long? He died at the beginning of the month?" Pedro asked.

"Yeah, I know. But the hospital kept him in the morgue, then the autopsy, some doctors want tests or something. Kingie wasn't very explanatory, but the funeral may not be for another week or two. And then the business needs to be sorted out. He lived above the bar. God, I'm going to miss him and *Love Stick*. It used to be such a great place. You could have a meal for lunch, and then at night they'd remove some of the tables, turn on the dance floor, there would be a lounging area on one side, the music was current, you'd put a suit and nice shirt on and just relax and have fun."

"It sounds like a nice place," Jenny said.

"Yeah, it was," Roger replied wistfully. "A lot like some of the places we've been here in New York. Friendly, casual, just a cool place to be, and no violence allowed."

"Did you go a lot?" Carlos asked, casually sipping his beer.

"I did before I met Tomas." Roger glanced at his forlorn lover. "I took him there on our first date after a day at the beach." He watched a soft smile light up Tomas's lips. "We went a couple more times before…" He sighed. "*Him* and the kidnapping. After that, we've been here."

"I suppose we should be grateful to Stefano's man for saving you from him," Jenny told Tomas. "And I am because God knows what harm *he* would have done."

"I keep telling you I don't want to talk about him, Mama," Tomas said, rubbing his eyes. "I've had enough of hearing about him."

"I know," Jenny said. "But he made such an impact on this family. Not just on you, personally."

Tomas sighed and looked at her. "I know, it's just that…it's almost four years, and Roger and I have been married for almost all of the time, and *he's* not a part of my life anymore."

"Okay, we'll move on." Jenny patted his hand. "Are everybody else's friends still intact?"

"Viv's lost a few acquaintances," Carlos said softly from behind his beer. "In London and France. We're not sure if it's the same thing, but a couple of model friends have passed away."

"Oh, that's horrible," Jenny murmured. "On top of those other photographer friends."

"Yeah, they've passed too. Sick like Cabot Conroy," Carlos replied.

"They were all gay?" Mike asked from between Roger and Pedro.

"Yeah," Carlos took another swig of beer to drown his sorrows.

"Like Leon, Stan, how many others have we lost from 69?" Mike asked Pedro.

"If you include Jamal Devron and Stephano DeLuca," Pedro cast a glance at Carlos, "even though they weren't regulars, then I think we've long surpassed double digits."

"Oh, that's horrible too." Jenny's hand went to her mouth.

"And they're just the ones we do know about," Pedro replied. "What about the ones we don't? All the regulars we don't know by name, all the elite that bypass the dance floor and go straight downstairs. How many of them have gone?"

Mike shrugged. "No idea. I think only Eddie would know that, and he keeps downstairs a closely guarded secret."

"I bet he's participating," Carlos said. "From the way he eyes us off, I'd say he's all over men."

Pedro looked thoughtfully at him. "Yeah. I did ask him, but he never said anything."

"So, he could be gone in a few years, too?" Jenny asked.

A deep sigh deflated Pedro as he leaned back, hands behind head, and looked at the ceiling. "Yeah. I suggested that and he didn't like it, but didn't deny it either."

"I have a very strong feeling that this thing, this disease, is going to take a hell of a lot more people yet. Including every gay person you boys know," Jenny said.

"Don't say that, Mama. I can't keep doing this," Tomas murmured and rubbed the bridge of his nose. "I can't do any more deaths."

"I know, my baby, and you don't have to." Jenny squeezed his arm, studying the dark circles under his eyes. "Have you not been sleeping?"

He shook his head gently. "No. I can't. I close my eyes, and everyone I met in Miami is dead, and they're reaching out their bony hands to get me. It's horrible."

"How awful that you should dream that," Jenny told him. "Oh, my poor baby." She wondered silently if he was having premonitions about his own death. "And the women who helped you in Miami, are they still okay?"

"Bette, Bertha, yeah." A soft smile touched his lips. "They're still okay. They'll probably die of old age soon."

"T, they're not that old." Roger chuckled. "They're only in their 60s or 70s."

"With all the men they've had, I bet they're hoping they'll die of old age," Tomas said. "And not this disease. Luiz *was* engaged to Bertha at the time."

"Yeah." Roger slid his fingers through his husband's hair. "I know, but you don't want to talk about Luiz, so let's talk about something else."

Alena and Diana took that moment to sneak up and scare everyone. "Cay!" they yelled, making everyone jump and cry out as the girls giggled.

*****

Finally, on April the 25th, Roger flew into Miami for the funeral of Frederique Montague Highmore, affectionately known as Freddy. He'd owned *Love Stick* for over ten years, having built it from the ground up, finding the perfect place to turn into a restaurant bar that turned into a party at night. It had been a success, turning over one million dollars within its first year, and to save money, and for the convenience, he had lived in the apartment above it.

But sadly, with the decline in patrons over the last two years, and giving money to those who needed it, paying for funerals when the dead and dying couldn't, *Love Stick* just couldn't stay afloat any longer, and once Freddy's health declined, that was it. *Love Stick, and* Freddy came to an end.

Roger stood staring at the bar from across the street. The 'reserved for a private party' sign was on the door. *The Love Stick* sign was a bit worn out and tatty. The bar was in a popular part of Miami, central to almost everything, and had been the best hangout for gays. That's why he'd taken Tomas there on their first date, to help him slip into the scene. The same scene that had so easily taken him in back in '75, two years before he'd met Tomas. The place was thriving back then, the whole strip was, but now, it was derelict, worn out, run down, and really, really damn sad.

Taking a deep breath, he walked across the road and up the stairs to Freddy's apartment. Kingie, Freddy's manager, had told him to go there first. He knocked.

"Hey, man." Jamaican born and bred, Kingie answered the door in bare feet and dreadlocks. His neon green t-shirt and Hawaiian shorts were way too festive for the occasion.

"Hey, Kingie." Roger hugged him. "How you doing?"

"Not so good, man, come in, come in." Kingie waved him in. "Tomas not with you?"

"No." Roger looked around Freddy's apartment. "He couldn't face another funeral, and I'm not sure I can either."

"I know what you mean, man." Kingie pulled out a chair at the kitchen table. "Sit, sit, what can I get you?"

"Nothing, thanks. I just want to know where the funeral is, so I can get it over and done with."

"Ya, ya." Kingie dug around in a pile of paperwork. "Same church where all tha others have been. It's at…" He found the paper and read it. "Twelve-thirty, man. And then we can come back here until five-thirty."

"I won't be staying that long. I'll stay an hour or so to send Freddy off, but after that, I'm gone. Who else is coming?"

"Anyone who's still alive I s'pose." Kingie swigged back some beer. "There have been more deaths, man. Did Freddy call you?"

Roger nodded slightly. "Yeah, almost ten a month, give or take a few either side. That's a lot, Kingie."

"Ya, man, it is. But we're not all sure it's tha gay disease. Some committed suicide, and we don't know why. Others were fine one day, dead tha next. And it's always tha same, man, cancer, pneumonia, some fungus, or sex disease. When you read tha papers, you see tha same line. Dies of cancer, dies of pneumonia. You can pick it after a while."

"Yeah, I know. My family and I check the papers daily. We've all lost someone we know."

"Ya, man. Whatever this disease is, it's killing off tha men."

Roger glanced at his watch. Nearly twelve. "So, what's happening with this place?"

Kingie shrugged. "Freddy was in debt; he owed tha bank, they want to collect. They're waiting until next month, so we have time to get everything out, everything cleared."

"Where are Freddy's possessions going?"

"Freddy didn't have much besides this place. Being in debt he won't have money, and what personal effects he had, he wanted buried with him."

"Like what?" Roger was curious to learn more about the man he'd called a friend.

"His heavy metal albums, his black leather jacket, a few pieces of jewellery that he wore. Some love letters from his ex-wife."

Roger's brows flew up. "Freddy had an ex-wife?"

"Many a year ago, man." Kingie grinned. "He asked me to post her a letter he wrote before he died. No idea what it said, though."

"Jesus. I always thought Freddy was as gay as the rest of us," Roger said.

"Hey, man, speak for yourself. I'm not gay," Kingie protested. "Had me a wife for fifteen years now, five kids to go with, man."

"Well, I didn't know that either," Roger told him. "From the way you flirted with all the guys, I just assumed you were gay too."

"Nah, man, just all part of tha job." Kingie's grin grew bigger. "But Freddy, he had a couple of partners back in tha early years and tha odd one here or there. It didn't really interest him, though. He may have changed courses, but he didn't like running. Said sex bored him as he got old."

"How old was he?"

"Fifty-five."

"Jesus, is that all?" Roger shook his head. "I thought he was in his sixties, nearly seventy at least. He *looked* old."

"All tha years had worn him down. Especially tha last few." Kingie looked at the clock. "We'd better get going. You go ahead. I'll just lock up and check downstairs."

"I came by taxi from the airport. Do you have a car?"

"Need a lift, man? Wait five minutes and I'll be down."

Roger slowly walked down the stairs and waited by the only car parked out back, assuming it was Kingie's, thinking about all he'd just heard, all it meant, and all that were now dead. He and Tomas hadn't been there since November when so many had died. Now, there were more, including Freddy, and it was only late April.

Kingie came out from the restaurant and locked up. "Ready to go, man?"

"Yeah." Roger heaved a sigh. "Let's get it over with."

Ten minutes later they were standing in the church for the funeral and what Roger saw shocked him. Only half the people he expected turned up. "Does this mean the other half that were here last November are dead?" he asked Kingie.

"Ya man. I doubt tha rest will last tha year."

"Roger?"

Roger turned and saw David, Zack and Adam walking up to him. "Hey, guys, you made it. Still alive I see."

"Yeah, man," David gave him a hug. "You, too. Tomas here with you?" He looked around at the half-empty church.

"No. He couldn't deal with this anymore, so he stayed home."

"Yeah, I know what he means," David murmured. "Jesus, don't tell me they're all dead."

"Apparently, the photo board is going to be huge today," Roger said. "A lot more have gone."

"Fuck, man," David breathed. "Yeah, I know where Tomas is coming from. I think this will be my last. We'll do it for Freddy, and that's it."

"That's why I'm here. Otherwise, I wouldn't be. It's too depressing," Roger said, turning as the priest called for everyone to be seated.

The service lasted about half an hour, and several people moved to the front to speak. Roger, Kingie, and David included. Roger thanked Freddy for giving them all a safe place to play, reminding him that he'd taken Tomas there on their first date. Kissing his fingers, he touched them to Freddy's coffin, which was closed to all who passed. The service ended, and they made their way to the cemetery for the burial, then back to *Love Stick* to toast their dearly departed friend.

Finding the photo board, Roger stood shocked, more so than in November when there had been thirty-six familiar faces. Now, there was nearly a hundred. The board was so big it extended ten feet long and six feet high. All in order of passing starting with the four *Seralift* porn stars Luiz had killed. The four that David had suggested started it all. Spreading the disease one after the other to people he knew, people he'd known, people he'd loved and cared about. The crevice between his eyes deepened as his frown did. *Seralift* guys, *Love Stick* regulars, *The Joy Stick* staff. More waiters and regulars from *The Bat and Balls* and *Wood*. Plus, he recognised friends he'd hung out with before meeting Tomas, and those he'd met after. "Jesus, even Freddy's picture is on here."

"Sad, isn't it?" David, Zack and Adam stopped to look.

"Yeah, it is," Roger replied. "I can't believe how many. Jesus fucking Christ."

"Yeah, our whole life is all but gone here. Everyone I know personally is either on that board, or in this room." David turned to look at the sick men left. "And once the last one of them is gone, who'll put their photos on this board?" He turned back. "At least another fifty plus will be added, if not more. Could even be hundreds."

"Fucking hell," Roger murmured, feeling the energy slide straight out of him, out through his feet, and into the floor. "Fucking hell."

"Yep. I have a feeling there will only be us left." David sighed. "The five of us."

"We're the only ones who still look alive." Zack watched the crowd. "And they're not even dead yet."

Looking from the board to the room, they saw nothing but death and destruction.

Destruction of the safety they once knew. Destruction of the lifestyle, their way of life, their sexual freedom, the place they all felt safe. But, they were safe no more.

They saw Kingie get up on stage and raise a glass. "Everyone, gather round and get your glass. Fill tha glasses will you." He pointed to the waiters and waited a moment. "Okay, everyone, get a glass, raise it to Freddy."

Roger held his up, watching Kingie the whole time.

"To Freddy. Tha man who started *Love Stick*, who worked hard to provide a safe haven, a happy place, a place for gay men to come to enjoy themselves freely and openly. He was tha life of tha party and will be deeply missed. To Freddy."

"To Freddy."

Roger went to put the glass to his lips, but stopped. His brain and gut were telling him not to drink from it. "Don't," he told the others sharply, quickly and inconspicuously stopping David, Zack and Adam drinking from theirs. "We don't know who's touched them, or drank from them before us. Just pretend you've drunk and find a place to put it down.

They nodded and found a table nearby with empty trays. When no one was looking they put their glasses down and walked over to Kingie.

"Great speech, man," Roger said. "Much like Freddy gave the last few times."

"He told me what he wanted," Kingie said. "Sweet and simple like he had been."

"It was great, but now we need to say goodbye," David said. "Kingie." He held out his hand. "We probably won't be back. Too many heartaches to deal with. We hope you stay safe and stay alive to see this thing through."

"Thanks, man, thanks for coming. Freddy would have wanted you to. You're tha only healthy-looking ones here," Kingie said.

"That's because we got out," David replied. "And now it's going to be permanent. It's been great knowing you, Kingie."

"You too, man, you too. Say goodbye to everyone on your way out, and I hope you all stay safe and sound."

"Thanks, Kingie," Roger said. "You too." Looking around, he decided to take some photos before he left. He snapped the picture board of the fallen, the décor, the people remaining, the wall of famous photos of the celebrities that had come to Freddy's *Love Stick* over the years.

He had a waiter take a picture of him, David, Zack and Adam underneath the sign that said *Love Stick* inside the door, but before taking the photo, the waiter sneezed then handed the camera back to Roger who carefully held it out while he grabbed a hanky to wrap it in. He put it in his bag and grimaced. "Can't be too careful," he told the others, and they went to say goodbye to the few remaining friends and acquaintances from their old Miami days, murmuring kind words and goodbyes while they still could. Telling them how sorry they were that they were going through this, and that they hoped they all had someone there for them at the end. With a final wave at the people, and a final longing look at the place, they walked outside, took a last glance at the dilapidated sign that said *Love Stick*, and hailed a taxi to the airport.

Roger walked into his apartment that evening, tired, worn out, and emotional. He wandered into the laundry and carefully removed his camera from his bag. Filling the sink with bleach and water he dumped the hanky in, thinking he should just throw it out. He removed the finished film from his camera, and carefully wiped the camera and his hands. Once he was clean, he wiped out his bag and left it to dry overnight. Taking the camera and roll of film into the lounge room, he found a canister to put the film in, and stuck a red dot on the lid to remind him to get it developed.

A quick shower and he was upstairs in the penthouse kissing his husband deeply, holding him, telling him he loved him.

"It was that bad?" Tomas asked from his husband's arms, waiting while Roger gained the emotional energy to speak. He could feel how worn out he was, lacked the energy he had before he'd left that morning.

"It was horrible." Roger sighed and glanced over at his family gathered around the fireplace. "Let's go over for a few minutes and then head downstairs.

"Okay." Tomas pulled back, worried by his lover's state of mind, and led him over to the lounge.

"How was it?" Jenny asked from between her granddaughters who were snuggled up on either side of her.

Taking a deep breath, Roger slowly let it out and sat on the couch arm. "Bloody horrible."

"Was the funeral okay?" Tomas asked, standing beside Roger, and slowly rubbing his shoulders.

"Small." Roger looked up at him. "More have passed."

Tomas frowned. "There weren't many there then?"

"Less than half from November," Roger said. "And the rest will go."

"How many?" Tomas asked even though he didn't want to know.

"Fifty or so."

"Jesus." Tomas covered his mouth with both hands and walked away, unable to bear death and destruction any longer.

"How many in total?" Pedro asked.

"Nearly a hundred, including Freddy. The photo board last November had thirty-six photos, now there's nearly a hundred." He shook his head sadly. "It was about ten feet long by six feet high. And from the look of those left, they'll be on the board by the end of the year."

"Oh, that's so sad," Viv said, the magazine on her lap forgotten.

"Yeah, it was," Roger told her. "But David, Zack and Adam turned up, and they're still alive and well so far. Kingie, Freddy's manager, is still okay, but that's because he's straight." He gave a laugh. "I never knew he had a wife and five kids."

"You're kidding." Tomas came back over. "I thought he was gay."

"That's what *I* told him, and he said flirting was all part of the job. And get this, back in the day, *Freddy* had a wife."

"What!" Tomas exclaimed. "I thought he was gay, too."

"Apparently, he was, tried out women first and then changed later in life. He only had a few male lovers according to Kingie, and he'd given him a letter to send off to his ex."

"Whoa." Tomas's eyes went wide. "The things you learn."

"Yeah, I took a bunch of photos of the place. I'll get the roll developed next week. It's sad. The place looks so lost and lonely, and in desperate need of a makeover; it's horribly sad what it's turned into."

"I'm sorry. It must have been awful to see." Tomas rubbed Roger's back to comfort him.

"Yeah." Roger shook his head. "Compared to just a few years ago when I took you there, the place is just dilapidated, almost in ruins. But then we noticed a few other places looked the same."

"All gay places?" Carlos asked.

"Yeah," Roger replied. "With the staff and regulars dying from *Wood, The Bat and Balls, The Joy Stick* and so many more, they're all looking worse for wear. Clearly, those that aren't sick are staying away while the rest are dying off."

Everyone sat lost in thought for a few moments.

"It's happening everywhere," Pedro finally said. "We've lost more regulars from 69. Eddie's now letting *anyone* in just to fill the place. The people that were once left out on the sidewalk are now being let in. I don't know how much more I can take. How much longer I can deal with it."

"It's going to get a whole lot worse before it gets better," Jenny murmured, hugging her grandbabies closer. "I have a feeling you're going to lose every gay person you know."

Scared eyes went to Tomas and Roger, but they only had eyes for each other.

"I've kept a list," Viv said, gazing into the fire. "How can I not. The people I worked with were more than co-workers, they were friends, some even more like my family than my real family. We'd spend Christmas and New Years on shoots in Milan, Tokyo, Paris, London. Looking back, it was an incredible life, and at the time, I was depressed at being away from home. But I'm glad it happened. I'm glad I spent those times with them."

"How many for you?" Jenny asked.

"I've just lost the eleventh," Viv murmured, gazing at her daughter snuggled under Jenny's arm, reading her storybook and colouring it in. She knew she was damn lucky to have the life she had now, and the husband and daughter bestowed upon her. And she gave her thanks every day.

"How many from 69?" Jenny asked Pedro.

He shrugged and struggled with a number. "I haven't actually counted, but probably up near thirty, or forty I think it was. The ones I know of."

Jenny glanced at Tomas and Roger. "And it's nearly a hundred for you?"

Roger nodded. "Yeah, not sure exactly, but nearly there."

Jenny breathed deeply. All this death, this sadness, was horrific, and a part of it was making her want to run back to Mykonos, or Australia. "Can you two take time off this summer?" she asked Carlos and Viv. "I think it's time we get out of here and go on holiday. Angie will be out of school, Pedro out of work. The boys don't work, so it will be just the two of you. We can celebrate the girls' birthdays somewhere like Australia…or Mykonos for the summer."

"Are you saying you finally want to go home?" Spiros was incredulous.

"No," Jenny told him. "I'm saying we need to get away to some place where there's no disease, no friends dying, no sickness, no funerals. Get away from it all for a while."

"What about work?" Viv asked.

"Depending on how long we're gone, maybe you can hire a film crew and do some exercise videos," Jenny suggested. "Think of the backdrops you could use, do exercises from around the world. You could get new ideas for perfumes, or other cosmetics."

Viv and Carlos traded glances. "It sounds good," she said. "If we knew for sure where we were going, we could set it up."

"Well, *I* don't know yet," Jenny replied. "We have another month for Angie to do exams, and then there's graduation. I'm sure we can come up with an idea in the next month."

"Could Maggie and Mike come?" Angie asked, the excitement creeping up inside her. "If we're going back to Mykonos that is."

Jenny smiled at her growing enthusiasm. "Sure, why not. They can come over at some stage once we're settled in. I'll pay their airfare."

Angie excitedly clapped her hands and Alena, seeing her mother so excited, clapped her hands too, lightening the mood for the evening.

Tomas and Roger smiled and said their goodnights before retiring for the evening to their apartment.

"That sounds like an awesome holiday. If we go to Mykonos, you can show me where you went to school, where you had your first job, where you had your first kiss…" He stopped as Tomas pulled out of his arms. "What is it, T?"

"My first kiss was Luiz," Tomas whispered. "In the steam room at the resort gym where I worked."

"Oh." Roger softened. "Forgot."

"It's okay. I do most times," Tomas told him, pulling off Roger's shirt.

"And then someone says something to make you remember." Roger helped Tomas out of his pants.

"And then I remember," Tomas said, taking hold of Roger's manhood. "And then I want to forget all over again." His tongue enticed Roger's out of his mouth.

"Then let me help you forget," Roger breathed, picking Tomas up so he straddled him and they fell back onto the bed.

Tomas lay full out on his lover until Roger rolled over and he was underneath. Not that who was on top mattered. He loved being underneath his husband. The masculine power that was Roger was a heady experience. One that made him feel like the prize. Roger wanted him and him alone, and Tomas didn't mind being the subordinate one. He loved it when Roger took control in the bedroom, preferred that he did. He had the muscle strength, the power, the uninhibited imagination and masculinity to take charge, and Tomas loved being underneath him, having his lover on top so he could wrap his arms and legs around him, hold him, show him he was his.

"Mmm," he breathed as Roger's tongue invaded his mouth. Small noises came from both of them during the throes of passion as they rocked back and forth, melding together as one. They didn't let anything stop them, didn't let *anyone* stop them, not even sure if they could. All they knew was that every time they were together they had to let it play out until its climatic end.

May 1981

Roger raced into his apartment to find Tomas lying on the couch. "I finally got the roll of film back from the pharmacy. Do you want to see, or shall I keep them from you?" He glanced down at his husband who looked tired. "You okay, T? You don't look so good." Sitting beside him, he felt his forehead. "Mmm, you're a bit warm."

"Mmm," Tomas moaned. "I don't feel good. Tired all the time."

"That's the nightmares," Roger said. "In which case, you won't want to look at Freddy's place. It will just add to them."

"Keep them." Tomas gently pushed his hand away. "I'll remember Freddy's the way it was. God…I'm so tired."

"Maybe you should get some air, get back into exercising some more. You need oxygen."

Tomas's soft grin slid into place. "Yeah. I haven't exercised much lately." He struggled to sit up. "I don't seem to have much energy either. Even to sit."

"Maybe you're coming down with something." Frozen tentacles of fear slid through Roger's heart.

"I probably caught a spring bug or something. Or maybe it's just from not sleeping." Tomas yawned and covered his mouth.

"Maybe," Roger said. "In that case, maybe you *should* get more air and some sun. I'm gonna get my photo albums to show your family the way Freddy's has changed. They upstairs?" He headed into the bedroom.

"Don't know." Tomas lay back down. "Tired."

After dinner, Roger passed around the album and new pictures. "I can't believe how much it's changed," he said from his spot on the couch between Tomas and Jenny. "It's sad, so goddamn sad."

"Aw, look at you two." Jenny found two pages of photos with Tomas and Roger.

Roger leaned over her shoulder. "Our first date at the beach and *Love Stick* later."

"You both look so happy." She smiled at the pictures of her son. "So happy."

"Yeah, we were," Roger replied. "Still are, aren't we, T?"

Silence.

"T?" Roger turned his head to look at his lover.

Everyone looked at Tomas to find him asleep, cheek resting on his hand as his elbow rested on the couch arm.

"He's tired." Jenny watched her son. "Hasn't been sleeping well, has he?"

"No," Roger replied. "Awake, or tossing and turning most nights. He was asleep on the couch when I came back from the pharmacy."

"How has his general health been?" Jenny asked. "Have the two of you seen that new doctor your friends suggested?"

"Not yet," Roger said. "For some reason, we never got around to it."

"New doctor?" Spiros inquired from beside Jenny. "You're not seeing Dr Hubbard?"

"No," Roger told him. "We heard about a doctor months back, around Christmas. He comes highly recommended by gay friends because he has a lot of gay patients. Some even said he was gay himself, that's why they all went to him. Figured he'd understand their problems better."

"Maybe you should have an all over exam," Jenny suggested, watching her son with that creeping fear that always arose. "If we're travelling over summer, we all should."

"Yeah, maybe," Roger said thoughtfully. "He felt a bit warm this afternoon." Reaching out a hand, he felt Tomas's forehead. "He's a bit warm now."

"We are coming into warm weather. All of the knits have been put away, and summer gear is just around the corner," Jenny said.

"And in two more weeks, I graduate." Angie squealed. She was sitting next to Pedro on the couch opposite her parents. "Yay."

"Yay, Mama," Alena said from her spot on the coffee table where she and Diana were colouring the pictures in the books Gamma and Gampa had bought them.

"Yay, Alena, Mama's nearly out of school," Angie said.

"Shool? Was that?" Diana asked, her golden curls moving as she bounced her head up and down.

"Somewhere you'll be going soon," Viv told her as she wrote a plan for filming overseas.

"Me?" Diana turned to look at her mother with wide, worried eyes. "Me go to shool?"

Viv laughed softly. "Yes, my darling. You and Alena will be going to school. You'll learn how to read and write and do arithmetic."

"I no go to shool, Mama." Diana fiercely shook her head. "Gamma will learn me how to wead, wite an' do wifmetic."

"School will also teach you how to pronounce your Rs," Viv said.

"Ahs, what are ahs?" Diana asked.

"Oh, Bubba, that's why children go to school. To learn what these things are," Viv told her, shaking her head in amusement.

Tomas's head fell off his hand and he woke, startled.

"You okay, T?" Roger asked. "You fell asleep."

Tomas yawned. "Oh…excuse me. I'm just so tired all the time."

"Are you still taking your vitamins?" Jenny asked. "I figured they'd been helping all these years."

"Yeah, maybe. I don't know," Tomas said sleepily. "Maybe I need to get out in the air more. Get some sun after a long winter. I probably have a bug."

Jenny looked up sharply from the photo album in her lap. "Well, I suggest you get that bug looked at. We have a few busy weeks ahead of us. There's my birthday, Angie's graduation, our anniversary, all in three days. And that's only two weeks away. Pedro, when are you leaving 69?"

Pedro looked up from his spot slouching on the sofa. "I told Eddie I'd last until the end of the month, give him a big Saturday night bash on the 30th, then I'm done."

"And then we have all summer to have fun and celebrate the girls' birthdays," Jenny told everyone.

"Berfday?" The girls turned in unison, turning to their Gamma. "My berfday?"

"No, Da-anna, *my* berfday," Alena told her cousin.

"No, A-ena, *my* berfday," Diana chastised right back.

Jenny laughed. "It's *both* your birthdays, my babies, but we have to decide where we're going yet. Where do you girls want to go for your birthday?"

Alena and Diana took one look at each other and told their Gamma the same thing. "Disneyand."

*****

That night, as Roger lay asleep, Tomas woke. He was shivering, despite it being late spring, and despite it being quite warm in the room. He was cold, and his body shook uncontrollably, muscles tense, nerves near breaking point. Pulling the blankets over him, he tried to get warm, but couldn't.

"Mmm." Roger breathed in. "T?"

Tomas couldn't speak, his jaw was clenched tight.

"T? You okay?" Turning on the light, Roger saw his husband shivering under the blankets. "Tomas?" He pulled back the covers and found him shaking. "Tomas." Feeling his forehead, he found he was burning up. "Jesus, Tomas, what's wrong with you?"

"So cold." Tomas's teeth chattered. "So cold."

"Come on, let's get you into the shower and get you warm." Roger rolled out of bed and carried him into the bathroom, setting him down in the shower; he turned the hot tap on. "Considering you're actually hot, I'm not sure I should be making you hotter," Roger said as the water warmed up.

"So cold." Tomas hugged himself. "So cold."

"How can you be cold when you're burning up? I think I should put you under cold water."

"No, no." Tomas reached out to stop Roger changing the taps. "Hot, need hot, so good…helping…" His teeth slowly stopped moving, and his muscles relaxed. "So good."

Roger added cold water so it wouldn't burn him. "Feel better?"

Tomas stood still, letting his muscles work out the cramps. "Yes."

"Good, but if you're still running a temperature, we should see a doctor."

With a sigh, Tomas agreed. "Tomorrow. We'll see one tomorrow."

*****

The next day they managed to get into their new doctor.

"And what's wrong with you today?" Melvin Crush MD asked. He was in his forties with brown hair, blue eyes and yes, he was gay.

Tomas glanced at Roger. "I think I have a bug. I've been tired this last week; I'm always sleeping, even though I can't sleep at night. I have night sweats and chills."

"Last night I woke up and he was shaking, saying how cold he was. But when I felt him, his skin was burning," Roger added.

"Okay, tell me why you think you can't sleep?" Crush asked.

Tomas rubbed his sweaty palms on his jeans and sighed. He did not want to be there discussing his personal issue with anyone.

"I can't help you unless you tell me," Crush said, studying both boys.

"Go on, T. Tell him," Roger urged.

"I…" Tomas glanced at Roger. "I have nightmares."

"About?"

Another deep breath and his eyes moved to the ceiling. "About… all of our friends…"

"And…"

"And they're all dead. In real life and my dreams, and they're reaching out their long bony hands to me." Tomas breathed, shuddering at the thought.

"Are the two of you gay? Partners?" Crush asked.

"Yes," Roger answered.

"Monogamous?" Crush went on.

"Yes." Roger did the talking while Tomas sat there staring anywhere but at them.

"All your friends are dying from this so-called gay disease we've all heard about?" Crush casually asked.

"Yes."

"Absolutely understandable," Crush said. "A lot of people are losing friends. It's depressing, and I'd say you're suffering from depression. The nightmares result in lack of sleep, so the body is always tired and trying to catch up. I'm going to give you a prescription for Nomifensine. It's an antidepressant. It should help lighten your mood. I also suggest a good diet high in protein and to make a sleep timetable. Every morning you get up at the same time regardless of how tired you are. Get out in the sun and get your body working for the day. Then, at night, go to bed at the same time. Try to relax for half an hour beforehand. No TV. No telephone. Some relaxing music, hot milk, and don't nap during the day. Have you been having headaches?"

"Sometimes," Tomas replied.

"Purely from lack of good sleep. I suggest getting a professional massage to help you relax. Come back in two weeks and let me know how you went. I'll see you then." He handed over the prescription and waited for them to leave.

"I'm depressed?" Tomas asked Roger as they walked from the surgery.

"It's understandable that all this death has made you miserable." They checked for cars and crossed the street. They had walked there in the warm spring sun and were heading back.

"Yeah, I know, but he's just a doctor. Don't I need to see a shrink about depression?"

"I suppose, but I guess he knows what he's doing," Roger replied.

"I...I don't even know if I should get these, Roger." Tomas looked at the paper in his hand. He'd never heard of Nomifensine before. "I don't know what they'll do to me."

"At least give them a go," Roger suggested. "For two weeks anyway, and if you're no better in a couple of weeks when we go back to see him, then you can try something else."

*****

That night, around the dinner table, Tomas told the family what the doctor had said; disappointed that it wasn't something definite.

"I suppose he knows what he's doing," Jenny said, watching him closely. "Do *you* think you could be depressed with everything that's happened?"

Tomas thought about it and shrugged. "I guess."

"As much as we try and stay positive and do happy things, death always knocks on our door once more," Roger said.

"Yes…I suppose you would be depressed with everything that's happening," Jenny murmured. "It must be so hard to lose friends."

"It is," Pedro murmured in return, watching his brother and worrying.

*****

Over the next two weeks, Tomas got up every morning, took his pills, and went for a one-hour walk around the park. He went to bed at the same time every night, took his vitamins, ate healthily like he used to, and did not take naps in the afternoon. If he became tired, he went for another walk. And while the prognosis was expected to be good, Tomas was not. He developed a sore throat, more headaches, muscle and bone pain, and a non productive cough

So did Roger…

They both lost weight, but that could have been from the occasional bout of vomiting, and both suffered from abdominal pain. They went back to the doctor and told him all of their symptoms.

He felt their glands, swollen and lumpy, looked in their throats and made them say ah, and did a general check-up. "You seem to have developed the flu," Dr Crush told them. "Which is strange. Have you been taking the pills?"

"Yes."

"Every day?"

"Yes."

"And getting exercise and fresh air?"

"We both have," Roger said.

"Mmm, and yet you've developed flu-like symptoms. Well, it looks like you've picked up a bug after all. I'll give you both pills to take and come and see me in another two weeks."

"We may not be here in another two weeks," Tomas said. "Our family is going away for the summer."

"Then see me the day before you go." Crush dismissed them.

Once again, they walked out of his office, wondering what it was he'd given them.

"How can we have the flu when it's May?" Tomas asked as he and Roger took a taxi because they didn't feel well enough to walk home.

Roger sighed. "Don't know, T. But I'm beginning to think we need to see another doctor."

*****

Two days later, they barely made it upstairs for Jenny's fifty-third birthday.

"Oh, my boys, you look horrible." Jenny rushed over to them as they came through the door.

"Feel awful," Roger croaked, barely having the strength to close the door and feeling like a bag of wet cement.

"Sorry, Mama," Tomas whispered in her ear, which was all he could do. "I know you wanted to go out tonight."

She held her son tight. "It doesn't matter. If my babies are sick, then a restaurant doesn't matter. Have you taken your pills?"

"I don't think they're working, Mama." Tomas stumbled into the sitting area. "My throat's still sore, I can't eat, or I vomit what I do eat. God, I feel like I'm dying."

"Don't say that," Jenny cried and sat beside him. "Don't *you dare* say that." She felt his forehead and looked into his eyes. His skin had a yellow tinge, and the cough was worse. "Maybe we should get you into the hospital to get a proper examination."

"I don't know, Mama. I hate hospitals." Tomas moaned.

"Because of what Luiz did?" Jenny asked. "This has nothing to do with him, Tomas. If you have the flu, it needs to be sorted out, and if you have something else then…" She left the sentence unfinished, and all heads turned to her.

"Don't even say that, Mama," Tomas warned with a shake of his head. "Don't even."

Jenny breathed in. "Then I suggest we get you to a hospital tomorrow my baby because there is no way I'm going to let you die from that. Now, let's get on with celebrating. It's my birthday, and I have cake to cut and presents to open."

"Pwesents?" Alena excitedly clapped. "Gamma has pwesents, Da-anna."

"An' cay, A-ena," Diana added. "Cay an' pwesents."

Their excitement over cake and presents made everyone lighten up and laugh, even Tomas and Roger.

Thank God for the girls, Jenny thought. *They've lightened the mood.*

Munching their way through dinner and cake, Jenny worried for her son. She felt it. Felt it was coming, and knew there wasn't a damn thing she could do about it but fight till the bitter end. Tomas had barely eaten, only a mouthful here and there. He'd lost weight, lost strength, and generally looked ill. After opening presents of jewellery and photos, they spent the night being a family.

*****

"Oh, my God, I can't believe we've graduated," Angie squealed as she hugged Maggie. After four years of triumphs and tribulations, deaths and despair, loss and pain, she had finally made it to her graduation.

"Neither can I." Maggie held on tight as they bounced around in circles.

"Are you girls going to 69 to celebrate?" Jenny asked. The whole family was there; even Tomas and Roger who'd mustered the strength to make it with the help of Spiros and Carlos. Mike had also turned up to see his girl graduate.

"Oh, I don't know, are you all going to make it?" Angie stopped to stare at her family. "I don't want to go and have fun while the two of you are so sick."

"Don't worry about us, Angie, you go and have fun," Tomas rasped.

"Why don't we all have dinner at home, and then you can go off later to celebrate. I know the boys have to be there early as usual, but you girls don't have to rush," Jenny said.

Angie and Maggie traded glances before Maggie looked at her parents standing nearby.

"I have to have dinner with my folks, but I can meet you there later," Maggie told Angie.

"Or come over to my place, and we'll go together," Angie said.

"Okay, I'll see you later. Bye Mr and Mrs Stephanopoulos." Maggie waved and ran off to her parents.

"Bye, Maggie," Jenny called then turned to her ill sons. "Okay, let's get you two home."

*****

While Pedro went to work, and Angie went off and partied, Jenny kept an eye on her grandbabies and babies. Tomas wasn't any better, and she knew she needed to get him to the hospital. But fear was stopping her. She knew she had to get him there, but if she did, and found out he was sick, then it would make it all real, and she didn't want it to be real. Couldn't deal with it if it was…

*****

Saturday the twenty-third dawned bright, warm, and sunny, and Jenny and Spiros celebrated their 29th wedding anniversary in style by making love three times in two hours.

"Oh, God, I love you." Jenny shuddered from her third orgasm for the morning.

"Oh, I know you do," Spiros gasped as he rolled off his wife and lay back on a pile of pillows.

Jenny laughed. "Oh, yes, you know I do." She rolled on top of him and smothered him in kisses. "And you can definitely keep up with your sons."

"More like they need to keep up with me," Spiros told her. "I don't think Carlos or Pedro have had sex with the girls since before the babies were born."

A snort left Jenny, and she laughingly collapsed on his chest. "Oh, *my* God. I can't believe you said that." Looking up she added. "But for the record, they have *definitely* had sex since the babies came along."

"Well, then, they really *do* need to catch up with me then," Spiros said and rolled her over for their fourth time for the morning.

*****

"Oh, God, Roger," Tomas moaned. "I feel awful. And I can't breathe properly...Roger. Roger?" He shoved his lover, who woke.

"Wha...wha...what's wrong?"

"I feel awful."

"Yeah, so do I."

"I think we need to go to the hospital," Tomas said. "I think Mama's right. This isn't getting any better."

"Yeah, I know. It's different to the other flu we had back in '77."

"Yeah, it's worse."

"If we can make it through today, then we should go see another doctor."

"Yeah, we should..."

"Okay, we'll go after lunch."

"Maybe we can wait until tomorrow?"

"Do you have the energy to wait?"

"I don't want to ruin Mama's day."

"I'm sure they'd rather know their sons are getting the proper treatment than spend their anniversary worrying."

"Yeah, I suppose."

*****

Jenny fluttered around the kitchen. They would be having anniversary lunch, it being a Saturday, so everyone could go their separate ways later. It was a beautiful spring day, the windows let in the light and scented floral air, and a happy anniversary banner hung across the side wall. Even though it was their anniversary, Jenny had no problem decorating the penthouse for her own party.

Carlos and Viv stumbled in with Diana just after twelve.

"Gamma." Diana ran over to her. "Happy anniversawy, Gamma."

"Oh, my baby." Jenny lifted her and smothered her in kisses. "Thank you."

"Does Gampa get a hug too?" Spiros asked his granddaughter as he moved to Jenny's side.

"Gampa?" Diana reached over, and Jenny let her go into Spiros's arms. "Happy anniversawy."

"Thank you, Diana," Spiros said. "Did we get a pwesent?"

Alena burst through the door. "Pwesents."

"Oh, God, Alena, not so loud," Pedro groaned. He'd only had five hours sleep and Angie not much more.

"Yes. Did you bring us pwesents, Alena?" Spiros asked her as she clung to his legs.

"Why would I bwing you pwesents, Gampa?" Alena asked innocently.

"Because it's their wedding anniversary, silly," Angie told her, laying the brightly wrapped box on the table beside the couch in the sitting area. "Happy anniversary." She hugged them after Pedro.

"Thank you, Angie," Jenny said, seeing Tomas and Roger slowly come through the door.

"Mama...Papa," Tomas rasped, his gait faltering. "Happy anniversary..."

"Yes, Mr and Mrs S," Roger said. "Happy...anniversary."

"Tomas?" Jenny saw it and frowned.

He staggered, coming to a stop. "Mama…I don't feel good. I'm sorry, but I don't think I'll make…the…" His vision blurred, his brain slowed, his legs gave out beneath him.

"Tomas." Jenny saw his eyes roll back in his head. "Tomas," she screamed, seeing him fall to his knees and sway, running towards him, seeing him land on his back, landing beside him as she fell to her knees. "Tomas, don't you dare leave me, don't you dare." She grabbed his face, shook him, felt his skin, looked into his eyes, felt for a pulse.

"Tomas." Roger collapsed weakly next to his husband. "Tomas."

Jenny looked from one to another, fear making her weak.

"Call an ambulance," Spiros directed Carlos who was frozen to the spot. "Call two ambulances," he yelled.

Carlos moved in a daze toward the phone, scared that his brother was dead.

The rest stood frozen in fear, holding back the girls who were crying, staring down at Tomas unconscious on the floor, Roger almost the same beside him, and Jenny screaming her son's name.

The ambulances arrived; the paramedics intubated both of them and rushed them to the hospital, where they were rushed into emergency with the family following.

Jenny rushed through the door, wildly looking around for her son, seeing him in a small room off to the side. *"Help him,"* she yelled. *"Do something."*

Spiros pulled her back as the nurse closed the curtain on them, but that just infuriated Jenny who went into Mama Bear mode with eyes ablazing. Ripping back the curtain so that it came halfway off the rod, she spat, "don't you dare shut the curtain on me. You *will not* shut me out of my son's treatment. Do you understand me?"

The wild passion and hard steely determination surprised them, for they looked up wide-eyed at her before going back to caring for her son.

"I need a chest x ray, blood panel, and any fluid test you can get," Doctor Dan Ardent, a five-ten brunet said. Flicking a light into Tomas's eyes, he asked, "Can you tell me your name?" Another flick of the light. "Nope, he's out. Get him a ventilator until we know what we're dealing with. What about the other one?"

"Conscious, barely breathing."

"Get oxygen on him." Dan made his way around Tomas's bed and stopped at Jenny, Spiros and the boys. Angie and Viv had stayed at the penthouse with the girls. "What's his name?"

"Tomas Stephanopoulos," Jenny told him.

"And how long's he been sick?" the green-eyed doctor asked, noticing how good-looking the men in the family were.

Jenny's eyes twitched. "We don't actually know."

Dan looked at her sharply. "Has he not seen a doctor?"

The comment just made Jenny angrier than she already was. "*He saw a doctor* on the 5th of May who told him his lack of sleep, headaches and excessive tiredness was due to depression. He prescribed Nomifensine and told Tomas to come back in two weeks. During those two weeks, Tomas and Roger complained of muscle and bone aches, bad stomach pain, sore throat, vomiting, weight loss and other things. They went *back to that doctor* on the 19th of May, and he told them they had the flu and prescribed another pill. In the last two days they've become worse. Before that, they hadn't been sick since Christmas '77 *when a different doctor* diagnosed the flu, and *before that,*" her eye twitched again, "he was poisoned with Nerium Oleander in October. He was treated in hospital and recovered. *Before that,* he hadn't been sick in over twelve years. He was fit, strong and healthy." She came to a shuddering stop.

Dan was quiet while he pondered his next move. "Your son is gay."

Jenny eyed him. "Yes."

"And the other man is his partner?"

"Yes." She waited for his reply. "Don't...you *dare* tell me..."

Dan ran a hand through his hair. "He's gay, it's possible...but we'll do tests."

Jenny moved closer and stuck her finger in his face. "*Don't you dare* tell me it's *that thing, not that.* They have lost too many friends to it, and I will *not* lose my son and his husband to it as well. You do every test there is on the face of the planet. You get in every doctor, every specialist. I don't care what the cost is, but you *will* find out what my sons have, do you understand me?"

Dan's eyes narrowed at the passion he was just blasted with. "You said…his husband?"

"Four years ago, they had a church ceremony where they married; they exchanged rings and vows and declared themselves married. It may not be legal in this country, but Roger Dencott is our son-in-law, and you will treat them both with the respect and dignity they deserve. Now, find out what's wrong with my sons," she snapped.

Dan gave a nod, surprised to see such a determined mother and family in the hospital. Most parents didn't care, didn't come. Most gay patients died alone. But he saw the fire in this mother's eyes and the fear in her husband's and sons'. "We'll do our best, Mrs Stephanopoulos."

"You'd better," Jenny told him and started pacing back and forth at the end of her sons' beds. She'd had them move Roger so they were side by side, and watched the nurses take blood, samples, x-rays and scans. Watched over them as doctors came in to examine their bodies from top to bottom, and murmur and mutter to each other until finally, Dan came over to talk.

"Well?" Jenny demanded.

"We've run a bunch of tests, but…unfortunately the early diagnosis isn't good."

"What does that mean?" Jenny asked, arms folded, looking the doctor square in the eye. There was no way she'd take the easy road.

Dan inwardly sighed. "Early diagnosis shows your son has pneumonia."

"That's not bad, is it?" Carlos asked from behind his parents.

Dan took a breath. "Well…this one is. It's called Pneumocystis Pneumonia…and it's bad, especially…in gays."

"And what does that mean?" Jenny inquired, refusing to hear the word bad.

"We've seen some male patients present with different ailments, but they all have this. It seems they are susceptible to it." His stomach was in knots, but the determination in this woman's face made him power on.

"Okay…" Jenny thought about it. "Then fix it."

He sighed. "We can put him on treatment, but it more than likely won't work."

"Why not?" she asked, refusing to give up.

"Because of the initial findings."

"Which are?" God, it was like pulling teeth to get an answer.

He took another breath. This was a job he hated doing. "Your son presents with a hell of a lot of problems, Mrs Stephanopoulos. Mr Dencott isn't so bad, but your son is full of issues."

"For the love of God, spit it out," Jenny snapped. "Issues like what? Can't you give him medicine?"

"For some of them, yes, for some, no."

"Why not?" She was over the time wasting.

"Because there aren't any."

That froze Jenny to the spot. "Are you telling me," the tears welled, "that my son has diseases you can't treat?"

"I'm telling you I don't know if we can make him better and that…" God how he hated this job. "You may have to prepare yourself."

The rage inside her flowed. Poking her finger into his chest, making him back up, she raged, "I don't care how many tests you run, how many orifices you swab, how many times you do it, how many x-rays, scans, diagnoses you do, you *will* find out what is wrong with my son. I told you to call in the specialists, so bloody well do it because my sons are *not* dying, doctor. *Do you understand me?* Money is no object, but you *will* properly diagnose my sons. Do you understand?" She didn't notice the rest of the staff staring in wonderment, or horror; she just wanted to get her point across about how bloody important this was, and Tomas and Roger were to her.

Dan nodded, intrigued and surprised by the fiery woman before him. "Yes, ma'am. We'll keep running the tests." He walked away, took a deep breath, and went back to work.

"Jenny," Spiros said quietly. "You can't—"

"Don't bloody tell me what I can't do," she snapped. "I will do *whatever* it takes to keep my baby alive." Stopping in front of Tomas's bed she stared at every tube, every needle, every machine keeping him alive. "I will *not* let you die from this," she told him as the family gathered around. "I will *not* let you die, my baby boy. I just won't."

*****

"Mama, where's evwyone gone?" Alena asked as Angie and Viv removed the Happy Anniversary banner and let down the other decorations.

"An' are we having cay?" Diana added.

Viv and Angie turned to see their daughters in front of them looking up with identical blue eyes. It had taken a good half hour to get them to stop crying, even though Viv and Angie were crying themselves.

"Oh, my baby, no. We're not having cake after all," Viv told Diana. "Maybe some other time."

"No cay?" Diana teared up again. Her pretty blue party dress was from Gamma, and it was the first time she'd worn it, but Gamma hadn't noticed.

"No, my baby, no cay today," Viv touched her daughter's cheek.

"Mama, where Dada an' Gamma an' Gampa?" Alena asked.

"They had to go and help Uncles Tomas and Roger." Angie folded the banner.

"So, no pahty?" Alena asked, wearing the pretty white dress Gamma had bought for her. The shoes were new and fancy too.

"No, Bubba, no party today," Angie said.

"Aw," Alena whined. "You told me we have pahty."

"I know, Alena." Angie was firm. "But Uncles Tomas and Roger have become very sick and need everyone's help, so the party's on hold." She saw her daughter's face scrunch up and knew what was coming. "Don't whine. If you want something to eat, I can get you some food."

"Cay?" Diana asked hopefully, holding her chubby little hands in front of her.

Viv laughed softly. "No, my baby, food, not cake."

They settled the girls down with a plate of food each, and out of earshot spoke in whispered tones.

"What do you think is going on?" Angie asked, scared out of her brain. After losing Leon, and Viv losing her friends, and Roger and Tomas having gone through so much, it was going to be hard if they had the gay cancer as some were calling it.

"I don't know," Viv whispered, keeping her voice low. Glancing over at the girls at the dining table she added, "After everyone we've lost…Jenny was always so scared that she'd lose Tomas too. Not like this, God, I wish someone would call."

The phone rang, making them jump and nervously giggle.

"Phone, Mama," Diana called before stuffing a rolled slice of ham into her mouth.

"Yes, I know, Bubba." Viv picked up the phone. "Hello."

"Babe, Carlos."

"Oh, my God, what's happening?" she whispered fiercely and turned away from the girls.

Angie quickly moved to her side, swept her hair over her shoulder, and stuck her ear to the phone while facing the girls to keep an eye on them.

Carlos sighed and glanced down the hall to see his parents watching Tomas while Pedro was by his side. He caught his eye before speaking. "They think it's bad. He has some sort of bad pneumonia that they've been seeing in gay men."

"Oh, my God," Viv breathed. "Does that mean—"

"Don't know," Carlos cut her off. "Mama doesn't want to think that way, and she stuck her finger in the doctor's face and told him to re-run every test. So far, not good."

"And the results are?" Viv asked.

"The doctor said he has a lot of issues, but he hasn't said what most of them are."

"Why not?"

"Don't know. Maybe it has something to do with Mama demanding they get every specialist in the world to check Tomas and Roger over. To re-do the tests over and over to make sure."

"Oh, God." Viv wiped a tear away. "What now? Will you be home?"

"I doubt it. He's our brother." He glanced at Pedro beside him who gave a sad smile in return. "We're here until the end."

"Of course," Viv said. "You stay as long as you need and call if you need anything. We'll be here in the penthouse. One of us will be here the whole time; we won't leave the phone. Anything you need, just call."

"Thanks, Viv, I needed to hear that. I'll call if anything changes." He hung up and glanced down the hallway to his parents and sighed. "What will we do if we lose him…them?"

"Don't." Pedro vehemently shook his head. "I don't want to hear it." He shuddered at the thought, his heart almost stopping as his breath came in gasps. "Is this…what Mama…warned us about…what she knew…years ago?" he sobbed. "Is this it? Is this what Luiz did to him?"

Carlos pulled him into his arms, and they clung to each other. "I don't know. I don't know, little brother, but I do know I don't want him to die. He can't die." They cried on each other's shoulders for a few moments. "We need to get back, so we don't miss anything." Wiping their faces, they walked back to their brother's room.

"Mrs S," Roger rasped, trying to remove his mask.

"Roger, no baby, keep it on." Jenny moved to his side and gently released it from his hand. "It's helping you breathe, keep it on."

"Tomas." Roger's eyes burned, his throat burned, his whole damn body burned, and he vaguely wondered if this is what all of his friends had gone through.

Jenny glanced at her son; the machine said he was still breathing, his heart still beating. "Still with us," she told Roger. "Still with us."

"Good." Roger breathed slowly. "I feel so sick."

"I know you do. But you both have to hang on because I'm not about to let you die. Not on my watch," Jenny said.

"Thanks, Mrs S." Roger drifted off.

"Mmm," Tomas moaned.

"Tomas?" Jenny moved to his side as did the others. "Tomas." She stroked his face, held his hand, and rubbed his arm. "My baby."

"Mama," he murmured and tried to open his eyes.

"Come on, baby." Jenny brushed his hair back. "Come on, come back to us, baby."

"Mama." His eyes opened a slit.

"Come on, Tomas," Jenny encouraged. "Come on, open your eyes and come back."

"Mama." His eyes opened, and everyone gathered around.

"Look at me, Tomas, show me you're in there," Jenny demanded, squeezing his hand harder.

"Mama." He turned his head to her slowly, blinking, looking at his mother. "Mama." His left hand lifted to his mouth to remove the mask. "Mama."

"No, baby, leave it on, it's helping you breathe."

"Mama," he rasped. "What's…wrong…with me?"

Jenny shook her head. "We don't know, baby. We don't know. The doctor's running every test possible, so we don't know yet."

"I…feel…so sick," he murmured. His whole being was on fire and in pain.

"I know," she soothed him, smoothing his hair back. "I know. But we hope they will start giving you something soon, and it will help. You rest now. You rest."

He dazedly glanced at his family and held out his fingers for them to take his hand. His eyes closed.

"Mrs Stephanopoulos."

Jenny turned to see the doctor and left her son to talk to him. Spiros took her spot at Tomas's bedside.

"Well, what have the tests revealed?" she asked.

Steeling himself, Dan looked at the paperwork in his hand to avoid her gaze. "Tests definitely show he has Pneumocystis Pneumonia which has attacked his lungs. He more than likely got this because his positive T cells are less than two hundred microlitres. It's why he's been having trouble breathing; it's the weight loss, the coughing, the night sweats. So that explains those symptoms. We can treat it, but it may or may not work."

"Why not?"

"Because he has a CD4 count of less than two hundred microlitres. He has all of the receptors of the disease…"

"No. Do not tell me that," Jenny told him, wild-eyed with boiling anger.

"When the CD4 count goes below two hundred microlitres, opportunistic infections occur, which is why he has the PCP."

"Then at least *try* and stop it by giving him the medication for it. You won't know unless you try."

"Ah…we could," he said. "But he has other infections too."

"Such as?"

"Such as parasites."

"What?" She shook her head, not even comprehending where, when, or how he could have gotten parasites. "Then kill them."

"We can try."

"Then that's what we have to do," Jenny told him. "Hit them with every treatment you can." She really didn't understand his reluctance in all of this.

He sighed. "We'll do what we can, Mrs Stephanopoulos, but when the blood cells die off, it usually means the end. You might want to prepare."

"I already did a long time ago doctor," Jenny told him. "Now, start giving him the bloody medication."

Nodding, Dan backed away to start the treatment.

Jenny went to Tomas's side. "Baby, the doctor's going to start giving you the medication, so you can get better. And hopefully, within a day or two, you'll be much better and they'll fix you, and you can come home with us. Okay, baby."

"Mama," he sighed, looking at her before his eyes slid shut.

"You rest, baby, you rest." Jenny stroked his face which looked so pale against the white sheets on the bed. Her lip quivered, and she was unable to keep it in. Rushing into the corridor, she landed against a wall and collapsed as the tears came.

"Jenny." Spiros pulled her into his arms, kneeling on the floor behind her. "Jenny, what did the doctor say?" Pedro and Carlos kneeled beside them.

She couldn't talk; every part of her body was clenched shut. Burying her head in Spiro's neck, she sobbed.

"Jenny," Spiros said and held her tightly. "What did the doctor say?"

"He," breath, "said," breath, "that Tomas has all the receptors of the disease that," breath, "gay men get."

"No," the boys murmured, tears coming to their eyes. "No, not Tomas."

"His blood had gone under two hundred microlitres. That's when gay men get opportunistic infections, which is why he has the bad pneumonia. He also said that he has other infections. Parasites."

"Oh, my God," Pedro said. "Did he tell you which ones?"

Jenny finally raised her head. "I didn't ask. I just told him to get all the medications he needed and give them to him. He said he would."

"Well…that's good then…right?" Carlos asked, hopeful that his brother and Roger would get help and be okay. Again.

"He told me," Jenny breathed, "that I needed to prepare."

"For what?" Pedro asked.

Jenny looked at him. "The end."

"Of…" Pedro shook his head in puzzlement.

Her blue eyes stared hard into his. "My son's life."

The boys sat back on their heels. "No, Mama," Carlos said. "No. We're not going to give up on him. On *them*."

"No, no we're not," Jenny told him and patted Spiros's hand. "Help me up. We have to be by our son's side. He can't be left alone, not for one moment." They made their way back to the room to find Dan administering the drugs. "How long before they take effect?" she asked.

He finished up injecting the tube. "The treatment for the pneumonia needs to be at least twenty-one days; the others vary from a week to two weeks."

"So, he'll be here for at least three weeks?" Jenny asked. "And Roger?"

Dan stopped at the end of the bed. "We're not actually sure what your son-in-law has, Mrs Stephanopoulos. Right now, it's showing as malaria."

Jenny's head shook in micro spasms of shock. "What? What do you mean, *malaria*?"

"That's what it's showing as, but we'll be testing for similar infections just in case it's something else, but it's slowly affecting him, and he will go the same way as your son."

"But how did he…how would he…?" Jenny was amazed and confused.

"We'll keep on testing to make sure, and start him on the medication for it. But as I said, it has started affecting him the same way, and we see OIs creeping in. We'll keep them both in ICU for a couple of days and see how they go. That will depend on whether we keep them there, or move them into a room," he paused, "Mrs Stephanopoulos, your son…"

"Is gay doctor, but does not have *that* disease!"

His heart went out to the woman before him. The mix of anger and sorrow in her eyes ripped his heart out. But she was full of fiery determination to help her son through something he was not going to survive. His voice softened. "Mrs Stephanopoulos, so far, all we know, is that every gay man that presents with illnesses like your son has, ends up dying within months. Now, there is a disease your son doesn't have that's common among the men, but overall, that doesn't mean much. Your son presents with the same issues, same diseases, and his blood cells are low along with his CD4 T cells. He has enlarged lymph glands and a respiratory throat infection. He has severe bacterial infections, he's," he paused and died a little on the inside, "not going to live long, Mrs Stephanopoulos. He has all the signs."

"You said there was one he didn't have?" she said.

"He doesn't have a cancer called Kaposi's sarcoma. Which is actually kind of surprising since he's of Mediterranean descent."

"What do you mean?" All the medical jargon was making her dizzy.

"Older Mediterranean men start getting blotches, or nodules in red-purple, brown, or black. Gay men have been getting them too."

"My um…" she thought back, "my husband's grandfather had those he's… *was* Greek. My boys are half Greek; we just thought they were sunspots, or something old men get."

"Well, that in part is true," Dan said.

"So, what else doesn't he have?" Jenny prayed there was an answer somewhere.

"Has he had diarrhea yet?"

"What?" She frowned. "Not that I know of."

"That normally comes along with the bacterial infections," he said. "But it could still happen."

"What else doesn't he have?" She was desperately hanging on to hope.

"He doesn't have, neither of them do, sexually transmitted diseases. A lot of gay men do."

"Roger was Tomas's second partner. They've been safe the whole time."

Dan nodded. "That's helped in a big way. It means we don't have those suckers to deal with, and they can be a bitch to deal with. But the diseases he does have means he has *the* disease. He's not going to survive it, Mrs Stephanopoulos. He's too sick, and even if we manage to get everything under control, it doesn't mean it will last long. He'll more than likely relapse and get sick again. You need to prepare for it." He looked at the family. "All of you need to prepare for your son's passing."

"You clearly don't know us, doctor," Jenny told him, the fire coming back to her belly. "I've fought hard for my babies, and will not stop until the day I die, and I don't plan on doing that for a very, very long time. I will fight with every fibre of the being God made me, and so will my family, to find out what's wrong with my boys and make them better, you can be damn straight I'll do that because Tomas and Roger's lives do not end here. *Tomas does not end here.*"

June 1981

"Jenny, it's Diana's birthday today," Spiros told her as he stood by Tomas's bed. "Should we take it in turns to go?"

With a weak sigh, she looked up at her husband. "What?"

He smiled softly down at her, brushing her hair from her eyes. "It's Diana's birthday. Are we going home to celebrate?"

Looking at her son, she didn't want to leave, but he was breathing better after two weeks and occasionally opened his eyes. More tubes were poking out of him, feeding him high doses of protein and medication to combat the dreaded parasites in his body. In part, it seemed to be working, but the onset of diarrhea had started, and that worried the doctors.

"Birthday?" Roger breathed from the bed beside his husband. Jenny had insisted on a room together and had received it. "Whose birthday?"

"Diana's," Spiros reminded him. "I can call to find out when they plan on starting. The parties will be a little smaller this year, but they decided to go ahead with them."

"And they should," Jenny said, feeling empty of all energy, all power, all...everything. "The girls shouldn't miss out. We should try and be as normal as possible."

For the last week, Pedro and Carlos had spent their free time at the hospital. Pedro was now out of work, so he didn't mind; his brother was more important. Eddie had tried convincing him to stay, but working for the last week of May had nearly killed him because it took him away from his brother, so he'd spent his days at the hospital and his nights at 69, which made him ragged and drained. And even though he'd wanted to up and quit, his mother had persuaded him to work out his contract.

Jenny was there twenty-four hours a day. There was no way in hell she'd leave her son's side for anything else because nothing else was important, nothing else mattered. Until today. "Call and find out when they're starting. I'll go for a shower and a change of clothes, and spend an hour or so. Call me if anything happens, then I'll come back, and you can go. The girls need to see us there. We'll do the same tomorrow."

"Okay, I'll make the call." Using a payphone down the hall, Spiros rang home.

Carlos snatched it up. "Mama, Papa?"

"It's your father. When is Diana's party starting?"

"Whenever you're able to come." Carlos looked at the dining room of the penthouse decorated with Diana's favourite colours of pink and blue. "Viv has her downstairs playing with Alena."

Spiros sighed, torn between being with his son and granddaughter. "We're going to come home one at a time. I'll send your mother home just before the party starts. Let her shower and change first. She'll spend an hour or so there and come back to the hospital; then I'll come home for an hour or so. Once the girls have cake and open presents it's basically all over anyway. As long as we turn up for them, that's what's important."

"Okay. How are Tomas and Roger?"

"Breathing, waking sporadically. His lungs are better, so he can breathe easier, but the doctors aren't hopeful for a positive outcome."

"Oh, Papa," Carlos murmured. "We can't lose him."

"I know. Your mother's fighting like hell and praying to God. I have a feeling, though, that we're all going to have to prepare."

"For his death?"

"No, not just that. Something else I think your mother has planned. But I'm sure she'll tell us when the time comes. I'll send her home, so meet her and give her time to shower and change before the party."

"Okay, I'll be waiting."

Spiros went back to the boys' room, just off the ICU. "Jenny, it's time to go home."

She breathed in and lifted her head from her hand. "I don't—"

"You need to." Spiros helped her to her feet. "You need to celebrate your granddaughter's birthday."

"I know, I just…" Her fingers reached out to Tomas.

"I'll be here. I'll call," Spiros told her. "It's only for an hour or so."

"A lot can happen in an hour."

"I know, my love, but I'll be here. You need to go and sing Happy Birthday to Diana."

She sighed, her fingers closing around Tomas's, her eyes drifting shut.

"Go, Mama," he rasped.

She opened her eyes to see him looking at her.

"Diana needs her Gamma on her berfday." He gazed adoringly at his mother, grateful for all she was doing for him.

"I don't want to leave you, my baby." She brushed his hair back.

"I know, Mama, but Diana's little, she needs her Gamma." He drifted off to sleep.

"Okay, my baby boy, I'll go." After kissing his cheek, she checked on Roger before turning to her husband. "If any—"

"Thing happens I'll call straight away," he finished the sentence and held his wife's face lovingly. "I love you, we *will* do this, but you need to go and tell Diana you love her and sing her Happy Birthday."

"But I—"

"No buts," Spiros said. "Grab your bag and take a taxi home. Have a nice hot shower, something to eat, sing Happy Birthday." He led her to the hallway. "Go home, my love, your grandbabies need you, too." He kissed her forehead, saw her smile, and watched her walk off down the hall. Once she was gone from sight, he walked back into his sons' room, sat down, picked up the family bible, and began to pray.

Jenny made it back to the penthouse in fifteen minutes due to a traffic jam and rushed inside and upstairs.

"Mama." Carlos ran after her.

"Make it quick; I need a shower." She ran into her room, into the bathroom, and started stripping off.

"Ah." Carlos stopped short at the door and turned around. "How's Tomas?"

Jenny stepped under the steaming hot water. "He's breathing, not on his own, but it's better."

"And Papa will be back?"

"Once I get back to the hospital he'll leave."

"Pedro and I want to come."

"Stay." Jenny stepped out and grabbed a towel. "The girls need to see their Mamas and Papas together as a family. It doesn't really matter if Uncle Tomas and Roger aren't there, but they need to see their parents on their birthdays." Coming out of the bathroom, she walked into the closet.

"But we want to come to the hospital." Carlos sat on the bed, so he didn't see his mother getting dressed.

"Then wait until the girls are napping this afternoon, or come tonight when they go to bed. There's not a whole lot to do."

"I know, it's just that we want to be there…with him…in case—"

"Don't even finish that sentence," Jenny told him as she came into the bedroom in summer pants and a top. "I don't want to hear it." She walked into the bathroom, hung up her towel and quickly dried her hair. "Is everyone on the way up?"

"I told them to be on the lookout and to come up and wait," Carlos said, crossing his arms and leaning against the door jamb.

With a last look in the mirror, Jenny said, "We'd better get downstairs and sing Happy Birthday to your daughter." Hurrying from the room and downstairs, Jenny saw Diana in the pink party dress she'd bought her and launched into Happy Birthday. The rest of the family joined in while Diana excitedly jumped up and down, clapping her hands and clinging to her Gamma's legs.

"Happy birthday, my darling." Jenny picked her up and kissed her. "And how old are you today?"

"Fwee!" Diana held up three fingers.

"Yes, you are, Princess Diana." Jenny carried her over to the sitting area. "You are three today and look at all of these presents."

"Pwesents," Diana yelled and ripped into the first one. Angie took photos and Pedro filmed, so Viv and Carlos could be in the photos and help Diana unwrap her presents.

With more storybooks, pretty clothes, and toys that any one child could possibly need, they moved over to the dining table where the castle cake was brought out, and the candles were lit.

"Blow out your candles, Diana," Jenny said, standing beside her to help her blow as she stood on a chair. "One, two, three, blow."

Diana blew the candles out, and Jenny proceeded to cut the cake and pass slices around.

"Gamma, where's Gampa?" Diana asked around her full mouth.

"He's watching Uncles Tomas and Roger," Jenny replied, scooping the creamy chocolate cake into her mouth.

"Why's he watching dem?" Alena asked from across the table.

"Because Uncles Tomas and Roger are very sick. That's why Gamma and Gampa haven't been around much. We're watching over them."

"Will dey die?" Diana asked, and the room went quiet.

"Not if I can help it, Bubba," Jenny said. "We're doing everything we can to make them better. That's why we have to be there. But Gampa will come back in an hour or so after Gamma goes to watch over your uncles. We're just taking it in turns."

"So, you won't stay all day?" Diana held her plate out for another piece, and Jenny cut it for her.

"I can't stay all day, Bubba, no. I have to get back to Uncle Tomas. But Gampa will come home for a while, and you can show him what you got for your birthday and give him some cake, so we'd better save him some."

"Okay." Diana nodded. "Save Gampa some cay, Mama."

"We will, sweetie, we will," Viv told her daughter and popped the cake back in the fridge.

"Gampa didn't get to sing me Happy Berfday," Diana went on.

"Then you'll have to sing it all over again when he gets home," Jenny said.

"And he didn't get to see my castle cay."

"Oh, sweetie, he did when he came home yesterday." Jenny nuzzled Diana's cheek.

She giggled. "Gamma."

"Diana." Jenny nuzzled some more. "Besides, we have photos and film to watch, so Gampa will see it again, don't worry." With a glance at the clock, she finished off her cake. "Speaking of Gampa, I'd better get back, so Gampa can come home and you can celebrate all over again." She tickled Diana's tummy. "And you can eat more cay."

"Yay, cay." Diana swung her legs. "Gampa cay."

A half hour later, Spiros was celebrating Diana's birthday, and Jenny was by her son's side. She had plans to make and people to call, and it was a plan on a huge scale. The plan had been weeks in the making, and now was the time to execute it. While her son lay ill in the hospital unable to breathe on his own, unable to do much, she was taking charge, and that's all there was to it.

*****

The next day they went through it all again.

"Happy birthday, dear Alena, happy birthday to you."

Alena blew out the candles and didn't wait for it to be cut up. Her hand dived straight into her princess cake and shoved a pile of it right into her mouth, making everyone laugh. This time, Carlos and Viv filmed and took photos, so Pedro and Angie could be with their daughter, making birthday memories for the future to come.

Alena had already opened her presents, finding the toys, teddies, dolls, and books to her satisfaction. She and Diana played games and danced around to the latest music on the radio, and that was when Jenny took her leave.

While the girls were singing and dancing, she slipped quietly out the door and back to the hospital, relieving Spiros of his nursemaid duties. "Go enjoy Alena's birthday," she told him. "They were singing and dancing when I left."

"Okay, my love, I'll be back soon."

She watched him leave then turned to her son. "Tomas, my baby, you okay? Today is Alena's birthday."

His eyes slowly opened. "A-ena," he whispered, a soft smile coming to his lips.

Jenny smiled. "A-ena's birthday is today. Both she and Diana wanted to save you some cake. I don't know if I'll be able to bring it in, or whether it will stay in the fridge until you come home."

"Cay," Roger said from his bed. "I love cay."

Jenny and Tomas turned to a smiling Roger, smiles on their own faces. "I'll check with the doctor, but I doubt he'll let you eat it. They have you on high protein mixes and medications. You're getting high doses of everything at the moment."

"Save it, Mama, you took pictures, didn't you?" Tomas breathed.

"Yes, I did, as I do with all the cakes I make or get made, so you'll get to see it at least. There were very yummy."

"As they always are, Mama," Tomas said and looked around the room. "How long have we been in the hospital?"

"Two weeks."

"What?" Tomas was shocked. They had been there for two weeks already? Hell, he didn't even remember coming in.

"Yes, my babies. You're both very sick," Jenny told him, lifting his hand and kissing it. "You are very sick, Tomas. The doctors are trying to make you better."

"But I don't feel better, Mama." He thought about it in his drowsy state. "Well, I feel a little better than before, but breathing's hard."

"I know." She rubbed her face on his hand. "And you have another week on the meds for your lungs, but the doctors aren't overly hopeful."

"Hopeful of what, Mama?" He wasn't focussing, his eyes hurt, and the light was too bright.

"That..." She nearly choked, but managed a deep breath. "That you'll survive this disease. They say you have the...the gay disease."

"What! No, Mama, no," Tomas rasped, struggling to take the

breathing mask off. "No, we've been careful."

"I know, my baby, I know." Jenny gently set the mask back in place. "I know, but apparently, you have low cells in your body, and that's the main thing they've noticed in all the gay men they've treated. And you have the infections all gay men are getting."

"No," he cried, tearing up. "No…how could I, how could I get this? I've only been with Roger. No, Mama, no." The panic rose, and his life flashed before his eyes.

"There…was…Luiz," Jenny said quietly.

"No," he gasped and stopped, looking at her with blurry eyes. "Luiz?" He drew a ragged breath. "Luiz?"

"He was your first, my baby." She stroked his forehead. "He was your first and…" She glanced behind her to see Roger on his side looking painfully at his lover, "there were Roger's partners."

Tomas looked across at Roger who was only marginally better than when he'd come in. "Roger," he drew breath, struggling to see his husband. "Roger."

"I don't know, T," Roger breathed. "If I don't have the same things as you, then it can't be me. It has to be you."

"No." Tomas's body shuddered with the first sobs coming moments later. "No, Mama, no, not Luiz," he cried, sobbing at the realisation that the first lover he'd ever had had done this to him, and he'd potentially passed it on to his husband. "No." He coughed and kept coughing the same dry hack he'd had for three weeks.

"Easy, my baby, easy." Jenny held the mask on as he coughed, and Dan came in, upping the dose of Ventolin to ease his breathing. "Easy, Tomas, easy," Jenny soothed. "It's okay, my baby boy." She nodded her thanks to the doctor who quickly checked Tomas over, noticing the excrement leaking from the adult diaper Tomas had on.

Jenny looked at him. "Bring the cart in, and I'll do it."

He nodded, knowing full well no parent had ever wanted to see such a thing done, let alone do it themselves. He came back with a cart laden with disinfectant, gloves, masks, a new diaper, wipers, cleaners, new sheets, and a contamination bin. After closing the door behind him, he handed gloves and a mask to Jenny, then put his own on, double layering on the gloves. Preparing everything, he stood across the bed from her.

That surprised her. "I can do this. I've *been* doing it."

"I know." He nodded. "Everyone has been too scared to, and I completely understand it. But your husband isn't here, and you'll need help, so here I am. What do you do first?"

Once again she acknowledged her thanks, and they proceeded to clean Tomas, taking note of the thinner arms and legs, all part of the wasting disease she'd been told he had, another disease that loved to kill gay people and eat them away bit by bit. Removing the diaper, she put it in a bag, along with the sponges they wiped him down with.

"Does that feel better, my baby?" Jenny murmured once they were done. "I'll give you a bath while I'm here, make you feel better." Washing him down she noticed he kept staring at Roger. *More than likely ashamed of what's happening,* she thought. She cleaned his face and neck, moving down to his arms while Dan did his legs and prepared new sheets.

"I'm surprised you're helping," Jenny told him. "No one else does."

"I know, and as a doctor, I'm ashamed of it," he said. "Helping people is what we're supposed to do. But they're all scared."

"I understand." Jenny dried Tomas off. "It must be hard to work in a place like this. Where you're always susceptible to germs and diseases."

"More so now," he said, helping to slide the bottom sheet down under Tomas, so he didn't have to move much. "This has everyone freaked out."

"But not you, you're here now, helping," Jenny said as they slid the sheet out and put it in the bin.

"Oh, believe me, I am," he said. "And I should be more freaked out than anyone else here." They removed their gloves and set the clean sheet in place.

"Why's that?"

"Because I'm gay."

Jenny looked up in shock, Roger's eyes moved from Tomas to the doctor, and even Tomas turned his head to look at him.

"Yes." Dan looked from Tomas to Jenny. "I'm gay too, and this thing has scared the absolute crap out of me."

"When did…?" Jenny started.

"I haven't come out yet. Not publically." Dan laid the top sheet over Tomas. "I've been in the closet for a while, not really discovering my sexuality until a few years ago. But I was so scared of doing it with men, you know," he blushed, "up the butt, that I haven't been with anyone yet. And now this comes along, and it makes me want to stay in the closet." They spread the blanket over and tucked it in.

"That's very interesting," Jenny said. "So, you're seeing all of this firsthand."

"Yes." Dan pulled his mask off and threw it in the contamination bin. "I'm seeing it destroy perfectly healthy people. And I'm seeing what human nature does."

"How so?" Jenny added her mask to the bin.

"Out of all the sick patients, the gay men we've had here, no one does this." Dan waved a hand at Tomas. "No one helps, or touches, their dying son, or brother, or friend. No one touches them for fear of catching it, but you," he shook his head in amazement, "you're quite a woman, Mrs Stephanopoulos. You demand specialists and tests, you research and read, you do your damndest to help your son even though there's nothing more than can be done, and you and your husband do this. Clean him up when he needs to be changed."

"It's not the first time I've changed his soiled nappy. I did it a lot when he was a kid." She smiled despite the circumstances.

"Mama." Tomas blushed and pulled the covers up to his eyes, covering most of his face. "That's embarrassing."

Jenny laughed as she hadn't done in weeks. "Maybe so, my boy, but it's true. I've done this many, many times over the years."

"Yeah, but not for decades, and the doctor doesn't have to know," Tomas told her, a surprisingly light sparkle in his eye.

Jenny looked on hopefully. "You sound better, can move a little more."

"I'm okay," he murmured. "Just embarrassed by my mother."

Dan smiled. "Don't be. Believe me, no one else's mother has done this for her gay son. Count yourself lucky; you have an incredible mother that loves you like no other I've seen. She's not only accepted you as being gay, but also arranged a wedding ceremony and rings, and a reception with the whole family." Jenny had told him things over the last two weeks, and being gay, he'd been curious. "Not all of us are loved and accepted like that, believe me. You're incredibly lucky to have such an amazing mother, Tomas."

"I know," Tomas murmured, his face lighting up as his mother took his hand and kissed it. "And I love you so much for it, Mama."

"I know you do, baby. I know you do." She smoothed back his hair from his forehead.

Dan checked the tubes and needles on both of them before wheeling the bin out. Spiros walked in, crossing paths with the good doctor. "Mr Stephanopoulos." He nodded.

"Doctor." Spiros watched him walk off before moving to his wife's side. "Had a bath, did we?"

"Yes, we did," Jenny replied, leaning against the bed, still holding her son's hand. "And we found out something very interesting about our doctor, didn't we?" she said to Tomas and Roger.

"And what's that?" Spiros asked.

Jenny glanced at the open door and then murmured over her shoulder. "He's gay, and this disease has made him too scared to come out of the closet."

Spiros's brows rose. "Really? Well, I never."

"Neither did I. Now." She turned back to Tomas. "I'm going to fight this to the bitter end for you, and I expect you to as well, *but...*if what the doctor says is true...and we have to prepare for your," she stumbled, "passing," she breathed, "would you like to do it in your own bed at home?" God, she hated the thought of that and using those words and phrase.

"I'd love to go home, but I don't want to die, Mama." Tomas teared up once more. "I don't want to die."

"We all do some time, my baby." Jenny cried hot tears as she stroked his face. "But if you do, if it *does* happen, do you want it to be in your own bed, in your own home when it happens? And by home, I mean Mykonos."

Once the shock wore off and she told him her plan, Tomas told her it was what he wanted. She arranged to have a doctor fly to Mykonos with them the following week to watch him on the plane and to help care for him at home. But instead of finding someone else, Dan Ardent volunteered himself free of charge. And while he organised for the equipment to use on the plane and in Mykonos, Jenny organised everything else. She rang her sons and told them the family was going home. To pack their clothes, belongings, and anything else they wanted to take. Pack up the kids, and their toys and teddies into cases and bags and the rest would be done by a professional removalist company. Empty fridges, say goodbye to friends, get down photos from the walls, and pack photo albums and personal papers and effects.

She made lists of things to do, and on Tomas and Roger's last day in the hospital, she executed them. "Have you got everything you need personally?" Jenny asked Dan as they stood in the hospital.

"I have my case, my bag, my passport, personal effects. I'm ready to go." The excitement of travelling to Greece made his stomach knotty, but the reason he was going made him sick and full of fear of catching whatever it was killing gay men.

"And everything Tomas and Roger need?" she asked.

"Considering you paid for it all, it's all yours and ready to go. I set it up on the plane personally." He stood beside her in the boys' room.

"Good." Jenny glanced at her sons who were sitting up in bed. "How are you both feeling?"

"Better," Roger said. He was still in a weakened state, but his symptoms seemed to have dissipated. For now.

"Can't wait to go home," Tomas said through his mask. "My old room, the ocean, the house, it's been so long."

"Yes, it has, my baby, and it's all been aired out and freshened up. Just you wait. Right, I need to go home and get everything done there. Spiros will stay here just in case, and then we'll stop here on the way to the airport and pick you all up. Have you organised the ambulances to take them?" she asked Dan.

"Considering that you're paying for them, they are at your disposal," Dan said.

"Right, I shall go and be back in a couple of hours." She looked at her watch. "It's nearly ten now; I'll be back at lunch. Doctor, a word." She kept talking as they walked down the hall. "Now, I rang the Mykonos hospital and told them you'd be calling with very specific medicine that you'd need, did that go okay?"

"Absolutely," he told her. "I asked if they had specialists in Athens we could call in and they gave me a list. I rang them, and they said they'd be available whenever I needed them."

"Good." The lift opened, and Jenny entered. "Unfortunately, Mykonos is small and probably not as equipped as they should be, so we may have to fly everyone and everything in. See you soon."

Five minutes later she strode into the penthouse.

"Mama, is he okay?" Angie bounded up from her seat.

"Hanging in there. Everything done?"

"Bags packed, fridges empty, everything else ready for the removalists," Viv told her as they stood in the sitting area.

"Tomas and Roger's apartment?" Jenny asked, walking up the stairs to her room.

Angie and Viv followed. "Pictures and albums packed and en route to the airport with Pedro and Carlos, along with our things."

"And my—" Jenny stopped, seeing her and Spiros's cases gone. They had been on the bed that morning.

"On the way," Viv said. "You said they were packed." She watched Jenny's face. "Did we do the wrong thing?"

"What?" Jenny was distracted. "Ah, no, they were ready." Walking into the closet, she saw all of the winter clothes and shoes. "They can definitely be packed and sent over. If it's one thing you need in Mykonos in winter," she said as she walked back into the bedroom, "it's a fur coat. Right." She stopped and looked around. "Have all the personal effects been packed from downstairs?"

"Yes."

"So, I just have ours to go?" Checking Spiros's bedside table, she gathered the things left and put them in his travel bag. "That's done."

She walked into the bathroom and pulled out drawers and opened cupboards before coming back into the bedroom to her bedside cupboard. Alena's urn sat in its prime spot with a family photo of all of them and the silver bible ornament from Tomas and Roger. A few bits and pieces rested on the cupboard. She removed a box from the drawer, and placed the urn in the velvet cushion and locked the box, laying it in her bag along with the ornament and photo. Her make-up and jewellery purses were already in there. "Does everyone have their jewellery all accounted for, bits and pieces?"

"Yes, Mama," Angie said. "We've been checking and double checking for the last week."

"Can't be too careful," Jenny said. "The packers and cleaners should be here any minute along with everyone else." With one last look, they went downstairs to find the boys back from the airport.

"All packed, Mama," Carlos said. "What now?"

"What now is we check the apartments one last time, turn off power, shut windows. The cleaners are coming though…" She trailed off as she looked around. The penthouse had been their home for nearly four years. They had loved, cried, partied, and had an amazing time there. She deflated. "A part of me doesn't want to go. It's been so great here these last years, birthdays, anniversaries."

"I think we travelled more than we stayed here." Pedro smiled.

Jenny sadly smiled back. "Yeah, I know." The downstairs phone rang, and she answered it. "Yes, Brewster?"

"Ma'am, the packers are here."

"Send them up to the penthouse please." Moments later the whole crew arrived. "Oh, goodness, so many." She directed two upstairs to the bedroom for their winter clothes and took the rest down to the other apartments for the girls' toys and belongings. "Overall, it's not a lot of stuff," Jenny told them. "But it's what we can't take at the moment, so it needs to be packed and shipped. Other than that, it's just about time to go. I will leave you to it, and Mr Brewster will see you out at the end. Thank you all, so much." Jenny went back up to the penthouse for her and Spiros's bags and saw the family was still there. "I'm going down to talk to Mr Brewster, and hope everyone else will turn up. Grab the girls and tell Maggie and Mike to wait."

"We're coming downstairs too, Mama," Angie said. "Maggie and Mike have the girls across the road until we're ready to go and we have our bags here."

They all grabbed their carry-ons and went down in the lift.

The cleaning crew arrived as they stepped out. "Ah, good, they're here." After conferring, they went up while the boys put their bags in the car and the girls went for Mike, Maggie, and the girls.

"Now, Mr Brewster," Jenny started, but was interrupted by Rich Sable, the fifty-something, tall, dirty-blond real estate agent who had found her the apartment building and handled the subsequent sale in the first place. "Mr Sable, right on time."

"Mrs Stephanopoulos, long time no see." He shook her hand, holding it between both of his large manly ones.

"Yes, it is." She saw Mike and Maggie come through the door. "Right, now everyone, Mr Brewster, the removalists should be done shortly, but the cleaning crew might be the rest of the day, so please stay until they are gone and lock up on your way out. Tomorrow there will be new beds arriving for each apartment, and a company is coming to remove and replace all of the linen, so it's all fresh and clean. Mr Sable." She turned to him. "I want to rent out the building, Apartments 2, 3, and 4, and the penthouse. Well paid people, refined people, I don't want damage being done. Now, I've set up an account for the money to go into, and out of that you will pay yourself and Mr Brewster." She looked at him. "I hope you stay, Mr Brewster. You'll be in my employment as always, so you," she eyed Sable, "can't fire him and hire someone else. He's *my* employee, not yours."

"Of course," Rich agreed.

"Now," she turned to Mike and Maggie and pulled the key for Apartment 1 from her handbag. "This is for you. Angie said the two of you were looking for a place together and this is for you. Rent free," she glanced at Sable, "the whole time you're tenants. I'll pay your utilities for the first year, again, out of the account, but after that, you'll have to pay your own way."

"Oh, Mrs Stephanopoulos." Maggie was shaking as she took the key, staring in amazement. "This is too much."

"You've been friends with Angie and Pedro, and this is for helping them through a rough time all round. For being their support system."

"Thank you, Mrs Stephanopoulos," Mike said. "This is unbelievable."

"With everything happening this week you can move in over the weekend. Mr Sable, the cleaning crew is upstairs. As my intermediary can you make sure they do a decent job?"

"Of course, Mrs Stephanopoulos." He slid into the lift and went upstairs.

"Mike, Maggie, go and say your goodbyes; we'll be leaving in a moment." Waiting for them to leave she turned to Brewster. "Mr Brewster, I'd like you to stay on as you've been nothing but a faithful employee. I'd like you to stay at least a week or so until Mike and Maggie move in, and then, if you like, you can go on a holiday over summer before coming back to work." She pulled a bulky envelope from her bag and handed it over. "Here's a bonus for all the years you've worked. I'm giving you cash in case you don't want to tell the tax man, but then there's a receipt in there if you do."

He opened the envelope, and his eyes grew wide at the pile of cash. It was nearly ten thousand dollars.

"For all the weeks you've worked for us. And you'll still receive your wage over summer while you're holidaying somewhere."

"*Thank you*, Mrs Stephanopoulos, thank you so much, this is more than…with everything else you've done, the birthday and Christmas presents, always too much." He was overwhelmed by his boss's generosity over the years towards him and his huge family.

"Nonsense," Jenny said. "You've been a loyal employee, helping when we needed it. And we need it again now." She told him what she wanted him to do every week and let him know she would send money for his trouble.

"Just a pity I can't help you now," he said. "I'm sorry about your sons."

"Thank you, Mr Brewster, and speaking of them, we'd better go." She looked around the lobby, and good memories came flooding back over her. "I'm going to miss this place." She looked out the door to across the road. "The zoo, the park, taking the girls there." She sighed. "I'm going to miss this."

"Do you know if you'll be back?" Brewster asked.

"I don't know." Shaking her head, she added, "I just don't know, and that's a pity."

"Yes…it is, Mrs Stephanopoulos."

Jenny saw Carlos wave from the car. "I'd better go, Mr Brewster. Thank you for your services with us all these years. Goodbye."

"Goodbye, Mrs Stephanopoulos." He opened the door for her one last time.

Jenny walked out and stepped into the limo, anxiously waiting while they travelled to the hospital. Once there, they parked near the emergency bay where Dan had the boys waiting.

Spiros came out to greet them, and Pedro and Carlos followed Jenny across the car park to the waiting ambulances.

"They're ready to go," Spiros said as Dan and some orderlies wheeled Tomas out.

He was sitting up at a forty-five-degree angle, mask over his face, looking weak with hair that had thinned over the last two weeks, but there was still a sparkle in his eyes. "Hey." He weakly held a hand out to his mother. "We're going home."

"Yes, my baby, we're going home." She gently squeezed his hand as he was rolled into the back, but let go so they could strap him in.

"You okay, Tomas?" Carlos asked. He and Pedro stood with their mother, watching their infirm brother be strapped in and drugged up.

"I'm okay," he rasped, giving a little wave.

They watched Roger be wheeled out and placed into the second ambulance.

"Are we done here?" Dan asked the paramedics.

"Done and ready to go."

"I'll go with Tomas, your father with Roger. Get back in the car and we'll go, and take Doctor Ardent's bags with you," Jenny told her sons.

"Okay, Mama," they said and left with Dan's bag and case.

Dan helped Jenny climb into the back of the ambulance. The

orderlies shut the doors, and they left for the airport. Fifteen minutes later they arrived and pulled to a stop at the hangar. The plane was outside and ready to go.

On alighting from the ambulance, they rolled Tomas over to the stairs where they unhooked him. Spiros took hold of his son and lifted him, walking slowly up the stairs with Carlos in front and Pedro behind in case he needed help. Once inside, they helped him into the bedroom they had specifically set up as a medical unit. The bed had been stripped and covered in plastic; there was a medical waste unit in the room opposite, and machinery all around.

Laying Tomas down, they let Dan check him over and hook him up before going back for Roger.

"I don't think you can carry me, Mr S," Roger softly joked as he was rolled over to the plane.

"We're going to try, Roger," Spiros said and put his arms and legs into position. "One, two, three." He lifted and carried Roger up the stairs the same way he had Tomas. They settled him next to his husband in the bed, and Dan hooked him up.

Jenny checked the boys' diapers.

"It's okay, Mama, I don't think I've done anything," Tomas said, watching her.

"Just making sure before we go, my baby," she replied and covered them both with the blanket.

Carlos popped his head into the room. "We're ready to go, Mama. They've shut the door and just need word on when to leave."

"Have you got Doctor Ardent's bags?" she asked.

"In the room across the hall. Ours are in the spare bedroom," he replied.

"Then we're ready to go. Let the pilot know." She helped Dan secure the patients and went to take her seat while he stayed with them. Ten minutes later they were in the air, and she was in her sons' bedroom. "It's going to be a long flight, and we'll probably land in darkness, but we won't let that stop us. The house is ready, and your bedroom is waiting for you."

Tomas smiled. "How did that happen?"

"I had help," was all Jenny said, and saw Tomas's eyes move to the door. She looked over her shoulder. "Hey, Bubbas, want to come say hello to Uncle Tomas and Uncle Roger?"

Alena and Diana stood staring at them, two identical twins but with opposite hair colour. Big blue eyes looked worried, and Diana turned and ran away. They hadn't seen their uncles in three weeks.

"Come on, Bubba." Jenny held her arm out to Alena. "Come say hello, come on. There's no need to be scared. Uncle Tomas is sick, that's all."

Alena slowly moved into the room, her eyes flitting from Tomas to Jenny.

"Come on, Alena, come here." Jenny lifted her onto her lap. "Uncle Tomas is okay; he's just sick, that's all. What book do you have?"

Alena looked from Tomas to Jenny to her book. *"Gween Eggs an' Ham."*

"Do you want to read that to Uncle Tomas?" Jenny asked. "He might like to hear you read."

"Yes, please, Alena," Tomas rasped. "Please read to me."

Again, looking from her Gamma to Uncle Tomas, she opened her book and started reading, bringing a smile to Tomas who hadn't seen his two munchkins in weeks.

Jenny spotted Diana in the doorway. "Come on, Diana." She put her arm out and waved her in. "Come say hello to Uncle Tomas, come on."

Diana hesitated, putting one foot in front of the other, sliding against the wall until she was level with the gap between Jenny and the bedside table, then flung herself at the bed.

"Easy." Jenny caught her. "Easy does it. You have to be gentle with Uncle Tomas okay, be gentle."

Backing up against Gamma's legs, Diana didn't take her eyes off Tomas the whole time. But her hand wriggled across the bedspread until it reached his.

He wiggled his fingers against hers, bringing a smile to her face and his. "Diana." He wiggled some more.

"Unca Tomas." She wiggled back.

"Da-anna, no. A-ena twying to wead," Alena crossly told her cousin.

"Shh," Jenny said in her ear, making her look up. "Keep your voice low, no need for fighting, especially around Uncle Tomas, okay. Keep your voice soft and gentle and keep reading to Uncles Tomas and Roger."

Alena, thoroughly chastised by her grandmother, went back to reading the book while Diana stood playing with Tomas's hand.

"Everything okay in here?" Pedro asked from the door.

Jenny turned her head. "We're fine."

"Little Miss Bossy Boots telling her cousin what to do again? We heard her from out there." Pedro nodded in the direction of the seating area.

Carlos was beside him. "We weren't sure what the girls were doing. We don't want them wearing him out."

"I'm fine," Tomas said. "I want my family around me, especially the girls. I've missed them so much."

"An' we missed Unca Tomas," Diana said.

"Yes, we have." Carlos stood behind his daughter. "Hanging in there, bro?" He laid a hand on his brother's face.

"Hanging in there, bro," Tomas replied, smiling up at his big brother.

"Good." Carlos turned his attention to Roger. "How you doin', Roger?"

"Not too bad," Roger replied. "First class service, can't complain."

Jenny smiled. "No, you can't."

Carlos looked at his brother and bent down to kiss his forehead. "You get better, Tomas, you hear me. You get through this, and we're gonna be here every step of the way egging you on. Okay."

Tomas breathed, tears springing to his eyes. "Okay, big brother."

"Mrs Stephanopoulos, a word," Dan said, indicating for her to follow him into the passage.

"Of course." She lifted Alena up and placed her on the bed. "Now, you be careful and don't hurt Uncle Tomas. Just keep reading to him."

"Okey-dokey, Gamma," she said and turned to pat her uncle's hand. "I wiw wead to you, Unca Tomas, an' make you aww better."

Jenny heard her say it and all but collapsed into the passageway.

"Oh, my God, did you hear that?" she asked Spiros. Her chest deflated and the pang hurt. "Oh, my God, she thinks by reading to him it will make him better."

"It might," Dan said. "Emotionally. It will lift his spirits a little, but look, he's finished his PCP treatment, but it's come back, and we're attacking the parasites, but just when we think we're turning a corner, *they* come back. Between the PCP, the CMV, and the Cachexia, the diarrhea, and all the other symptoms, your son doesn't stand a chance, and your son-in-law's last test results showed he has Toxoplasmosis and Cryptosporidiosis. And all of that together is no good. It's weakened his immune system, and both of your sons have shown signs of anaemia for the last two weeks." He shook his head. "I'm sorry, but I don't know how long they have left."

"I know my son, Doctor Ardent." Jenny stepped closer to him. "If I tell him to fight this, he will fight it, and if he can't, then we will. I refuse to believe he has this gay disease that all of his friends had, and I refuse to believe that he's dying. So, whatever doctors, whatever tests, we will do them, and you will give him every medication known to man to fight off all of these bastard parasites in his body. I'm a very determined woman, doctor. I lost one child at birth in 1959; I'm not about to lose another one twenty-two years later. We *will* fight this. We will *all* fight for my sons."

In the bedroom, the girls were still by Tomas's bed.

"Pooh, Da-anna, you pooped your pants." Alena screwed up her nose at her cousin. "You stink."

"No, I didn't!" Diana exclaimed. "I did not poop my pants. A-ena poop here."

Carlos saw Tomas blush and look at Roger who squeezed his hand, embarrassed by the truth. "Okay, girls, enough. You're both poopy pants, and we're going to go and check you both just in case. Come on." He picked up Diana. "You can come see Uncle Tomas and Roger later. Let them have a nap. I think you two might need a nap too."

"Yep." Pedro picked up Alena. "Come on, poopy pants."

"Dada." Alena giggled. "I no poopy pants."

"Well, one of you is." Carlos looked at his parents as they left the room. "One of you girls is a poopy pants." He gave a discreet nod at Tomas and left with Diana.

Jenny nodded, and she, Spiros, and Dan went into the room to clean up with Pedro and Carlos coming back a moment later to help.

"Figured we'd do our bit," Carlos said. "Viv and Angie have the girls."

Together they cleaned up Tomas and wiped down the bed, helping Roger as well. Redressing them, they cleaned up the room and loaded everything into the contamination bin that went back into the room across the hall. It didn't matter what they had to do, Carlos and Pedro would be there for their brothers. Through thick and thin, for better or worse, in sickness and in health, till death do them part. That's what the family was all about, and there was no way in hell they'd forfeit their last moments with their brother for anything.

*****

They arrived in Mykonos after dark, coming to a stop on the small airstrip next to two ambulances Jenny had hired. They carried Tomas and Roger down the stairs and settled them in, while the boys offloaded their bags and sleeping children into the vans the airport was lending them. The airport authorities were quickly checking passports and documents, knowing who the Stephanopoulos family was, and the money and power they were coming home with. Forty minutes later, they stopped outside their home.

Jenny alighted from Tomas's ambulance to knock on her own door.

Her mother, Sarah Marsh, opened it, and several family members came out to help.

"What…what's going on?" Spiros asked as he and the boys stood staring in shock.

"I called my parents a week ago and asked them to come over because the boys were sick. And to see if other family could come too," Jenny told her husband and sons.

"But where will we put them all?" Spiros asked as Tomas was rolled out of the van.

He was shocked to see his cousins helping, and they touched his arms and murmured kind words, making him tear up at the reunion.

"Don't worry; it's all planned. Let's just get them inside." Jenny watched Dan and her sons roll Tomas's stretcher into the house and down the hall to his room, thanking God the room was big enough for them to get him in there. Standing the stretcher around the window side of the bed, Jenny directed Spiros into position. "Okay, you're going to pick him up and boys, you'll quickly take the bed away. Okay, on the count of three… One, two, three."

Spiros lifted Tomas, and Carlos and Pedro rolled the bed back and out of the room while Spiros laid Tomas in his bed and Jenny put a pile of pillows behind him.

"There you go, baby." Jenny tucked the blanket over him while Dan hooked him up. "We'll go and get Roger."

"You stay," Dan told her and followed Spiros out to retrieve Roger, while Viv and Angie took care of the girls, and aunts, uncles and cousins helped bring the luggage and boxes in from the vans and put them in the right rooms.

Dan, Spiros, Carlos and Pedro rolled Roger in and repeated the process. While the boys dealt with the bed and vans outside, Dan, Spiros and Jenny settled the boys in.

"Can you open the curtains, Mama?" Tomas asked. "I want to see the lights."

"You sure you don't want to sleep?" Jenny tucked the bedding in.

"I want to see, Mama," he pleaded with hooded eyes.

"Okay, well then I have a surprise for you." She flung back the curtains to reveal the normal window gone and a huge floor-to-ceiling sliding door window in its place. "I think that turned out well." She opened the window to let the sea air in.

"You changed the window," Tomas managed.

"Yes, and when did this happen?" Spiros asked, astounded by everything that was going on.

"Well," she glanced from her husband to her son, "I figured you might want a better view of the place, and it lets more air in. And being summer, the air will do you good. Just wait until sunrise."

"That's what I'm waiting for, Mama," Tomas said, gazing out at the lights of Mykonos, his island home. He pulled his mask down to breathe in the ocean-scented breeze. "That's so good."

"Don't keep that off for long," Dan warned. "It's what's helping your lungs expand."

"I know." Tomas breathed in again. "I know."

"Let's hope the warm tropical breeze helps you get better," Jenny said, stroking her son's cheek. "You get some rest. I'm going to pop out to talk to Grandma and Grandpa."

"I can't believe they're here," Tomas said.

"Why wouldn't they be? They're family." Jenny smiled and left Dan watching over her sons to enter the fray in the lounge room. Her boys were catching up with their cousins; the girls were catching up with their in-laws.

"When did you organise all of this?" Spiros asked. "And where is everyone going to be staying?"

"First thing's first," Jenny told him. "Mum, Dad, thanks for coming." She hugged them both, seeing some of her sisters and brothers and the boys' cousins over their shoulders. "Is this all that came?"

"It's all that could get away," Sarah said. "The rest send their condolences."

Jenny sighed tiredly. "Well, thanks for coming. Now," she told her husband. "Last week I took it upon myself to get my family over here to open the place up and give it a freshen up, and you've done a great job with the new window." She glanced over the thirty strong crowd in her lounge room.

"All the companies were quite accommodating when they heard you were coming back. The lawyer you hired helped a lot," Sarah told her.

"Lawyer?" Spiros asked, his brows rising. "Why do we need a lawyer?"

Jenny glanced at her husband. "It's Giorgio's attorney. I rang and asked him for help, plus I made a few purchases, and dealt with the estate agent here on the island."

"And why would you do that?" Spiros had no idea where the

conversation was going.

"Because we needed more room for the growing families, so I bought the houses either side of this house. Plus…the three below." Jenny waited for his reply.

"You what?" Spiros stared open-mouthed at his wife while the rest of the family looked on. "What for?"

Jenny frowned. "Take a look around; we need accommodation. We have grandkids, the family's here, and all of the hotels would be booked out, so, I managed to get the estate agent to buy up the properties. Did you get them freshened up in time?" She looked at her parents.

"Oh, absolutely. Fresh paint, cleaning crew, new furniture and curtains," Sarah said.

"And from the look of this place, it's like I never left." Jenny glanced around. "Is the fridge stocked?"

"In every house," Sarah said. "All the rooms are ready to go just like when you left."

"I can't believe it was all done in a week," Jenny told them. "But then I guess when you hire every company on the island everyone makes money out of it. Ah, has the fridge been stocked with all of the medication?"

"Yes. We bought a small fridge as recommended and it's in the laundry," Sarah said.

"Fantastic. Right, we just need to get unpacked. Boys, why don't you get your things done and then we'll start on Tomas and Roger's. Has anyone made food? I'm a bit hungry." Jenny heard her stomach grumble.

"We weren't sure when you'd get here, so we made up some meals. We can reheat them," Rebecca, Jenny's sister, replied.

Jenny sighed. "That sounds good, let us know when it's ready. We'll go unpack." Quickly emptying their cases and hanging their belongings, Jenny realised she'd have to get rid of the old clothes she'd left behind. *Just another chore to do, bagging up and taking them to the local charity store. Maybe I could get my sisters to do that.* She quickly filled up an old case with the things she didn't want, and once finished, they went to Tomas's room.

"How are my babies?" she asked, carrying a box into their room and placing it on the end of the bed.

"Better for being home, Mama," Tomas said. "It's so good to be here."

"I'm glad it's made you better." She opened the box. "Because we're going to make you even better. Mum, can you unload their bags please, and I'll get started on this."

"What are you doing, Mrs S?" Roger asked.

"You'll see," was all Jenny said, and proceeded to measure out spaces on the blank wall opposite the bed with Spiros. When the spots were marked, Pedro banged nails into the walls, and then Jenny started hanging Tomas and Roger's photos that they'd hung on their wall in New York.

"Hey, it's our photos," Roger said. "Look, T, our photos."

First date, wedding, holding their newborn nieces, Christmas, New Year, birthday, anniversary, holiday snaps, they all went up on the wall in chronological order until Jenny was done. Any extras sat on the long chest of drawers underneath.

"Wow." Dan wandered over when Jenny stepped aside. "You did give them a wedding ceremony."

"I told you I did." Jenny smiled and unpacked the boys' personal belongings. Their wedding and anniversary rings went on top of the chest with the photos of the family at Christmas '77; along with the other jewellery they had given each other and the watches from Jenny, because since wasting away, they couldn't wear any of it. Personal papers were already in a large envelope, and that went into a drawer.

"Well?" She turned to the boys. "What do you think?"

"It's great, Mama." Tomas smiled, remembering all the times in the pictures.

"Just like back home," Roger added. "In New York, I mean. We get to see them all the time."

"That's the point." Jenny sat carefully next to her son. "I want you to look at these photos every day and remember the good times. Remember everything you've done together, everywhere you've been, the fun you had, the love you shared, remember it all and use it to help you live. You need to fight this, with every ounce of mental strength you have. Both of you. Don't let this get you." She laid her hand on Tomas's. "Fight with everything we taught you. Everything we raised you to be. Will you do that for me?"

He squeezed her hand. "Yes, Mama. For you."

"That's my boy. Between the photos and the view and sea breeze, we're counting on all of it to make you better. You were always sick in Australia, but once we moved here, you became better and weren't sick again until you moved to America. So, I expect it to make you better again. And I expect you to help yourself, too. We'll let you rest, have something to eat and a shower, and we need to set Doctor Ardent up with somewhere to sleep." Jenny rose from the bed and turned to him. "We have a cot bed we can put in here if you want to stay close. Otherwise, we could put it in the hall. You'll have to share the bathroom with the boys, and now the girls and kids, or you can use ours every day."

"I should be in here with them, so I can hear the machines," Dan said. "The cot will be fine."

"Okay, we'll get that set up and get you something to eat and drink. There's plenty of family around if you need help. Mum used to be a nurse, and one of my sisters is one now, so there's plenty of help."

"That's fantastic," Dan said. "Thank you. I do need to use the bathroom at the moment."

Jenny smiled. "Down the end of the hall. I'll stay while you go."

A few moments later he was back, and Jenny was having a hot shower. After nearly four years she was back in her own home, her own shower, her own bedroom. Everything was different, yet just as it had been when Carlos and then Pedro had left. Then the Tomas and Luiz thing, and leaving for Miami. But there was no way she would give up. No way she'd let her son die from any disease let alone *that* one. *Not* that one. No way in hell would he die from that one. She didn't care what Doctor Ardent said, he didn't have it, and that's all there was to it.

Was she in denial? Sure. Was she refusing to believe what every doctor had told her? Absolutely. Was she willing to lose her son? Hell bloody no. There was no way she was going to lose young, pure, innocent, and sexually naïve Tomas to Luiz all over again. Knowing he had been poisoned and not being there to help him was bad enough, but there was no way in hell she was going to let Tomas's dead lover take him a second time. No way in bloody hell was Luiz going to win this time.

*****

The sun slowly rose to a warm Mykonos day, and Tomas opened his eyes to see the sky change in all its glorious colours.

"Roger." He moved his hand over to his lover. "Roger, look."

"Mmm," Roger breathed and lifted his fingers to entwine with his husband's. "What is it, my love?"

"Look," Tomas said. "Look at the sky. It's so beautiful." A small smile played on his lips as he watched the world awaken on his island. He'd never known *what* it was about Mykonos that had him. As much as he'd loved Australia and growing up with family, and had hated the thought of moving halfway around the world to a tiny island in the Aegean Sea, he'd loved it the moment he saw it from the ferry. The azure of the ocean, the turquoise of the sky, the brilliant aureolin of the sun. It had his heart from the moment he saw it as a twelve-year-old boy, and had explored the streets with his mother and brothers to find out about the new place he would be living in. His Greek was already fluent, having been taught from a baby boy by their father, so he could carry on a conversation with anyone. And his mother had used him as a translator between her English and their Greek.

He sighed, remembering back to their early years. They had lived at the beach in summer and played near the windmills, running with kites as they flew high through the air. They had taught their classmates cricket and football, and the fact he spoke Greek and looked Greek, especially like his father and grandfather, meant he blended in better than Carlos, but that didn't matter, Carlos would always be an Aussie kid at heart while he would be a Greek kid at heart. Mykonos was *his* island, *his island home.*

He had flourished there, and become a far healthier version of himself. He hadn't been sick, hadn't broken bones. He'd been healthy, and it was one of the most beautiful places to be, especially late spring through early autumn. Winter could be downright chilly, but he'd taken to the winters by watching the sea beat across the rocky outcrops every day. He would watch the ferry come in, and watch ocean liners deposit tourists at the docks. It was an amazing place to be. Far different from New York, and as amazing as The Big Apple was, there was no place like home. Not Europe, not Miami, not Australia. Mykonos was where he would always be. Even in death.

The pang hit his heart. The pang of fear, the pang of death. He didn't want to die, not this way, not at twenty-six. As much as he'd lived life, a lot in the last three and a half years, he did not want to leave the planet yet. He wanted to see the world again. To see all of Australia and America and Europe again. Hell, he even wanted to take the girls back to Disneyland again.

He sighed. *Oh, Mama. For all of your fears the last few years, especially after Luiz, the pain and fear I saw in your eyes, the trepidation, the determination of giving Roger and me the money to travel, you did it because you knew this was coming when I didn't. I had no clue. I was in denial. All I knew was, when I met Luiz, I had the most incredible first experience. And then came Roger.*

He slowly moved his head so he could look into Roger's eyes as he stared out the window at the sunrise. "Roger," he rasped. "I love you, so much, I'm so glad I met you. I'm so glad you wanted to marry me."

Roger turned his eyes to his husband. "I'm glad you wanted to marry me, my love, my darling Tomas. I'm glad it's me you chose." A smile crossed his lips. "I've been so happy with you, my love. Happier than I've ever been. Ever." His fingers gently squeezed his lover's.

"Me too," Tomas told him. "Until you came along I didn't know what real love was. I didn't know what love in general was. But you made it all happen for me, and I will love you until my dying day."

"In sickness and in health, till death do us part," Roger murmured. "We will definitely be living up to our vows."

Dan sat up from his spot on his cot and faced them. "How many men have the two of you slept with?"

Roger and Tomas looked toward the end of the bed in surprise, having forgotten he was there with them. "What?"

"How many men have the two of you slept with, and were you always safe?" Dan was on his feet now, a germ of an idea floating in his head as he watched the two of them. "But I need to write it all down." He grabbed a clipboard and stuck a notepad to it. "Go ahead."

"Why would you be…?" Roger started, feeling a panic rise. He'd slept with the four *Seralift* stablemates that Luiz had killed, and now a hundred were dead and possibly because of them. So, if he'd contracted this gay disease and passed it on to Tomas, it would be all his fault. And he'd lied to everyone about sleeping with them, especially Tomas who he'd vowed to never tell. Shit!

"Because it could be important," Dan said. "Now, who's had the least amount?"

"That would be me," Tomas said. "Roger's my second."

"And your first?"

"Luiz…"

"Luiz who?"

"Luiz Manning…"

Jenny walked into the room. "What's this about Luiz Manning?"

"I need to know how many lovers your sons have had and who *they've* had sex with," Dan said.

"And why do you need to know that?" Jenny asked.

"Don't know," Dan said. "But I have a feeling it could be important."

Jenny blinked. "Okay, Luiz Manning was my daughter-in-law's half-brother."

Dan's brows rose to his hairline. "Really? Which one?"

"Angelina," Jenny told him. "Not that *she* knew. Luiz was illegitimate, born six or seven years before her. He lived with his mother, Sheila Manning, in New York. I vaguely remember something about her kicking him out at seventeen, and he was engaged to Bertha St John when he met Tomas. I finally saw a picture of him a few months back. He was very good-looking."

Dan's eyebrows moved higher. "Wow, what a web this family is."

"You don't know the half of it." Jenny sighed.

"I hope we have the time for you to tell me. This is a very interesting family indeed, Mrs Stephanopoulos, but right now, I need to know all of your sexual partners," he told the boys. "And whether all sex was safe." He wrote down all of the names and times the boys could remember.

Roger kept the four *Seralift* co-workers a secret. Still. Even though they were both on their death bed, the agonising decision to tell Tomas was eating him more than the disease was. *Maybe in a moment alone. But will he forgive me for lying? And what if it was from them? But then I was with them long before Luiz killed them, so maybe they were safe then. And maybe I'm being a dickhead now.* He inwardly collapsed, and the inner turmoil grew worse.

You need to fucking tell him.

No, I need to keep it a secret.

But he's your husband, your soulmate, your one true love.

And so I can't hurt him by revealing the truth.

But the truth will set you free.

The truth will make him hate me.

You don't know that.

Yes, I do.

No, you don't.

I don't want him to hate me and never trust me again. I love him too much.

You assume too much. You're assuming he'll hate you and never forgive you. You're both dying, spit it out, and if it can help you live, then by God do it.

"Mrs Stephanopoulos?"

"I think it's time you called me Jenny," she told Dan with a small smile.

He blushed at the thought. "Oh, ah, Jenny. Guess you'd better call me Dan then. Do you have a lot of notepaper, pens, and something I can put the notes on, like a corkboard?"

Jenny thought. "We don't, but we do have thumb tacks, so just stick it all on the wall in the hallway. Probably better to keep those notes close by anyway. And we can always replaster it."

He raised a brow at the unconventional suggestion. "Are you sure?"

"Do anything you need, Dan, we're here to save my sons, so if there's anything you need to do, or want, just ask."

"Okay, well then I'm going to need a shower, lots of coffee, a high protein breakfast, lots of notepaper, a phone, plus any medical journals the local library or hospital can give me. I'll also need the phone numbers of all your exes' partners," he said to the boys. "But if you don't have them, I'll also need American phone books. But that can all wait until we give your sons their medication and get them cleaned up."

"I'll get my mother and sister," Jenny said and brought them back with the medications. They spent fifteen minutes administering them and writing down every little detail before they left, and Spiros and the boys walked in to help clean Tomas and Roger up. With the precision of teamwork, they were bathed and clean in fifteen minutes. "There's something I want to do, need to do," Jenny told Dan. "It will just take a minute."

"What's that?" he asked.

"Can you roll Roger toward Tomas?" she instructed and rolled Tomas toward Roger. "I figured you two haven't had a kiss in a while."

Smiling, the boys removed their masks and kissed, with Tomas stroking Roger's face. Their eyes were bright and sparkling; the fire was back in them.

"I love you, Roger," Tomas rasped. "So much."

"I love you too, T," Roger replied. "Till death do us part."

"I thought you two might need that." Jenny gently rested Tomas back on his pillows. "You wouldn't have done that in what, weeks."

"Since we got sick, Mrs S," Roger said, replacing his mask.

"I want you two to hold hands and kiss and talk about everything you've done. That's what we're here for, to remind you of all the good times you've had and that you'll have many more. Maybe we can even take you out on the balcony later." She looked at Dan for approval, and he nodded. "It looks like it's going to be a glorious day today." Moving the curtains back further, she saw blue sky for miles. "Perfect. A perfect summer's day in Mykonos. You know, I think it's even four years since Carlos and Viv met and he left to fly off to L.A."

Carlos popped up at the door. "Yes, it is, Mama. When Connie and Viv…" his voice trailed off.

"This must be hard for you," Jenny said gazing wistfully at her son. "With Connie and Antonio."

"Yeah, it is." With a frown, he left to go back to the lounge.

"Who's…?" Dan wanted to ask more.

"Connie was a friend of Viv's, Carlos's wife. The two of them helped Carlos out of Mykonos in Connie's Luis Vuitton trunk to Athens, and then on a plane to L.A. after some trouble, but that's another story. Connie's son, Antonio, worked with Carlos as a bartender on the beach for three years. Antonio's father, Connie's estranged husband, was the bullfighter, Stephano DeLuca. Well, Connie and Stephano were estranged, but that didn't stop them having other lovers, and it turns out that Stephano's lovers were male." Jenny raised a brow at Dan. "Stephano had all the same issues the boys have, this gay thing, and he and Connie had a fling last year when they met up. Stephano died in October last year on top of his male Filipino housemaid, and the autopsy showed he was riddled with sexually transmitted diseases and a whole bunch of other stuff that, wouldn't you know it, he had passed on to Connie, making her very sick and heartbroken that her husband was gay and having sex with young men. So, she killed herself at the beginning of the year, and sadder still, for their son Antonio, not being able to deal with his father's infidelities with the male persuasion, or his mother's suicide, the shame and heartache was all too much for him, and he killed himself, leaving behind a young wife and child. It cut Carlos and Viv pretty deep. Antonio came to their wedding in '77. And to think it's all because of this gay disease."

"Do you know that for sure?" Dan asked, intrigued by all the family had gone through.

"Well, a co-worker of Pedro's, at *Studio 69* in New York, died of it early last year, and in his little black book was a police officer we knew, and Stephano DeLuca to name two. They also died last year, as did a few other people who revealed all before *they* left this mortal coil."

"Ahh, interesting," Dan murmured, thinking something through. "Mrs, ah, Jenny, I'm going to need a list of every person your family knows who has gone through this disease. Is sick from it, or died from it."

"Any reason why?"

He looked at her thoughtfully. "I don't know the reason why, I just have a feeling it will be important."

"Mmm, Pedro called everyone for Leon when he passed. I don't think he has the book, but he might have a list somewhere."

After a large protein-powered breakfast, a hot shower, and lots of coffee, Dan got to work on his lists and on finding all those phone numbers and addresses. There were plenty to call and talk to, and being a doctor afforded him information most people wouldn't have received. The hospitals faxed through papers, and several ex-lovers told him plenty, especially Bertha St John. She knew all about Luiz's exploits and gave him ex-lovers' names. Dan suggested she get checked out, and she insisted she was fine. But when told Tomas and Roger were on their death bed, she quietened down and agreed to be tested and have her doctor fax through the results. She gave Dan her doctor's number and asked him to pass on her condolences.

After a long day, he had plenty of information, but not many answers, and pinning the last piece of paper to the wall he looked at all it meant.

If only *he* knew what it all meant.

*****

"I still can't believe you did nothing with Berry Wilder," Chris chastised Carlos as the boys all sat in Tomas's room. After a morning out on the balcony, Tomas and Roger had taken a nap and were now surrounded by male cousins.

"You deserved it for all the cracks you made at my wedding." Carlos flicked through the wedding album his mother had made him. "I always knew the way to get to you was through Berry."

"That's low down, cuz." Chris took a swig of beer and glanced around at the ten or so others in the room. "Can you believe he did that?"

"Of course I can." David grinned. "He's Carlos."

That brought a smile to Tomas's face. Anything that had to do with bashing Carlos was always funny.

"What are you laughing at?" Carlos asked Tomas, thankful his brother still had the energy to smile and have a laugh.

"It's fun remembering old times," Tomas breathed. "We should get the photo albums out. There's a picture of you in your room with Viv's poster."

The blood drained from Carlos's face, and the boys laughed.

"You mean the one where he's lying on the bed like some stud with his hair slicked back and his jacket open to the waist?" Blake asked. He was one of the younger cousins, closer to Pedro's age.

"That's the one," Tomas said. "Mama's still got it."

"Aw." Chris laughed. "I gotta see that again."

"No, you don't," Carlos snapped. "What about you, Christopher? Did you ever get it on with Berry after I'd gone, or wasn't she interested?"

"She wasn't," Lawrence said. "She turned her nose up at all of us. If we weren't Carlos, we weren't wanted."

"Hang on." Greg put his hands out to calm everyone. "What about Barbara Weston? She got rejected by Carlos. Whatever happened to her, does anyone know?"

The cousins all glanced at each other, shaking their heads, while Carlos and Pedro exchanged frowns.

"Go on," Tomas told his brothers, and they looked at him. "Tell them."

"Tell us what?" Hayden asked. "Do you boys know what happened to Barbara?"

Carlos sighed and ran a hand through his hair. "Yeah, yeah we do."

"Go on," Chris urged.

"Well, it started four years ago…" Carlos went on to tell them the story of his encounter with Barbara, her run-in with Viv, how Barbara had gone to his parents and told them she was pregnant, and then about the legal letter his father had sent her.

"Fucking hell!" Chris exclaimed. "She turned into a real psycho. So what happened?"

Carlos turned to Pedro. "Time for you to tell the story, little brother."

Pedro talked about Barbara stalking him and Angie at the club, the attacks on both of them, and then the demented gifts she had sent in New York. He also regaled them with the details of how she drove his car into his future father-in-law.

"Fuck man," Greg said. "That's sick shit."

"Yeah, yeah it is." Pedro finished off his beer.

"Bloody hell," Richard, a cousin Tomas's age, said. "Is she the only psycho you guys have had, or are there more?"

"Besides all of the guys that kidnapped us who were Papadopoulos's men, there was Luiz." Carlos turned to his brother and saw him wince.

"Not someone I like talking about," Tomas rasped.

"I know," Carlos replied. "But he became obsessed with you, and not only poisoned you, but killed four of your co-workers and tried to frame Roger for it. Even left a dead body in their apartment's car park," Carlos told everyone.

"Jesus, what i*s it* with you lot?" Richard asked. "You attract trouble like no tomorrow."

"Well…" Carlos leaned back in his seat. "You know…that's what happens to good-looking people like me."

"Aw, get your hand off it," Chris said as guffaws went around the room.

"Hey." Carlos put his hands up in protest. "My hands aren't on it."

"Your hands have always been on it," Greg reminded him. "Ever since puberty."

The boys spent several more hours reminiscing, looking through old photo albums, talking about old times, and at the end of the day, Tomas and Roger had their spirits lifted. And that was all that mattered.

July 1981

Jenny dialled an Australian phone number. It was the first week of July, and she should have done this sooner.

"Hello."

"Yes, hello. Mrs Dencott?"

"Yes."

"My name is Jenny Stephanopoulos, and I'm calling about your son, Roger."

"I don't have a son called Roger."

"I know you do, Mrs Dencott. I also know you disowned him when he told you he was gay. What I'm calling for, is that he was wondering if you still had his belongings, and if so, could you send them to me?"

"And why would I do that?" Marsha Dencott was suspicious. She hadn't heard from Roger since '78 when he'd called to say he was in Australia and could he come around to see them. She'd refused, him being a poof and all. So, why was this woman calling now?

"Because he'd like his belongings if you still have them." Jenny didn't want to give too much away too soon. "I'll pay for them to be sent, Mrs Dencott."

"Why does he need them?" Marsha asked.

"Because they're his belongings, Mrs Dencott. He'd like his things, and any photos you might have that you would be willing to part with."

"Shacked up with some poof, has he?" Marsha asked. "Why are

you calling? You're a woman. What do you have to do with a poof like him?"

Jenny finally had to reveal it. "Because he's my son's partner and I would like to put together an album of his photos for him and get the rest of his belongings if I can."

"He's your son's partner?" Marsha asked, incredulous. "You put up with this abomination?"

"I was raised Catholic by my parents. God teaches us to love, forgive, and accept, as well as have compassion. I'm not about to hate my son because he's gay, Mrs Dencott, and that's just all there is to it. We have accepted Roger into the family, and I'm calling you in the hope you still have his things, or some photos we can have. Do you?"

"No. I threw it all out when he left. And even if I did I wouldn't send it to the mother of his partner. Partner, ha! What a joke. If you want to be a poof lover go right ahead, Mrs whatever your name is."

"Stephanopoulos, Mrs Dencott," Jenny said icily. "It's Stephanopoulos."

"That sounds like a queer name. What is it?"

"It's Greek, Mrs Dencott, and throughout Greek history, homosexuality was always accepted, and I will accept my son and the partner he chooses. And he chose *your* son. So, quite frankly, Mrs Dencott, I don't care what you think of my son *or* me. All I'm after is Roger's things. Do you have them or not?"

Marsha paused. She certainly hadn't expected a woman to ring up about her poof son. When Roger had tried contacting her, she'd rejected him, more for her husband, Roger's father, than herself.

"If you have anything, Mrs Dencott, please send it express post. I'll send you a check for your time and shipping."

Marsha thought about the things she *did* have left, packed in a box in the attic. A few stuffed toys, photos, and different school things. But did she want to send them to some strange woman?

"Mrs Dencott," Jenny said softly. "Your son is sick. So far, the doctors haven't been able to cure him. They say he has malaria, but they can't fix him..." pause... "I can pay your way over here if you wish, Mrs Dencott. If you want to see your son before he dies. I'm more than willing to bring you over to stay with us while his days pass. We don't know how long he has."

"Oh, my God," Marsha murmured, completely shocked at the sudden change in conversation. "Oh, my boy."

"Will you come, Mrs Dencott? And bring Roger's belongings and any photos you have. Once he's…at the end, I'll pay your way back."

"I…" Marsha thought some more and worried. "I can't just leave. My husband…won't want me too."

"If he works, pack your bag and leave during the day. I'll wire you the money, Mrs Dencott. Pack Roger's things into a case and bring them with you. Please come, Mrs Dencott. Say goodbye to your son before it's too late."

Marsha quickly figured out when and how she could leave and made a plan. She had always desperately wanted to see her son, but never did because of her husband. And if he was dying, she didn't want him to die without saying goodbye. The guilt would kill her. "Wire me the money, and I'll leave tomorrow."

*****

Marsha Dencott arrived two days later and was met at the airport by Jenny's mother and father. Arriving at the Stephanopoulos home, Jenny greeted her.

"Mrs Dencott, Jenny Stephanopoulos, good to see you." They shook hands.

"Mrs Stephan—"

"Call me Jenny, please. Let me take you to the guest room so you can freshen up." Carrying Marsha's bags, Jenny led her to the room off the hallway at the other end of the house. "Here we go." She placed the cases on the bed. "You have a small closet and ensuite."

"Roger…" Marsha paused. "How…?"

Jenny saw fear on her face. "Very sick, Mrs Dencott. Both of our sons are."

"Both?" Marsha laid her coat on the bed. "You said…,"

"That Roger has been diagnosed with malaria and he has hung in there. My son is also sick with a similar bug. It's ravaged their systems, and they are not the men they used to be. They are anaemic and have wasting disease."

"What's that?" Marsha stood almost as tall as Jenny at five feet seven, but was plumper.

"It's a disease that eats away muscle, so they look very thin, very ill, and…" Jenny swallowed, "very sunken. Their cheeks, their eyes. Mrs Dencott." Jenny took her hand. "I have no idea how much longer your son will be here, or mine for that matter," a breath, "I would love for you to make up for lost time and…clearly, you want to, otherwise you wouldn't be here. I'm hoping that you can accept him the way he is, and love him in his dying days. But if not, please tell me now so we can keep the visit short, because if you're just going to call him names and tell him it's all his fault, then I will have to make you leave. We need him to pass happy, Mrs Dencott. Please make your son happy in his last days on Earth." Jenny tried prevailing to her sense of motherhood, and it looked as if she had succeeded.

Marsha blinked away tears. "Yes. Yes, all right."

"Why don't you freshen up and prepare yourself, and I'll get a box for Roger's things. I can't wait to see what they are." Leaving her to change, Jenny went and fetched a large box and came back to find Marsha with the case open. Jenny saw a teddy bear, some toys and artwork. "Oh, my, look at those things." Putting the box on the bed, she picked up the teddy.

"He had that until he was about eleven," Marsha said softly, a small smile on her lips.

"I think he'll love to see it now," Jenny told her. "Let's take these things to him." Packing the box, she led Marsha through the house and to the boys' bedroom. "Roger, I have a surprise for you." She set the box on the bed and saw Roger turn his head to her.

Seeing something in the corner of his eye, he turned his head further, seeing her standing in the hallway, he frowned, unsure if he was seeing things. "Mum?"

Jenny moved to her side. "Come, Mrs Dencott, please." Slipping an arm around her, she pulled her into the room.

"Mum?" Roger felt himself heave. "Mum?"

"Oh." Marsha's hand flew to her mouth at the sight of her boy strung up to so many tubes and wires looking so gaunt and ill.

"Shhh." Jenny comforted her. "He's very ill with malaria, isn't he, doctor." Jenny eyed Dan. The lie had been told. Everyone knew to stay away so it *could* be told.

"Yes, Mrs Dencott," Dan said. "I'm Dan Ardent, your son's physician. "Mrs, ah, Jenny, hired me to look after them both in their final days."

"Oh, what's wrong with him? Why is he dying?" Marsha slowly moved closer to the bed.

"The disease attacked his immune system before we knew about it, and it attacked hard. All we can do is keep him comfortable," Dan told her.

"Oh, my boy." Marsha went to his side and sat slowly. "My boy."

"Mum." Roger's eyes pleaded with her. "Mum...please..."

Marsha remembered Jenny's words from her phone call about being Catholic and compassionate and loving. In fact, that's all she'd been doing the last two days, remembering those words. "Oh, my boy. I have missed you so much."

"Mum. I've missed you, too." Roger reached out with both hands.

Marsha looked from her son's hands to the doctor. "Will I?"

"It's not contagious, Mrs Dencott. You can touch your son."

She slowly reached out and took his hands, bending her head to kiss them. "Oh, my boy. My son. I have missed you, so much."

"I've missed you, too, Mum. I've missed all of you, so much." Roger stared in a daze, through tear-filled eyes, in disbelief that his mother was right there, on the bed beside him.

Looking into his eyes, she saw the sadness she was sure reflected in her own. "I'm so sorry this happened. I'm so sorry I never saw you again. I've missed you so much." She reached out and stroked his face. "You're so sick, my boy. Jenny says you're dying."

He nodded and painfully closed his eyes as his heart lurched. "Yes, Mum. We're dying."

Marsha looked at the man beside him. "Are you my son's partner?"

"Yes, Mrs Dencott," Tomas rasped.

"That's my son, Tomas," Jenny said quietly, pulling Roger's teddy bear out of the box.

"Jupiter." Roger's eyes lit up. "You brought Jupiter."

Marsha turned and Jenny handed her the bear, which she passed to Roger. "Yes. Jenny asked if I still had some of your belongings. I did." Watching him light up at the sight of his teddy bear made her heart soar back to the times he was young. "I brought your artwork and your photos." Indicating for Jenny to pass them over, she showed them to Roger. "Do you remember these?"

"Oh, Jumbo at the amusement park, and there's my brother and sister, our school, my school photos. God, look at me, T, I was a dork." He showed Tomas his school photos from when he was fifteen.

"You look awesome, Roger, just like you do now," Tomas told him.

"You're just trying to flatter me," Roger joked.

"No." Tomas gazed into his eyes. "I'm telling you the truth. You'll always look awesome to me."

"Aw, T." His hand went to Tomas's cheek. "You say the sweetest things. I love you."

"And I love you," Tomas replied.

Marsha, seeing the love between the two, welled up inside. She had never seen her son look like that. Look that happy, that in love, and she wondered what she had missed out on. Sobbing, and overwhelmed by it all, she ran from the room.

"Mum?" Roger called.

"It's okay. I'll go. It must be too much for her." Jenny went after her, finding her in the guest room. "Mrs Dencott, I know it's upsetting, but you must be strong."

"I," Marsha gulped. "Can't bear to see him like that."

"I know," Jenny soothed, rubbing her arms as she stood behind her. "I know it's so very hard to know they're not long for this world."

"I…" Marsha shook her head. "I can't."

"Please," Jenny said. "Why don't you refresh yourself and come into the lounge room for a cool drink. Please."

Sniffing, Marsha nodded and fled for the bathroom.

Jenny went into the kitchen and served drinks. Her family came from the balcony to help. Carrying the tray to the dining table, Jenny turned when Marsha came out. "Mrs Dencott, this is my husband, Spiros Stephanopoulos." She indicated to her husband standing beside her. "My son Carlos and his wife, Vivian." She moved a hand to her right as they came to her side. "And my son Pedro and his wife, Angelina." They stood to Spiro's left. "We are Tomas's family. We are Roger's family."

Marsha stared from one to the other, rung her hands and fretted, feeling very overwhelmed at all of the people suddenly there. "How can you…how do you…?"

"Accept him?" Jenny asked.

"Yes. He's not…" Marsha closed her eyes a moment.

"Normal?" Jenny inquired.

Marsha sighed. "Yes."

"He *is* normal, Mrs Dencott. And he's our son," Jenny replied.

"And *our* brother," Carlos said.

"And *our* brother-in-law," Viv added.

"But it's not normal. It's a sin," Marsha murmured. She too had grown up Catholic.

"According to the Bible, homosexuality *is* a sin," Jenny said. "But then the Bible also taught us that Jesus forgave all for their sins and loved them anyway, regardless of their status, regardless of their flaws. He taught us love and forgiveness, love and compassion. And I love my son, Mrs Dencott, no matter what. He chose your son to be with, and your son chose him. They love each other. Who are we to stand between two people loving each other?"

"Yes." Marsha felt herself relenting. "I saw it in their eyes."

"Then let me show you more, Mrs Dencott." Jenny motioned for her to sit at the table and brought out several photo albums to look over. Opening one, it showed photos of Tomas and Roger together. "Look at all of those, Mrs Dencott. Birthdays, Christmases, New Years. They travelled, they celebrated, they loved each other with pure abandon." Pausing to watch Marsha's face light up, she went on, "I have never seen two people more in love. I believe they are soulmates, true mates, true lovers. It's in their eyes when they look at each other.

It's in their touch when they touch each other. It's there, Mrs Dencott, all over their faces. It's in their body language, their expressions. It's there for all to see."

Flipping through the albums, Marsha smiled. She had missed out on so much with her son, and now she was regretting it. The pain from not seeing him in over ten years was overwhelming her, strangling her throat. Closing the book, she thought, and then shook her head. "I can't stay. I have to go home."

Surprised, Jenny recoiled. "He's your son, Mrs Dencott. He needs you."

"I know, it's just that my husband—"

"Threw him out," Jenny said.

Marsha nodded in shame. "Yes, he did. But I can't stay too long. I must go home. Get back to my home. I told my husband I was going to my sister's as she was sick. She's in on it."

"Do you not want to be here for Roger in his last days?" Jenny asked.

Marsha looked up sadly. "I can't lose him again. Not for real." The tears came. "At least I knew he was alive before, but this time he won't be, and I can't face that. I just can't."

"It's okay." Jenny gently rubbed her back. "It's okay. How about staying for a day or two and then you can go? But I think he needs to hear this from you, Mrs Dencott. I think once and for all the two of you need to have a heart to heart and get all of your emotions out on the table. Then, if you do decide to still go home, you can at least say that you told him everything you wanted him to know. You'll have a full heart knowing he knew how much you loved him in his final days. Will you come with me now, Mrs Dencott? Come with me and have a heart to heart with your son? See what an amazing man he is. How much he is loved by my son and this family? Will you come with me now and learn what he's been doing, and how much he still loves you?"

Marsha gulped. "Yes."

"Okay, come, Mrs Dencott. Let's go talk with your son." Jenny led her back into the bedroom where they found Dan had put up all the artwork and left the toys on the bed.

Roger was flicking through the photos when they entered. "Mum?"

"Oh, my boy. There's so much I want to say to you." She sat by his side and took his hand.

For the next several hours Marsha and Roger talked about everything. The day he left, the pain, the hurt, the tears she had cried at losing him. He told her about his life with Tomas and living in America, how happy he'd been that the Stephanopouloses had accepted him so willingly.

Marsha spoke with Tomas about his love for her son, and with Dan about the medication and treatment, especially when he administered the hourly doses. She spoke to Jenny about taking care of him, and was shown the wall of photos, with Jenny explaining how they had organized a wedding ceremony so her gay son could have what his straight brothers were having. There was a photo of Tomas and Roger's wedding on the chest of drawers with all six Stephanopouloses in the shot. Tomas and Roger were beaming. In fact, they all were.

Jenny saw how Marsha longingly looked at it. "I have copies of all the photos if you'd like some."

"Oh, yes, but I…" Marsha looked up longingly.

"Your husband?" Jenny nodded.

"Yes." Marsha became downcast.

"Then hide them from him," Jenny suggested. "You hid the box of Roger's things all these years, so hide the album. I made an album for you to take back."

Marsha looked at her in surprise. "Thank you."

"You're most welcome." Jenny smiled. "Spend some more time with your son."

"Ah, but not yet," Dan said. "It's time for a change."

"Right." Jenny nodded and turned back to Marsha. "Why don't you come with me and wait in the lounge room, relax a little, and have a drink." Jenny led her out. "Talk to my daughters-in-law about your son, and we will help them with something and be back shortly. Girls, can you take Mrs Dencott. Boys, you're needed."

Jenny, Spiros and the boys went back while Marsha asked what was happening.

"Tomas and Roger need help freshening up," Viv said politely.

"Freshening up?" Marsha frowned.

"Changing." Viv blinked. "This disease means they need to be changed regularly."

Marsha thought about it. "Are you saying my son needs changing? As in…a nappy?"

"He's ill, Mrs Dencott," Angie said. "They both are, and the disease they have means they have no control and need help to…*freshen up*."

"Oh…" A hand flew to Marsha's mouth. "My poor boy."

With the situation taking its toll, Marsha decided to stay for two days and talked with Roger at length. As much as she wanted to be there, she had to get home.

"Stop letting Dad control you," Roger told her. "He's dictated all our lives how things should be, and you've let him. Mum, please, stay. I don't know how much longer I have."

"And I don't know if I can watch you die, my boy." She stroked his face. "I can't watch you die. I can't lose you a second time."

He sighed. "I know, Mum. It must be so hard, and I'm so sorry."

"It's not your fault," she said. "You've been struck down with a disease they can't fix. And now you're wasting away on me." Sadly shaking her head, she went on. "I can't bear to see you like this. I just can't." Kissing his hand, she sobbed.

"Oh, Mum." Roger stroked her head. "I understand."

"My boy, please, please understand. This is gut-wrenching for me seeing you like this. Seeing you waste away." She lifted her head. "But at least you're with a family that loves you. That's taking care of you, and I will forever be grateful to Jenny and her family for doing that. For taking you in and loving you when I couldn't."

"That's okay, Mum," Roger told her. "I'm grateful to them too. The boys treat me like another brother, and the girls are like sisters. Mr and Mrs S are like substitute parents, reminding me to wear sunscreen, and be safe, get out in the sun and exercise. I know you couldn't be there for me, and I'm sorry that none of you could accept me for the way I turned out, but I didn't stop loving any of you. And as much as I'd love you to stay, I understand if you can't. At least we've had this time together, and that's more than anything I could have ever hoped for. It's okay, Mum. I know you feel guilty and I forgive you. I forgive all of you for what was said and done. It's okay, Mum, it's okay."

Marsha sobbed. All the years of missing out on her son, seeing him happy, even if it was with a man, seeing him married and living life the way he wanted. It was all too much. "I don't want to lose you."

"I know, Mum, I know. But we all die, we all go. I'm just going sooner than you. It's okay, Mum. If you can't bear to see the end, it's okay. I forgive you. Please don't cry anymore. It's okay."

After much forgiveness and many more tears, Marsha Dencott left her son in the very capable hands of his mother-in-law, Jenny Stephanopoulos, begging for word once it happened, but to please send anything to her sister's address.

Jenny promised she would, and sent a tearful Marsha Dencott back to the airport with her parents as escorts. Wandering back to Tomas's room, she stopped at the doorway, seeing Roger's body racked with almighty sobs in Tomas's arms.

Dan was quietly making notes in the hallway and glanced at her.

She smiled sadly at him and left her sons to grieve in private.

*****

That weekend, Jenny had a surprise for her boys. "Okay, we're going to get you two up and out of the house today. We have a surprise for you."

"A surprise?" Tomas asked, his face lighting up. "What is it?"

"Well, it wouldn't be a surprise if I told you, would it?" Jenny laughed. "But I definitely think you need it." She glanced at Dan who nodded. "Once the two of you have breakfast and are cleaned up, we'll go."

Half an hour later, once the boys were refreshed, Spiros wheeled the first chair in.

"It's not a normal wheelchair," Jenny told Tomas. "More like a recliner on wheels." It was a wicker rocking chair on two huge wheels that had been used in convalescent homes. "And Roger, there's one for you, so we can get you both to where you need to be."

Jenny directed Spiros on how to pick Tomas up and set him in the chair, and Dan attached the tubes and bags to the metal rod on the back.

Carlos and Pedro wheeled another chair in, and Spiros lifted Roger into it.

"Okay, we'll pop a light blanket over both of you." Jenny tucked in the hospital grade blanket around Tomas. "And we'll go."

"What if we….need to…" Tomas blushed and let the sentence stop.

Jenny smiled grimly at his discomfort. "We have plenty of supplies, and you're sitting on waterproof bed covers, so nothing will leak. Now, let's go. Got everything, Dan?" She wheeled Tomas past him and into the lounge room where four cousins stood along with Rebecca and Sarah in case they were needed to help with the boys.

"We do." Dan grabbed his bag. Not expecting a day out, he'd had to borrow clothes from the boys' wardrobes, being close to the same size Tomas had been.

"Okay, let's go then." They wheeled the boys outside, and Jenny stood between the chairs holding one umbrella over Tomas, and another over Roger to keep the sun off.

After making their way down various streets, they came to a small private cove at the beach where Jenny had sent the family to set up massive tents, towels, a barbecue, and seating for everyone.

"Oh, my God, Mama," Tomas cried. "You did this for us?"

"Of course I did, my babies. You deserve to see the ocean. We should have gotten you here sooner. It would have done you a world of good." She waved at her family, and more of the boys' cousins came over to help carry the chairs down the stairs and across the sand to the tents where they settled Tomas and Roger in a suitable spot out of the sun.

"Look at the ocean." Jenny gazed across the blue water and along the coastline. "Smell it." Breathing deeply, she turned to the boys. "Would you like to go out in it?"

"What?" Tomas looked up from the water to her. "We can't, Mama."

"Nonsense! We've already decided how we're going to do it, and first off, we need to get you two into some shorts."

"I'm going to need more than that, Mama." Tomas looked away in embarrassment.

"Tent flaps down everyone, we're getting the boys ready," Jenny called, and they cleaned and changed them. Once finished, she called for Chris's help.

"One, two, three." Spiros lifted Tomas into his arms while Pedro held the chair's metal rod up, so the bag and tubes didn't get tangled. The boys' arms were wrapped in cling wrap to keep the water from getting in. Carlos and Chris lifted Roger, while Hayden held his bag and tubes up. They slowly made their way to the water, walking in until they were chest deep and side by side.

"Oh, my God, this is so good." Tomas breathed in, his arms around his father's neck.

"Let it heal you, my babies." Jenny was right with them, as was Dan and the other cousins who were helping. "Let it wash over you and heal you. Make you feel better."

Tomas lifted his face to the sun, letting it warm him. "It's been so long."

"It certainly has," Spiros murmured as Jenny gently washed water over their son's back and chest.

Breathing as deeply as he could, Tomas gazed across the ocean, and, as Spiros slowly turned, the coastline they called home. "Oh… look how beautiful it is, Roger. It's so beautiful."

"Yeah, it is, T," Roger said from Carlos's and Chris's arms. "Absolutely beautiful.

"It always is in the summer," Jenny said, seeing the boys' faces. Even Dan looked impressed. "It always was amazing late spring, summer and early autumn. Just beautiful."

"I've never been here before," Dan said, marvelling at the coast. "Definitely a place I'd like to spend more time."

"Once this is over…you should stay for a holiday," Jenny said as they floated.

"I can't. I already had to take leave to come. I'm not even sure they'll want me back." He frowned at the thought of losing a job he loved and was good at.

"Of course they will. They'd be stupid not to," Jenny said. "How long have we been in?"

Dan looked toward the beach to see Jenny's parents waving them back in. "Fifteen minutes from all accounts." Sarah and Matthew had timed them as the boys could only be in for so long with everything that was happening.

Everyone slowly made their way back to the tent where they changed the boys back into their diapers, and the family sat chatting, enjoying the quiet until Alena and Diana came screaming down the beach toward them. Viv and Angie had taken them for a long walk while the family had spent their time together.

"Go in water, Dada," Alena cried. "Mama chasing A-ena."

Pedro grinned. "That's my girl." He grabbed her as she tore into his arms and he swung her high in the air and around in circles.

"Water, Dada, A-ena swim." Her little blue bathing suit sparkled in the sun, and her black curls were damp.

"Okay, Bubba, let's go for a quick swim." Running down to the beach he waded out until he was waist deep and helped Alena paddle back and forth.

"Da-anna swim, Dada?" Diana ran up to her father and launched herself at his legs.

"You wanna swim too, do you?" Carlos looked at her in her little pink bathing suit and matching hat covering her golden curls.

"Yes, Dada. Da-anna swim wiv A-ena."

"Okay, let's go." Before he was up, she was off and racing toward the water. "Wait up, Diana," he yelled, but his daughter was determined to get to her cousin and doggy paddled her way out. Daddy caught up to her and splashed her.

"Dada," she screamed in delight, giggling her way to her cousin as her daddy swam beside her.

"My God those two are a handful." Viv sat down on a towel and took the drink Jenny offered her. "They've been screaming and running and playing since we got here."

Jenny laughed lightly. "Little kids do have a lot of energy. They take after their fathers." They all watched the boys with their daughters, screaming, laughing and splashing.

"Definitely like their fathers," Chris agreed, and the cousins laughed.

An hour later they were cooking meat on the barbecue and setting out mouth-watering salads.

"Oh, that smells so good," Tomas groaned. "I miss Papa's meats and your home-cooked meals, Mama."

"I'm sure you do, sweetie." She brushed his thinning hair aside. "And I wish you could have some, but you know it all goes through you."

"I know, Mama. It doesn't mean I can't miss it." His stomach grumbled.

Jenny's head twitched, thinking that strange, and asked Dan about it.

"It's possible for hunger to happen even though they are on extremely high doses of protein to stave off the Cachexia. But sometimes, when you get the scent of juicy, succulent meat, the stomach's gotta do what the stomach's gotta do. Growl for some."

Tomas smiled. "Yes. My stomach wants food."

To Jenny, that was a hopeful sign, but as Dan explained further, the protein from the medication could clash with the protein from the meat. The doses were pure, the meat not, and so it might only make them worse.

"I'll just have to sit here and salivate then," Tomas said. "I miss your cooking, Mama. All the lamb, the roasts, the desserts."

"There has to be something he can have?" Jenny asked Dan, feeling absolutely sickened that her poor son couldn't have food before he died. "You told us he was dying, so why can't he have something?" The thought of her baby never having another of her meals again was heartbreaking.

"Well…maybe some salad, or dessert." Dan knew it was hard for Jenny. The boys were hanging in there and prolonging the inevitable. So, why shouldn't they eat? "But just a few mouthfuls so they don't get sick. Otherwise, we may be cleaning up vomit as well."

"As long as it tastes good going down I don't care how it comes out," Tomas joked.

During lunch, Jenny carefully fed Tomas and Roger two mouthfuls each of salad.

Tomas closed his eyes in happiness. "Oh, that is so good, Mama."

"Thank you, my baby. It's been so long since your stomach's had food, I hope it doesn't make you ill."

"But it's so good." He weakly reached for her hand and squeezed it. "It's always been good, Mama."

For dessert, she fed them a mouthful of creamy chocolate pie and Roger groaned in pleasure.

"Aw, Mrs S, that is amazing."

"Thank you, Roger. Even with everything going on I still wanted to make some of the desserts."

"Definitely awesome, Aunt Jenny," Greg had a second bite of his piece.

"Do you want more, or would you like to try Grandma's raspberry chiffon pie?" Jenny asked Tomas and Roger.

"Oooh, wahsbwy?" Alena and Diana said, looking hopefully at them for more food even though they had already shared a piece of chocolate pie.

Jenny laughed. "You want some too, do you? Great-Grandma's pie?"

"Yes, pwease." The girls held up their plate, and Sarah cut a small portion for them to share.

"Tomas?" she asked.

"Yes, pwease," he joked, and Jenny fed him and Roger. It melted in his mouth. "Oh, Grandma, that's good."

"Glad you like it." Sarah gave the last slice to Dan. "And what do you think?"

"I think I'll be going home fatter than when I got here," he replied, making everyone laugh in agreement.

"It's the sea air," Jenny said. "Makes you hungry and then you can't stop eating."

During the afternoon, the family took Tomas and Roger out into the ocean, dunking them while keeping their arms out. Jenny gently held her son's head back and washed water over it.

"That's so good," Tomas murmured, eyes closed against the sun.

"Let it heal you, my baby," Jenny murmured in reply. "Let it heal you."

Dan did the same for Roger, getting a murmured thanks in return.

Back on the beach, the girls woke from their naps and were taken for a quick swim by their parents before wanting to talk to Uncle Tomas.

"Unca Tomas." Alena stood by his chair.

"A-ena." Tomas smiled down at her. "How are you, my baby girl?"

"Can I sit on your wap?" She gazed imploringly up at him with her big blue eyes.

"Oh, I'm sorry, sweetie, I'm not strong enough," he told her and weakly played with her curls. They were longer, shoulder length now she was three.

Pedro moved one of the beach chairs, which was actually a kitchen chair, over next to his brother. "Come on, Bubba, sit on my lap and then you can lean over." He lifted her, shifting her into his right arm so she could lean over and kiss Uncle Tomas on the forehead.

"Aw, A-ena," Tomas rasped. "I love you so much."

"I wuv you, Unca Tomas." She gently patted his face. "Why can't I sit on your wap?"

"Because I don't have the energy, baby," he replied. "I'm weak and sick, and I don't have the muscle strength anymore."

"Why are you sick?" she asked, looking at all the tubes sticking out of him.

"Because I have a germ that's making me sick," he said.

"Why can't da doctor make it go way?" Her big blue eyes stared into his and Pedro teared up.

"Because he doesn't have the medicine, Alena. There's no medicine that will make me better." Tomas saw his brother blink back tears.

"Wiw you aways be wike dis?" A frown crossed her pretty face.

"Yes, Bubba. And maybe worse," Tomas told her.

"Dat's not nice," she said.

"No, Bubba, it isn't," he replied. "Not very nice at all."

"So you can't pway wid me anymore?"

"No. But it doesn't mean that Alena can't read me books and tell me all about her day. What she does with Diana, and the games you play, and the songs you sing. I want to hear all about it. Can you tell me about it, Alena?" Tomas smiled at his adorable niece.

"Okey-dokey, Unca Tomas." She promptly went into a long conversation about her day so far, with Diana popping up to add her two cents worth, leaving Tomas and Roger with big smiles on their faces.

"An' now we're here," Alena finished. "Tawking to you, Unca Tomas."

"Thank you, Alena." He glanced down to his knees where Diana was hovering and leaning on them. "And you, Diana, for telling me. Will you do it all again tomorrow?"

"Yes, Unca Tomas. A-ena wiw tawk to you evwy day to make you better." She kissed his forehead, bringing tears to everyone's eyes.

"Thank you, Alena." He smiled. "Thank you, so much."

"Dat's okay, Unca Tomas. Dada, A-ena wants to swim." She wriggled out of his lap and went running with Diana down to the water, with Viv and Angie running after them and wiping tears away.

"Those two." Pedro shook his head.

"Those two are precious little angels," Jenny said from behind them.

"Yes, they are," Tomas agreed, looking at his younger brother. "You all are."

Pedro looked back and couldn't stop himself from crying. Red hot tears flowed down his face and he leaned over and gently held his brother. "I love you, so much," he sobbed.

"I love you too, little brother," Tomas said as his own tears fell.

Jenny noticed everyone wiping away their tears and couldn't take it anymore. Turning, she quickly walked away, sobbing her own heartbreaking tears.

Spiros caught up with her as she reached the stairs. "You can't go."

"I'm not, I'm just…" She collapsed on the step. "I can't do this. I can't watch my baby die."

"I know. I know." He knelt behind her, arms around her. "I can't either, but we have to be strong."

"I don't know how much longer I can be." She sobbed between gasps of air. "I can't watch him die. Look at him; he's thinner, more gaunt, more sunken. I don't know how much longer I can watch him waste away."

"I know," Spiros murmured. "I know. But we have to put all of that aside to make his last weeks memorable and happy. Put him and Roger ahead of us."

"I know." She drew a ragged breath. "I know." Getting her breathing under control, she went back to the tent with her husband. "It's almost sunset, just wait till you see how it changes colour, you're going to love it." She stood between her son and son-in-law, a hand on each of their shoulders, and felt one lay upon hers. Glancing down, she saw Tomas looking up, tears in his big black eyes, eyes just like his father's. She felt herself falling, emotionally, at the desolation and infection she saw in them. Her eyes watered, and he removed his mask to kiss her hand. Her eyes closed, her tears fell, and she silently cried beside her son. When she did open her eyes, she found him crying just as much. "Oh, baby." She bent down and rested her face on his head, while her hands were on his face. They both sobbed. Cried for what had been, cried for what was. Cried for what would be, and would never be again.

Most were silent, quietly stepping away to let them have their moment, crying themselves, hugging their loved ones as Jenny and Spiros cried for their son. As Carlos and Pedro cried for their brother, and as Viv and Angie cried for their brothers-in-law.

Finally, Spiros pulled Jenny away. "The sun is setting, my love."

Gasping back air, Jenny wiped her face. "Okay, ah, okay, let's get you boys cleaned up, and then it's time for your final swim for the day."

Fifteen minutes later, they were back in the water all watching the magnificent Mykonos sunset, saying prayers, shedding tears, washing away their sons' sins and past mistakes to be redeemed in the eyes of God.

Tomas rested his head against his father's, stroking his face. "I love you, Papa. Thank you so much for everything you've done for me."

"You are more than welcome, my son," Spiros murmured. "More than welcome. You are my son…that is what fathers do for their sons."

Tomas gently slid his fingers over his father's moustache. "Promise me you'll keep this. It looks good on you, and shows me what I'd look like with one."

Spiros smiled sadly. "Of course I'll keep it. Your mother loves it."

Tomas grinned. "So do I."

"Come, my babies, time to go in," Jenny said. In the dying rays of the sun slipping behind the horizon, they carried the boys back to the tents. The towels and chairs had been collected by Jenny's sisters to make way for the gentle bath they gave the boys. With clean water and shampoo, they washed Tomas and Roger's hair, gave them a soft wash, and a freshen up, then changed them for bed.

The cousins carried the chairs up to the street where they all went home to tuck the boys into bed.

"Did you have a wonderful day, my baby?" Jenny asked from her spot on the bed next to Tomas.

"Oh, yes, Mama." Tomas's eyes sparkled. "So much. It was all so wonderful."

"I'm glad." Smiling, she patted his hand. "And we'll have many more days like that, don't you worry."

"Mama." He took her hand. "I know you're trying to stay positive for me, but…" His eyes searched hers.

"Don't even go there," she told him. "We *have* to stay positive." Tears sprang up. "We have to, and that's all there is to it. So, no more tears." She wiped away her own before wiping his away. "We all need to stay strong and stay positive."

"It's okay to fall apart, Mrs S," Roger told her.

"I don't like falling apart, especially in front of family," Jenny said. "I would rather do it in private. Plus, I believe we need to stay positive, not just for the two of you, but for each other."

"Mama." Tomas lifted her hand to his lips. "I love you so much. Thank you for everything you have ever done for me. The wedding, the money to travel, the holidays, everything, and now you're taking care of me like this."

"Of course I am." She smiled through her tears. "You're my baby. I'll always take care of my babies, regardless of what's wrong, or how old you are."

"I know, Mama." He nestled into her hand. "I know, and you have proved that time and time again these last twenty-six years, and especially for the last four. You've been my biggest supporter my whole life, and I have never been as grateful as I am now. I love you, Mama. I love you and Papa, and Carlos and Pedro, and Viv and Angie, and the girls and Roger. I love you all, so much."

"I know you do, my baby. I know you do." Jenny gently laid her head on her son's chest and sobbed.

Tomas slowly stroked her hair. "It's okay, Mama. It's okay to cry. It's okay."

"No, no it's not," she sobbed. "I feel like I'm letting you down."

"You've never let me down, Mama, never. Not even when you're angry can you ever let me down."

"I know. I just feel so helpless. I can't do anything to fix you. I just…"

"I know, Mama. I know." He kissed her head. "I know you can't fix this. But I love you so much for trying."

*****

At Jenny's request, Martin Brewster bought all of the newspapers Jenny had asked for every day, wrapped them in cling wrap, boxed them up, and sent them every Friday by express post to her in Mykonos. She received them every Tuesday and would hand out each paper to a different family member. Whether it be the L.A., San Francisco, Miami, or New York papers, they had the major ones sent every week.

Jenny scoured each day's *New York Times*, telling the others to look for anything, any medical article, any story, any obituary that might mean something. Flicking open the July 3rd edition of the paper, Jenny finally found something. An article talking about a rare cancer seen in forty-one homosexuals. Her eyes quickly flew over it; then she ran into the boys' bedroom. "Dan, Dan, look at this, quickly." She handed over the paper as he stepped out of the room.

Poring over it, his eyes widened. "Well, I'll be," he muttered when he'd finished. Turning, he grabbed a pair of gloves. "I need to check you boys over." Rolling back the bed covers, he carefully checked each limb and their chests, and with the help of Jenny, and Spiros who had come to see what was going on, their backs. But he found nothing. Covering the boys back up, he pulled off the gloves.

"Well?" Jenny asked, hoping for a miracle.

"Well, they don't seem to have it. But they do have the other infections mentioned. I need to get my hands on that report. I'm going to need to use your phone and fax."

"Go for it," Jenny told him.

"What was that about?" Spiros asked her.

"A new finding." Jenny picked up the paper and showed him while the boys looked silently on, almost too scared to hope for a miracle or cure.

Spiros glanced over the article. "But Dan just said they don't have it."

"No, but they have everything else." Jenny bit her lip in frustration.

"So, what does that mean?" Spiros asked her.

"I don't know," she said, silently crossing everything she had.

*****

An hour later, Dan pulled her aside. "I was faxed through the MMWRs reports from last month and last week about the diseases your son has."

"MMWRs?" Jenny inquired.

"Morbidity and Mortality Weekly Reports. It's a little-known publication from the Centre for Disease Control, or the CDC. Here's last month's."

Jenny took the paper and read about five young men struck down with Pneumocystis Pneumonia, all treated in the last eight months. All five also had CMV infections, while three had sexually transmitted diseases. "So, they all had what Tomas has? What does that mean?"

"Not sure." He sighed. "It shows that it's prevalent among gay men. It shows it can be a killer. The Kaposi's sarcoma strikes and doesn't let go, but your son doesn't have that. Here's the second report from the day after the newspaper article."

Jenny read the report about Kaposi's and Pneumocystis Pneumonia, how more gay men had been diagnosed with them, and most were dead. Other patients had severe STDs as well. Finishing it, she sighed. "At the end of the day, Dan, I have no idea what any of this means. What does it mean for my son? For Roger?" She waved a hand at all of the paper pinned to the hall walls in the boys' wing of the house. "Does any of this mean anything?"

"I don't know, Jenny. What I *do* know is I keep getting ideas, just little snippets of information floating through my head that throw ideas at me, and I try and grab it. I'm trying to make sense of it all. I check the boys' tests every week that the doctors fax through from Athens. I'm reading every medical journal I can get my hands on; including those I've had friends send me. We've spoken to all manner of doctors, specialists, herbalists, from everything we know, and even based on these reports," he held up the reports, "Tomas has everything. Low CD4 T cells which are the things we look at that leads to opportunistic infections which he has, and they are the same infections everyone else is getting. Except for the KS."

"So, at the end of the day?" Jenny was desperately clinging to her faith, but her hope was draining away.

Dan sighed. "I just don't know, Jenny. I'm going to contact a few of the doctors in the report, especially the ones in New York and San Fran, see what else they can help me with."

Jenny felt her soul starting to drain away. "I hope they can help, Dan, because my sons are fading, and I don't know how much longer they'll last. If you can pull a rabbit out of your hat…"

Despite the circumstances, he chuckled. "I wish I could, because I would."

"Please, try for my sons and me," Jenny pleaded with tearful eyes and a quivering lip. "Please. Whatever you need, whatever they have to have, and money is no object as you know."

"I know, Jenny. It's just, so far, there's not a whole lot left to do."

She silently pleaded with him for a moment before speaking. "Whatever that whole lot is, do it."

*****

A couple of hours later, they rolled the boys out to the lounge room and set them up to watch old home movies.

"What's going on?" Tomas asked, looking at all of his family crowding around.

"We're going to watch all of your old home movies," Jenny told him.

"Oh, Mama, no." Tomas grinned. "We don't need to see Carlos being a show-off. We live it every day."

"Hey," Carlos protested. "Just because I reached puberty before you lot and became the world's greatest lover—"

"Aw, get your hand off it," Chris said as he sat on the floor near Carlos. "It isn't always about you."

"Hey, I didn't bring it up," Carlos retorted.

"Are we ready?" Jenny asked everyone and took a seat next to Tomas.

"Just need to turn…it…on." Spiros clicked the button and the old film footage projected onto the white screen hanging in front of the fireplace.

"Oh, look at Carlos," Jenny cried out. "He was such a golden child. Diana's going to be just like him."

"Da-anna?" Diana looked up from her spot in front of her grandmother. "Me, Gamma?"

"Yes, Bubba. You're going to be just like your Dada, look." Jenny pointed to the screen. "That's Dada when he was young." She turned Diana around to look. Both girls were hovering near her and Tomas.

"Dada?" Diana asked, pointing to the screen.

"Yes, Bubba, that's me." Carlos was sitting on the floor in front of his brother.

"You, Dada?" Diana leaned on her father's broad shoulders.

"Yes, Diana." Carlos kissed her cheek.

"Oh, and there's Pedro," Jenny said. "Oh, my baby."

"Oh, for God's sake, Mama." Pedro shook his head in embarrassment.

"Well, you are, oh, look, Roger, there's Tomas when he was eight."

"Hey, T," Roger breathed. "You were such a cute kid. Look at those dark, soulful eyes and jet-black hair. Tomas Stephanopoulos, little

Greek God, right from the moment he was born." Laughter went around the room.

"Roger." Tomas smiled. "That's so sweet."

"Greek God, huh!" Carlos got a cheeky grin on his face and looked over his shoulder. "That reminds me of a particular movie we all made."

"Oh, don't you dare put that on, Carlos. I don't want to see it," Jenny told him.

"Just kidding, Mama, don't worry," he said as Diana somersaulted over his shoulder to fall into his lap. "Hey, Bubba." He kissed her chubby cheek.

"Hey, Dada." She smiled brightly up at him.

Tomas smiled. Those moments were so precious, and he was going to miss out. He didn't know how long he had left. Didn't know how many more precious moments he was going to have with his parents, his brothers, his sisters, even his precious little angels Alena and Diana. Such precious little babies he wished he'd had. He wished he'd had a child of his own, an offspring to call Bubba. A son or daughter to call him Dada. But that was something he'd never experience. Something he'd never have because he didn't have long. Was not long for this world, and that sucked.

He saw himself on the screen, running around the front yard of their house in Australia. Running around with their cousins, their aunts and uncles. He missed it, longed for it, longed for the days of his childhood when he ran around barefoot on the grass with his brothers and cousins when he had nothing to worry about, and life was carefree. Oh, God, how his heart ached for those days again. Those carefree days that he'd never have again. Never feel the grass of Australia, or the sandy beach of Mykonos. Never feel the breeze on his face, in his hair, his thinning hair. Never smell the ocean's scent; never eat any of his mother's food again.

Never hear his father tell her he loved her, never hear his mother tell him she loved him in return. Never work in the meat shop, never hear Carlos talk about himself, never see any of his siblings turn thirty, never turn thirty himself, never see Angie turn thirty, or the girls became teenagers, or turn sixteen, eighteen, or twenty-one, let alone thirty. Never see any more nieces, or nephews he might have. Never see the day gay people could legally get married in America, or Greece, or Australia.

He'd never be able to adopt or have a surrogate. He'd never be able to do anything. Not run on the sand, swim in the ocean, be a personal trainer again. Not love Roger, not *make* love to Roger.

He turned his head to look at his lover. *For all Mama has done for us, giving us a wedding ceremony and reception, being able to fly around the world and travel and see it, being able to do whatever we wanted, Mama understood. Understood what being gay meant. What Luiz had done meant. She* knew *this was coming. Knew something was coming. She never knew what, but here it is. It is now, it is happening now, and I hate it.*

Hate Luiz for doing this to me, hate Luiz for making me love what he did to me, hate Luiz for trying to frame Roger for murder, for poisoning me, for kidnapping me. For doing God knows what to me while I was unconscious. I hate Luiz with every fibre of my being for doing this to me because I know Roger didn't. I know Roger hadn't, so it had to be Luiz. He was the only one who could have given me this damn gay disease that's now killing both of us, and I hate it. I hate it, I hate it, I hate it. Unable to help himself, he cried out in anguish while his heart broke in two.

"Oh, my baby, no." Jenny pulled her crying son into her arms. "Oh, my baby." She wept with him as animalistic howls came from him with what little energy he had left in his weakened body. "Oh, my baby."

Spiros turned off the projector, and family members walked outside to give them a moment. Viv and Angie took the girls out and tried to explain to their frightened expressions that Uncle Tomas was just very upset about being sick.

"Oh, my baby." Jenny bawled her eyes out along with her son. "We didn't mean to make you cry. We wanted you to remember all the good times you had. All the things we did in Australia. We haven't gotten to Mykonos when you were twelve, or your wedding. Oh, my baby."

Slowly, Tomas's sobs softened, turning to gasps before they stopped.

Jenny wiped his face and helped him blow his nose. "Oh, my baby.

I am so, so sorry."

"You knew," he said to her. "You knew this was coming four years ago."

She frowned. "I knew something bad was coming, but I didn't expect it to be this. I prayed that it wasn't, and thanked God every day you were alive."

"You knew," he said sadly. "And that's why you gave us the money to travel and see the world. That's why you did everything for us."

She brushed his greying hair from his forehead. "I wanted you to do everything, see everything, *be* everything you wanted to be. To have all the experiences only a very few get to have. And I wanted to give you the world," she breathed. "I wanted to give you the world."

"You did, Mama. You did." Tomas's breathing became laboured, and Dan upped the Ventolin on his machine.

"You need to stay calm, my baby," Jenny said, kissing his forehead. "Stay calm so you can breathe, baby. Oh, my Tomas." She gazed at him with every ounce of love she had for him, and every ounce of sorrow she felt for the life he would not have.

"Mama." He gazed back. "I love you. Thank you for being my mother."

That set Jenny off, with a fresh round of tears falling down her face.

Tomas's eyes moved up to his father. "And Papa. I love you, too. Thank you for being my father. The both of you have been the most amazing parents to me."

"Oh, my son." Spiros bent over Tomas's chair to kiss the top of his head. "You have been the most amazing son to us."

Tomas looked adoringly up at his father just as he had as a child. His father was his hero, and he worshipped him. "Mama, Papa, don't ever feel guilty for bringing us to Mykonos. I love the place so much, and even though we were away from our family, I don't want you to regret the choice because I loved it. And I love you both, so much."

Jenny couldn't speak, her face crumpled, her throat constricted, the tears would not stop coming.

Tomas looked at his brothers kneeling at his knees. "Carlos, Pedro, the best big and little brothers in the world. I love you both, so much.

Everything you said at my wedding was the most amazing, incredible things, and I have cherished every moment I've had with you. I love you both, so much."

"We love you, Tomas." Pedro gently squeezed his arm that Carlos was holding. "So much. And you were the best big brother. Even better than Carlos."

That brought a smile out of Tomas. "I know," he said. "I know."

"And you were the best little brother," Carlos said, bringing Tomas's hand to his mouth to kiss. "And then Pedro came along."

Tomas's smile widened, and they laughed softly. "Yeah, I know." He turned his head to Roger. "And Roger. You've been the best lover, husband, partner, best friend that any man could hope for. I love you with every fibre of the being God made me, and I am so proud and so grateful, that you chose me to be with. I love you, so much."

"Oh, T." Roger reached out and laid a hand on Tomas's arm. "I loved you from the moment I met you at *The Joy Stick*. You were so gorgeous in your black suit. The way you danced, the way you moved. You were beautiful. Just like the Greek God you are." Tiny laughs came from the family. "I love you, so much, Tomas Stephanopoulos. So, so much."

Tomas covered Roger's hand with his. "I love you too, my husband."

"For better or worse, in sickness and in health, till death do us part," they said together.

The family were silent for a few moments while those words sank in.

"I'd like to finish watching the movies," Tomas said. "And see our wedding movie. But I need to freshen up first."

"I'll get everything," a teary Dan said and went off to collect the cart.

"Can you tell everyone to wait until they're called back in," Jenny told Spiros, and they spent the next few minutes cleaning up the boys before the family came back in.

"Are you okay, cuz?" Richard asked. They were all puffy eyed, having cried out on the street, or next door.

"I'm okay," Tomas breathed through his ventilator. "Let's finish watching."

Alena shuffled up to her uncle. "You okey-dokey, Unca Tomas?

You no need be so sad anymore," she said softly and crawled onto Jenny's lap to be next to him. She patted his arm. "You no need to be so sad anymore, Unca Tomas. We wuv you."

Diana hovered at his legs. "I wuv you too, Unca Tomas."

Tears threatened to start again, and Jenny furiously blinked back hers while Tomas crumpled.

"It's okay, my babies. I wuv you both, too." He pouted his lips to give Alena a kiss and tried to bend down to give one to Diana. But Carlos lifted her for him instead, and he planted it on her chubby cheek. "And you, Diana. Unca Tomas wuvs you both."

They settled back in and watched the rest of the videos from Australia. Birthdays, Christmas, New Year's, school fetes and plays, then came the film from their move to Mykonos and their ferry trip across the ocean from Athens. Tomas's face lit up. How he loved that. His twelve-year-old self was smiling broadly at the camera, waving and pointing to the island as they approached. Then there were videos with their Greek grandmother whom they had two years with before she passed.

"Hey, she's glowing," Tomas said, all dreamy-eyed. "It's like she has a halo."

Jenny looked at him in concern, for there was no halo around her mother-in-law in the video. She turned her gaze to Dan, but all he did was frown and give a slight shrug.

More birthdays, Christmases, and New Year movies, then it was on to the weddings with Carlos and Viv going first.

"Look, Bubba, that's Mama and Dada getting married," Carlos told Diana who was in his lap.

Diana stared at the ceremony. "Where was I, Dada? Da-anna not dere."

"Oh, Bubba." Viv laughed. "You were in my tummy." She was sitting beside Carlos on the floor.

"Your tummy, Mama. Why?" Diana turned her big blue eyes to Viv in confusion.

"Because I was in the process of having you," Viv told her. "Diana was in Mama's tummy."

Still too young to understand, Diana just stared at the movie, seeing her parents and aunts and uncles and Gamma and Gampa have fun and dance.

"Oh." Carlos breathed when Antonio came on screen. "Oh." He and Antonio were waving at the camera, acting stupid. "That's all I have of him. That and the photos from the reception," he murmured and his vision blurred. "In all the years I never got a picture of the two of us. Or with Connie." The room grew sombre, as the family had been told the story of their deaths.

"I have a few pictures of me with her. I treasure them dearly," Viv said quietly. "I look at them often. If it weren't for her and Harriet, you and I would never have met." She nudged her husband.

He wiped away a tear. "Yeah. I guess we have Antonio and Connie to be grateful to. Without working with Antonio, I wouldn't have met Connie, and I wouldn't have met you." He gazed lovingly at his wife. "I love you, Viv."

She smiled back. "And I love you."

Next, it was Pedro and Angie's wedding.

"Oh, look at my babies," Jenny said, still holding Tomas's hand.

"God, we're an awesome-looking couple, babe," Pedro told Angie. "And you were so beautiful in that gown."

"Aw, thanks, babe." She blushed from her spot beside him on the floor.

"Where was A-ena?" Alena stood with her hands on her hips in front of her grandma. "Where A-ena, Dada? Why A-ena not dere?"

"Because you were in your Mama's tummy too, Bubba." Pedro tweaked her ear.

"How could I be, Dada? I no see A-ena dere." She walked over to the screen, blocking everyone's view. "Where A-ena?"

Laughter filled the room, and Pedro crawled over to his daughter and pointed to Angie's stomach. "You were in there, Bubba. Growing in Mama's tummy. You weren't born yet, like Diana."

She pouted, hands still on hips, and finally said. "Dat's not fair. Mama an' Dada got to have fun an' A-ena didn't."

No one could stop laughing; even Tomas and Roger were smiling at their niece's antics.

"Okay, Bubba, that's enough. Come and watch Uncle Tomas get married." He pulled her back to sit down, and they watched while Tomas and Roger walked down the aisle, went through the ceremony, and said their vows.

Jenny glanced at them. Their hands were joined, their fingers entwined as they smiled at the film, memories bringing back wonderful times in their lives.

"Wow," Dan murmured, looking at the reception. "That looked incredible."

"It was," Roger told him. "Every single minute of our lives together has been incredible."

"Aw, Roger," Tomas breathed. "That's so sweet."

"Well, it has been, T." Roger looked at his husband. "Every single minute has been amazing."

More film of Thanksgiving, Christmases, New Years, birthdays, the births, the babies, all the way up until that year was shown. But finally, Spiros turned the projector off, a deep sigh slowly leaving his body. He was going to miss his son. Just as he had missed his family when he immigrated to Australia, and missed his parents when they passed. He was going to miss his son. His spitting image. The quiet introvert who took to Greece and the Greek life with wild abandon and had proved better at the language than him. Had taken to the island better than expected and thrived. He was going to miss his son. The pain killed him inside. They had nearly lost all three boys four years ago, and now he was not only losing a son, but a son-in-law as well. He helped wheel the boys into the bedroom and laid them on the bed.

As he picked up Tomas, he cried. For all the years he had done that when he was a child, and then back in '77 at Christmas when he had the flu, and here he was, picking him up and carrying him once again.

"Papa, it's okay," Tomas told him as he was set down. "It's all going to be okay."

"Oh, my son." Spiros pulled the covers over him and sat on the bed. "I really hope it is. I hope and pray every minute of the day that it is." He brushed aside Tomas's tears and then his own. "I love you, my son. And I am so glad that God gave you to us to look after and raise, because you have turned into a magnificent young man, Tomas Giorgio Stephanopoulos."

Tomas smiled. "Thank you, Papa. Knowing you love me means the world to me."

"I do." Spiros nodded. "I do, so much. But you boys must rest a while. You must be tired. It was an emotional day."

"It was," Tomas agreed and settled in for a long sleep. "I'll see you on the other side, Papa." He closed his eyes and drifted off to sleep, his right hand in the middle of the bed holding onto Roger's.

Jenny noticed, knew they always fell asleep that way, holding hands between them. With a tear in her eye, she and Spiros left Dan in charge.

"Jenny," he called softly, stopping her while Spiros went into the lounge room. "I need more paper. Big paper, like never-ending paper that I can cover the wall with."

"Well, we don't have anything like that," she paused, "not here anyway. Give me ten minutes." She spoke to Spiros who went to the meat shop and returned with a roll of butcher's paper. "Will that do?" she asked Dan.

"Oh, absolutely," he said. "I think I'm going to be busy all night."

"I'll let you get on with it then." Jenny glanced in Tomas's room, and saw by the machines her son was still alive.

"Oh, before you go." Dan stopped her. "Can you tell me what it was that Luiz actually did?"

"Why?" She was puzzled by the question.

Dan shrugged. "You never know."

Jenny launched into the whole sordid mess, detailing Luiz being engaged to Bertha St John, but having sex with Tomas, and then following him to Miami, then the murders and poisoning.

"Which poison?" he asked.

"Nerium Oleander. Didn't I mention it in New York when he was brought in?"

"I think so, but just checking. Go on."

Jenny continued up until Tomas and Roger were sick in '77 with the flu. "He never was a hundred percent after the poisoning. He said he felt it. That he wasn't the same after it happened, even though he's been on vitamins and a good healthy diet, he just never felt the way he had before the poisoning."

"And which hospital did he go to in Miami?"

"Miami General, back in October '77."

"And you said he saw a doctor here in Greece?"

"Yes. A Doctor Ethos in Athens in October '77, barely days after he was kidnapped from Miami. He declared him all right."

"Any others?" Dan was writing it all down.

"Just the doctor before he ended up in your ER."

"Okay. I've got names. I just need numbers. Do you have those?"

"I can get them for you. What are you thinking, Dan?"

"Don't know, Jenny. I just want to get all the facts, so if there's anything you or the family can think of, it's important that you tell me. Regardless of how insignificant you think it might be."

*****

Pedro awoke early, in his teen years bed, in his teen years room. Angie was beside him, with Alena in the cot beside her. Both were sound asleep. But he wasn't. He couldn't rest. Not after the fitful sleep he'd had. Not after the last couple of days where all they'd done was cry or hold Tomas while he cried, or watched their Mama and Papa cry, or the rest of the family cry. And he and Carlos had taken a few moments every night to fall apart in each other's arms, crying for the brother they were losing.

Restless, he turned away from the window, away from Angie. But that didn't help. With glimpses of light coming in around the curtain, he quietly slipped out of bed and into the bathroom for a quick shower and shave. Opening the window, he saw the sun rise over the glorious coast of Mykonos before there was a quiet knock on the door. He opened it to Carlos. "Hey."

"Couldn't sleep either?" Carlos walked in and shut the door.

"Nope."

"The last few days have sucked big time."

Pedro sighed. "They certainly have."

"How are we…?" Carlos started then stopped, not knowing *how* to finish the sentence.

"Going to deal with losing him?" Pedro stared miserably at his brother.

Carlos deflated. He hadn't slept all night except for the few times he'd drifted in and out. Most of the night he'd lain on his back staring at the ceiling, trying to come up with a way to keep his brother alive. But not being a doctor, and not knowing the full extent of Tomas and Roger's illnesses, there wasn't anything he *could* come up with. "We can't."

"I know," Pedro replied. "But I don't know what to do about it."

"Neither do I." The two of them stood staring at each other as they tried to hold back tears.

The three brothers, for all of their jokes, had been insanely close. Their parents saw to that, especially Jenny. She had raised them to love each other, honour and defend each other, and look after each other no matter what, and to do it all while protecting their mother and defending their parents. All three were close, that's just the way they were, and now that one of them was sick and possibly leaving them, it was way too much to bear.

"So, what do we do?" a stunned Pedro mumbled.

"What *can* we do?" Carlos asked in return.

Pedro sighed, and his shoulders flagged. "Love our brother and Roger as much as we can, and tell them we love them and are here for them until the end."

"Yeah." Carlos blinked back tears. "But when *is* the end coming? Because I don't want it to end. I want him to get better."

"So do I." Pedro's voice was raspy and he cleared his throat. "So do I. But it looks like there's nothing more we *can* do, so let's do what we *can* and be with our brother." He left Carlos to himself and quietly dressed before going into Tomas's room. All were still asleep. Dan was on the cot in front of the dresser, Tomas and Roger were sleeping while holding hands. He slid past Dan and made his way to his brother's side. Sitting in the chair his mother had placed by the bed, he watched his brother's chest go up and down. It was frail, brittle-looking, as Tomas had lost all of the muscle mass he once had.

He's so thin, Pedro thought, frowning at the sight of his brothers lying there. *So thin, so bony. God, it's so sad.*

The morning light drifted through the open window along with the ocean breeze, stirring Tomas.

Pedro watched as his brother struggled to open his eyes. Struggled to breathe. Struggled to live. There was nothing he could do for him. Couldn't find a cure, couldn't find medications. He was already receiving all he could, and *still* it wasn't enough. He remembered back to Leon, lying there in the hospital, tubes and needles and the ventilator. God, how awful it must have been. He recalled the stories from Viv about Cabot Conroy and some of her friends. Recalled the stories from Roger about their friends and the people they knew in Miami. People were dying left, right and centre, and doctors couldn't tell anyone what it was. Just that gay men were dying from this fungal pneumonia and some cancer that luckily Tomas and Roger didn't have. But they had everything else to indicate it was the same. The same as Leon. The same as Cabot. The same as Jamal Devron, Stephano DeLuca and Freddy. The same as Thomas Derbon and Stan Kosnov and other 69 regulars. This damn disease was killing off all the gay people they knew, and it sucked. It bloody sucked, and now it was attacking his brother and brother-in-law and eating the family apart. And there was nothing they could do to stop it. Not a damn thing anyone could do to stop it, and it bloody sucked.

Tears rolled silently down his face as the misery seeped through him. For all the positivity Mama went on about, he was miserable. The *whole family* was miserable. They were losing a son, a brother, an uncle, and it bloody sucked. He allowed the tears to fall. It's not as if he could stop them anyway. They came when they wanted, stopped when the well was dry, and once it was refilled, out they poured again. He felt himself falling. But he was really just bending forward until his arms rested on his legs and his head rested in his hands, and he sat there, hunched over beside his brother, crying hot silent tears for what he was losing, what he would never have again, until he felt a hand on his head.

At first, he thought it was the hand of God, because a beam of warmth spread through him. But when he looked up, he saw Tomas smiling gently at him, his hand on his little brother's head. Taking Tomas's hand, he kissed it, clinging to it as he cried.

"It's okay," Tomas said softly. "Let them fall. Let them out. It will all be over soon."

"I don't want it to be over." Pedro gulped. "I don't want you to die."

"I know," Tomas told him. "I don't want that either, but this is the way it is, and there's nothing we can do."

"There must be," Pedro sobbed. "We must be able to do something. This can't be it."

"Oh, my little baby brother," Tomas murmured. "There will come a time when we will all go. Mama and Papa, Grandma and Grandpa, our aunts and uncles, our cousins. We will all go one day, my little Pedro."

"But I don't want you to go now." Pedro gasped for air. "I want us to be old and grey before we go. I want us to all go together, so we don't have to mourn all the time. It's not fair. You're only twenty-six. We haven't lived life yet."

"I know," Tomas said. "It sucks, and I don't want to die. I want to grow old and grey with you and Roger. I want to see Alena grow up and have her own family, along with any other children you and Angie have. I want to see Diana grow up and see both girls succeed. But that's not going to happen, so it's best to think about what we *do* have and how amazing it all is, and remember everything we've done instead of getting miserable over things we'll never see, or experience. Let's just be happy in this moment. We're here in Mykonos; we have our family here, Roger got to see his mother because of Mama. Let's be grateful for what we have and not worry about what we don't."

Pedro wiped his face. "It's hard not to. Just like you cried the other day after watching the home movies. You knew all of that was never going to happen again. You knew you'd never get to eat Mama's food, or see the girls grow up. That's why you cried."

"Yes," Tomas told him. "Yes, it was. And I've realised that I can't be crying over what might or might not happen in the future. That I have to live in the moment, and be grateful and blessed to have the parents and the siblings and family I've got. Because you are *all* amazing."

"And you're pretty damn amazing yourself, Tomas Stephanopoulos," Pedro replied. "Pretty damn amazing yourself."

That brought another smile to Tomas's face. "I've tried."

"You've more than that," Pedro said. "You've been the best big brother a boy could ever hope for. You held my hand; you looked after me, helped me with my Greek, and school projects. You've been the *best* big brother ever." He gazed adoringly into his brother's eyes, seeing the sparkle still there. "I love you, so much. I feel like I'm losing a limb. That someone's going to cut off my arm or leg. That's how I feel. You're a part of me, Tomas. So is Carlos. My brothers are a part of me, and that's the way it always will be."

"Oh, Pedro," Tomas murmured. "Oh, my boy, my little baby brother. Come here." He pulled his not so little baby brother into his arms, so Pedro was lying beside him on the bed. Wrapping his frail arms around him, he stroked his head, smoothing back the jet-black mop that lay unruly. "At least you still have your hair."

Pedro couldn't help it. The chuckle rose from his stomach to his throat, and glancing up at Tomas's thinning greyish hair, let it out. "Sorry, bro. You don't look like Papa so much with almost no hair."

"At least you know what Papa will look like when he gets older and grey and thin."

"Yeah, like you." The sadness came back to Pedro's soul. "I love you."

Tomas looked into his brother's sad eyes and stroked his cheek. "And I love you, my little Pedro. Always remember that, even long after I'm gone."

The tears welled again. "Don't say that." Pedro's eyes closed against the onslaught, and he buried his head in his brother's bony chest. "Don't say that. I don't want you to be gone. Ever!"

"I know, my baby Pedro," Tomas soothed. "I know. But it's going to happen. We may as well prepare for it."

"No. I don't want to," Pedro sobbed. "I don't want to. I can't."

"But you have to."

"I don't want to."

A beeping sound set the machines off, and Dan wiped away his tears. He'd heard all of it, and it killed him inside, breaking his own heart for what was and what could be. As a gay man, he knew this could be his future, and he had to be careful. He arose from his cot at the end of the bed. "Sorry to interrupt the moment, but it's time for your meds."

"We have them," Jenny said as she, Rebecca and Sarah came slowly through the door. She'd heard and seen some of her sons' moments and hadn't wanted to interrupt their time together, so they'd stopped in the hallway to shed their own tears.

A short time later the boys were refreshed and sitting out on the balcony watching the day start on the island. One by one, the family took their plates out to sit with them and eat; talking about their last time there and the adventures they'd gotten up to.

"We've known each other for just over four years now, Viv," Carlos told her as they sat around sipping juice. "June '77 after you'd spent a month on Santorini."

"Yes, that's right," Viv remembered. "Connie told Harriet, Harriet told me. I had to come and see for myself the gorgeous Greek God that had so captured their hearts."

"Yeah." Carlos softened. "Connie."

"Yeah," Viv repeated, her own memories coming back. "Connie."

"And it's almost Pedro and Angie's first date anniversary," Jenny said. "Or has that happened?"

"Yeah." Pedro nodded. "Earlier this month. I saw this hot little number waiting backstage for me and decided to go and say hello. Do you still have that red dress you were wearing, babe?"

Angie blushed in embarrassment, remembering their first time backstage, screwing while the music played, and her father was up in his office. "I remember." She tucked a strand of hair behind her ear. "And yes, I still have that dress somewhere."

"Then it will be four years next month since Tomas and Roger met." Jenny turned to them as they held hands and smiled.

"Yes, Mama. August," Tomas said, gazing at his husband.

"At *The Joy Stick*," Roger added. "When it was hip and happening and full of life and love and music. God, it was such a great club to hang out."

"And if it weren't for Bette, Bertha and Willow taking me there that night, we wouldn't have met," Tomas told him.

"Not necessarily true," Roger said. "Bette brought you to *Seralift* later, and I ran into you. So glad I did. We had our first date because of that."

"Yes, we did." Tomas smiled with all the love he had for his husband. "A day at the beach, and the night at *Love Stick* with Freddy rockin' out to his own place." He saddened. "God how things can change in just a few short years."

"They changed for everyone," Jenny said. "Look what Papadopoulos did. Set up Carlos and made *him* run. Andros set up Pedro and made *him* run, and you felt left out and decided to leave." She patted Tomas on the hand. "And then they all ruined your lives, but luckily, it brought us all back together again. To be one big happy family with three new in-laws and two new grandbabies."

"A-ena, Gamma," Alena said from her father's lap. She was dressed in a pretty blue summer dress that Jenny had bought her.

"Yes." Jenny turned to her two grandbabies. "Alena and Diana joined the family just three years ago."

"I'm fwee." Diana held up three fingers. Sitting on her father's knee, being bounced up and down, she was wearing a pretty pink dress that Jenny had bought her.

"Yes, you are, my baby," Jenny told her. "You and Alena are both three."

"No, Gamma, fwee," Diana repeated. "Da-anna is fwee."

"Okay, Diana, you and Alena are fwee." Jenny smiled at her babies. Turning her attention back to her dying sons, she added, "and you two need to get better so you can celebrate the anniversary of the first time you met, and when you became a couple, and then your fourth wedding anniversary in November."

"I don't think I can hang on, Mama. Not for that long," Tomas said weakly. "I don't have much left in me. And then you'll want Thanksgiving and Christmas and New Year, then next birthday."

"You have to, baby, you have to," Jenny cried, clinging to his hand. "You *have* to keep hanging in there. Keep staying strong, keep staying with us. *For* us. Keep hanging in there, and we'll find a cure for you and make you all better. Just keep hanging in there, and we will find a way to make you better."

"Mama," Tomas murmured, staring at his mother with tired disease-filled eyes. "I love you for everything you've done and everything you're doing. But I don't have much longer."

Jenny's head turned sharply. "Girls, can you go inside for a few minutes, we need to talk to Uncle Tomas."

"Aw, why do we—" Alena started whining.

"I'll take them," Dan said. He'd been hovering around, keeping an eye on his patients, never being far from them. "Come on, girls. Have you ever seen a stethoscope? You can listen to each other's heartbeat with it."

Grateful, Jenny smiled as the girls went inside and Spiros closed the balcony doors. Jenny turned back to Tomas. "Don't you dare tell me you don't have much longer. I will *not* watch my son die from some Godforsaken gay disease that he doesn't deserve. I will *not* let you die, Tomas, do you hear me. I will not let you die, and I will fight to the bloody bitter end for all of my babies, do you hear me. I will fight for you until neither of us can fight anymore. But I *know* there is more inside of you. I *know* that you want to live, so fight goddamn it, fight. *Do not* give up on me, Tomas. Fight for your life. Fight for Roger, fight for the girls, fight for yourself."

"Mama, stop, please," he tearfully begged. "You're only postponing the inevitable. We have to deal with the fact I don't have long. Neither does Roger. He's not much better than me." Tomas glanced at his husband. "You're sick too."

"I know I am, T. I know. But you're much sicker, and I don't want to watch you die," Roger rasped. "I'd rather die with you at the same time so we can go up to heaven together."

"Oh, my God," Jenny cried and bent her head. "Stop, stop, stop saying those things. I can't bear for my babies to die, so just stop it." She felt Spiros's hand on her shoulder and raised her head to look at her teary sons. "I *am not* going to let you die, goddamn it. I'm *not* going to let you die." Storming inside, she gathered all of the current medical journals they'd gotten and scoured all of Dan's paperwork on the walls, leaving her family to mourn alone on the balcony.

"What are you doing?" Dan asked, leaning on the door jamb.

"I'm memorising your notes, so I know what symptoms to look for, and then I'm going through each and every goddamn disease until I find the one my son has. Because he *does not* have the goddamn gay disease. He *doesn't,* that's just all there is to it."

"Then I'll help." Dan picked up a medical book and started on the first page. By lunchtime, he'd made notes, tacked them to the wall, and circled words on the butcher's paper already there. He'd covered the wall with the whole roll Jenny had given him and made circles and connecting lines everywhere. But for the life of him, he just couldn't connect the dots in his head to what all of the information meant.

All of the tests, each and every week, showed low CD4 T cells, he had opportunistic infections, he had parasites eating him away. So did Roger. That's what fitted. *Nothing* else. The gay disease fitted and *nothing* else.

After lunch, the boys were brought in for a freshen up and a nap, and as Jenny tucked them in, Tomas rested his hand on her cheek.

"Mama."

She looked up. Her puffy eyes were as hollow, sunken and full of tears as her son's.

"I love you for *everything* you've done and *everything* you're doing." He gazed imploringly at her. "But it's nearly time, Mama. It's time to let it go."

"Never!" she exclaimed. "I will *never* let it go. I will *never* let *you* go."

"Gamma?"

They looked toward the door to see Alena and Diana standing

there in pyjama short-suits, clasping their teddies in front of them.

"Yes, my baby girls," Jenny said. "Is it nap time for you, too?"

The girls looked at each other. "Can we have our nap wiv Unca Tomas an' Unca Oger?" Alena asked.

Jenny cast a glance at the boys. "Are you able?"

"Absolutely." Tomas smiled. "Come, my baby girls." He held his arms out.

"Round this way," Jenny told them, directing them to her side of the bed, and they excitedly ran around to her. Picking up Alena, she laid her by Tomas's side in the crook of his arm. "You need to be very careful, very gentle. And don't move so much, okay. You don't want to hurt Uncle Tomas."

"No, Gamma. A-ena no hurt Unca Tomas," Alena said, resting her head on his shoulder so she could look up at him.

"Come, Diana." Jenny picked her up. "And, you be careful between them okay? No throwing your arms around." She set Diana down in the middle under Tomas's arm. "There we go."

Tomas looked at his nieces, thanking God he'd had the time with them and seen both of them born.

Roger rolled over so he could cuddle them, laying a hand gently on Tomas's torso. It had been a long time for the two of them, and oh how he wished they could make love one last time. To hold each other, kiss, touch, caress each other. Be inside of and wrapped around each other. God how he missed the intimacy they shared almost right from the start. He remembered back to their first European vacation. They had made love everywhere, even on the Orient Express. The heady days of the '70s were gone. The sexual revolution for men was grinding to a very bitter end. If this disease was anything to go by, it was going to bring *all of them* to a very bitter end.

"Unca Tomas." Alena yawned and tucked her teddy under her chin. "Did you have a teddy when you were wike us?"

"Yes, I did," Tomas told her. "I had a patchwork teddy that I called Ted."

Jenny picked the bear up from Tomas's beside cupboard where she'd placed it after Roger had gotten Jupiter from Marsha.

"There's Ted," Tomas said as Jenny placed it on his chest. "And Roger has Jupiter."

Pedro came through the door. "And Daddy has Raggles, and Uncle Carlos has Fred somewhere. There you two are." He stood at the end of the bed watching the girls. "Will they be okay there?"

"Of course." Tomas smiled brightly.

"Are the girls there?" Angie and Viv came through the door. "Oh, there you are. We put you two to bed, and you disappear."

"And here they are right next door." Jenny smiled at her granddaughters. "They'll be fine. I've told them they have to be careful and to not move too much, so they don't hurt Uncle Tomas. They'll be fine, and I'll be here watching." She sat in the chair by the bed. "Why don't you go and get Raggles and show the girls," she told Pedro. "He's up top in your wardrobe."

Pedro went and came back within a minute, but the girls and Tomas and Roger were already out like a light. He stood there, gripping his teddy under his chin, watching all four of them sleep. Watching his mother resting in the chair beside them. Watching his wife and sister-in-law sitting on Dan's cot bed, all just watching the girls with their teddies curled up in Tomas and Roger's arms.

Taking a seat beside his wife, he kept watching. Watched while Carlos came in to see where everyone was, and watched as Carlos sat on the cot bed next to Viv. Watched as his father came in to see if there was anything that was needed, and watched as his mother told his father to go and get the camera and take pictures. Watched as his father took pictures of the girls sleeping in their uncle's arms all surrounded by love and teddy bears.

Watched as his mother kept wiping away her tears, and watched as Angie, Viv and Carlos wiped away theirs. Watched as his brother and brother-in-law gasped for air and woke briefly, and watched as Jenny adjusted the Ventolin levels and soothed her sons back to sleep. Watched while he wiped away his own tears, heard his heartbreak for the billionth time, felt his stomach sink at the thought, the prospect of his brother dying.

Just four years ago they had all been there. All been getting married, all stayed in this house before their big day. Given out cufflinks, helped with tuxedos and bowties. Watched Tomas tear up at never having his own wedding. And then they'd given him one, and the joy on his face was the most beautiful thing to see.

He turned around and looked up at the photos on the wall behind him. The joy on Tomas's face when he realised his family had organised a ceremony in a church, the look on his face Christmas '77 when they had the photo taken of them all wearing Christmas jumpers. The photo that Cabot Conroy had taken of all six of them for their parents and grandparents, of which they had received copies for themselves as well.

The holiday snaps, the anniversary pics, all candid, all full of love and happiness and endless tomorrows, all coming to a crushing, fruitless, senseless end that should not be. Not with the love and happiness in those photos. No. The love and happiness in those photos should not be coming to an end like this.

He spied the boys' wedding and forever first anniversary rings on the dresser behind him, along with the watches their mother had given them Christmas '77, and the jewellery they had given each other since. The love, the happiness, the endless tomorrows should not be coming to an end. No, they should be continuing. They should be endless with no end…

Wiping his face, he turned back to the bed, watching his brothers die before his eyes.

No, they should be endless with no end…

*****

Angie wandered through the house, after taking a nap herself. She'd changed Alena when she'd woken, and given her a snack. Answered multiple questions about Uncles Tomas and Roger, and not very well at that, having no answers to give her inquisitive child about whether Uncle Tomas would be able to play with her again, or lift her up and carry her, or if she'd be able to sit on his lap, or when he would get better. That question she had teared up at, not knowing what to tell her daughter.

She ended up in the lounge room as family members drifted in and out. Running her fingers along the upright piano that sat against the wall beside the fireplace, she sat down and lifted the lid. Her fingers ran over the keys, launching into something she'd done at Juilliard.

In the bedroom they all looked up, hearing the tune waft through the air.

"Angie," Tomas breathed, glancing toward the door.

"Sounds like," Jenny replied, laying a hand on his cheek. "Do you want to hear more?"

"Yes, please."

Out in the lounge room, Alena hovered at the piano seat, watching her mother's fingers move over the top.

"I don't think you should be doing that," Ned Marsh, one of Jenny's brothers said. "Too much noise. Quiet now."

Incensed by his tone and attitude to thinking he knew what was best for Tomas and Roger, Angie seethed inside, pleased to be vindicated when Spiros, Carlos and Pedro walked into the lounge room.

"Tomas wants to hear you play, so we're moving the piano down the hallway."

With a sly glance at Jenny's brother, who looked amazed at having been wrong, Angie carried the stool and followed the others. They placed it against the wall opposite Tomas's door. "Any requests?" Angie jokingly asked and set the stool in place.

"Anything you can think of," Roger said. "New stuff, disco, pop, whatever Pedro used to play at 69."

"Okay, disco coming up." Angie sat down and started belting out '70s tunes they all used to dance to at 69 with Alena and Diana dancing to them.

"Aw, look at them, T." Roger watched his nieces bounce around. "Aren't they cute?"

"Yes, they are," Tomas agreed, smiling at his two little baby girls as they shook their little tushies off. Those memories he'd have forever. From them falling asleep in his arms, patting his cheek and telling him he was going to be okay, to them patting his hand and telling him he'd get better soon. He'd wondered if Alena had some sort of insight. Knew things that the rest of them didn't. Wondered if she was his reincarnated sister as Mama had suggested. That maybe she knew something all of them didn't. Or maybe she was just being sweet and comforting since she didn't know any better. Didn't know just how sick her uncles were because there was no way she and Diana would understand the complexities of the disease, or that he had the disease because he was gay and that he'd given it to Uncle Roger. Neither of the girls comprehended what being gay meant. They had never questioned why he was with a man and not a woman like their daddies. They just accepted and loved Roger as their uncle as they did him. And the girls loved both of them as he and Roger did the girls. His little baby girls, Alena and Diana; only children until Viv and Angie had more. Not that he'd ever see more nieces and nephews; he'd be long gone before they came along. Like Great-Grandpa Giorgio. He had survived long enough to see his great-grandchildren married, and then let himself go a week later while they were flying to New York to live. They hadn't had much time with him, but had cherished what time they did have. The few days at the weddings, the lunch at home. The last time they'd seen him was in this house in the dining room when Jenny announced she would be going to New York to set up Pedro and Angie. Not to mention his grandfather had died in this house, and his grandmother. He'd only had two years with her, and she'd taken to him like he was a second son. "*The spitting image of your father and grandfather,*" she'd told him. Sometimes, at the end, she confused him with them. But he didn't mind. If it gave her comfort in her final days, then all the better. She had passed peacefully in her bedroom, now the guest room, and they had buried her with her husband. "Mama."

"Yes, my baby." She reached across and held his hand.

"Where will I be buried?"

She blinked while the others stared in shock. Another blink. "What?"

"Where will I be buried? Next to Grandma and Grandpa? Great-Grandpa? Do we have a family burial plot? Will Roger be allowed to be buried in it?" For him, they were all very serious and important questions.

For Jenny, she wanted them left unanswered because she didn't want to think about burying her son.

"Unca Tomas, wook at A-ena," Alena called. "A-ena dancing."

"Yes, Bubba, she is," he said to her, smiling. "A-ena dance with Diana."

"A-ena an' Da-anna dance." Alena grabbed her cousin's hands and they skipped around in circles.

"Mama." Tomas turned back to her. "Where will you bury me?"

Jenny choked. Her sons, daughters, and husband were watching her. "I won't," she started, took a breath and went on. "I won't. I'll cremate you."

"And what will you do with the ashes?" he asked, intrigued by the idea.

Another choke. "Put half in with Alena, and the other I'll scatter to the wind across your favourite place." The tears fell, whether she wanted them to or not. They had been constantly falling, whether she liked it or not.

"That's nice, Mama." Tomas dreamily stared out the window. "Spread our ashes from the top of a windmill, or across the bay out on a boat, so I can swim in the water one last time."

The tears became sobs as they racked her body and she bent, her head going to his hand, holding it to her forehead as she cried. "I can't...I can't."

"Oh, Mama, you don't have to. You can bury me if you want to," Tomas told her.

"I don't want you buried in the ground to rot away," she managed. "I don't want you in the ground."

"Then cremation is good enough. If it was good enough for my sister, it's good enough for me."

Unable to bear any more, Jenny rushed from the room, past her sobbing children, and into her own bedroom, throwing herself onto her bed, screaming into her pillow. Letting out the anguish, the fear, the gut-wrenching pain of losing another child, and him thinking how nice it would be to be scattered on the wind. She couldn't, she just couldn't.

Spiros quietly closed the door and lay next to his wife, taking her into his arms, holding her tight until her sobs abated and she lay still.

"I can't do this again."

"I know, my love." He smoothed back her hair. "I know."

"And not just one, but two."

"I know. I wasn't expecting him to ask about the burial plot either."

"I don't want him in the ground."

"I know. You want him next to your heart."

Jenny glanced at her bedside cupboard where Alena's urn sat with the pictures of the family in their Christmas jumpers from '77. Tomas and Roger had been ill then, and she had often wondered these last few months if that was the start of it all. The disease. The end. But what she *did* know was she couldn't lose another child. Not another one.

Carlos sat by Tomas's side on the bed. Angie had stopped playing when his mother blew out of the room, the girls had stopped dancing, and the others had gone into the lounge room. It was just him for some one-on-one time with his brothers.

"I upset Mama," Tomas breathed through his mask. "I didn't mean to. I was just thinking about how Grandma and Grandpa died in this house, and now we are too."

"Don't think that," Carlos said, holding his brother's hand. "Don't think about death and where you'll be buried. Don't think it. Don't speak it."

"But I need to," Tomas said. "I'd like to know where I'll be buried when I die. Don't you?"

"Nope." Carlos vehemently shook his head. "None of us are dying yet. I won't accept it." He could feel himself crumbling, and his breathing came in gasps. "I can't, I won't accept it. I'm with Mama. I don't want you to die. I couldn't bear it. I couldn't bear it if any of you died. Mama, Papa, Pedro, Angie, Viv, you and Roger, hell, even the girls. Look at the way I went to pieces when Harry sent me the letter about Connie and Antonio, and here we are, four years later back in the spot where it all happened. I was getting paid by Connie, worked with Antonio, met Viv through Connie and Harriet. And they're gone. Leon's gone, Officer Devron, Cabot, Viv's friends, your friends.

I can't bear to lose you too. Not you, little brother. Not you. Not after the last four years we've had together. Finding out what Papadopoulos did, being reunited, and coming home to Mama and Papa only to meet each other's partners, get married, spend time with our great-grandfather, move to New York, and celebrate our first Thanksgiving in a new country as a family."

"Papa wasn't there yet," Tomas reminded him.

"Yeah, but still. Mama bought us that amazing apartment building to live in. We had Christmas, New Year, our birthdays. You got to go home to Australia with Grandma and Grandpa and see the family. And besides the horrible few months of Mama and Papa breaking up and being separated, Viv and Angie gave birth."

"And Mama and Papa got back together," Tomas added.

"And we all lived happily ever after," Carlos said. "Our first wedding anniversaries, although you guys were travelling, and then you were home in time for the girls' first Christmas, which was awesome."

"It was." Tomas smiled at his big brother, watching his face light up at every word he was saying, every memory.

"And then our birthdays again, Viv's and Angie's, Roger's, Mama's and Papa's birthdays and anniversary, the girls' birthdays, travelling through Europe for three months, now *that* was bloody awesome."

"It was so nice seeing it again with family," Roger murmured.

"Yeah, it was," Carlos agreed. "Italy was beautiful, London, France and Paris, walking up the Eiffel Tower, Germany, Switzerland, it was all amazing. Then we're back in New York for Halloween, and our second anniversaries and Thanksgiving, then off to Australia. God, I miss home." He absentmindedly rubbed Tomas's hand. "The cousins, the freedom, the running around."

"Yeah. It was great," Tomas murmured. "So great."

"And then back to New York for another birthday and more birthdays."

"More deaths," Tomas added.

"And now we're back in Mykonos. Back home where it all started." Carlos smiled sadly. "Four years that started with fun, continued with hell, and ended in fun until this. All in four years." He glanced at the machines helping to keep his brothers alive. "It was fine until this. In only four years..." his voice trailed off as he thought about it. "So much has happened in only four years. We leave, we live, we party and travel, and marry and give birth, and celebrate and return. Return to this. Return *because* of this." He waved a hand at the machines. "It takes you getting sick to get us all back here." A choking sob went through him. "It takes a tragedy to get us all back home."

"Yeah, but look at everything we've done," Tomas said. "In four years we've done so much, and we should be happy. You have Viv and Diana, Pedro has Angie and Alena. I have Roger." He reached over and grasped his lover's hand. "It may have only been four years, but we've all done so, so much Carlos. All of us."

"And that's why it shouldn't end this way. Not for you, not for us," Carlos said. "I'm with Mama; *this is not it.* This *is not* the end. I don't *and won't* accept that this is it. I just won't."

Tomas smiled. "You always were like Mama. So much."

"Just like you were always like Papa, so much," Carlos told him. "Right down to being his spitting image."

The smile widened. "So everyone always told me. I think it's a good thing. I'm proud of looking like Papa."

A soft smile lit up Carlos's face. "I'm proud that you look like Papa too." His head shook slightly. "I love you, so much, Tomas. So, so much. Everything I've said about you is true. Everything at your wedding, everything since. I'm so glad that you're my brother and I love you so, so much." Tears fell. "There are no other words I can put my feelings into."

"I know." Tomas pulled him close and hugged him. "I know. I love you, too. So, so much. My big brother. Carlo Stefan."

Carlos couldn't help himself. The chuckle turned into a laugh, and Tomas was laughing too, albeit softly so he didn't cough.

"Oh, God, thank Harry for that name," Carlos said. "But I gotta say it was a damn good one."

"So good Greta and Marcus took the name and ran with it, banking on us being brothers to make more money."

"Yeah," Carlos agreed. "And it worked until you and Pedro quit, and neither got royalties from *The Greek Gods* movie. I can't believe we weren't in the business that long."

"I was barely in it for two months in total," Tomas said. "I only got into it to be with Roger."

"Porn worked out well for you." Carlos lifted his head to look into his brother's eyes. "Maybe I should get our awards out and show the family while they're here."

"Don't you dare," Tomas jokingly warned. "Or I'll kill you."

The joke hung heavy in the air, and all three of them became silent.

"I love you, Tomas."

"I love you, too, Carlos."

*****

Dan took some more samples on Friday morning, blood, urine, faccal, saliva, wrapped them up in padding and a plastic bag, and ran it to the airport where a doctor was waiting to take it back to Athens for testing.

They did this once a week, every Friday, and had done it since getting there. Every week he'd take samples, run it to one of the specialists waiting in the plane Jenny had hired, and it was flown back to the mainland to be analysed over the weekend. On Monday morning they'd fax through the results. The results were always similar, each condition varying a little as time went on, each condition getting worse, each condition eating them alive. And each Monday he'd give them the same medication, or up the levels, trying to make sure they were comfortable and fairly pain-free. It worked, for the most part. The painkillers, the morphine. But they were still dying. In fact, Dan wasn't sure how much longer they had, certainly not months like at the beginning when they'd come to the hospital in May. They'd hung in there for two months, staying strong for Jenny, strong for their family, strong for themselves.

But he could see it. He could hear it. And medically, he knew it. They were dying. A small part of him hoped Jenny would, or could, find a cure, a medication, one small thing that would, or could, reverse this whole thing around, but, so far, she hadn't. And neither had he. For all the journals, for all the doctors, for all the long-distance phone calls to experts, and sample testing, there was just absolutely nothing they could do to stop the inevitable…

*****

They made it through the weekend, barely. The family kept constant vigil with Jenny always by her sons' sides, and Spiros, Carlos and Pedro taking turns to come and sit. Sometimes all of them were in there talking, holding hands and crying. It was evident the end was fast approaching, but Jenny was in denial. Denial that it was the end for her son. Denial that it was the gay disease. Denial that death was upon them once more after all the friends her children had lost, that this thing had affected the family on a more personal, deeper, level. A level that hit home. Right in the heart and soul of it.

After freshening up the boys, noticing they were thinner, they helped roll Roger onto his side so they could be in each other's arms.

"Hello, husband," Roger breathed, gazing deeply into his lover's eyes as Tomas put his arms around Roger's neck.

"Hello, husband," Tomas breathed back, a soft smile lighting up his face. "I love you."

"I love you, too."

Tomas stroked Roger's face, gazing deeply into his eyes while Roger rested his hand on his shoulder. Removing his mask, he laid a kiss on Roger's forehead. He knew it wouldn't be long, probably a matter of days if not hours. He felt himself weaken, letting go. His breath became more laboured, but he kept gazing into his husband's eyes.

Roger removed his mask, and they kissed. "I love you, Tomas, so much." He caressed his husband's cheek. "I wish we could make love one last time."

"So do I," Tomas whispered, feeling himself become lighter. "So do I."

"Put your mask back on, baby, it helps you breathe." Jenny was by his side, watching her boys suffering in hell. Spiros was leaning against the chest of drawers on Roger's side. Pedro was sitting on the end of the bed, while Carlos was standing behind his mother. All four of them looked on, knowing it could be soon. Knowing they had to be there. Knowing that Tomas and Roger *needed* them to be there.

Angie and Viv wandered in and out, as did other family members. All smiled, told the boys they loved them, and to be at peace.

The boys drifted in and out of sleep, but the family remained on vigil. Not eating, only drinking when Sarah and the others brought something in, and Dan kept an eye on everyone and everything, wondering where that day's test results were. So far, they hadn't been faxed in, and he wanted to know why.

As a gay man, he was seeing the disease firsthand. What it did to gay men. The wasting disease, the pneumonia, the way it ate away everything that was a human being. And it made him sick. Sick that God could make such a disease, and whether it would even stop. *Ever* stop. Or would it go until it killed every single gay man on the planet? He stood back, watching as Tomas and Roger's breathing laboured. By the look of the machines, Tomas would be the one to go first. And soon.

"Roger," Tomas whispered and removed his mask, his family forgotten. "What Mama said is true. We *are* soulmates. True lovers experiencing true love. Our souls connected on another plane, in another time, in another place. And we were loved then, just like we are now."

Jenny crossed herself and said a little prayer, silently, so no one heard.

But Spiros heard it in his head, and said his own prayer, crossing himself, and Pedro and Carlos did the same. So did Angie and Viv.

Dan saw this, saw everyone cross themselves and murmur something. So did he. Even though he wasn't religious.

"I love you, Tomas," Roger said. "And I believe it, too. That's why I want you to hang on, so we can die together. Or maybe Dan can administer something so we can die in each other's arms. I don't want to die without you, Tomas. Will you wait for me?" Roger implored his dying husband. "Will you wait for me, my true love, my soulmate, my lover, my husband, my best friend? Will you wait for me?"

"Roger." Tomas fell further. "Come with me."

Rebecca stopped at Dan's side. "Still no fax," she whispered, hearing the boys' words. "Is there anything we can give them?"

Dan glanced at her. "Like what?"

She shrugged a shoulder. "A dose of morphine each so they're not in pain, and they die in each other's arms."

His head tilted. "*We* can't do that; it's unethical."

"Do you really think anyone is going to do anything about it given who my sister is and the money she has? She'll have Tomas and Roger cremated before an autopsy can take place," Rebecca all but scoffed at him.

"But *I* would know," Dan whispered.

"Can you live with yourself if you don't help them?" she whispered urgently.

He frowned, misery etching his face. No, he couldn't, he couldn't live with himself if he had to let more gay men die from a disease no one had a cure for because no one knew what the hell it was.

"It's a pity," Rebecca said, watching her nephew slide away. "That so many damn diseases all have the same symptoms. That these things can't be diagnosed and separated from each other."

"Tomas, stay with us, baby," Jenny sobbed, her eyes puffy, her nose blocked and dripping. "Stay with us, Tomas, stay with us."

"Mama." He barely looked up from Roger's face. "Let me go, Mama."

"No. No, I won't," Jenny cried. "I won't let you go; I won't. *We* won't. Stay with us, Tomas. I demand that you stay with us."

"Mama…let me go…" He continued gazing into Roger's eyes. "I love you all, so much. Say goodbye to Alena and Diana. The lawyer has my will and legal documents. I, we, don't have much, but we want all of you to have it. We want to be cremated with our wedding and forever anniversary rings on Mama, in our black suits with our cufflinks from Pedro and Carlos."

Diseases all have the same symptoms, went through Dan's head. The cross sign they'd all made drifted back and forth as imagery. It triggered. He turned to look at the notes on the walls in the hallway.

"No, baby, no. I won't do it. I won't let you go." Jenny moved closer and put her hands on his frail arms. "No, I won't let you go. No, my baby. I won't let you go."

Pedro and Carlos were openly sobbing. Spiros, being stoic, was trying to stay calm, but losing his son was too much to bear, and he too openly sobbed.

"Goodbye, Mama," Tomas whispered. "Goodbye, Papa, Pedro, Carlos. Thank you for loving Roger and me all these years. I love you all. I love you, Roger. I love you all…"

The machine beeped, telling her his heart had stopped. "Tomas." Jenny looked up, stunned, and her head moved in short, sharp motions as her eyes went back and forth from Tomas to the machine, and she held her breath, the realization coming in short, stunted moments. "Tomas? Tomas?" she screamed. "No. No, my baby. No." She clung to him as Carlos clung to her, all of them sobbing, all of them clinging to each other. "Tomas, no…"

*****

A few days later, the family stood on the beach in the small cove they had taken the boys to. Carlos held Diana with Viv beside him. Pedro held Alena and had an arm around Angie. Spiros and Jenny clung to each other while they sobbed.

Jenny held her daughter's urn close to her chest, not wanting to let another baby go. Another baby die. But the stress was all too much, and she fell to her knees on the sand, sobbing for all that was and all that would be, and all that never would be again.

It was a private moment, just immediate family, although her parents stood back behind them, waiting while they took their time, the rest of the family were back at their homes. She hadn't wanted them there.

Spiros held his wife tightly, feeling the months of agony and pain, both emotional and physical, finally make their way out of her. Blocking his ears to her screams, wanting to scream himself. But she had to do this. She had to vent. Had to let it all out so she could begin to deal with it and find a way to move on. And move on they must.

Carlos stared across the water. This had been his home for ten years, and he had never appreciated it for anything other than the female tourists it had afforded him in summer. But, times were vastly different. Now, he could finally appreciate the island for what it was.

Home.

"Viv."

"Mmm?"

"I've made a decision."

"What is it?"

"It's time to come home."

She saw the look in his eyes and knew he was as determined to be there for his family, his mother, just as he had been in '78 when his parents had separated. And just as she had understood and rearranged her life back then, so she would now. She gave a nod. "Okay. It's time to come home."

Pedro watched intently, hearing the exchange, and knew it was the answer. The *only* answer. With a knowing look at Angie, who had heard it too, she nodded her consent, and they made the decision. "Thank you," he told her, kissing the top of her head.

When the family finally walked in the door hours later, it was quiet, and eerily so. Everyone else was in their homes; there was no one around. No one in the Stephanopoulos household except for them.

Wandering, in faltering steps, over to the mantel above the fireplace, Jenny gently kissed the urn and set it down in the centre. On the left was the Christmas photo Cabot had taken of all six of them. On the right was the Christmas jumper photo. Looking at it, she noticed Tomas's sour expression at wearing the jumper and smiled.

Spiros held out his two photos in front of her; the ones he had carried around for twenty-two years. The photo of Jenny pregnant with their baby daughter and the boys around her legs, and the one of her holding their daughter, asleep for all eternity.

Spiros set them in front of the Christmas jumper photo, making sure they stood proudly as part of the family.

Looking at them, at all of the photos, Jenny felt herself fall and didn't stop it. Emotionally, psychologically, physically. She fell and kept on falling deep into an ocean of never-ending tears.

*****

FRIDAY, 31ST JULY, 1981

GAY PORN STAR BROTHER, DEAD AT TWENTY-SIX

Miami's Porn Star Brother, Tomas Stefan, and his real life and on-screen lover, Roger Dencott, passed away in Mykonos, Greece, Stefan's homeland, on Monday the 27th of July. Reports say they had the disease affecting gay men all across the country, Pneumocystis pneumonia, a fungus seen in many gay men, and multiple other infections. Their ashes were scattered off the coast of Mykonos. Roger's family were not in attendance, but the rest of the Stefans, and their partners and parents, were there. Roger and Tomas are survived by their families.

Stefan and Dencott worked for Seralift Productions making gay porn and were the bestselling stars of the late '70s. Their last movie together, 1978's The Greek Gods, also starring Carlo and Pedro Stefan, was the biggest grossing film of all time and still continues to hit the number one position regularly. Maybe his death will create a resurgence in sales.

Retired detective, Jeremiah Barden, formerly of the Miami PD, finished reading the article in *The Miami Report* and slowly put the paper down. He'd always known something would happen. But hadn't known it would be this, and had made a note to keep an eye out for any mention. With all of the gay men of Miami dying, he had wondered if Tomas and Roger had survived it. Apparently not. Was it all because of Luiz, or the mere fact they were gay and in the porn industry?

"Oh, well," he muttered. "The end of their story has come full circle." Making a cross sign, he said a small prayer and went back to reading about the never-ending gay deaths in Miami.

*****

Marcus Seralift stared at the half page picture of Tomas and Roger. It was a picture from one of their promotional posters and did both boys justice. If only it did *him* justice. *Seralift Productions* was failing. If they weren't dead, they were dying, and there weren't many gay men left to do movies. And he couldn't trust that they would be clean. The only thing to do was to go back to the way they were and make straight porn again. Because *Seralift* needed money and needed it now if it was to stay afloat.

He wondered if he could sell off his back catalogue. *Maybe Harry or Greta will want Tomas and Roger's movies, or any of the others.* The fact that his biggest stars were dead sickened him. They were such great boys, so talented, so big in more ways than where it mattered. But matter it did, and it wasn't keeping him afloat.

But who knew, maybe the death of a Stefan would prove to be a boon for *Seralift.* With all the awards they won in '78, their movies were still the most popular he had. Maybe with the news of their deaths, they would stay that way.

*****

At the *Coral Gables Country Club*, Bette, Bertha, and Willow read the paper out loud and remembered with all of their friends. All who had known Tomas and Roger loved them, and had been there from day one when they'd met at *The Joy Stick*, been on their first date, and had fallen in love. Been through all of the Luiz garbage and what came next. They had been so happy when the boys had come back to visit, finding them healthy and very indecently happy. But now they were gone, along with all of the staff at *Sexe et Faveurs* and many other hangouts for older, or gay people. They were all gone, and they had no one left but themselves.

Even many of their ex-husbands were dead from it…

Oh, the shame…

*****

In New York, Greta read the news and instantly thought of Thomas Derbon. He had wanted to say goodbye to Pedro before he died, and Jenny had generously allowed it, making Thomas happy in his final days. She mourned for Pedro's brother and brother-in-law, two of the hottest men in the porn industry, and Tomas was one-third of the Porn Star Brothers. But that was a long, long time ago.

Calling in her assistant, she dictated a letter of condolence to the Stephanopoulos family, mourning not only the loss of Tomas and Roger, but her Thomas all over again. She hadn't replaced him, had only hired someone to do the job, but just not replaced *him*. Because no one would ever be as good at publicity, as Thomas Derbon.

*****

Giancarlo Gardo read the paper with interest. The last time he'd seen Tomas was at the department store the previous year when he'd run into Jenny. It had been a long time since seeing her too; the woman he'd once been so infatuated with he'd wished her husband dead, just so he could have her. But that had all changed when Sheila Manning had her makeover thanks to Jenny giving her five million dollars from the Papadopoulos estate for the death of her son Luiz.

The makeover had been just the thing Sheila needed to become the woman she wanted to be, and had made him look at her differently. Not just as a woman he occasionally had sex with, but as a potential partner. A partner who had given him his only child when he was at the ripe old age of fifty-four. He glanced over at James who was playing on the lounge room floor with his toys. He was now two, and as full of life as any kid his age.

James looked up with his big aqua blue eyes and smiled. "Dada."

"James." Giancarlo smiled at the love of his life and went back to the paper, his heart going out to Jenny and what she must be going through. With all Papadopoulos and Andros Poulos had done to her children, she had pulled through. And now that he had a son, he couldn't imagine losing him to something like that. *Poor Jenny, how her heart must be breaking,* he thought.

351

James toddled over to his father and looked at the paper. "Tomas." He pointed to Tomas in the picture, sending icy cold tendrils of fear, surprise, shock and apprehension through his father's insides as to what and how he could possibly know or remember. "Tomas, Dada. Tomas."

*****

In Hollywood, Harry, Harriet, Aneeka, Tony, and the rest of the cast and crew that were left at *De Ville*, gathered in Harry's living room. They had read the paper, mourned for the loss to the porn world, and then mourned for the loss for their colleague, Carlos. His brother and brother-in-law were gone, passed on from the horrible gay plague affecting many. It had even hit *De Ville*, with Harry losing many closeted gay stars and crew. Even Suzy Q, his maid, had become ill and passed away. He knew of her side job of servicing his crew when they were horny, and since finding out some of the crew were tapping both parties, they had passed on all manner of diseases to Suzy. Harry was now looking after her son, nine-year-old Alfonso. He had promised her he would, even though he and Harriet were on the older side of life. But he felt it his responsibility to do so, and Suzy had told Alfonso they would look after him.

He thought about Carlos, the son he'd had for a while, and how this had to be hitting him hard. He'd met the family in Greece, and been impressed by the brothers' closeness, been torn a new one by their mother, and then gotten *The Greek Gods* movie plus a hundred others out of Carlos as writer and co-producer.

"This must be killing him," Aneeka said. The sadness exuding from her eyes said it all. "I met those boys, and they were an amazing family. Even Jenny. She loved them so much. This must be killing all of them."

*****

At the precinct, Detective Star's smirk grew bigger. "Well, well, well, porn star's got his at last."

"What'd you say?" Drew, his partner, glanced up from his paperwork.

"See this?" Star flashed the paper at Drew. "Porn Star's brother is dead. Apparently, Carlos Stephan-freakin'-opoulos's brother and brother-in-law died from that fag disease going round. They were cremated, and the ashes scattered."

"Why are you happy about that?" Drew asked, remembering back to '77 when they'd had to track a kidnapped Carlos and Aneeka Ne Masta down. Turned out, his ex-great-uncle was behind all the trouble.

"Ah, well." Star threw down the paper onto his desk and leaned back. "Looks like Stephan-freakin'-opoulos finally got what was comin' to him." The smirk grew bigger still.

"What? A dead brother and brother-in-law? You have a really sick way of thinking someone gets what they deserve. His brothers *are dead* for Christ's sake. Have some compassion." Drew's comment cut the smirk short.

Star stared at Drew's face, showing he gave no fucks whatsoever about Carlos Stephan-freakin'-opoulos! "Coffee?" he asked and stalked away.

July 1982

ONE YEAR LATER

"Good evening everybody and welcome to the opening night of *SB3*," Pedro called from behind his decks on stage in the family's brand-new nightclub. "This is our grand opening, and because we love you all for coming, the drinks and food are free all night." The crowd cheered loudly, giving whistles and screams. "Get your party shoes on and get on down to *I Love Rock 'n Roll* by Joan Jett and the Blackhearts." He let the record fly and danced. It was so good to be back behind his decks again, and brand-new top of the line ones they were.

It had been a rough year, and this club was just one of his mother's brilliant ideas to get them all out of depression. He saw *Studio 69* regulars Bev Marie, Sara Holdare and Martine Krevnokov front and centre, just like the last four years in New York. They had come over for the summer to see him. He even saw Eddie in the crowd having a nosey at what his star DJ was now up to. And from what he'd heard, 69 had faltered without him bringing in the crowds, the ones still alive and kicking that was, as many more had passed away since. Even Eddie looked ill. 69 had shut its doors four months earlier, and Eddie was in Greece for the summer.

Gazing out across the crowd to the bar at the back of the room, his eyes moved up to the balcony above it that was attached to the office. He saw Angie and Alena with his father and Diana, and Mike and Maggie who were on holiday. But he didn't see his mother.

Once last summer was all over, and the rest of the family had gone home to Australia, Jenny had moved Carlos and Viv into the house next door to the left, and him and Angie into the house on the right. They had their own homes right next door to Gamma and Gampa, and Mike and Maggie were staying with them. Mike had lost his job at 69, and Maggie was between jobs. They still lived in Apartment 1 in the family's building in New York. They could stay as long as they wanted rent free, Jenny had seen to that.

In the office, Jenny was reading a bunch of papers from the CDC that Dan had given her, plus many American newspapers. All announced what the gay disease was. They had named it AIDS. Acquired Immunodeficiency Syndrome. Named so because it didn't just attack gay men, it also attacked straight men, women and children, haemophiliacs, heroin users, and Haitians. There had been many names the last six months. The 4-H Disease (homosexuals, haemophiliacs, Haitians, and heroin users), GRID (gay-related immune deficiency), and gay cancer. But now it was just AIDS. And now they all knew what had killed their friends, their co-workers, their loved ones.

"My boys," she murmured, putting down the paper and seeing the manuscript for the book she had written. For all the pain and torment, she had kept a diary of her daily thoughts and schedule about living with the disease. When she and Viv had shopped it around, the publishers had jumped at the chance and offered big money. She was the Porn Star Brothers' mother, and mother-in-law to big-time supermodel Vivian Villiers. They had also managed to get Dan a book deal, writing about AIDS and the gay men's health crisis. She needed to do the edits for her book, but it would be ready for the printers soon.

Sighing, she wandered onto the balcony. It had been a long year for the family, living with what had happened, being emotionally drained and physically exhausted, but they had gone on. Celebrating the boys' anniversaries, Thanksgiving, then Christmas and New Year's, the boys' birthdays and Valentine's, the in-laws' birthdays, hers and Spiros's birthdays and 30th anniversary, and then the girls' birthdays when they turned four. Not to mention celebrating Mothers' and Fathers' Day. There had been a lot of things to celebrate through the year, and here was the grand opening of the family's brand-new nightclub, *SB3*.

It was an idea she'd had in the months following it all. She needed to get the family back on track and give the boys what they needed. For Pedro, it was a place to play his music, so a nightclub-slash-function room more than made up for it. All year round at night it was a club, but by day it was a restaurant and entertainment zone for people to book functions of all kinds. They had to make it profitable all year round, and if opening night was anything to go by, it would be a roaring success.

She and Spiros were owner-managers, Pedro DJ, and she, Angie and Viv did publicity. As well as the nightclub, she had set up a music publishing company, *Sync*, with a recording studio for Pedro and Angie to make beautiful music together, and they had, writing and recording several songs that would be played tonight.

Plus, a small film studio called *S'Reel* had been set up for Carlos and Viv. Being in Mykonos, they had set up the two studios next to each other in a compound on a hill overlooking the town, and Viv had kept up with her exercise videos while Carlos filmed, directed and produced. They filmed across many of Greece's islands as well as in Athens. The ones currently skyrocketing in sales were the pregnancy videos she had done, because in the last year Viv had become pregnant again and was due to give birth, which is why she and Carlos weren't there, they were in the hospital. The cosmetics and perfume part of the company was still going gangbusters, with a new fragrance being released that past May.

And, as part of the Stephanopoulos legacy Jenny hoped to achieve, she had helped Carlos buy up all of the boys' porn films from Harry, Greta, and Marcus, and locked them in the mega-sized vault he'd had installed in the office at his studio.

Glancing across the crowd, Jenny saw a very happy Dan Ardent, the doctor who had helped her like no man had. And she'd repaid him for his generosity; not only suggesting he write a book and medical paper on his experience, but allowing him to stay in their home until he went back to America. He'd stayed until after Valentine's Day, relishing in all of Mykonos's beauty before going home. Now, he was back, not only with a well-received paper, but a boyfriend. His first. Another doctor by the name of Derek Blaine, a tall, good-looking brunet with sharp blue eyes and a sharper wit, whom he'd met while trying to get his job back at the hospital. Apparently, the hospital had hired Derek to replace him, and it was love at first sight for both of them. With some reservations about jumping into gay sex, Dan had told Derek all about his experience with the family, and both had been tested for every STD and disease they could test for, just to put Dan's mind at rest. Once he was satisfied that neither of them was infected in any way, shape, or form, they dated, and now happily lived together. His experience with the family had changed him, and they were forever in his debt to the point they insisted he stay with them every time he was in town. Derek too.

Jenny saw Eddie Monteif who looked as if he had the disease, friends of Angie and Viv, and old friends of Roger's, David Marks, Zack Bryant and Adam Zevon. She spoke in Spiros's ear and pointed to the boys. He left Diana to her to go downstairs and get them. "Diana, dance," she said to her baby.

"Dance, Gamma." Diana's hair was longer, less curly, but still golden-brown like her parents'. She was taller, and wore a pretty blue dress Jenny had bought her.

Jenny spotted family members in the crowd, her brothers and sisters, the boys' cousins. She had invited them all over for the opening of the club and had booked out *The Windmill Hotel* ahead of time.

Spiros came back with the boys, and she stepped into the office to welcome them. "Boys, good to see you again. You still look well."

"Mrs Stephanopoulos." David shook her hand. "I'm so glad you invited us to the opening, but so sorry about Tomas and Roger. This damn disease finally got them too."

"Are you boys still clean and free from it?" she asked, studying each closely.

"So far, so good, Mrs Stephanopoulos," Adam said. "Sorry about Tomas and Roger."

She smiled. "Well, don't believe everything you read. This way."

Leading them onto the balcony, she looked to her left to see her two beautiful boys sitting there enjoying the show.

"Oh, my God, Tomas, Roger," David yelled. "You're alive."

"Hey, guys." Roger jumped up to hug them and slap each on the back. "Yeah, we are; a case of mistaken identity it seems."

The family couldn't figure out how, but something had leaked out about them dying, and they'd all decided to go with it. It was a chance for them to start afresh, away from their porn history, and have a private life to themselves.

Jenny gazed at Tomas who looked back with a sweet smile on his aged face.

His hair had grown back thick, but it had a dusting of grey through it and made him look older than twenty-seven. She thought it made him look a little distinguished; Roger called it a little sexy. He needed glasses as his eyesight never fully recovered from the CMV, and the thick black frames suited his colouring. His black suit and matching shirt highlighted the tan he had after spending time in the sun over spring getting his health back on track.

She smiled, so glad her baby boy was alive and thriving every day. She listened to the boys tell their friends the story.

Tomas *had* died that day a year ago. His heart had just stopped beating, and she had collapsed on him screaming his name as Dan and two doctors rushed into the room. One doctor ordered Spiros to get Roger off the bed, and they sat him in the chair beside it while he administered a needle of medication straight into the line in his hand. Dan jumped on the bed and performed CPR on Tomas with the other doctor, pushing hard on Tomas's chest to get his heart started. Finally, they administered something to kick his heart into gear, and when it did, they injected the same medication they had just given Roger. It was a mix of Atovaquone and Azithromycin, drugs to treat Babesiosis, a disease transmitted by ticks they had somehow contracted.

Dan had told his story later, how all of them making the cross symbol had triggered a memory. In the blood cells, there is a Maltese cross structure made by parasites, which may infect less than one percent of circulating blood cells, and can be easily overlooked. It's quite similar to malaria, which they believed Roger had, causes many of the same symptoms as the pneumonia Tomas had, and is of the same parasitic family that causes toxoplasmosis and cryptosporidiosis, which is why Roger tested positive for all of them. From what dots Dan could connect, Roger and Tomas had somehow contracted the disease and Tomas, whose immune system was never a hundred percent after the Nerium Oleander poisoning, had borne the brunt of it all.

Opportunistic infections struck, including the pneumonia and other parasites, but it was why he'd never contracted the Kaposi's sarcoma cancer so many other gay men had. The Babesiosis had eaten his blood cells, causing the anaemia and the wasting disease, Cachexia, which had taken a hold, and so he had all the symptoms of the gay disease except for the STDs and the cancer.

The two other doctors had been from Italy, experts in parasitic diseases that had flown in for a conference and been asked to look at the last samples Dan had sent in. After studying all the paperwork and checking the blood, they had found the Maltese cross in the samples blood and instantly flew to Mykonos to see Dan and the patients, getting to the house in time to resuscitate Tomas, and give them both the medication for the Babesiosis.

Jenny vaguely remembered Dan looking at her after resuscitating Tomas, and breathing hard, as he managed to speak. Something about how she was right, he didn't have the disease, but something else, and they had just found out what it was and could finally help them. Then he'd looked at Tomas and told him he needed to fight because this wasn't the end, but he'd need to go to the hospital for weeks, if not months, of medication and around the clock care. It all came through foggy to Jenny, as if she was underwater and could only capture bits and pieces of what he was saying as she fell apart in Carlos's arms, reaching out to her dead son.

That's why they had all gone to the cove, to purge their grief over all that had happened as a family. Tomas and Roger were alive and in the hospital getting care from the world's top experts, and Jenny and the boys could finally let their grief go.

After ten days on the drugs, and with high doses of everything else,

Roger had stabilised and could get out of bed and sit, as the Cachexia hadn't destroyed him. He was healthy after three months, and could walk on his own after intensive physio.

Tomas was slower. He had taken time getting better. Once the parasites were gone, the Cachexia stopped, and the CMV and PCP cleared up. But he was weak and frail and his eyesight not as good as it had been, so Jenny brought in a team of experts to help. He had physiotherapists to build up his muscles, chiropractors to keep bones in shape, nutritionists to get his diet back on track, and continued high doses of protein to build his muscles back up. He had been able to stand on his own by six months, and walk on his own after a year.

It had been a lot of work, and Jenny, Spiros, and the boys had been there every step of the way. But once he had come back, he fought every goddamn day. He fought and fought hard to get back to his old self, grateful that everyone hadn't given up on him at all. And he showed what he could do by way of getting better, and with his family's help, plus support from Dan who'd stayed on, he slowly recovered.

One year on, he still wasn't a hundred percent like his old self before Luiz poisoned him, but he knew he would get there one day. He wasn't as broad or muscular as he once was, but he was getting there too. Still smiling at his mother, he was grateful that she and Dan hadn't given up. That she had loved him enough to fight for him, and fight she had. Although he had a feeling it wasn't *all* his mother.

A few months after it had happened, and he was off the ventilator, and the PCP had cleared up for him to breathe better, he told his mother one night when she was tucking him into the brand-new bed she had bought him, the story of his death.

When he'd died, he had seen a soft golden light. And people. Some he knew, some he didn't. One was his grandmother, who looked healthy. One was his great-grandfather, Giorgio, looking fit and out of his wheelchair. The third was his grandfather whom he had never met, but who looked exactly like him and Spiros. He told Jenny that all three had greeted him, hugged him, told him they loved him, and welcomed him to the family. But they had also told him it wasn't his time and he had to go back, for he had much to do on the planet. He had much to say, and would know where and when and how to make the biggest impact. And so, with love and light, they told him they loved him, and sent him home.

Jenny had cried and hugged him tightly, thanking God that he, Giorgio, Giorgio junior, and Katyana had been there for her son when he needed it the most, and had sent him back to be loved by his family.

Everything they had gone through made their fourth wedding anniversary extra special that year. Carlos and Pedro had held up Tomas and Roger as they danced together. They exchanged vows again, but since their rings didn't fit them, Jenny had bought necklaces for them to wear the rings on until their fingers could accept the rings back on their hands. Thanksgiving had also held extra special meaning. The entire family was thankful for Tomas and Roger still being with them.

He sat talking to his and Roger's friends, catching up on the latest news.

The phone rang, and Jenny ran to answer it. "Carlos?"

"Mama, we're on the last leg. The doctor says she's about to blow, gotta go."

Jenny called down to the backstage area where Mikos, an ex-bartender friend of Pedro's when he worked at SantorPoulos, Andros Poulos's old club on Santorini, was helping out. He relayed Jenny's message onto Pedro.

"Ladies and gentlemen." Pedro turned down the music. "I have to go, so I will leave you in the capable hands of Ricky K our fill-in DJ." The crowd booed. "Now, now," he grinned. "My sister-in-law, supermodel Vivian Villiers, is about to pop out my twin nephews, so the whole family needs to go. Remember, you have free food and free drinks for the rest of the night, and we will give you all a free ticket to come back another time. Enjoy the rest of your evening." He left his decks and raced towards the back office where his family was exiting en mass. "How long?" he asked his mother.

"About to blow, Carlos said," Jenny told everyone. "We'd better go." Racing up the hill, they made it to the hospital in record time, although Tomas and Roger took their time walking with some male cousins keeping them company in case they needed help. But they arrived in time to hear Viv screaming down the hospital.

"Oooh," she growled. "Get them out of me. Give me more drugs."

"Oh, that's definitely Viv." Angie laughed, and another scream came tearing down the corridor.

Then all was quiet.

For about three point nought seconds.

The cries of a baby followed, then the cries of two babies came down the corridor.

"Oh, babies," Jenny cried, grabbing Spiros's arms. "Babies."

An hour later they were allowed into Viv's room while the rest of the family stayed back to let them have their time.

Jenny and Spiros went first, with Jenny poking her head around the door. "Well?"

Carlos turned around. "Come, Mama. See your grandsons."

She walked over to him and stared down at the two beautiful baby boys, wrapped in the blue blankets she had knitted for them, lying in the crib. "Oh, look at them," she told Spiros who was beside her. "They're beautiful."

Pedro and Angie set Diana and Alena on the side of Viv's bed, so Diana could see her brothers and Alena her cousins.

"Diana, say hello to your baby brothers," Viv told her.

"Brovers, Mama?" Diana looked from the two babies to her mother. "Da-anna no want no brovers. Da-anna want to be only baby of family."

Everyone chuckled, and Jenny moved aside for Tomas and Roger to take a look. "Look at them," she breathed. "They look exactly like Carlos."

"That's all we need," Tomas moaned. "More Carloses."

Pedro grinned from beside his father. "Imagine what they'll be like when they grow up."

They groaned. "Just like Carlos," everyone but Carlos said.

"Okay, okay." Carlos waved a hand in protest. "I'm the butt of everyone's jokes. But look at them. They're *not* identical."

Staring, they all studied the golden-haired boys before them, seeing nothing to separate them until one opened his eyes.

"Well, blue just like his father," Jenny said. "He looks exactly like you did as a baby. So why did you say they're *not* identical?"

"Because of this." Carlos gently stroked the other twin on the cheek and he opened his eyes.

Sleepy eyelids opened, and huge emerald green eyes stared back.

"Oh, he has Viv's eyes." Jenny leaned over both of them. "How extraordinary. Each one has a different eye colour. I don't think I've ever seen identical twins with different eye colours. But either way, they both look like you did as a baby. You have beautiful babies, Carlos. I hope they all take after Viv when they grow up." She gazed adoringly from her grandsons to her son.

"Hardy har har, Mama." Carlos rolled his eyes, but couldn't help kissing her on the cheek.

"Have you picked out names, yet?" Angie asked, staring down at her nephews. She'd never had nephews before, and wasn't sure she wanted them now.

"Well...we were considering Tomas and Roger, but those names were already taken," Carlos joked, more than grateful that they were still alive. He squeezed his brother's shoulder and received smiles from Tomas and Roger. "And Greek names don't really seem to suit them so...we narrowed it down to...Cabot Conroy Stephanopoulos and Antonio DeLuca Stephanopoulos, after our dear departed friends."

"Oh, you named them after Cabot and Antonio, that's so sweet." Jenny smiled sadly. "That must still hurt?"

"It does," Carlos said, looking down at his sons. Now he knew how his father had felt every time his mother had given birth. He had two strong, healthy boys. "But we have so much to be grateful for this year. Our brothers came back to us, our businesses are doing well, and we have two healthy baby boys."

"Cheers, to *all* of that." Jenny hugged him, and the family crowded around.

About the Author

L.J. has been writing since 2006, when her first of many novels, *The Road To Vegas,* was born. In 2016 she created the *Porn Star Brothers* series about three sizzlingly hot Australian born Greek Island raised brothers who became the hottest porn stars in '70s America.

L.J. lives in Australia, loves '80s music, disaster movies, and collecting Jackie Collins books as Jackie is her inspiration and mentor.

L.J. Diva is the adult pen name for author Tiara King. You can find more about Tiara on her website; follow her on social media, or visit her publishing house, Royal Star Publishing.

Have you read these?

THE PORN STAR BROTHERS SERIES

Porn Star Brothers
Forever
Love Never Dies
Stefan: The New Generation
DeLuca
Spiros & Jenny
And Always

THE ILLICIT THINGS SERIES

Her
Him
Madam X

A NOVEL INVESTIGATIONS SERIES

Designs in Crime
A Killer Plot
Murder on the Set
A Novel Investigation (omnibus)

Or these?

NOVELS

Burning Desires
Anything for You
Falling for London
The Road To Vegas
Hollywood Dreams
The Billionaire's Dirty Little Secret

SHORT STORIES

The Body
The Perfect Plot
The Star of Your Own Crime Scene

www.ingramcontent.com/pod-product-compliance
Lightning Source LLC
Chambersburg PA
CBHW032204180726
48284CB00001B/187